Edith

*To Dr Carlo Gébler and Dr Paul Delaney
of Trinity College Dublin. With thanks.*

A NOVEL

MARTINA DEVLIN

THE LILLIPUT PRESS
DUBLIN

First published 2022 by
THE LILLIPUT PRESS
62–63 Sitric Road, Arbour Hill
Dublin 7, Ireland
www.lilliputpress.ie

The map of Castletownshend is based on a version from *Somerville & Ross: The World of the Irish R.M.* (Penguin, 1987) by Gifford Lewis. This version © Niall McCormack.

Paperback ISBN 9781843518303

A CIP record for this title is available from The British Library.

1 3 5 7 9 10 8 6 4 2

The Lilliput Press gratefully acknowledges the financial support of the Arts Council/An Chomhairle Ealaíon.

Set in 12.75pt on 16pt Perpetua by iota (www.iota-books.ie)
Printed in Kerry by Walsh Colour Print

'Only connect.' — *Howards End*, E.M. Forster

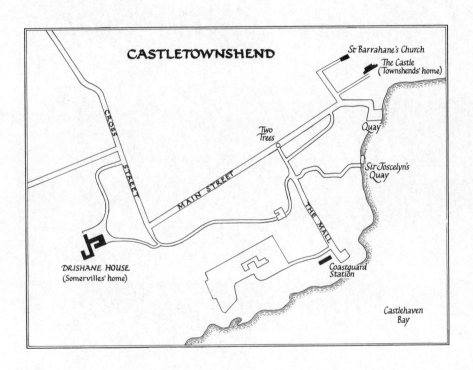

CASTLETOWNSHEND

St Barrahane's Church
The Castle
(Townshends' home)

CROSS STREET

Two
Trees

Quay

MAIN STREET

Sir Joscelyn's
Quay

THE MALL

DRISHANE HOUSE
(Somervilles' home)

Coastguard
Station

Castlehaven
Bay

Dramatis Personae

Edith Somerville (1858–1949) from Castletownshend in County Cork was one half of the bestselling Somerville and Ross writing partnership. In their day they were critically and commercially acclaimed, producing novels, short stories, travel books and journalism. Their three collections of Irish R.M. stories (beginning with *Some Experiences of an Irish R.M.* in 1899) became the duo's most popular work. Edith was also a trained artist and illustrated their books.

Violet Martin (1862–1915) from Connemara in County Galway, who wrote under the pen name Martin Ross, was the other half of Somerville and Ross. She and Edith were second cousins, and closely attuned to one another. After Martin's death, Edith continued to give her co-author status on new work, believing they were in regular contact through automatic writing and seances.

Ethel Smyth (1858–1944) was an English composer, a member of the women's suffrage movement who was jailed for her activities, and the first woman to be made a dame for services to music. She and Edith were friends for a time following Martin's death.

Flurry Knox, a roguish horse-lover memorably described as a 'half-sir', is a key character in Somerville and Ross's Irish R.M. short stories.

Time

A guerrilla war known at the time as the Anglo-Irish War, and later the War of Independence, has been fought for two-and-half years between the Irish Republican Army or IRA and the British administration in Ireland. A truce is called in July 1922. Now, leaders on both sides are engaged in negotiations. But the ceasefire hasn't yet delivered peace. Parts of the country are lawless, with IRA flying columns treating it as an opportunity to re-arm and prepare for the resumption of warfare. A deal will soon be struck which delivers independence for most of Ireland – but, controversially, accepts partition. The north-east is reconfigured as Northern Ireland, while the remainder becomes the Irish Free State. And all around Ireland, people are forced to consider where their loyalty lies.

one

Edith Somerville proceeds along Skibbereen's North Street, past the town hall with its broken clock face, her mind buzzing with errands. Family silver left in the Bank of Ireland safety deposit box. A birthday gift chosen for a godchild, despite the shops being light on stock because of the Troubles. Letters and packages posted, although no guarantee when they'll arrive with IRA interruptions to the postal service. She's earned herself some luncheon in the West Cork Hotel before setting off homewards. In high good humour amid the late September sunshine, she makes her way towards the riverfront.

'Beggin' your pardon, Miss Somerville,' comes a voice from behind her. Apologetic. But undeniably an interruption.

Shirtsleeves rolled to the elbow, apron smeared, the butcher has darted out.

'What is it, Mattie?'

His Adam's apple works. 'C-c-could you ... could you spare me a minute, your honour-ma'am? Inside in the shop?'

'Spit it out now, like a good fellow.'

He approaches, lowering his voice to a whisper. 'The Drishane account. Four months, it is, since 'twas settled.'

'Gracious me, Mattie, you shouldn't leave it so long. Have your boy drop in the bill the next time he's doing a delivery.'

'Won't you oblige me and step inside where we can talk in private, ma'am? It won't take up much of your time.'

She glances at the yellow premises with its black and white sign over the doorway.

Dwyer
Father & Son
Master Victuallers

In the window, trays of interleafed chops and sausage spirals are arranged, flies congregating around their moist pinkness. Sawdust leads from his boots back to the door, like a fairy-tale trail of crumbs through the forest. A stray mongrel materializes to sniff at it.

As abruptly as a hunter refusing an easy jump, her serenity is ruffled. Perhaps it's his persistence. Or it might be a flash of foreboding. 'It's not convenient today, Mattie. Now do as I say and send in your bill.'

His voice is somewhat louder and a shade less humble. 'We've handed it in at the kitchen door over and over, Miss Somerville. Mrs O'Shea says she's passed it on to Mr Somerville and what more can she do? Two weeks ago, I took the bull by the horns and went up meself. Waited about for a word with Mr Somerville. He wrote me out a cheque there and then, so he did, and I lodged it the self-same day. But the bank wouldn't honour it. Said the cheque was ...'

A mumble.

Colour floods Edith's face. That word she couldn't quite catch sounded like worthless. Lately, Cameron has become evasive. When the post does manage to get through, she has noticed a shiftiness in her brother. Anything resembling a bill is jammed, unopened, in his pocket.

A rag-and-bone cart jangles by, churning up mud. A customer exits the shop and dawdles past, not troubling to hide her curiosity. One of the Finnegan girls, if she's not mistaken. How much has the chit overheard?

Edith hooks Mattie Dwyer with her gaze. 'There must be some mis-understanding. Never mind, I'll settle the account on the spot. If I may, I'll take you up on that offer of a few moments in private on your premises.'

'I wouldn't put you to the trouble if the bill hadn't shot up so high, ma'am. It's an honour to have the Somerville account, like me father before me.'

She makes a chopping gesture. *Stop discussing our business in public*, says her gloved hand.

Almost bowing, he stands back, and she precedes him into the shop. Flitches of bacon dangle by their fat outer sides from hooks on the ceiling.

'Keep an eye on things, Pat,' he tells a youth in a striped apron behind the counter. 'Mrs Nagle's cook will be in shortly to place her order. She'll want three pounds of rashers and half a dozen rings of black pudding, at least. Make a start, parcel them up.'

Dwyer parts a curtain and ushers Edith into a nondescript room overlooking the back yard. Beneath the window is a table. Dwyer dusts off one of two chairs beside it and holds it back, inviting her to sit. He does not presume to occupy the remaining one. Edith stares through a grimy net curtain at the butcher boy's delivery bicycle. If Cameron was caught short, why didn't he borrow from her? She's lent him cash before. Granted, he owes her a sizeable sum already. But she'd advance him every last farthing rather than discover he'd handed over a duff cheque with a Somerville's signature on it.

Behind her, at a sideboard covered in brown paper and balls of string, overspill from the shop, Dwyer rustles his accounts book. She hears him breathing through his mouth. And no wonder with those blocked nasal passages. An even more alarming possibility occurs to her. There may be overdue bills with other tradesmen. At the fishmonger's and grocer's.

Dwyer clears his throat. 'Here it is. Colonel Somerville, Drishane House, Castletownshend.' He hands the account to Edith.

Her eyes skim over the figures and snag on the total. An intake of breath, rapidly suppressed. How on earth did Cameron allow it to mount to such a level? A tower of pork chops as tall as the Fastnet lighthouse wobbles before her eyes. Sausages laid in a line, reaching all the way into

Cork city. Who is eating all this meat? It's an age since they had a dinner party. The only house guest they entertained was her friend Ethel Smyth a year ago, and she insisted on paying a share of the household expenses.

Edith thought when the Great War ended, money worries would ease. But it's quite the reverse – things keep getting tighter. Hospitality stuttering to a halt is one among many economies they've had to practise. Not least because Ireland's been in a state of ferment for close on two years. Nobody wants to risk driving after dark for the sake of some duck *à l'orange* and a couple of glasses of Merlot. Rents are difficult to prise out of the tenants. Drishane's paddocks have never held so few horses – horse-coping has been a lucrative sideline for her but it's no longer generating much income. The estate's farm produce is unsaleable, with craters in the roads and blown-up bridges preventing goods from going to market. The IRA is bent on making roads impassable for the forces of law and order, but getting about is a nuisance for everyone else, too. As for the book business, once her cash cow – sales are modest. Her latest hasn't set the literary world on fire.

If times turn any harder they'll be reduced to vegetarianism, like that crank George Bernard Shaw. How her cousin Charlotte puts up with his peculiar eating habits, she'll never understand. An amusing man. But unsound.

All at once, Edith recalls giving Cameron her share of the butcher's bill. Whatever he spent her cash on, it certainly wasn't to pay the butcher. No wonder he refused to take a run into Skib this morning when she suggested it at breakfast. He must have known the bill wouldn't disappear into thin air.

Mattie Dwyer clears his throat. 'I trust everything is in order, your honour-ma'am?'

'Perfectly in order, Mattie. But it's somewhat steeper than I anticipated.' She knows to the last shilling how much her purse contains. 'I find I don't have enough cash on me at present and I've left my chequebook in Drishane. Let me make some inroads into it, at least.' She produces three banknotes and an assortment of crowns, half-crowns and florins from her bag. 'Count this up, please, and deduct it from the total. I'll make arrangements to pay the remainder in due course.'

Except she does not know when that will be. Meanwhile, they must trust to the butcher's good nature to continue meeting their orders. An ugly word occurs to her. The Somervilles must rely on his charity.

'And may I check what's on order with you for the weekend, Mattie?'

'A mutton joint, ma'am, and some liver and kidney.'

'Cancel them.'

'Ah, now, there's no need for that, Miss Somerville. I wouldn't see you go without, above in Drishane. That wouldn't be right at all. I dare say you'll let me have what's owing as soon as you find it convenient.'

'There is no question of us going hungry, Mattie. The cook has fallen into wasteful habits, ordering meat we don't need with just my brother and me echoing about in the house.'

'Whatever you say, ma'am.' He licks the pencil stub and enters the sum paid in his ledger.

It represents three-quarters of what's due. And now she is stony broke.

—

Edith waits while the stable boy from the West Cork Hotel fetches her dogcart. Does she have a coin in her pocket to tip him? Her right leg throbs. She uses a walking stick at home but won't carry one into Skibbereen, in case the townspeople say she's ageing. Which is nonsense. She's a youthful sixty-three – plenty of vim and vigour in her yet.

The boy, one of the Connors clan judging by those curls, has harnessed Tara and leads her back. The chestnut horse huffs out a breath in recognition, and she strokes the mare's forehead along the white flash. Quick to spook, Tara is wearing blinkers for this trip to town.

'Any packages, Miss Somerville?'

'Just myself, if you'll lend me your arm.' She allows him to hand her up the steps, although once she'd have sprung into the dogcart under her own steam. 'Are you a Connors?'

He tucks the tartan blanket over her knees, attentive as a lady's maid. 'Yes, ma'am.'

'Roddy's boy?'

'No, ma'am. He's me uncle. Philip was me da.'

She remembers Philip, he died in prison. Caught fever a year into his sentence. He was jailed for something political. A hothead, they tried him out in the Drishane stables, but he wouldn't take orders.

Edith fumbles in a pocket and her gloved fingers close over a disc. A stray button? Too slender and even. Feels like a sixpence. She slides it into the boy's palm. 'Thank you, young man.'

He tugs his cap brim. 'That's a grand animal you have, Miss Somerville.'

'Tara's from a good bloodline.'

'I hear tell you've a stable full of fine beasts above in Drishane.'

She frowns. What business is it of his? Without answering, she clicks her tongue at Tara, who springs forward. The tub-shaped vehicle clatters over the cobblestones and onto the street. By the bridge near the hotel, she meets a neighbour's son, and pulls on Tara's reins.

'Need a lift, Harry?'

Lieutenant Harry Beasley removes his uniform cap. 'No, thank you, Miss Somerville. I've just arrived here. Haven't had a chance to sample Skib's delights yet.'

'How are things across the water?'

'I've been stationed in France. But from what I saw travelling through England last week, there are problems. Nothing that can't be sorted, of course. But shortages, definitely. Too few jobs, too many mouths.'

'Oh dear. Still, I'm sure your mama is delighted to have you home from your regiment. I expect the fatted calf was prepared.'

'She didn't know I was coming. Telegram wasn't delivered.'

'Ah, that's because the telegraph wires have been cut by the flying columns. It's to delay reinforcements when they engage the soldiers.'

He runs a palm over his sleek head. 'Things seem edgy in Skib.'

'Times are tense.'

'The place has taken a bit of a battering. I see the courthouse is burned out, and the town hall looks pretty shot up. Mother hadn't told me.'

'I suppose she didn't want to worry you. But Ireland's had a rough time of it.'

'Self-inflicted woes.'

'Skibbereen has received a fair amount of attention from the Crown forces, Harry.'

'What can people expect if they turn rebel? Anyhow, there's a lot of bored uniforms confined to barracks now.'

'Thank heavens for the ceasefire. Hopefully the two sides will knuckle down to peace talks soon. Once a deal is struck, the country will settle itself.'

'The savages are running wild, truce or no truce. They need to be culled. Mother goes to bed every night expecting to wake to a house in flames.'

'You know, the Black and Tans and Auxiliaries are just as bad as the Republicans. The people are being terrorized.'

'I say, Miss Somerville!'

'It's true. Ask your mama. Some think the Tans' behaviour might persuade America to join the fight.'

'Impossible. America would never side with Ireland against Britain. We were allies in the war. Great Britain needs to take a firmer hand. Swamp the country with troops and crush resistance. That's the only language rebels understand.'

'Hmm. Well, I must be pushing along. Oh, Harry, if you happen to know anyone in the market for a horse, I have a couple of beauties I'm willing to part with. Hunters both. Stallions.'

'I thought Mother said the hunt had been stopped.'

'The IRA has forbidden it. Some nonsense about putting an end to the gentry's days of riding roughshod over the Irish people's land. Any damage was always paid for.'

'I'm surprised at our sort, taking orders from those fellows.'

'They left out poisoned bait for packs where the chase went ahead. Have you ever seen an animal die from a dose of strychnine? Agony for the poor hound. Anyhow, enjoy your leave, Harry.'

The Angelus bell begins tolling for noon. She waves, and guides Tara towards Main Street, with its honeysuckle- and fuchsia-coloured shop fronts. Chicken wire is pinned over windows facing the street. As they clop along, Edith remembers what Mike Hurley told her. The Sinn

Féiners are doing American lecture tours. They have friends in high places there. No point in saying that to a young man in khaki, home on furlough.

A wagon delivering laundry to Mrs Nagle's boarding house holds up the traffic. By rights, the driver ought to use the service entrance. Edith prepares to wait it out. A couple of idlers lean against a hardware shop, and she notices them taking an interest in Tara, whispering together.

'Move that nag of yours. We've a train to catch.' A head emerges from a yellow motor car in front. She didn't know they came in such a colour. The head belongs to a chauffeur, judging by the peaked cap.

'Sure what's stopping you? You could sail an ocean liner down this road,' shouts the laundryman.

From habit, Edith casts an eye over the dray horse between the shafts of his delivery cart. It looks half-starved – she can't abide people mistreating animals. Urchins scamper over, pointing and jostling at the chugging motor car. Its passenger door flings open and a man steps out. He paces up and down the footpath, watch in hand. An American, by the looks of him. No Irish or Englishman would wear a coat woven from such violently checked cloth.

Enough is enough. She swings Tara around the blunt-nosed motor car, past the delivery cart, keeping a sharp eye out for pedestrians – the townspeople are demons for stepping onto the road without looking first.

Beyond Skibbereen and heading east, she has five miles of obstacle-strewn country lanes hedged by flaming furze to negotiate. But with a horse which knows the way home, there is time to consider Cameron's behaviour. Her indignation against him simmers. He's always had an irresponsible streak, but instead of fading over time it has intensified. Perhaps it's more apparent since he retired from the army two years ago and is living full-time with her in Drishane. That squirmer with Dwyer is due directly to her brother.

Remembering a pit in the middle of the road near the O'Mahony farm, its danger camouflaged by branches, she climbs down to lead Tara past. Cameron is in a financial pickle, she realizes – the signs were there all along but she's been slow to detect them. And the disruption to the postal service has allowed bills to mount. Timmy the Post works like a Trojan to scramble through, but he's only human. She climbs into the cart again and Tara whizzes along, eager for the paddocks.

Ahead, a man is standing by the side of the narrow road. He's in his late twenties, wearing knee-high riding boots and a hacking jacket. There's something familiar about him. She squints at his face but he's bending over, adjusting a bootstrap. Just as they are parallel, a flash of autumn sunlight blinds her. The dogcart bowls past without her catching a clear sight. Yet the prickle of perspiration against her hairline and in her armpits identifies him. Her body has recognized this man.

No, it's not possible.

It can't be who she thinks it is.

She drives on in a daze.

Martin speaks. 'I saw him, too.'

Edith knows the voice is inside her head. That Violet Martin, otherwise known as Martin Ross – friend, cousin, literary collaborator – isn't here with her in the dogcart. She's dead and buried – gone almost six years now. Even so, their conversations help her to tease out dilemmas.

'Perhaps it was a figment of my imagination,' suggests Edith.

'And perhaps not. Anyway where's the harm?'

The bend for home appears ahead, followed by her first sight of the sea, a hat ribbon on the horizon. Edith continues her conversation with Martin, who isn't there, except in her heart.

'Something will have to be done about Cameron, Martin.'

'Cameron's always hidden from unpleasantness.'

'He simply can't leave bills unpaid. Above all, he can't do it here, where we live. Tongues will wag. They may be flapping already. The family has to live up to its good name.'

'Cameron's Cameron. He'll never change.'

'He must.'

'You know what you have to do, Edith.'

'He can't be left in charge. I thought he could. But I was wrong.'

Edith waits for a denial, a defence of Cameron.

A sigh, whisper faint. It's corroboration.

When Martin doesn't speak, Edith does. 'I'm going to have to do something about him.'

She needs to know how bad things are. A thought occurs to her. One so dreadful that her vision blurs. Has the staff been paid? Or is a backlog building up for Mike Hurley, Philomena Minihane, Mrs O'Shea and Jeremiah O'Mahony? And for the others they use occasionally from the village? She shakes her head to dislodge the appalling possibility. Even Cameron wouldn't be so irresponsible.

Would he?

two

Edith is unpinning her hat as the luncheon gong sounds. It conjures up her brother on the staircase – punctuality was drummed into them from childhood.

Cameron's expression brightens. Only two years separate them and they've always been friends. 'Hello, Peg, I thought you were intending to lunch in the West Cork.' He hurries downstairs. 'Good of you to come back. Never much cared to eat alone.'

Edith knows Cameron misses the companionship of military life as much as its certainties. But she's in no mood to be sympathetic. She tosses her hat on the hall stand and pats her hair. 'I did mean to eat out but there was a change of plan.'

'The Murphys will be inconsolable. They depend on the celebrated authoress making an appearance now and again in their dining room – raises the tone of the place. That hotel must be a goldmine for them. It's always heaving whenever I stick my head in. Shall we sit up? The gong's gone.'

'I'll come through directly after I wash my hands. Mustn't keep Philomena waiting – the servants have enough to put up with, I suspect.'

'Oh dear. You're using Mama's precise tone of voice when she had a bone to pick with someone. Me, usually.'

That pulls her up short. If he thinks she's attacking him it will prove counterproductive. This situation requires diplomacy.

Just then, Philomena stomps by carrying a tray. Their housemaid always walks as though she's wearing Wellington boots.

'Shan't be a jiffy, Chimp.' Deliberately, Edith uses her pet name for him. 'By the way, I collected our post in Skib. Couple of letters for you. Left them on the table there.'

Edith washes off the grime from her morning's business in the downstairs cloakroom and joins her brother in the dining room. It's excessive, just the two of them eating here in lofty splendour, but neither likes to break with tradition. As soon as Edith is seated, Philomena serves steaming soup from a tureen. Her stomach gurgles at the smell.

'You must be hungry after gadding to Skibbereen and back in a morning,' says Cameron. 'Any news from the bright lights?'

Philomena tracks between Edith and Cameron with a basket, offering thinly-sliced toast triangles. Surprised, Edith glances up at her small face crowded with features. It's a face she knows as intimately as her own.

'Mrs O'Shea wasn't able to bake rolls this morning, Miss Edith. The range is acting up again.'

'We really must have that looked at. Thank you, Philomena, that will be all.'

Alone now, Edith assesses Cameron. He doesn't come across like a man on his uppers. Look at him, ladling butter on his toast without a care in the world. 'Any news in your letters?'

'Weekend shooting party over Ballycotton way's been cancelled. English guns won't travel on account of the Troubles.'

'How disappointing.'

'Can't be helped.'

'How are we fixed as regards bills, Cam? Keeping our heads above water?'

A wave of his hand. An attempt at bravado. 'Nothing out of the ordinary. Leave them to me to sort out.'

'But are you taking care of them?'

He blinks. 'Don't quite follow you.'

'Or are you crumpling them up? Throwing them in the wastepaper bin?'

He wets his lips, about to speak. Reconsiders. Lifts his soup spoon and manages a few mouthfuls of oxtail.

She presses the starched linen napkin against her mouth. 'The bills aren't going to be abracadabra-ed away in a puff of smoke, Cam. We need to work out how to meet them. I was accosted by the butcher on the street in Skibbereen, in full view of every corner boy. He mentioned an account of four months' standing.'

'I don't remember any bill from Dwyer.'

'He's been sending it in, week after week.'

'No, I expect it went astray. Can't rely on the post these days.'

'His boy hands it in at the kitchen door. You know that perfectly well.'

His colour heightens. 'Stop hectoring me, Edith. You don't have the right.'

She concentrates on her soup, trying to work out how best to proceed. Cameron may be risking cash he can ill afford on the Stock Exchange. The men in her family have always had a taste for financial speculation.

A tap, the door opens, and Philomena backs in with a platter. At once, Edith's expression turns neutral, as does Cameron's.

'Thank you, Philomena. Leave it on the sideboard and I'll serve us.'

'Sure, whatever you like, Miss Edith. If that suits you it suits me. I've plenty to be gettin' on with. There's lovely fresh peas from the kitchen garden to go with Mrs O'Shea's fish pie.'

A soft thud and the door closes again. Edith rises and scoops a helping of fish pie onto a plate, adds some vegetables and places his luncheon on the tablecloth in front of Cameron. In the process, she rests her hand on his shoulder. 'Come on, Chimp. Let's put our heads together. Any ideas? How about your army pension, could you funnel a little more of that into the estate?'

He stares at the plate. 'That's a drop in the ocean when it comes to Drishane.'

'What do you mean?'

'You seem to imagine I'm in receipt of a massive pension from His Majesty's grateful government. Quite the contrary. Modest is the best description. And it doesn't stretch far enough.'

Nonplussed, Edith fetches her own plate and sits down. A brooding atmosphere seeps out through the dark-green wallpaper. If only Cameron had married an heiress. He never even made a serious try at bagging one. Either of the Payne-Townshend girls would have been perfect for him. Not only related to the Somervilles, so the right sort, but rich as Croesus. It seems positively sinful those fortunes left the family. Her second brother, Aylmer, could afford to help, having had the good sense to court a wealthy widow. But it's possible he feels tapped once too often. In any case, he and Emmie live in England and are distant – both geographically and mentally – from Drishane's expenses. There are three other boys, and a sister, Hildegarde, but none of them is flush. And they have their own families to consider.

Only she and Cameron never married. There was no requirement for Edith to do so, unless she could pull off a suitable match, which she didn't manage. A few offers were made but none deemed fitting by Papa and Mama. She shed tears at the time, but it's water under the bridge now. However, Cameron has neglected his duty. He neither bagged an heiress to buttress their house, nor provided an heir to inherit it.

'Plenty of chaps in the next generation. One of them can take the place on,' he always says, at any mention of a successor.

But why would their nephews want to be saddled with it? Especially if they didn't grow up in the house, learning to love its idiosyncrasies? His logic is self-serving. Very well. If her brother lacks the gumption to behave like a responsible Master of Drishane, he'll have to hand over the reins to her. He can be governor in name. But she'll be the one who makes sure the family seat is passed on intact to the next generation.

'This isn't good enough, Cam. Somervilles have always paid their way. You're letting the side down.'

'And I suppose you're the resident expert?'

'At least I care about doing the right thing. All you seem to care about are your own selfish pleasures.'

'Pleasures? Stuck here in the middle of nowhere with all sorts of blackguard behaviour happening under our noses? Believe me, if it was pleasure I was after, I wouldn't look to Castletownshend. I'm fed up with Ireland and her endless quarrels.'

Silence settles. Cutlery scrapes on bone china. Edith realizes the conversation has taken an unfortunate turn. If they start talking politics an almighty row will brew up. Covertly, she watches her brother at the head of the table. He has extravagant tastes. But even Cameron must realize the well has run dry. Granted, retrenchment is challenging. Papa struggled with it too. But Cameron only has himself to consider, whereas Papa had the burden of settling five sons into careers and making arrangements for two daughters. Not that she required much arranging, she aimed to be self-financing from the outset. Earned her first money at the age of sixteen, designing greeting cards.

'Chimp, frugalities are needed. Let's just face up to it and introduce them.'

'I really don't see how I can frugalize any further.'

'In that case, there's no help for it – we'll have to sell something.'

'Land?'

'Certainly not! There's been enough of that already. You'd have to let it go for half nothing and then it's gone for good. No, I was thinking of the houses in the Mall.'

'Your retirement nest egg.'

She shrugs, as if it's irrelevant. For years, Edith has been using her literary earnings to buy up properties in the village, amassing a modest portfolio. She rents the houses to suburbans who clamour to stay in Castletownshend during the sailing season, and sometimes she persuades a member of their extended family to take out a lease.

Cameron strokes his moustache. 'It might be the answer, Peg. If you don't mind letting one or two of them go.'

Outrage flares at the easy way he accepts her sacrifice. Before she can help herself, Edith exclaims, 'It most certainly is not the answer! It's a stopgap. I won't get one-quarter of the true value, with the state of the country. Cameron, you must go through the household accounts with me and put everything on an honest footing. This may be your house but it's my home and I work bally hard to help keep it going. Shutting me out is unjust!'

Crimson patches his cheeks. 'I loathe this blasted old heap! I'm only living here because you nagged me into it. Told me it's my duty as the eldest son. I'd gladly hand it over to Aylmer, or Boyle, or any of the boys who'd take it off my hands. But none of them will touch it. They've more sense. The tin it costs to keep the house running beggars belief. And you could sink your life savings into the estate without making a jot of difference.'

'Do stop exaggerating, Cam. The house is sound. It simply needs some maintenance. As for running costs, the servants have taken a cut in wages, as well you know.'

'We still have to feed them and keep everything up to scratch. This place is a swamp – gobbles up every last pound in a man's possession, gives an almighty belch and stands ready for more. But you've always been blind to its faults, Peg. Grandpapa made a pet of you and filled you full of stories about the importance of the Somervilles holding tight to Drishane. Trying to do right by it made Papa miserable.'

'At least he didn't sell off fields for ready cash. You don't even drive a good bargain.'

'The land is mine to dispose of as I see fit.'

'It was given to you to hold in trust – not peddle, to supplement your income.'

'For two pins I'd put the entire estate, house included, on the market tomorrow. Sell it all, lock, stock and barrel.'

'You can't mean that, Cam!'

'Try me.' A curious note spikes his voice. It almost sounds like relief.

'Do you really want to go down in family lore as the Somerville who let it all slip through your fingers?'

'The blasted family myth! Just because you've bought into it doesn't mean I have to. Anyway, who made you the voice of my conscience? You look to yours and I'll look to mine.'

Edith mangles her fingers. The conversation isn't going the way she expected. She presumed Cameron would be touchy enough, proud enough, to wince at the thought of having 'The Somerville Who Lost Drishane' as his legacy.

'Chimp, don't let's fall out. We're on the same side, remember? Together, we can handle this.'

'The best way to handle this is to sell up and find a nice serviced apartment in Kensington or Westminster.'

'You'd hate it.'

'You might. I wouldn't.'

'I know the estate is going through a bit of a drought. And you're bound to be worried, as the head of the family. Why don't we think about ways to economize? Hold our nerve, stand our ground?'

'Cutting corners won't do the needful, I'm afraid. That horse has long since bolted.'

'What do you mean?'

'You might as well know the truth. We're in a bad way. I'm in a bad way. We could lose Drishane.'

Lose Drishane.

The room blurs. She hears a rushing sound like applause in her head.

The next thing she knows, Cameron is holding a glass of water to her lips. 'Here, drink something. I think you may have passed out, old girl.'

Trembling, she manages a few sips. When the mist clears, she sees her cutlery has been knocked to the floor. Cameron picks it up.

'I'm all right. I just had a bit of a turn. Really, I'm fine.'

'You don't look fine.'

Her mind begins to recalibrate. She knew they were in a tight spot but not how bleak their prospects were. She hasn't taken such a knock since her hunting days. With an effort of will, she sits up straight. 'Cam, what I need from you now is to know exactly where we stand.'

Cameron retreats to the sideboard, pours himself a brandy, and tosses it off in a single swallow. 'Will you have one?'

'No thank you.' She dips her napkin in her water tumbler and presses it against her right temple. 'Why don't we strike while the iron is hot? Spend the afternoon going through the household accounts?'

He lifts the decanter again. 'Come on, Peg, what's the use? We're survivors of a bygone age, you and me. Let's just chuck it over. You could live with me in London – we could share the expenses there just as well as here. And we'd have some capital from the sale.'

'I could never leave Drishane.'

'Why not? It's a draughty old house with rats under the floorboards and walls dripping with damp. It's in the middle of nowhere. And the natives don't really want us here – you know they don't. However much they pile on the flattery.'

She raises a hand, palm outwards. 'I won't listen to another word. We've been in Ireland nearly as long as the potato. We belong here. Now, let's order coffee and get down to brass tacks about finances.'

'Not right now, Peg. Fact of the matter is, I promised to take a run down to the castle this afternoon. Give the place the once-over for the Townshends. You can't rely on caretakers. Sooner or later they take liberties. Believe I'll stretch my legs in that direction now.'

'Chimp, we can't carry on like this. You're behaving as if it's ill-bred to discuss money. Please stay and thrash it out with me.'

'Sorry, old thing, can't oblige. We'll do it later.'

'When later?'

'Soon. Although, I give you fair warning, you won't like what you hear.' He sets down his empty brandy balloon, jams his hands in his pockets and saunters towards the door.

Edith knows this invented engagement on behalf of their cousins from the castle is a deferral tactic. Her brother is behaving like a twelve-year-old whose pocket money has been withheld for smashing a pane of greenhouse glass.

Her face sinks into her hands. And to think she imagined that scene with Mattie Dwyer was the worst the day could throw at her. By and by, she rallies and rings the bell for Philomena.

'Was that the colonel I saw going out without his coffee, Miss Edith? It's not like him.'

'We're skipping coffee today, Philomena. You may clear the table now.'

Edith leaves her to it. In need of fresh air, she throws on a battered old hat and jacket – her Skibbereen clothes are too good for the bluebell woods – and stands on the back step, whistling. An answering commotion, and her fox terrier bolts up. Tongue panting, he wags his tail, spraying water in all directions.

'Were you paddling in the horses' water trough again, Dooley?'

She marches along, Dooley trotting at her heels. As she walks, she swipes at clumps of thistles and dandelions with her ivory-handled walking stick. It belonged to her grandfather, Master of Drishane when she was growing up. The Big Master, he was called. Cameron is right. From the outset, she was Grandpapa's pet. He used to hold her hand taking prayers every morning – staff, family and guests alike assembled for the ritual. It was then she began to feel she occupied a privileged position within the family. Edith could never hope to inherit, despite being the firstborn – too many brothers ahead of her in the pecking order – but she felt herself charged with the role of guardian. A sense of responsibility for Drishane House and the Somerville position in Castletownshend was bred into her.

Cameron, however, is willing to sell the family seat for a song – see it turned into a rest home for Roman Catholic priests, she shouldn't wonder. Four full-time staff out of a job, never mind the occasional workers. As for Edith, she'd be forced to make her home among dull English people – worthy, granted, but lacking any joy in life's quirks.

Even the servants in Ireland have more poetry in them than her own sort in England. Only yesterday, Nora Treacy, who helps Mrs O'Shea with the rough work, told her she'd never marry. Edith took it with a pinch of salt since Nora was all of nineteen. Still, she was impressed by the scullery maid's reasoning. 'I had this off my Granny, ma'am,' she said. 'Two things every woman should keep from a man: a corner in her pocket and a corner in her heart. If you have to love, let you not do it extravagantly. But to my mind, if you're not going to do it with a heart and a half, you'd best not do it at all. So I'm planning to stay single. Same as yourself, ma'am.'

Edith finds such conversations invigorating. It's their subtlety, unexpectedness, and the confidential nature of these exchanges. And, yes, the meeting of equals. Drishane's servants always retain something of their independence despite the economic relationship.

A swipe at a clump of nettles. Mrs O'Shea swears by nettle soup. Says there's nothing to beat it for taste. So far, they haven't had to stoop to adding it to the Drishane menu but anything is possible. For decades, it's been a struggle to balance the books, but robbing Peter to pay Paul or sending out an SOS to their brothers in England won't be sufficient this time, judging by Cameron's gloomy prognosis.

How disappointed Papa would be in Cameron. She feels a burst of compassion for her brother. Drishane is his birthright. But he didn't ask for it – it was just landed on him. And he's out of his depth.

'We have to find a new income stream, Dooley,' she tells the foxhound.

He yips, acknowledging that she's addressing him but too distracted by a variety of scents near a tree root to spare her his full attention. Sometimes, that's exactly how her brothers treat her.

A breeze whips against her legs. A blackbird opens its bill, a songburst in yellow. 'All shall be well,' said Martin, in their last automatic-writing session. And maybe it will. Meantime, bills take no account of cash flow. There was a time when writing a shilling shocker with Martin was all it took to rustle up the readies. Those were the days. *An Enthusiast*, her latest, is racking up only modest sales. Does she even have another novel in her? 'Would Longman's bother to publish it?' she asks Dooley. Low in his throat, he growls. Perhaps he's picked up the scent of a woodland animal. He's a demon for chasing hedgehogs, never learns how much damage they can do.

Generally, exercise eases her mind. But today, the outdoors can't soothe her. Uphill she labours, ignoring the ache which causes one leg to drag on the slope. If Martin was with her, she'd say something to make Edith giggle, forgetting the pain. Martin is always with you, she reminds herself. Even so, there are days when her presence is not as vivid as Edith would like.

She whistles for Dooley, who has skulked off into the undergrowth. A series of yaps, a bustle of paws, and he reappears to rub himself against her calf, intelligence sparkling in his black eyes. She stoops to pat his smooth coat, white but for an autumn leaf patch over one eye. 'I wouldn't want to go to heaven if there were no dogs in it,' she tells him, and he nuzzles her palm. Fortunately, Martin is reassuring on that score. Every pet dog she's ever owned will be waiting to greet her when she presents herself at the Pearly Gates.

Edith straightens, pain jolting through her right knee. The nip of sciatica is a legacy from a lifetime spent riding side-saddle. Even when ladies began to ride astride, she always declined to change her habits. It felt improper. To rest her leg, she sits on a tree stump, the remnants of a diseased elm. A gardener took a saw to it on Papa's orders. Papa hated losing trees. 'Our job is to plant them not cut them down,' he used to say. Grandpapa was the same. But Cameron has no money for tree-planting, and nor does she, for that matter.

Overhead, a flock of pale-bellied wild geese in wedge formation forges steadily ahead, arriving in Ireland to hibernate for the winter. The wind increases in intensity, causing the boughs above her to creak. She slides off the tree base and prepares to press on.

And then it happens. She hears a snatch of song.

> *In seventeen hundred and forty-four*
> *The fifth of December – I think 'twas no more*
> *At five in the morning by most of the clocks,*
> *We rode for Kilruddery to try for a fox.*

She closes her eyes, sensing his presence as the singer draws closer. There's his horsey smell and the tang of fresh sweat. No Paris colognes for him. So, it was Flurry Knox there on the side of the road!

'What's wrong with you, gerrill? You look off colour.'

She allows herself a smile. Girl, indeed.

A sideways glance is slid at the slim figure with muscular legs next to her, in case staring might scare him away. He's holding his bowler hat in one hand and a riding crop in the other, tucked under his armpit. His hair is slick against the outline of his head, and his eyes make you think he's up to no good. Just as she first sketched him all those years ago. If his likeness were used for a pack of cards, he'd be the Jack of Spades.

'Advancing years, Flurry. That's what has me out of sorts. And a few other troubles besides.'

'Come on out of that, gerrill. You're a long way off from the finishing line – there's decades in you yet. Take a stroll with me. You'll feel the better of it. And sure, if you tell me your problems, who knows but I might be able to help? Two heads are better than one.'

Edith falls into step beside him. He replaces the bowler, defying gravity with its tilt at the back of his head, and whistles a jaunty tune. *Hunting the Hare*, if she's not mistaken. She's cheered just having him beside her. It's impossible to be in Flurry Knox's company without feeling optimistic.

'So what's eating at you, Edith?'

'I hardly know where to begin. But it's serious. Maybe too serious for me to fix.'

He makes no reply. All the same, she knows he's listening. He has an intent air – the one that transfixes him when the hounds are straining at the leash, immediately before a blast from the horn.

'Mind you, you've helped enormously with my finances over the years, Flurry. You patched the roof, built a glasshouse, paved the avenue and paid my taxes.'

'Steady, now. Don't be accusing me of doing an honest day's work or my reputation might never recover. How did I manage such impressive toil?'

'The Irish R.M. stories. The public lapped them up. There now, I'll give you a fat head.'

His grin stretches from ear to ear, dislodging his bowler. He catches it gliding off and tucks it under his arm. 'The public has excellent taste, Edith, if I say so myself.'

They reach the viewing point at the crest of the hill, the beat of the sea below them and the bay spread out as if for their particular pleasure. There's Horse Island, and Reen Point – America is the next parish over. In the harbour, four fishing vessels bob on the choppy water. Edith sighs with contentment. She can't imagine Flurry anywhere but here. He belongs to the barony of West Carbery. Both of them do. When she has looked her fill, she surveys her companion. In the quarter-century since she and Martin talked Florence McCarthy Knox into life, he isn't a day older or a hair greyer. Martin is lying in St Barrahane's churchyard and Edith's hunting days are long behind her, but Flurry remains capable of springing onto a flighty mount at a moment's notice and charging off in the thick of a foxhound pack.

He could be her son now. Is she sorry she never married and produced a flesh-and-blood son rather than this literary version? She is not. He's more her son than Martin's, of that she's certain. Flurry shares her appreciation for horseflesh. His fondness for the hounds is another characteristic she embedded in him. She can't lay claim to his financial shiftiness – she prefers paying her bills, on the whole, as did Martin. That unsteadiness blended with charm was borrowed from several of her brothers.

Her eyes linger on Flurry's profile. What is there of Martin in him? His sense of humour, perhaps. Martin had a serious veneer but burst into hoults of laughter at the least provocation.

'What's bothering you, Edith? You know you can tell me anything. I'm unshockable.'

'Money worries, Flurry.'

'To the seventeen divils I pitch them.' He snaps his fingers. 'I wouldn't let them weigh on me, indeed and I wouldn't. Money comes and money goes. That's just the way of it.'

'Aren't you the airy-fairy one, you and your Flurryisms. It's easy to be flippant about money when you've no need of it.'

'Here's what you do. Find a decent colt, buy it for a song and sell it for a king's ransom. That'll take care of any cash shortages. Never fails for me.'

'It's not that simple any more. The horse-coping business is in a poor way, between the Troubles and the public's taste for motor cars.'

He flashes a scandalized look. 'The day an Irishman of any class or creed loses interest in horseflesh is the day the world stops turning.' He scratches his leg with the riding crop. 'You could always write another Irish R.M. book. Them's the boys that were your crock of gold.'

'Out of the question. I haven't the heart for it with Martin gone. It took the two of us to catch the froth on those frolics and shape it into stories.' She bites her lip. 'The truth is I can't manage it on my own.'

'Sure where's the good in your automatic-writing sessions with herself, the two of you colloguing together, if you can't turn a profit from them? Rustle up a few hunting stories?'

Edith suspects a twist to his words. 'I won't be mocked, Flurry Knox.'

His smile is sly, and she knows she was right to doubt him.

'I have it, Edith. Why not take some of the stories the two of you wrote together, back in the day, and give them a new lease of life? Use them as scaffolding for a play, maybe? They say there's a fortune to be made on the stage.'

'Adapt the Irish R.M. for theatre?' She's surprised. What does Flurry Knox know about the world of greasepaint and footlights?

'Yes, for the stage. Why not?' Grinning, Flurry slaps his hat back on his head.

Edith is seized by a burst of enthusiasm to match Flurry's. It seems not just possible but probable. 'Once, Martin said we should grind West Carbery's bones to make our bread. Back when we were starting out. I can do it again, I know I can! How would you like to strut across the London stage, Florence McCarthy Knox? Are you ready for applause from a metropolitan audience?'

'Sure I don't mind at all if it gets you out of a hole, gerrill.'

three

A noise wakens Edith. She realizes it's Dooley, who is standing on the bed and growling. At first, she thinks it's just this old house disturbing him – like her, Drishane beds down for the night with snaps and groans. But then she hears a smack against gravel. Footsteps outside. A snarl rumbles from Dooley. 'Hush, boy,' she whispers.

Throwing back the covers, she shuffles barefoot to the window, the foxhound bristling at her ankles. Cautious, she parts the edge of a curtain. The lace of frost on windowpanes blurs the outside world. She squints past it to where moonlight floods the courtyard. Her eyes patrol the perimeters. No moving shadows.

But perhaps any trespassers are taking cover? They may have seen the curtain move. Maybe she's being watched. She waits, shallow breathing. Her toes curl up, trying to escape the icy floor. She can no longer feel her feet. Dooley skitters over to snuffle beneath the door to the landing.

By and by, she uncoils, too. Perhaps she misheard. It might have been a night creature hunting, or the wind whipping a tree branch against a windowpane. Everyone's nerves are stretched to breaking point, with the country in a state of lawlessness and no credible authorities to complain to about it. She might as well go back to bed.

Dooley remains at his post by the bedroom door, stubby tail erect. Edith considers her little Cerberus. To be on the safe side, she should investigate downstairs. She pokes her feet into a pair of slippers, wraps a wool dressing gown around her, and lifts the torch from her bedside table. She could find her way blindfolded about this house but it seems prudent to bring it. Dooley keeps his mistress in his sights. 'Come on, boy,' she whispers, and he pants with excitement but knows not to bark. Since a puppy, he has always read her moods.

She eases open the door and steps into the passageway. Mrs O'Shea and Philomena sleep near her room. No sound from that direction. Short of a cavalry charge through the rose garden, nothing rouses them. Her brother is three corridors away. Should she go up to his room and knock on the door? But it's at least thirty-five yards away. She decides to conduct her own investigation first. Back stairs or main staircase? The back stairs are a shortcut to the kitchen, directly below her bedroom, but the formal rooms are more likely to be targeted by intruders. She chooses the back stairs. Discretion is the better part of valour. Supposing there are intruders, she doesn't want to blunder into them.

Before entering the closed-in staircase, she stands and listens. Her concentration is fixed on identifying any unfamiliar noise. Dooley quivers, inclined to bolt downstairs, but knows he needs his mistress's permission. 'Stay, boy.' The house strikes her as intent. Does it hear her pattering heartbeat? A clock ticks. Mice rustle and scamper beneath the floorboards. Or rats, possibly – Cameron complained about them earlier. Usually, the dogs keep them under control but it might be time to lay poison again.

Shivering, Edith wonders if she's overreacting to an isolated sound. These are jumpy times. She'll manage no work tomorrow on her play if she tromps about the house at all hours. Just as she's on the point of returning to bed, a horse whinnies. She swivels her head. Sounds like Trumpeter. She decides to check the locks.

Edith switches on her torch, knowing it would be foolhardy to tear about in the dark. She's had her fair share of hunting spills down the years but broken bones at her age take longer to heal. Her descent follows its tapered beam, her enlarged shadow throwing up a distorted silhouette. It occurs to her she has all the components for an atmospheric painting – a woman, her shadow and a loyal fox terrier keeping her company in the fastness of night. The stairs bring her directly to the kitchen, where nothing is out of place. She plays the torchlight along the windows and back door, and is satisfied. Next, she makes her way to the morning room, where French doors open out to the lawn. That would be an easier entrance to break though than the front door. Once again, she shines the pool of light against locks. All is intact.

She and Dooley pass through the inner hall, where she flicks the torch towards the face of her parents' grandfather clock, a wedding gift sixty-four years ago, which continues to keep perfect time. Lasting better than her, in point of fact. It's almost two-thirty in the morning. The witching hour has passed, but the night has time left for mischief. This room leads to an outer hall dominated by a massive, nail-studded front door. She checks its bolts and hinges. Nothing appears to be tampered with. Satisfied, she flashes the torch towards the windows on either side of the doorway, which always remind her of squinting eyes framing a nose. Everything looks secure. Dooley conducts his own checks, sniffing along the lip of the door, a grumbling sound issuing from his throat. Inspection complete, he scampers through the darkness to continue his own investigations.

Edith's mouth feels dry. A glass of water and she'll return to bed. En route to the kitchen, she passes the glory hole, and notices its door is ajar. To be sure to be sure, as Mrs O'Shea likes to say, she sends the torchlight tiptoeing around an assortment of boots, rods, fishing baskets, umbrellas and sketching equipment. A three-year-old child would struggle to find a hiding place among such an excess of paraphernalia. Dooley reappears and barrels in, knocking over a discarded kite. She leaves him to root about.

Propping the torch on the table, she scans for matches, and finds them on a shelf on the dresser beside a pair of lamps. Soon, a yellow glow from one of the lamps reveals a shadowy kitchen. By day, it is homely – not that she often sets foot in it uninvited. The kitchen is the cook's domain. By night, it looks stark. Barred shutters at the windows give it a barracks appearance. Her eye lands on the range used for cooking and heating. Its warmth draws her forward, and she opens the range door to the fire inside, riddling the embers. Even in the middle of the night, the kitchen is cosy compared with the draughty hallways and corridors she's been wandering. She'll develop a chill in her kidneys from this night's work if she's not careful. Perhaps she should forget about water and heat some milk.

As Edith starts in the direction of the pantry, a loose stone outside is driven along the yard. Mid-step, she falters, a row of tiny hairs quivering against the back of her neck. This time, she distinctly hears footsteps. Her blood flow reduces to a sluggish trickle. The steps approach one of the windows. Metal against stone suggests their owner is wearing hob-nailed boots. Crunch, crunch, crunch. A man, and no lightweight. Just one set of feet. He walks directly up to the window and stops. He must see the lamplight and know somebody in the household is awake. Is it her imagination or can she hear breathing?

Paralyzed, she waits. Her eyes never leave the shutter fastening. It can't be opened from the outside – while the glass is intact. But removing a square of glass causes little difficulty to the determined housebreaker. She's watched her brothers do it to gain access to a locked boathouse: they wrap an elbow in sacking and push in the glass. A small pane shattering doesn't make much racket.

Dimly, she becomes aware of scuffling noises from the glory hole, punctuated by growling and rapid bursts of barking, but is too focused on the trespasser to pay Dooley any attention. Whatever he's up to, he'll have to deal with it himself. Now the footsteps begin their stamping again, this time ranging along the outer wall of the kitchen. As though searching for admission. There is a slit in the shutter nearest to her, where the wood has split. The footsteps stop there. After an eternity, a dark shape flits in front of the gap, moving away.

Belatedly, it occurs to her that she ought to cry out for help. Cameron would come charging downstairs with some weapon or other. Not his army gun, that was handed in to the RIC barracks. All firearms had to be surrendered. Otherwise, there's a risk of them falling into rebel hands. But before Cameron could arrive, the prowler might force an entry and use her as a hostage – he's just a few feet away whereas her brother is on another floor. Besides, her throat has seized up. She's not certain she can squeeze out more than a croak. Where's Dooley when she needs him? She hears him barking and scuffling, still wrestling with something in the glory hole. The noise is enough to waken the dead, but the household slumbers on.

Crunch, crunch, crunch. The intruder has passed along the rear of Drishane and is now heading back to where she waits. He's taking quite a chance. Her brother could throw open a window and fire a shot at him. This person doesn't know they have no guns. His confidence sends an adrenaline spike of fury coursing through Edith. Convulsively, her fingers tighten on the milk pan. If he does burst in, she'll clatter him with it.

After an eternity, the footsteps grow fainter. It sounds as if they are retreating across the stable yard, maybe hurdling the gate at the end of it leading to the woods. Exhausted, she slumps into a seat. The thought of malignant forces on the estate is horrible. She ought to raise the alarm, organize a search of the grounds. But what if there is more than one trespasser and Cam is injured – even killed? Her mind races, weighing alternatives. Leave well enough alone until the morning, she decides. All things considered, it's the safest course.

Drishane is too securely barricaded for any casual robber. Possibly, the footsteps belong to an advance scout. She'll talk to her brother in the morning, and together they can organize further precautions with Mike Hurley, Jeremiah O'Mahony and any of the villagers willing to lend a hand. There's a thought. Will the villagers stand by them? It's hard to know whose side they're on. Face to face, they're courteous to the Somervilles. But their loyalties may lie elsewhere. The people are seething at the Crown forces' violence, never mind towns under curfew and fairs and meetings banned.

When a truce in the fighting was called two months previously, she hoped they were over the worst. Normal life might resume. Much of the country remains outside the law, however, and units of IRA men are still operating – particularly in Munster. The Royal Irish Constabulary is depleted, with many constables calling it a day, while those digging in for their pensions are barricaded into barracks, police officers in name only. Last year, England sent over reinforcements – the RIC Auxiliaries, in their debonair Glengarry caps, but a bad situation was made worse with their wildness and tit-for-tat violence. As for the trigger-happy Black and Tans, if you weren't a rebel before meeting those soldiers, you'd be one for certain after an encounter with them. That's if you lived. Jeremiah O'Mahony's nephew was pulled over for not having a light on his donkey cart, taken away for being surly and flogged near death with a strip of wire. No wonder the people feel rancour.

Thuds and crashes continue to burst from the glory hole.

'Whatever you're doing, stop it at once, Dooley,' she cries.

Edith decides to sit up and keep watch. Sleep is impossible now. At least Martin will help. She has assured Edith there are good spirits in heaven who care about Drishane and can be called upon in emergency. Family members, and so on. Edith feels the dull poke of pain in her hand. Why, she's still holding the milk pan. When she sets it down, she sees a ridge in her palm scored by the handle.

Dooley reappears, swaggering, a dead rat between his jaws. He deposits it on the tiles and sits back on his haunches, tongue showing, dark eyes lambent.

'So that's what you've been busy with.'

He gives a triumphant yowl.

She tugs gently on one of his ears. 'Quite right, you deserve a prize. You've had rather more success with your unwanted visitor than I have with mine. Let's see what we can find in the pantry.'

Using coal tongs, Edith grasps the rat by its fat, furry middle and opens the range door, dropping it in. Next, she fetches a slice of chicken that seems to have been put by for tomorrow's lunch. Settling herself in Mrs O'Shea's armchair beside the range, she feeds it to Dooley from her hand, morsel by morsel. A final sniff at her fingers and lick of his chops, and he hops onto her lap, circles twice and settles down to sleep. The heat from his body spreads through Edith, a comfort to her racing mind.

The house has escaped tonight – touch wood – but the family's good name in the district won't shield them forever. Sooner or later, rebels will arrive looking for horses, guns and money. She warms her hands on Dooley's flanks. By and by, her eyes drift shut.

———

'Saints preserve us, Miss Edith, you're after giving me a desperate fright sitting there, so you are!' It's Philomena, first up to light the fires and carry tea on a tray to Cameron and Edith.

Edith blinks to absorb her surroundings. The previous night's events return to her with a sour spurt of juice in her mouth. 'Good morning, Philomena. I seem to have passed the night here.' She stretches her neck and adjusts her position to massage it, shifting Dooley's weight.

Just then, their cockerel crows.

'Imagine being awake before Roddy. I haven't been abroad this early since my hunting days.'

'Did something happen, Miss Edith? What were you thinking of, sleeping down here?'

'I'll tell you once I've had my cup of tea. I'm parched.'

'Miss Edith? What's going on? Were we – did you hear something in the night?'

'Tea first, please, Philomena. We'll talk then.'

Philomena looks mutinous, but bustles about the kitchen. She pushes the kettle onto a hot plate on the range, ferrets for wood in the basket by the pantry door and crashes open the shutters. Edith hears snatches of her complaint. 'Catch your death of cold at that aul' malarkey' … 'not twenty-one anymore.'

Edith knows she ought to stand up to do some stretches, and her weary bones deserve soaking in a hot bath. But she can't rustle up the energy to move quite yet. Dooley feels the same. He opens one eye, observes Philomena's activity and burrows into his mistress's lap. 'My warrior,' she croons, caressing his wiry fur. She's conscious of Philomena's shrewd glance but pretends not to notice.

'You'd hand that animal the moon out of the sky if he asked you for it, Miss Edith.'

'Dooley killed a king rat last night, a fellow as big as himself. I suppose there's no sign of the colonel yet?'

'Ah, sure, you won't see hide nor hair of him 'til I hit the breakfast gong. He's a man that's fond of his *leaba*, so he is. You'd imagine he'd be used to early rising after the army. But divil the bit of it. There's days I think if breakfast was changed to eleven o'clock in the morning, it would suit him just as—'

Enough is enough. Edith interrupts Philomena's flow. 'When you bring up his tea you might say I'd like a word with him before breakfast. As soon as he finds convenient. Tell him it's important.'

Philomena restricts herself to a tight nod.

Oh Lord, thinks Edith, now she has a cross Philomena on her hands. And if they are to keep Drishane safe, they need the staff onside. A cup and saucer is handed to her. 'You're an angel. Make sure you have some tea, too. There's nothing to beat it for starting the day.'

'I have to see to the colonel first. Tea and hot water for shaving, he needs.'

Edith sips at the steaming brew. Philomena has added extra sugar, a welcome treat – they are meant to be economizing on sugar, which is becoming hard to source. Dooley lays his front paws on her chest, pleading with every inch of his dear wee face. 'Down, boy. You'll have your share.' He looks a shade doubtful, but obeys. She splashes some tea into the saucer and sets it on the red quarry-tiled floor.

Philomena treats herself to an unmistakeable sniff before leaving the room with Cameron's tray. Edith creaks out of the chair and hobbles to the nearest window. She peers outside, alert for some sign of unusual activity. A fast-moving shape catches her eye. It's Mike Hurley arriving for work, bright and early, as usual. He lives with his family on Cross Street in the village, in the cottage where he was born. There's nothing Mike doesn't know about horses. He trained as a stable boy for the Dunravens at Adare Manor, but leapt at the chance to come home when Edith was able to take him on some years ago. She raps the window pane but he doesn't hear her. Wrenching open the sash window, she calls his name.

'Morning, Miss Edith. You're up with the lark. Did you want me to ready Tara for you? The road's worse than ever, mind you. Holes as big as bullocks. The boys have been busy. Must think there's a chance of the Tans or the Auxies coming this way on patrol.'

'No thank you, Mike. That won't be necessary.' She beckons with a finger. 'There's something I need to ask you.' When he's standing right outside the window, she leans forward, voice lowered, forefinger against her lips. 'Are all the horses in their stalls? None missing?'

An eyelid flicker ruffles his expression. 'Haven't checked them yet, miss. I'm just on my way in to them. Did something happen last night?'

'I believe there was an intruder on our property. I heard footsteps in the yard.'

'Are you all right, Miss Edith?'

'No harm done, I think. I'll have a word with you later, Mike, after I speak to the colonel. But please check everything carefully in the stables. And not just the horses. Look over the bridles, saddles and so on. We shall have to think what to do about the horses. They're an incitement to the robber class.'

'Right you be, Miss Edith.'

She tugs shut the window. Philomena returns while she's fiddling with the catch on the sash.

'The master says he'll be down directly. Won't you tell me what's going on, miss? I know something's not right.'

Edith hesitates. Maybe she should just tell Philomena. But paws skittering outside signal the arrival of Cameron's dog Loulou, who hurtles into the room, rushing straight to Dooley's empty saucer of tea. She gives the china an exploratory lap, more in hope than expectation. Dooley growls and Loulou backs under the table, trailing her plumed tail. The cream Pomeranian, only seven inches high, is dwarfed by the furniture. Dooley, more than twice her size, growls again to show who's top dog.

'Ignore him, Lou,' says Edith. 'Dooley, mind your temper.'

Where Loulou appears, Cameron is never far behind. He arrives now, scarlet in the face. To her surprise, he is still in his pyjamas and a navy woollen dressing gown. Childhood aside, Edith could count on one hand the number of times she has seen her brother in his night clothes, and still have fingers to spare.

Anxiety splinters his voice. 'What's this I hear about you sitting up all night?'

'Why don't we go into the morning room, Cam? We can talk there.'

A knock on the back door delays them. Edith and Cameron exchange glances while Philomena answers it, converses and returns to the kitchen. 'Mike Hurley says to tell you all present and correct, miss.' An inhalation of breath. 'He wouldn't say what he meant by it.'

'You'll know soon enough, Philomena. I need to talk to the colonel first.'

Edith leads the way, to where the table is ready for breakfast and preparations for a fire are lying in the grate. Ignoring her protesting kneecaps, she hunkers down and strikes a match. Paper twists catch fire instantly and begin sparking the wood. She hauls herself to her feet and meets her brother's eye.

'There was a man prowling about the stable yard last night, Cam.'

'Why the blazes didn't you call me?'

'I know, I should have. I think I must have been paralyzed by fright.'

'If someone is loitering on our property after dark, you can be sure they're up to no good. You really ought to have woken me, Edith.'

'I thought I heard something, but convinced myself I was imagining things. When I couldn't get back to sleep, I went downstairs to check the locks and bolts. It was just a precaution. Honestly, if I'd believed there was someone I'd have knocked on your door and sent you down. Then when I did realize it, I just sort of froze. By the time I pulled myself together he was gone. So I thought I might as well let you have a night's sleep while you could. Because ... we have to assume ... I mean, I expect he'll be back tonight. You'll have to sit up.'

'I still think you should have woken me, old girl.'

'It was stupid of me, Chimp. But honestly, I believed the danger had passed. I'm not idiotic enough to tackle a gang of men single-handed.'

'A gang? I thought you said one intruder.'

'Yes, just one. I think. Let me tell you what I heard.'

After Edith updates Cameron, he says, 'I've been expecting something of this nature.'

'At least we have some notice. We can be ready for them. They'll want guns, of course. You handed in all of yours, didn't you Chimp? We were warned to, in the springtime.'

'I've told you before, I gave our duck guns to the RIC. Along with that old shotgun Hildegarde's Egerton passed on to you. Then, after Skib courthouse was burned out last June, I handed in the small revolver with filigree work on its handle. The one I picked up in Paris. Let them shoot me, I thought, but not with my own gun.'

'And your army pistol? You've surrendered that, too?'

He fidgets with his moustache. 'Can't bear to part with it. But I've hidden it well. They'd have to tear the house apart to find it, Peg.'

'Are you mad, Cam? When Park House was broken into, not a mattress survived their bayonets. Nelly and Mimi's nerves were ground to shreds.'

'You can't expect young ladies to stand up to that kind of pressure.'

She lowers her voice. 'These men have a network of local sources. The servants could be passing on information. Not deliberately, perhaps, but you know how word gets about. What's to stop Philomena mentioning your revolver to Mrs O'Shea, and maybe she'd say something to her sister in the village about Colonel Somerville being armed. And she'd tell a neighbour, and so on. We're watched, Cam, whether we like it or not.'

He crosses to the French doors, which open onto a manicured lawn and flower beds blazing with lobelias, Japanese anemones and cactus dahlias. 'It all seems so peaceful out there.'

Edith thinks of the biplane which buzzed the nearby hills earlier in the year, trying to flush out a group of IRA men believed to be hiding there. 'Deceptively so.'

'I can't give up my service revolver. We'd be like lambs to the slaughter.'

'If they find it, your gun will be used against the Crown, dear.'

'They might not find it.'

'And they might.'

He slaps his hand against the door frame. 'Have it your own way. I'll go to Skib after breakfast and give in my revolver at the barracks.'

'Good. The sooner all our guns are off the premises the better. Your service pistol – and any others that might have slipped your mind. When they come, as come they will, you can look them in the eye and say you have no weapons. If you're straight with them, hopefully they'll spare the house. Dr Jim gave them a donation instead of weapons. But if you're caught telling an untruth, it gives these people permission to do their worst.'

'Donation my eye,' snorts Cameron.

Edith stands her ground. 'It saved face for the rebels – no one wants to leave empty-handed. I'm convinced that's what stopped Park House being set alight.'

'No wonder the Jim Somervilles sold up. We're fools to hang on here, Peg. At least we still have something to sell. If the house goes up in flames there'll be nothing worth putting on the market.'

So, he's back singing that song. Has Drishane ever had a more ineffectual master? She chokes back her impatience. 'Selling up is the easy answer. They won't get rid of us without a fight. After more than two hundred and fifty years here, we've earned our right to live in Ireland. Let's show them what we're made of, Cam. What we have we hold.' She joins him at the window, and pats him on the shoulder. 'Good times will come again.'

'But what's to happen to us meanwhile? We'll be sitting ducks.'

'What use is one gun or even two against a gang of men? Look, we can't protect the house indefinitely from them. Let's make the best of it, wait for them to come to us and give them some of what they want. If we co-operate, maybe they'll leave us alone.'

'Feed a crocodile and it always returns for more.'

'We don't have much choice. These are lawless times. The police can't defend us. Nor can the Tans. We must look to ourselves. What's the loss of a few possessions compared with keeping Drishane safe? If we get on the wrong side of the rebels, they're capable of torching the house out of spite.'

'You seem rattled, old girl.'

'That's because I am. We're powerless against them, Cam. The Somerville name means nothing to a flying column. I say let them in, be polite, give them a few odds and ends to keep them satisfied. Food, a couple of saddles, a horse if we must, some paste jewellery to sell on – they won't be able to tell it from the real thing.'

'Ever the pragmatist, Peg.'

Why must he be so obtuse? She reels in her exasperation. 'Do you have anything on the premises you shouldn't? Other than guns, I mean?'

'Not a thing.'

'Nothing at all? They'll come back if they think we're holding out on them.'

'Well, I might have something.'

'What? Cameron, what have you got? Tell me!'

'Some sovereigns. In my study, in the desk.'

With creditors unpaid? Edith is thunderstruck. But now is no time to challenge him about his stash. 'Lodge them in the bank when you go to the RIC with your gun. No matter how banjaxed the roads, you must get through to Skibbereen. I don't have any cash but I'd hate to lose Mama's jewellery. I'll wrap it up now. When you're in the bank, ask the manager to store it in his safe for me. Oh, and it would be a good idea to hold back a sovereign or two. Something to give the rebels.'

He rubs the stubble on his chin. 'By George, that's not a bad plan you've cooked up, old thing. Give a little, to make them think we bear no ill will. It'll buy us time until the rabble is routed.'

Edith isn't convinced these guerrilla fighters who call themselves soldiers in the Irish Republican Army will be beaten. They don't play by any of the rules of war her soldiering brothers understand. Her thumb pad strokes the gold Claddagh ring given to her by Martin, worn in her memory on her ring finger. 'So you'll go to Skib today with your revolver and Mama's jewels?'

'I'll go. But there's one thing that's staying in Drishane, whatever you say. Grandpapa's regimental sword.'

'I've heard of them taking those swords.'

'I'm not surrendering it and that's final! It's a family heirloom. It's hung on the wall since before either of us was born. The only time it was taken down was when we laid it on his coffin.'

She breathes in. Waits a beat. Looks contrite. *Choose your battles.* 'Whatever you say, Chimp.'

Edith knows where her priority lies. Preventing Drishane from going up in smoke.

four

Edith stands beside Cameron on Drishane's limestone steps, under the pillared front door with its arching skylight. Other houses may be tentatively placed, teetering apologetically in their settings, but Drishane is confident without being conspicuous. Its position welcomes in the countryside: open outlooks sweeping towards sheltering hills northwards, while to the south rears a craggy coastline with changeable seas.

A mass of foliage crowds the driveway, which curves downwards to join the only road in and out of the village. It's impossible to reach Castletownshend by road, or leave it by road, without passing the Somervilles' gate. Sea routes are a different matter. At the end of the avenue stands the gatehouse, home to their gardener, Jeremiah O'Mahony. Beyond it, to the right, the village begins its downhill meander. Nowhere in Castletownshend is more than a ten-minute walk from Drishane.

Brother and sister watch Mike lead the horse and trap – which Cameron prefers to the smaller dogcart – around the side of the house, towards the front sweep of pathway. Cameron turns to Edith and taps a bulge in his breast pocket, indicating his army pistol. She nods, and casts a practised eye over the way Tara is conducting herself.

'Madam here's gentle as a lamb for now, but don't be fooled. She's ready to shy at anything and everything today. A child running out, a white gatepost she doesn't like the look of, even a tree by the side of the road – she'll bolt. You'll need a firm hand on the reins or she'll dance you into a ditch.'

Cameron buttons his driving gloves at the wrist. 'Hold her there, Hurley. I'll soon show her who's boss if she acts up, Peg.' He mounts the trap and cracks his whip in the air. The sound causes Tara to set off at a lively lick, the conveyance wobbling as it corners too fast.

Oh dear, thinks Edith. He needs to humour Tara, not behave like her commanding officer. 'She's still inclined to be jittery around motor-cycles,' she shouts after him, but it's unlikely he hears her.

Mike Hurley shrugs, as much as to say Cameron will have to find that out for himself, and returns to the stables.

Edith's eyes stray across their land. Imagine having a deer park. But they need the fields for grazing. Tara jumps like a deer – it's a pity neither she nor Cameron is capable of putting the mare over West Cork's steep banks. Tempus fugit. She walks behind the ivy-covered house. Drishane isn't showy. It's built squarely of grey stone, well-proportioned and many windowed – elegant in its simplicity. Inside, there are smoky chimneys, dog hairs on the soft furnishings and holes blooming in the silk curtains. But the structure, undoubtedly, is a thing of beauty. As for the Atlantic setting, looking west by Cape Clear – it's inspired.

The artist in her wonders about Drishane's architect. His name must be listed on bills somewhere, but she doesn't know it. Clearly, he was a man who understood the value of symmetry. Of course, Tom the Merchant, her several times great-grandfather (she loses count), who commissioned the house in the 1700s, had the wit to choose the right man for the job. That earlier Somerville had a fleet trading with the West Indies and Newfoundland in sugar, rum and wine. He made the family's fortune. It's been in descent ever since. What was it Shaw called them, last time cousin Charlotte brought her beloved to lunch? Downstarts.

Just like himself, he claimed. An imp of a man, says what he likes and does it with a flourish.

Dooley yaps at a robin, which startles from a bush. Remembering his loyalty the previous night, she bends to pat his white bristles, with an extra stroke for the patch of autumn leaf above his eye. 'My little shadow.' As she straightens, a dart of sciatica jabs her right knee. A wooden leg would be a distinct improvement. By rights, she should sit with her feet up, but rest will have to wait its turn.

The smell of damp vegetation and fresh horse droppings signals the stables, where Mike is grooming Pilot with a curry comb. He nods at her but keeps going.

'I'm a bit behind here, Miss Edith, a lick and a promise will have to do them today. But I had a good look round and nothing was taken last night.'

'I wonder if some other house was their target instead?' The repetitive motion of his hand is soothing, and she watches it for a few moments. 'I dare say we'll hear soon enough.'

Trumpeter is in a sulky mood and kicks at the wooden partition, flicking his tail. But Samson pokes his head over the top of his stall and whinnies, his warm breath reaching across to her, friendly as a wink.

'Hello, old man. You never forget me.' Edith produces a windfall apple from her pocket. With delicate precision, the dappled grey horse takes it between his teeth from the palm of her hand, and munches through it in a couple of bites. He nuzzles her hand in hopes of another. 'That's your lot. We had some high times together, didn't we, Samson?' Once the strongest of hunters, he's now advanced in years and used for farm work.

On impulse, she takes down the hunting horn from its nail on the wall and blows. Samson pricks up his ears and neighs. Alarmed, Trumpeter and Pilot drum their hooves and snort.

'Easy, boy.' Mike pats Pilot, a smile lightening his solemn face. 'You too, Trumpeter. Easy.' Mike is not much past forty, but a life spent working in the open air has aged his skin.

Edith knots her fingers in Samson's mane. 'You'd like to be following the hounds, too, wouldn't you, Samson? Those were the days! Nothing like the music of the horn to stir the blood.'

The highest compliment she ever received was an overheard one, from the groom before Mike. 'Miss Edith spends more time on horseback than she does in bed,' he told a visitor's manservant. But no longer.

She rests her forehead against Samson's. Once, the stable yard was a beehive of activity, every stall occupied and half a dozen men from the village employed there. A place in the Drishane stables was prized by the locals. The hounds were kennelled nearby, and their yodelling and scrapping among one another fed into the rich soup of estate life. The kennels are silent now, even emptier than the stalls – the pack sold into Yorkshire.

Mike is the only one left to look after the stable's four inhabitants. A phantom parade of horses rises to her mind: her first pony when she was three, first hunter in her teens – never has she felt more intensely alive than when on horseback, leading the chase. The joy of those four-thirty morning starts when the world was new-minted: cannoning along with the wind at her back, grips spilling from her hair as she took a jump. She'll never know such exultation again.

Edith shakes herself. Surrendering to nostalgia won't safeguard the few horses left to her. 'I wish we'd been able to sell some of the mounts, at least, Mike. They'll be commandeered if we don't watch out.'

'Nothing's selling these days, Miss Edith.'

'I know. But if we don't move them on, they'll be taken by men who think they're patriots. And maybe they are,' she adds hastily. Mike's never been a Sinn Féiner, but people who were never Sinn Féiners before have turned to the Irish independence party.

'Ridden into the ground, then shot and ate. That's what'll happen the poor beasts,' says Mike.

Edith purses her mouth, conveniently forgetting her own set's habit of feeding horses to the hounds when they've outlived their usefulness, or broken legs and necks on the hunting field. She casts a critical eye over Pilot and Trumpeter, both as fat as butter from insufficient activity. If she could only mount a horse again, she'd exercise the devilment out of those two.

'This pair are prime hunters, Mike. There must be some way to find buyers in England, even if Ireland's in no mood for hunting these days. A lowish price would be better than nothing. A bird in the hand.'

'How would you even get them to England, miss? Word'd get out. They'd be taken off the train in Cork or Limerick. Mick Collins's boys are always in need of horses.' Mike lifts Pilot's hooves, one after another, and checks them. Between the second and third hoof, he says, 'I might see if I can find a safe berth for them. Tide them over the winter. Sure, who knows how the lie of the land might be by springtime.'

'Is there anywhere?'

'There's a farmer I know. Lives off the beaten track.'

She doesn't answer, still wedded to the idea of selling the hunters.

'I wouldn't take all day making my mind up, Miss Edith. Time's not on your side.'

His frankness startles her. 'He's reliable, your friend?'

'To the best of my knowledge. I don't deny it's a risk. But so is having them here, where the world and his wife knows the Somervilles keep decent horses.' Mike straightens and meets Edith's eye over Pilot's back.

'I suppose we should think about—'

'I'll ride over this morning.' He slaps Pilot on the rump. 'This boyo could use the exercise. It'll take me a while, though – I'll have to stay off the roads.'

'This morning?'

'No time like the present. I'll ride Pilot and lead Trumpeter. When the fella I have in mind sees them, he might maybe be minded to give the pair of them a home for the duration. He's a horse fancier like his father before him. He wouldn't want to see good horseflesh put at risk. They could easy take a bullet, the places them flying columns would take them.'

Edith hesitates. It's unlike Mike Hurley to be so insistent. Does he know something she doesn't? 'You mean leave them with him today?'

'It's for the best.'

She swallows. 'All right, Mike. If you say so. What about Tara and Samson?'

'You can't be without her ladyship for getting about. And Samson is handy for farm work.'

She's relieved about Tara. Without the mare, she can only go as far as these crocked legs will carry her, which is no distance at all. 'I'll give you something to cover their board and lodgings if your friend is willing to take them in. There'll be feed to buy over the winter.'

Mentally, she retrieves two sovereigns from Cameron's hoard. Just before leaving for Skibbereen, he stashed some coins. They discussed safe places, and ended up loosening a hat lining and placing the money inside it. The boater is hidden in the ancient wooden settle in the inner hall.

Samson blows through his nose, as though aware he's being discussed. Edith scratches his ears. 'You're solid gold, old fellow. We had some times of it, didn't we?'

'You could mount a child of two on him and he'd be as gentle as a lamb. Not like the other one, she's a contrary lady. But still and all, she's a well-made specimen with plenty of jizz. Your friend beyond in England, Dr Smyth, took quite a shine to her. Called her Tara-go-round-the-chimney-pots.'

'Tara likes to jump. Especially when you least expect it.'

Edith's mind starts to tick. Ethel Smyth is well-connected. She has neighbours and associates in Surrey who appreciate horseflesh. Could she help her to sell Pilot and Trumpeter? She's still reluctant to trust them to a stranger, who may or may not return them to her. Possession is nine-tenths of the law. There must be some way to ship the horses to England. Perhaps if she found a buyer she could arrange safe passage for the animals. Pay off someone, if necessary.

Yes, that's what she'll do: write and ask Ethel Smyth to make inquiries about buyers. If only she'd thought of it before Cameron set off – he could have posted the letter in Skibbereen. But there's always a chance Timmy the Post will manoeuvre his bicycle through to them. He lifts it over barbed wire and steers it around potholes in the road. Ireland still produces some people determined to do their duty. Although his diligence may be due to family feeling. As a nephew of their cook's, he's always inclined to go the extra mile to reach Drishane, where he can be sure of a mug of sweet tea and slice of apple tart the size of a cartwheel.

Except she can never be certain about his comings and goings, and she really shouldn't delay selling the horses. She chews her lip, and decides to send a letter via the destroyer in Castlehaven Bay, lying in wait to respond to possible emergencies. Her brother, Hugh, told her she could use it for important communications. All she has to do is ask the coast-guard to signal, and the captain will despatch a boat to the quay. Hugh is naval commander at Queenstown – it was his idea to send the destroyer from Haulbowline in Cork harbour, ready to protect His Majesty's loyal citizens if things turned hairy. A signal arrangement has been put in place. If she waves a red lamp from one of the top windows, fifty crew members will spring into action to evacuate her and Cameron. It's a comfort, of course. But she doesn't want to withdraw from Drishane. It may not be possible to return.

Ethel Smyth – Boney – is her closest friend. Ever since girlhood, Edith has needed an intimate friend. One particular soulmate to whom she can lay herself bare emotionally, sharing her innermost thoughts. There have been several, but none became a bosom friend on the same level as her dearest Martin. Boney comes closest – although there are times when she is fonder of Boney from a distance.

The notion of an intermediary who might sell her horses cheers Edith as she goes indoors, towards the panelled oak settle that's sat there forever. Or at least since the days of Tom the Merchant. From inside the seat, she extracts a hat, pokes open the lining and squeezes out a couple of sovereigns. She considers nesting there to write her letter because it always looks welcoming, with flowering plants carved on its upright back and 'Reste and Bee Thankful' inscribed on an upright panel. But appearances are deceptive. Wood offers no kindness to sore bones. Edith goes to the breakfast room to compose her missive. She must strike the right note. Not desperate to sell, frightened for Drishane's future – but expectant that a friend will do her a favour, if at all possible.

Drishane House
6 October 1921
My dear Boney,

I know I sometimes brandish that eminently sensible quote at you, 'Fools rush in where angels fear to tread,' but foolishness or angelic wisdom has overtaken me. One or the other. We shall see. I'm knee-deep in a project which excites me more than anything I've attempted since

45

Martin passed beyond the veil. I'm adapting some of our Irish R.M. stories for the theatre. I can't tell you how elevated I feel working on this material. Naturally, it is a labour of love. Nevertheless, I'm hoping virtue won't be my only reward and the project will reap shekels galore for my sorely depleted coffers.

This is a long-winded way of saying, dear Ethel, that I can't possibly leave Drishane until after Christmas. The play must take priority. In the meantime, you are most welcome to visit Castletownshend if you feel like a break from Woking, although I should warn you that this part of Cork continues to bear the brunt of the fighting. There is precious little sign of any ceasefire here. The post, trains and banks are all being held up and robbed 'for the cause' — where there is anything to steal. Houses, too, are being raided by armed men. I dare say it's only a matter of time before we are their target here in Drishane.

She considers telling her about the previous night's intruder and decides against it. The post is said to be opened and read by the rebels. On that basis, it's a risk to mention the horses but she has to take it.

We have nothing of worth here. It will be a frightful waste of their time if they do honour us with their presence. Meanwhile, we potter along as best we can. Cameron and I managed to have a game of croquet the other day — it was almost like old times. Apart from the unseasonal hailstones!

You don't happen to know of anyone who's in the market for a hunter or two? I have a couple of toppers here. One of them is black apart from two white socks on his hind legs. He has the courage of a lion — has never refused a jump in his life. The other is a long-backed roan stallion, a little on the short side but he'd suit a plucky lady rider. Do ask around for me if you can. You'd be doing me ever such a good turn.

Fond regards,

Edith

P.S. Mike Hurley would accompany them and guarantee to deliver them to their new owners in tip-top condition.

Edith puts the letter in an envelope and addresses it to Dr Ethel Smyth of Coign, Hook Heath, near Woking, Surrey, England. Boney was awarded an honorary doctorate in music by the University of Durham, and friends omit the title at their peril. This afternoon, she'll make arrangements for it to be sent to England via Hugh's destroyer. She doesn't like to abuse his generosity, but selling horses is no trivial business to her.

Now to the play. As she looks over yesterday's work, doubt nibbles. *Flurry's Wedding* tells of Flurry Knox's usual horsey shenanigans and the resident magistrate Major Yeates's attempts to rein him in. Flurry's pranks are all in a good cause, intended to raise the cash to marry his several-times-removed cousin Sally Knox. Edith is convinced it's a cracking piece, full of fun and frolics, which are sorely needed in these uncertain times, but how is she to place it?

She has no contacts in the theatrical field. None that count, anyhow. She knows Lady Gregory socially, of course, but has no intention of handing over her work to the Abbey Theatre. Martin would never approve. They manufacture their past, the Celtic Twilighters. That enterprise is too, too worthy. Besides, there's no money in a Dublin run. And even if she were to give it to the Abbey, nationalist Ireland has always been lukewarm about the Irish R.M., perceiving slights where none were intended. No, she doesn't care for the Dublin literary set, all long-haired male poets and short-haired female novelists. Flurry must be placed with a London producer. He deserves nothing less. Royalties lie at the end of the West End rainbow.

She considers unsealing the envelope and adding another postscript. Boney is a natural-born networker and bound to have ideas about whom to approach. But she is such a busybody. If Edith solicits her advice, she'll commandeer the play in its entirety. Before she knows it, her friend will be voicing opinions on plot, character, staging and scenery. Ethel Smyth is true-hearted, unflagging in her affections and enthusiasms. She charges out to meet the world head-on without ever pausing to check if her hat is sitting straight. But her conviction that she's an expert on virtually everything can be a little trying.

Edith sucks the lid of her fountain pen, and inspiration strikes. Her cousin Charlotte is married to George Bernard Shaw. Lottie has always had family feeling galore, besides being a helpful sort – nearly clever, but not quite. She'll send the play to Lottie for advice, and her cousin is bound to ask the great man to take a look. That will set it on its way. If Shaw likes it, he'll recommend it to someone influential. Edith is confident he will. The public loves those hunting stories – their agent, Mr Pinker, was always badgering the Somerville and Ross team for more. Admittedly, it's been a few years since the last R.M. collection. Nineteen-fifteen, in point of fact – such a sad year. She lost Martin a few months after publication. Not lost entirely, she's with her always. But it's not quite the same.

Edith sighs. She must go back out to the stables and give those sovereigns to Mike. Then she really should take a rest.

———

Dinner is a melancholy affair: hunters gone, jewellery gone, guns gone. So far as Edith can judge, Cameron has carried out her instructions. The problem is you can never tell with her brother. She wouldn't be surprised if he'd held back some dagger or spear from his soldiering days. But at least his army revolver is with the RIC and Mama's jewellery is in a Bank of Ireland safety deposit box. She expects him to take more of an interest when she tells him about Mike Hurley's scheme for hiding the hunters, but he's too wrapped up in his own day, chuntering on about detours taken and streams splashed through. You'd imagine he was navigating the Orinoco.

Nodding and looking outwardly sympathetic, she is preoccupied by a heart-stopping realization. She forgot to give Cameron the most important item of jewellery in her possession. She kept some paste jewellery to palm off on raiders, and handed over everything else in her jewellery box – apart from Mama's ruby ring. The last person to wear it was her sister Hildegarde, who borrowed it and noticed the stone was loose. When she returned it, Edith didn't put it back where the ring belonged, instead slipping it into the pocket of her travel bag because she meant to take it to London to be re-set. But the country was in such convulsions that any unnecessary journey seemed unwise. Which means Mama's ruby ring is in Drishane. Should she confess to Cameron? Not after the row she raised over his service pistol.

She needs a proper chat with Martin. If only she could manage a seance. But her neighbour Jem Barlow, who acts as her medium, has gone away for a time. The nightly diet of rifle shots and flames against the sky – not as distant as one would prefer – has taken its toll, and many of the more substantial properties in the village and surrounding area are deserted. Still, Miss Barlow's absence hasn't derailed Edith's communications with the spirit world. Edith, too, possesses the psychic spark – she's had it since girlhood. Her automatic-writing sessions are treasure troves of sensible conversation with Martin. She'll do some after dinner.

Over dessert, a measly affair of stewed fruit with insufficient sweetening, she considers asking her brother to join her. Sometimes, he plays Brahms on the piano to assist with atmosphere during seances. She gauges him through narrowed eyes. No, he's showing the strain of recent events. Look at him fidget – he'd never sit still long enough for her to go into a trance. Oh, he's feeding that chubby-chops of a Loulou some left-over slivers of fat cut from his meat. Deceitful little creature, just like her master. Cameron must have slid them into his napkin before his dinner plate was collected. A filthy habit, Mama would never have permitted it at the dinner table. No wonder that creature is like a waddling sofa. Dooley is much better behaved. As a reward for not begging, she goes to the sideboard and lifts a sugar cube from the bowl. She bends down and Dooley takes it from her, table manners as restrained as a duchess's.

'Any chance of a splash of coffee, old girl? Now you're on your feet.'

'Of course. I'm being terribly slow tonight, aren't I?'

'Not at all. As a matter of fact, I'm astounded you're still standing. Tough as ... Chip off the old block. Mama, I mean.'

'You were about to say old boots, weren't you?'

'Steady on, Edith, I was trying to pay you a compliment. But any attempt to flatter women – even a sister – is a risky business.'

Edith pours out their nightly aid to digestion and carries the cup and saucer to Cameron. She's had to tell Mrs O'Shea to brew the coffee weaker than usual because beans are in short supply at the grocer's. Fortunately, they're not reduced to reusing grinds yet. And at least her Townshend grandmother's silver coffee pot is safely in storage, along with its matching milk jug, sugar bowl, tongs and tray. She loved seeing them clustered there, like a plump mother goose with her goslings. But she's happier not seeing them, currently.

Cameron scratches one of his prominent ears, looking pleased with himself. 'You'll be glad to hear I've fixed things with Hurley and his nephew to share sentry duty in the grounds tonight. And I'll be sitting up, on guard in the house. Thought about roping in O'Mahony but Hurley said he was too old, it wouldn't be fair. Volunteered his nephew instead. So you mustn't fret, Peg. We have it all in hand. You can't lose a second night's sleep.'

She's about to protest at him making arrangements without consulting her. On second thoughts, Cameron needs to feel he's in charge. 'Well done, Chimp.'

'You do think Hurley's trustworthy, don't you? And the other servants?'

'They've worked for us for years. Surely you don't suspect them?'

'They might have divided loyalties, the way things stand. Maybe they're hunting with the hare and running with the hounds.'

Edith chews her thumb knuckle, slanting the thought this way and that. It's as hateful as it is logical. The British haven't ruled Ireland well – quite the reverse. Why shouldn't the common people support men of their own sort who tell them they can make a better job of government? Words are cheap, of course, but they may be effective.

'But they've never given us any grounds to doubt them,' she says. 'They must have known about your revolver but didn't breathe a word to anyone.'

'I suppose.'

Edith tries – and fails – to imagine running Drishane without staff. Who'd cook their meals and serve them? Set their fires and beat their carpets? Her play will never get written if she has to spend her time thinking about mincing leftover beef into sandwich meat or searching for eggs in the hens' hidey-holes.

'Anyhow, you've asked Mike Hurley now, Cam.'

'Didn't have much choice. There was no one else. Stopped off in the village on the way home from Skib. Thought I'd have a word with some of the men. See if they knew anything. Meant to ask them to help us keep watch. Didn't in the end. There was something odd about the behaviour of two of the Connors boys. Furtive – that's the best way to describe them. I didn't like it. So I said nothing. Came back up the hill to Drishane and fixed things with Hurley instead.'

'Some of those Connors boys are Sinn Féiners. At least one of them is on the run.'

'But their father saw service in the Boer War!'

'That was then.' A dragging sound outside causes her to startle. 'What's that? Are we expecting anyone?'

'The young O'Mahonys. Jeremiah's grandsons. I was able to lay my hands on some empty potato sacks in Skib. Stopped into the O'Mahony place on the way home and squared it with their father. I've put them to filling the sacks with sand. They're setting a battery of sandbags against all the outer doors so no one can force their way in.' He expands his chest, ready for her congratulations.

'Are they able for it? Can't be more than twelve or thirteen.'

'Looked strong enough to me, from farm work. Any chance of another splash?'

She tops up his coffee. Despite her apprehension, the artistic side of her brain admires the arc of the flow from spout to cup. The tree-trunk brown colour is perfect for a woodland painting – darker than toffee, lighter than chocolate. 'I hope you haven't asked the O'Mahonys to patrol with the Hurleys. They're only children.'

'I might use them as lookouts another night. We'll see how we go.'

'You know, I can't help wondering if we aren't better getting a raid over and done with, dear. We're in the IRA's sights. We can't hold them off indefinitely.'

'No reason to leave the henhouse door lying open.'

'I suppose.'

He drains his cup and stands. 'Believe I'll go out and inspect those sandbags. Might look in on O'Mahony, too. Tell him to keep an eye out from the gatehouse. I know Hurley says he's too old, but it's all hands to the pump in an emergency.'

When she's alone, Edith rings the bell for Philomena to clear away the dishes. She intends to work at the dining-room table where there is plenty of space to spread herself. She's seen arms flung about like windmills at trance writing, pots of ink and vases knocked over. She doesn't need many props – a thick pad of paper, a selection of pencils and Martin's tooled-leather cigarette case will be sufficient. Along with some peace – unfortunately, Philomena is inclined to linger and chat. Abstracted, Edith listens to the casement clock bonging eight-thirty. She had counted on starting now – it's a conducive time for Martin, apparently.

Her silence doesn't discourage Philomena. 'I saw Mike Hurley taking two of the horses away. Then back again on foot, without either one of them. Where he went, he wouldn't say. Just tapped the side of his nose and said, "that's for me to know and you to guess".'

Edith glances up. 'What you don't know you can't tell, Philomena. There's safety in ignorance. It's for your own good.'

Philomena's eyes round, catching her meaning. 'I hear you, Miss Edith. Shall I leave all the candles lit? Are you intendin' for to stay and have one of your ghostie-things here?'

'Yes, leave the candelabra lit. You may extinguish the oil lamp on the sideboard.'

'It's a mortal pity to think that you, who was always flourishing about as if you hadn't a bone in your body, running here there and everywhere, should be sitting in at nights at this aul' malarkey. Me, I'd have no truck with talking to the dead. Not for all the tea in China. And sure, wouldn't Father Lambe have me guts for garters if he heard I was at that aul' caper?'

'That'll do, Philomena. I know what I'm about. Incidentally, you may be reassured to know Mike Hurley and his nephew Ned are patrolling the grounds tonight. At least we'll get fair warning if intruders are about.'

Philomena gives a dramatic shiver. 'With the help of God. There's plenty of blackguards taking their chance to settle old scores. All for Ireland, indeed. We'd be greener than cabbage if we believed that yarn.'

She takes a last check that everything is back in place. Adjusting the cut-glass bowl of chrysanthemums so that it stands in the centre of the table, Philomena lifts a tray stacked with dirty crockery. Turning with her load, she almost trips over Dooley.

'I'll swing for that animal one day,' she mutters.

Edith chooses not to hear.

Alone, she sits upright in her usual seat at the foot of the dining-room table. Three candles burn with a steady flame in front of her. The paper and pencils rest near-hand, ready for the moment of connection. She never doubts her ability to communicate with Martin – Edith knows she possesses the necessary spark of psychical power, her shortcut to the beyond. Her right hand lies on the table, palm upwards, relaxed. Her left hand, heavy with Martin's ring, caresses Martin's cigarette case, thumb pad tracing the initials VM. Martin had a variety of cigarette cases, but this was her favourite. A faint scent of tobacco rises towards her nostrils.

Practice has taught Edith how to enter a trance. She closes her eyes and empties her mind. Pinpoints of light loom and fade behind her eyelids. Distant sounds honeycomb the silence, before the dream state takes over and noise dwindles into nothingness. She slows her breathing, conscious of taking air into her body and holding it in her lungs, feeling it swirl through them before being expelled. Her blood roars along her veins.

Now she feels a tingling, pricking sensation in her right arm. It is followed by a numbness in the arm from shoulder to hand. The limb becomes cold and disconnected, as if it no longer belongs to her. But Martin isn't here yet. Her mind has not yet emptied. It continues to intrude on her connection with the other world. Around her, Drishane is a patient presence. Head tilted to one side, she keeps stroking the case, aware of her ribcage rising and falling. Now she opens her eyes and fixes her gaze on the door opposite. She doesn't see the grain of the wood, nor its brass handle. Even the door's rectangular shape is indistinct. Blankness spreads across her vision, her mind lulled into a dream state.

The force begins to grow within her. A swollen sensation runs up and down the right arm, converging on her finger tips. Without conscious thought, she lifts one of the pencils, leaning it loosely against the web of skin between her thumb and forefinger. She listens, not with her ears but her body. All at once, her heartbeat trips and her hand jolts, fastening tightly on the pencil. It executes a series of circles in the air.

Martin is with her – Edith senses her presence. She knows she must initiate the conversation.

'Are we safe in Drishane, Martin?'

The pencil is propelled towards the paper. As soon as its point touches the page, words spill out: angular, downward strokes scoring deep onto the surface. Edith has no knowledge of what she's writing. She doesn't even look at the page, gazing instead into the candlelight. For now, her hand does not belong to her – the force causing it to move is external.

The pencil ceases its activity as abruptly as it began writing. Only when it stops moving does Edith feel that she, too, can stir. It's as if she has been held in a gentle but firm grip and is now released. She exhales, and reads the spiky script.

> You must be braveand resourceful a challenging tiem lies ahead
> but you are not alone tap into your reserves of courage believe and
> allshall b e well

The script has covered almost an entire page. She turns it over, presenting another blank surface. Cameron's doubts about the Connors boys are preying on her mind.

'Are the tenants loyal? And the villagers? Can we count on them?'

> some are and some are not youmust take sensible precautions
> but it will be impossibel to escape the attention of
> nabothsvineyardnabothsvineyard raiders entirely

She takes another page. 'What do you suggest?'

The pencil rises from the page and moves forwards and back a few times, indecisive, before crashing back down onto the paper.

You are not alone we who love you guardguardguardguard &&&&&
_ _ _ we guard you we patrol drishane and keep at baythe most
desperat among these menofviolence

'Dear Martin, I'm so relieved. Can we keep the house from being
burned?'

it will be spared your ancestors form a spirit shield a circleofprotection
that man you heard last night left because I gained entry into his mind
and convincd him to go

'I wondered why he turned away. Have there been other attempts on
the house?'

gang of ruffians bottom of the avenue severel nights ago your papa
made a great racket as though apackofhounds was charging them
and they lost their nerve swerve verve nervenervenerveyyyyyyyyy

'I wish you'd told me.'

not permitted to mention it until youdid our role is not to cause fear
but offr reasurance

'Advise me, Martin. How do we get through this?'
The pencil hovers over the paper, indecisive, before it rears against
her fingers like a nervous colt objecting to the bridle.

a stitch in time saves nine

'I don't understand.'
Nothing.
'Martin? Please help me.

give a littel to save a lot

'Yes! That's what I suggested to Cam. It's the practical way to deal with
these people. I'll tell him you urge it. Will the raiders be back tonight?'

theyare undecided

Edith places another blank folio beneath her pencil. 'Martin, Mama's
ruby ring is still in Drishane. Where should I hide it for safekeeping?'

The pencil wavers and dips. When it touches the page there is only a continuous line, broken in the middle.

——————————————— – – ———————————————

'I don't understand, dear.'

The pencil lies idle.

'I've hidden it but I'm worried it can be found. Won't you tell me where to put it?'

Still nothing.

Edith sighs. 'Martin, how do you think our play is going? I feel your hand in mine as I work.'

It is
sailingalong
with the wnid
in its sails

She reaches for more paper. 'Will it be a success?'

The pencil quivers but does not write.

'Will Flurry help me to keep Drishane in the family?'

The pencil lurches again, and this time the tip begins to shiver across the page.

there
is
a   n
impediment

'What is it?'

Nothing.

She waits.

Nothing.

Unable to help herself, she bursts out, 'Martin, don't desert me! What is it?'

The pencil almost slips from her grasp, so swiftly do the letters pour out.

pmihc

Edith can't make head or tail of the peculiar word but knows it for a riddle she must set aside to solve later. It is a significant answer, judging by the changed writing size.

'So this is the impediment. Can't I overcome it? Or is it too powerful for me?

Nothing.

'Is it a person?'

Now the pencil bucks between her fingers.

threeblindmice see how they run

'Is it someone I know?'

they all ran away from the farmerswife

Edith waits.

??

'I'm still here, Martin. Guide me, dear. I rely on you.'

The pencil fidgets, but is uncommunicative.

'I visited your grave yesterday. I placed some chrysanthemums from the hothouse in front of your headstone. Bronze ones. I always feel such a sense of contentment when I'm there. Dooley came with me. Dear, I'm in sore need of your strength and wisdom. Won't you advise me?'

always use your witsand strik a bargain whereyoucan

'Yes, I'll do that Martin. Anything else?'

Sur le pont d'Avignon on y danse on y danse.

'What times we had in France. Back when the world was young. Didn't we, dear?'

121-121-121-121-121-121-121-121-121-121-121-121-121-121

'Is that a psalm number? A house number? What is it?'

The pencil slips from her hand and Edith feels a sense of emptiness – as though she walked into a room expecting to see someone who is nowhere in sight. The connection with Martin is severed.

Pins and needs tingle in her right hand and arm. She massages it, sensation returning. The intelligence which moved her hand is gone. Still, it has been a reassuring encounter. Parched, she swallows a long drink of water, gathers the sheaf of papers and reads over the messages again. The writing – proof of her communication with Martin – is always a comfort to read back over.

Her eye snags on that one-word answer about an impediment to her plan to use *Flurry's Wedding* to save Drishane.

pmihc

How poisonous the Lilliputian word looks. She spells it out. P-M-I-H-C. Attempts to say it aloud – pim-ee-hic. What can it mean? She pulls another blank page towards her and doodles a rearrangement of the letters. Sometimes, when Martin is agitated, she gives Edith jumbled-up words for answers. A scribbled *michp* is followed by *himcp* – both meaningless. Is it possible it's mirror writing? She catches up the sheet of paper with automatic writing on it, and goes to a chiffonier surmounted by decorative etched glass. She holds up the page and reads the reverse image of the ominous word.

pmihc

Edith's reflection is grey-white in the mirror. The enemy is within.

five

Three nights later, a fox's bark wakens Edith. Instantly, she is fully alert. She hobbles to the window and parts the curtains by a whisker – enough to catch the moving arc of a torch beam outside. Her dressing gown and a tartan scarf are lying ready on a bedside chair. She pulls on both against the night chill. Next, she collects her old riding whip, which she has taken to sleeping with under her bed, and makes her way to Cameron's bedroom close to the top of the wide, graceful front staircase.

A tap on his door. 'Cam, there's someone outside.'

No answer. She raps again. Still nothing. She opens the door. A candle burning inside a globe on the bedside table shows the bed to be unoccupied, covers smooth. He must be sitting up again. Senses a-twitch, she hurries downstairs, fingers trailing along the banister – remembering which loose stair tread to avoid without counting. She passes portraits of her ancestors etched on cavernous walls with the clarity of India-ink sketches, Dooley skittering along behind, knowing instinctively to stay quiet. She can see where she's going because Philomena is now leaving paraffin lamps burning overnight at strategic points in the house, on Edith's instructions.

Near the bottom of the staircase, a dark shape jackhammers her heartbeat. Are they inside already?

'Who's there?' To her annoyance, her voice quavers a little.

'It's all right, Peg, it's me.'

She catches hold of the bannister, knees buckling. 'Are there men outside, Cam?'

'We think so. Young Hurley's just been in to say there's some activity down near the road. He's going to investigate. Mike Hurley's manning the back gate and I'm holding the fort here.'

Edith hauls herself down the last few stair treads. Cameron is fully dressed, a pool of buttery lamplight falling on an ancient fowling piece in his arms, which belonged to their grandfather. So much for handing over all of their weapons to the RIC.

'You told me you weren't going to stay up again tonight.'

'Changed my mind.'

'I could have shared the wait with you. Four hours each.'

'Next time.'

Loulou dances into view, emitting a series of self-important yips. Dooley circles her, the two sniffing one another.

'Pipe down, the pair of you,' says Cameron. 'You can do all the social-izing you like tomorrow.'

A whinny.

Edith stiffens. 'They're at the stables. They're after the horses.'

'We'll see about that.' He indicates his shotgun. 'Death or glory, like Uncle Kendal's Lancers!'

'Have you lost your mind? That antique will explode if you pull the trigger. It could blind you!'

'A man feels more secure when he has a firearm.'

'Cam, you never saw a gun fired in anger in the army. You ran the music school. Put it away!'

The sound of something being dragged at the rear of the house stalls their argument. Brother and sister exchange glances. Turning as one, they head for the back door.

'You two keep as quiet as mice,' hisses Edith, and the dogs wag their tails, understanding her, as dogs always do.

The dragging noise is louder here.

'They're moving away the sandbags,' whispers Cameron. 'I'll go out through the French doors in the drawing room and see if I can't take them by surprise from behind. You stay here.'

'Is that wise? Going outside?'

'Can't skulk in here leaving all the risk to the Hurleys.'

Something hard is drummed against the back door. A stick, perhaps, or a weapon handle. Instantly, the dogs unleash a high-pitched cacophony.

'Did you agree a code with the Hurleys?' hisses Edith.

He looks remorseful. She resists the urge to pull a face at him.

Cameron lays his forefinger against his mouth, gestures to stay where she is and approaches the source of the knock. The dogs follow. 'Who's there?'

The rat-a-tat-tat is repeated. The dogs begin baying.

'That you, Hurley?' cries Cameron.

Edith goes to stand beside her brother. She hears other voices outside, their words indistinct. Boots stamp on the cobblestones.

From outside: 'Open up in the name of the Irish Republic!'

The dogs intensify their racket.

'Shut up, Loulou, Dooley,' hisses Cameron. He calls out, 'State your business.'

'Our business is Ireland's. Now open the door or we'll break it open.'

Cameron hoists his gun to rest the butt against his shoulder. Fear presses against Edith, suffocating. He'll get himself killed if he carries on like this. 'No! Let them in, Cam!'

From outside: 'I'm going to count to three.'

'This house can't be defended, Cam. Do as he says.'

'Absolutely not.'

'The odds are against us.'

From outside: 'One!'

'A child could break in, never mind a gang of men!'

'Two!'

'Please, Cam!'

'Hold your horses. I'll open up!'

He unbolts the door, and gives ground, stepping back to join Edith. Even as he moves, the handle is turned from outside. On a blast of damp night air, a knot of men crowd into the passageway. Lamplight falls onto faces blackened by burnt cork to prevent recognition, heightening the menace they project. They surge forward and Edith and Cameron retreat into the kitchen. Edith counts five men. Two are holding rifles, another has a pistol and the others are armed with cudgels. One looks like a policeman's baton. So the stories are true about Republicans using captured weapons.

'I'll be relieving you of that, Colonel Somerville,' says the man with the pistol.

Edith notices his weapon is an army-issue Mauser. Robbed, no doubt. She also notices the men keep their caps on.

Cameron is gruff. 'Who are you? State your business here.'

'We're soldiers of the Irish Republic. I won't ask you again. Hand it over.' He wears authority like a familiar coat.

Cameron bites his moustache. Quickly, he bends forward and lays the fowling piece beside his feet.

Good for Cam, thinks Edith. Let the fellow stoop if he wants it.

The leader nods to one of his men, who lifts the weapon and moves closer to the lamplight to examine it. 'A woebegone aul' blunderbuss. Sure even the crows wouldn't be afeard of it.'

'Should be in a museum,' says another. 'Not sure we'll get much good out of it, Captain.'

'It might come in handy at a pinch.' The leader returns his attention to Edith and Cameron. 'Well, now, aren't you as snug as thrushes in here. How many in the household?'

Neither of them answers.

'Don't make this any harder than it has to be.'

Silence.

The leader pushes his face into Cameron's. 'I'm running out of patience. Did you hear me, soldier boy?' A beat. 'I'm waiting.'

'Four indoors. My sister and me, plus two servants.'

'I hope for your sake you're telling the truth, Colonel.'

Edith appraises their visitors, some detached part of her mind urging her to memorize what she sees. None of the trespassers are older than their twenties and one looks like a boy. All are in corduroy trousers and collarless shirts, but have puttees, caps and odds and ends of assorted uniform. Trying to look like an army, she supposes. Two wear filthy trench coats with bulging pockets. None are locals – she'd recognize them, blackened faces and caps pulled low or not. But villagers must have given them information and fed them, perhaps sheltered them. Yet they carry a smell of the woods and unwashed bodies. Perhaps they've been sleeping outdoors. Every one of the men has stubble, even the overgrown lad, suggesting no shaving opportunities for several days.

She pays closest attention to the man doing the talking. He has a Cork city accent and wears a leather motorcycle jacket. His face is lean but unlined beneath the slouch hat with one side pinned up. He's younger than she expected a leader to be, maybe twenty-three. She can tell he's like a wasp, ready to sting in a split second.

Dooley darts close to the men, unleashing a furious tirade of yelps. Loulou joins him, snarling, but when one of the men shouts at her the little Pomeranian reverses, yipping, to cower beside Cameron. Dooley holds his position, quivering with fury.

'What do you want with us?' demands Cameron.

'Donations to the cause, Colonel Somerville. You're nicely placed here. Time to do some sharing.'

'What cause do you mean?'

'Oh, I think you know perfectly well, Colonel.' He turns to one of his men and mutters a command.

'Right-o, Captain.'

'You go with him,' he tells the man with Cameron's fowling piece.

Sleek as silhouettes, the two leave the kitchen.

Incandescent, Dooley scoots after them.

'No, Dooley! Stay!' cries Edith. He crouches on the spot, sides heaving, sending a volley of barks after the men. 'To me, Dooley!' Reluctantly, he trots to her side. There, he fixes his gaze on the man addressed as captain and snarls, low in his throat.

One of the men turns his rifle so the stock is jutting out. He points it at Dooley. 'Either you make that fucker shut up or I will.'

Edith stoops to Dooley, shushing him, and he subsides.

'Noisy little beggar, isn't he?' says the leader. 'We'll have to lock your animal in a cupboard if you can't control him. Still, you have to admire his loyalty. Now, where were we, Colonel? Ah, to be sure, the cause. Irish freedom. Either you're for freedom or against it. We don't have much tolerance for them that faces both ways.'

'We're for it, of course,' Edith puts in. 'I gave one of you ten shillings not four months ago when I was stopped in the village.'

'Is that so, Miss Somerville? And grateful we are for each and every donation. But eaten bread is soon forgotten and we need to impose on your good nature again. I've a column of men to feed and arm.'

'Isn't there a peace deal being thrashed out?' says Cameron. 'Your chaps, Griffith and Collins, are over in London in the middle of talks with the Prime Minister. Why are you still arming?'

'Talks can go nowhere. We must be prepared for all eventualities.'

Cameron snorts.

'What have you done with the Hurleys?' Edith puts in. 'I hope you haven't hurt them.'

'Tied up in the stables, Miss Somerville. They'll come to no harm if they stay put. One of our lads is out there, keeping an eye on them. Now, about your donation.'

'We have no money,' Cameron protests.

'Ah-ah!' He wags a finger. 'Shame on you for fibbing, Colonel. The likes of you always has some of the readies. Your idea of hard up and mine are two entirely different things.' He pats the inside pockets of his jacket and extracts a cigar stub. 'Could I trouble one of you for a light?'

Edith glances at Cameron, who appears rooted to the spot. She fetches the matches kept by the stove and hands over the box.

He lights up, luxuriates in a long inhalation and rattles the matches. 'With your permission.' He pockets the box. 'Never know when a match might come in useful.'

The other men laugh.

Through a smoke ring, the leader squints at Edith. 'I believe you're a writer, Miss Somerville. I had a look at one or two of your hunting stories. They gallop along at a fair old lick. You know your stuff, I have to hand it to you. Of course, these parts would have been prime hunting country, back in the day.'

'The hounds have been stopped.'

A puff on his cigar and he shakes his head. 'We couldn't have the High-and-Mighties careering over decent folk's land, now could we? And not so much as a by-your-leave. What kind of a republic would that be? No, I didn't much care for your Irish R.M. stories, though I heard the voice of the people in some of them. There was too much forelock tugging and your honour-ing for my liking.' He taps his breast pocket. 'I prefer Shakespeare's sonnets. Carry a copy of them wherever I go. When I read, I want to be elevated. And the Bard never disappoints.'

Edith's lips purse to the size of a farthing. He doesn't speak like a gentleman, for all his cigar-smoking and bardolatry. 'We wrote as we found, my partner and me.'

'I dare say. But what you thought you saw, and what was there before your eyes, mightn't be one and the same. Your Ireland is a playground. A land of plucky mounts that never refuse a jump, woods filled with game for your shotguns and cunning foxes who get the chop after a merry chase enjoyed by all, foxy included. But that's not our Ireland. You know nothing of the people's struggles. The constant battle to make any kind of living that keeps body and soul together. The loss of children on the emigrants' ship.'

'The land is rich – there's plenty for all to share. Old grievances do nobody any good.'

'Share, is it? What do your lot know about sharing?'

'... ashamed of yourselves!' It's Philomena, who arrives in the kitchen with Mrs O'Shea, both wearing shawls over their nightgowns, their hair flopping in single plaits.

Edith's eyes darken. She has never glimpsed either woman with her hair exposed, although they've shared a roof for years. Somehow, it strikes her as more shocking than having a kitchen full of armed men.

Philomena's hair is still as black as wet coal, apart from some grey at the temples, but Mrs O'Shea's is white.

'It isn't decent, dragging folk out of their beds at this hour of the night!' Philomena is shrill with complaint – even the guns don't silence her.

The men grin with embarrassment, their teeth tobacco-stained.

'Nobody else here we can find, Captain,' says one of the men. 'No sign of any guns, either. We'd a good root about.'

The leader addresses Cameron. 'You bigwigs are operating on a skeletal staff. Are you certain there's no one else, Colonel?'

'I am not in the habit of telling lies. We take people on from the village now and again when we need them.'

'Are you sure Mike Hurley's all right?' asks Edith. 'And his nephew?'

'I told you already. Those boys are being looked after,' says the leader.

'You haven't hurt them?'

'Not a bother on them.'

Edith is about to mention Jeremiah in the gatehouse, but holds off. If they have him, nothing can be done about it. If they don't, so much the better.

Right, ladies, take a seat.' The captain ushers Edith, Philomena and Mrs O'Shea towards the kitchen table, pulling out chairs for each of them.

'I prefer to stand,' says Edith, despite a stabbing pain in her left hip.

'Then let you stand, Miss Somerville.'

Loulou darts across the room and springs onto Philomena's knee, tunnelling into her lap.

'There, there, *a leanbh*.' She pats the dog's head. 'I don't blame you for not wanting to see what's going on here.'

Unexpectedly, Mrs O'Shea explodes. 'Leave that alone, ya spalpeen! It's for tomorrow's dinner.'

One of the men has discovered a cooked chicken in the larder and is gnawing on a leg. He passes the platter of meat to a comrade, who pulls off the other leg.

'Tell them to stop, Colonel,' cries Mrs O'Shea.

Humiliation, as livid as a bruise, patches across Cameron's face. He shrugs.

Edith makes an inventory of the five strangers. Each man has a bandolier or khaki sling containing ammunition over a shoulder and crossed at his chest. The one who found the chicken has a hand grenade fixed to his belt. Edith shudders at the egg-shaped object. A single slip and they could all be blown to kingdom come – Somervilles, dogs, staff and Republicans alike.

The chicken is offered to the captain who waves it away, still chewing on his cigar. A third man, a soiled bandage on his hand, steps forward and breaks the carcass in two. He tears off a fistful of breast, eating it skin and all. The fourth disappears into the larder.

Mrs O'Shea spits out prayers between clenched teeth. 'Hail, holy queen, mother of mercy, may the divil toast yiz slowly, hail our life, our sweetness and our hope.'

The captain studies her for a moment, head to one side, while she treats him with majestic indifference. He runs a finger under the rim of his hat where it rests on his forehead. 'As I was saying, Colonel and Miss Somerville, we're here to collect donations for the Irish Republic. What can you offer us?'

'Nothing,' snaps Cameron.

'And I thought you claimed to be an honest man.'

'I have some jewellery you're welcome to,' says Edith. 'Let me fetch it for you.'

'Go with her,' the leader tells a young man licking his fingers. He falls in behind Edith.

Dooley chases round the side of the youth and attaches himself to Edith.

'Stay, boy.'

Ears pricked, his face betrays doubt. He studies hers for clues. Unusually, he disobeys and keeps trotting behind. The man with the hand grenade grabs for his collar. Dooley snaps at his fingers, landing a bite.

'Bastard!'

Scarlet, he lashes out with a boot. Dooley goes flying across the room. The little dog's head cracks against a metal handle on the range and he lets out a high-pitched wail.

'Fuck sake. What did you do that for?' says one of the men.

'Fuck off yourself. Bastard drew blood. Dogs give you rabies.' The hand-grenade man follows Dooley, foot raised to kick him again, but Edith darts forward.

'Don't you dare touch him, you viper!'

'Easy now. Easy,' says the captain. 'Everyone calm down.'

Edith drops to her knees beside the fox terrier, who is curled up and whimpering. Blood leaks from his mouth. She lays his head gently on her lap. His stubby tail moves feebly, acknowledging her presence. Edith's fingers part his fur, searching for cuts. Foam begins to gather on his muzzle and his eyes glaze over. Recognizing the signs, Edith's voice breaks. 'Dooley, oh Dooley, what have they done to you?'

Dooley moans and a shudder passes through his body.

Loulou gives a single howl, high-pitched, but is shushed by Philomena. She subsides into a string of whimpers, pressing her muzzle against Philomena's stomach.

Edith cups her palm under Dooley's chin. 'Don't leave me, little man, I couldn't bear it.'

His breath wheezes. With her free hand, Edith strokes Dooley. His body begins jerking. Helpless, she watches, keeping her hand in place on his fur. The juddering lasts for thirty seconds. Until the small body stops twitching.

Dooley heaves out a sigh. And is still.

Edith scoops him towards her, pressing her face against his, rocking him back and forth.

'Ah, Miss Edith,' says Philomena brokenly. 'Ah, miss.'

Edith raises her head, her eyes as blank as Dooley's. His blood is smeared on her cheek and chin.

six

'Someone help me with him,' says Edith. 'Dooley's been hurt.'

'I think, I'm afraid ... he's gone, old girl.' Cameron stoops and presses a hand on Edith's shoulder.

'No. He can't be. It's not true. Fetch a blanket, Philomena. We need to keep him warm.'

'Time's wasting. Leave the dog alone,' snaps the captain.

'Poor Dooley. Heart of a lion,' says Cameron.

'Put the bloody dog down or you'll really have something to cry about!'

Cameron shuffles onto his knees beside Edith and tries to take Dooley away from Edith. She resists. 'Let go, Edith. I'll look after him.' He lifts Dooley onto his lap.

'Get a fucken move on, we haven't got all night!' yells the captain.

Hand-grenade man yanks Edith to her feet.

'Murderer!'

He makes a fist. 'I'll give ya a taste of the same medicine, ya bitch.'

'Enough!' The leader pulls her by the elbow away from the other man. 'Watch that temper of yours,' he tells his companion. 'And you, missus, get the jewellery. Chop-chop.'

'Why should I? You've just taken away the thing I love best in the world!'

'Believe me, we can do worse.' The captain walks to the range, lifts the poker and flicks it along the shelf where crockery is stacked. Plates rain on top of Mrs O'Shea and Philomena, bouncing from them to the floor, hopping into fragments. The women cry out in alarm, covering their heads with their arms.

'Now, what's next?' The captain opens the range door and riddles the embers inside into flames. 'What to do with a hot poker?'

'Stop it, I'm going!' cries Edith. 'You can have whatever you want.'

'I know.' He skims his eyes over to her. 'Get a move on.'

'You'll mind him for me, Cam?'

'I won't let go of him. You can count on me, Edith.'

Edith kisses her fingertips and trails them along Dooley's nose. He'll never hear her call his name again. She stalks out of the kitchen.

The youngest member of the party follows her out of the kitchen, past the back stairs, pantry and glory hole, along a dim corridor. She leads him towards the dining room, lifting the hall lamp in passing. Her destination is the chiffonier. She places the lamp on its polished surface and opens a drawer, removing a cloth bag. In the mirror above the sideboard, she glances at her captor's reflection. He can't be more than eighteen or nineteen, composed entirely of angles, his corduroy trousers bagging against hips and backside. Her eyes flick from his blackened face to her own. She looks ghastly, Dooley's blood blotched on her.

'I'm sorry about your dog, ma'am. There was no call for it. Your man has a fierce bad temper on him. He'd kill a fella and ate him after.' A basso voice wells, incongruous, from his narrow frame.

Edith feels nauseous at the thought of her loyal little companion being kicked to death in his own home. She should have been able to protect him. Emotion wells up and she bites hard on her lower lip. What can't be cured must be endured.

'They get under your skin, a pet dog,' he goes on. 'I had one growing up. Lucky, I called him. Loved that dog like a brother. Everywhere I went, Lucky went.'

She glances at him, assessing. This one's talkative. 'What's your name?'

A shake of his head. 'No names. The captain warned us.'

A country voice. Soft-spoken. 'Where are you from? Kerry?'

'I'm not allowed to say.'

'They say Kerry is rebel country.'

He snuffles. 'Even the hens lay bullets there. That's what the captain says.'

'A determined sort of a fellow, isn't he?'

Hero worship flashes from moss-green eyes, their colour emphasized by the black streaks on his face. 'The captain's a man that can think things out. I'd follow him to hell and back. He was at the university, above in Dublin, 'til the Troubles come upon us.'

'He has death in his eyes. If you stay with him, you'll end up dead, too.'

'We give as good as we get. We hit back. Or more, maybe. The captain'll keep us safe. What's in the bag, ma'am?'

'Some jewellery. Your captain can sell it.'

'Can't be much in a small little bag like that. He'll want more. What else have you got?'

'Nothing. Look, I don't doubt you have your reasons, but this will end badly for you. You're too young to throw your life away. Go home to your family. Your mother must be at her wits' end with worry.'

'I have no home. The Tans burned us out. Me an' the boys, we live like foxes in dugouts or caves.' He tugs open the drawer she's closed and pokes around.

'The drawers are empty. We're as poor as church mice. All we have are the house and land.'

'Nobody's poor that has a house and land.' His eyes sweep the room and snag on the matching candelabra.

Edith pretends to be alarmed. 'No,' she says. 'They're family heirlooms.' In fact, they look more valuable than they are.

'Too bad.' He yanks open another drawer, finds a tablecloth and begins to tuck the silverware into its folds, making a sling of the material.

'It must be a tough life for you, always on the move. Don't you miss sleeping in a bed? Eating a meal without looking over your shoulder?'

'Freedom can't be won without some hardship. So the captain says.'

'Is he strict, your captain?'

'He likes us column men to shave regular, and keep ourselves clean, ma'am. When we can.' He rubs the shadow on his chin. 'We haven't managed too well this past week.'

The boy pulls open a cupboard door and rummages inside, looking for anything of value that's portable.

'But how do you manage to bathe if you're living in dugouts and caves?' Edith asks.

'We takes a dip in a stream while one of us keeps a lookout.'

'And what do you do for towels?'

'Roll in the grass.' He makes an impatient gesture. 'Enough of that aul' blarney, now. These candlesticks isn't enough. Where's your tin? The captain prefers cash, so he does. Get me tin when you can, says he.'

'No doubt. But we have none about the place. You can't draw blood from a stone. Shall we go back?'

'It's best to give him what'll get him to leave. The longer the lads are here, the greater the chances of . . . something. I dunno. Wouldn't like to say. But something.'

She finds him a canteen of cutlery and a set of silver-plated egg cups. 'What else?'

'Nothing. I told you, we've nothing left to give. You're not the first Republicans to pay us a social call.'

He rubs the back of his hand against his mouth. She can see he doesn't have it in him to order her around the way his captain does, or raise his fist to her like the hand-grenade man. 'Have you nothing else? It's for your own good I'm telling you. This won't satisfy him.'

Edith's meets his boy-bright eyes. 'This is no life for you. Are you trying to be a hero? A martyr for Ireland? Ireland gobbles up blood sacrifices. She'll suck you dry and spit out your bones. You'll be as stiff and dead as . . .' she gulps, caught in a wave of misery, '. . . poor Dooley in there.'

He stares at her, pupils widened. 'The taste of blood gets into your mouth. Once it's there, nothing shifts it.' Edith waits. 'But there's no going back now. I've crossed the line.'

'It's never too late.'

'It is. I've done things.'

'You could emigrate.'

His voice is almost inaudible. 'They'd never let me go, the others.'

'Your friends?'

He clears his throat. 'I'd never leave them. We're Volunteers.'

Edith feels compelled to recover this boy who's not yet a man, despite the bravado. 'I noticed you were limping. Are you injured?'

'No, ma'am. Thank God.'

'Is it your boots?'

He looks at them as if surprised to notice them on his feet. 'I did a swap with me da, the day I left. His were new. He thought he was doing me a favour. But I'm crippled with them.'

'One of my brothers left a pair here the last time he stayed over. They might fit you.'

She leads him to the boot cupboard at the bottom of the back stairs. Aylmer's knee-length hunting boots are near the front. They can hear voices from the kitchen but not the sense of what's being said. The youth sits on the floor to try on Aylmer's boots, his face excited, the way a child's is on Christmas morning.

'Holy mackerel, ma'am. Are you really giving them to me?'

'I am.' Edith notices his socks are soaking. 'You'll get chilblains wearing wet socks, you know.'

'I don't have a spare pair, ma'am. I did once. Nobody knits like me ma. But I left the spares after me, clearing out by a nose ahead of the Auxies.'

The Auxiliaries, the Black and Tans, the RIC. It's only a matter of time before military or police catch up with this boy. He feels for his big toe inside the boots, pressing his thumb against the leather. Will he be shot wearing her brother's riding boots? Or hanged? The odds are against him surviving – she's wasting the boots. But they may as well go to another as moulder among family debris. Aylmer's in no hurry to return to Drishane. As the captain has just pointed out, Treaty negotiations may be happening in London but the ceasefire is a provisional arrangement.

The boy peeks up at her shyly. 'Can I ask you something, ma'am?'

'Of course.'

'I heard something over the summer I'd love to believe, but dunno if I can. They say there was a butterfly found in Clare, striped green, white and orange. The people are calling it the Republican butterfly. Could such a thing be true?'

Edith opens her mouth to deny the possibility. The trust on his face makes her pause. 'Anything's possible.'

He smiles.

Another of the men looms over them. 'Captain says what the feck's keeping you?'

The boy scrambles to his feet, lifts the clunking tablecloth and escorts Edith back to the kitchen.

She drops the cloth jewellery bag into the captain's hand. 'With my compliments.' Turning on her heel, she goes to where Cameron is nursing Dooley. She holds out her arms and he transfers the fox terrier's body into them. 'My gallant boy. You're with Martin now. She'll take care of you.'

'Took a pounding, poor old fellow. Totally unnecessary behaviour. Utterly caddish,' says Cameron.

'Shut the fuck up,' says Dooley's killer.

Meanwhile, the captain loosens the drawstring, upends the bag and an assortment of paste pieces cascade into his cupped palm. One after another, he inspects them.

Cradling Dooley, Edith's gaze circumnavigates the room. Has anything changed in her absence? One of the men has a sack at his feet. Her forehead pleats.

Mrs O'Shea catches her eye. 'My kitchen supplies. They've helped themselves to what's in the larder. Like sheet lightning, they were, the speed they stripped the place.'

The captain strolls across to the dresser, and holds a drop earring to the lamplight there. He twirls it between his fingers. With his back to the room, he says, 'Now, I'm no jeweller, but these don't strike me as family heirlooms.' His head and upper body whip round towards Edith. 'You can do better than that, Miss Somerville.'

'They're all I have left.'

'She give us these candle sticks, too, captain.' The boy speaks up. 'Solid silver, they are. You should feel the weight of them. And some forks and things.'

'Good work. Nevertheless, I believe the lady can dig a little deeper.'

The captain looks around, spies a newspaper lying beside one of the chairs, and throws it on top of the range. He produces his box of matches and lights the paper. In an instant, it goes up in flames.

Everyone watches. Sparks and blackened embers fly about the kitchen.

One of the men laughs.

Edith swallows. 'If I had any more to give, don't you think I would, to make you leave? You can't imagine my brother and I have any wish to prolong this visit.'

'I've no doubt you'd be glad to see the back of us, Miss Somerville. Nevertheless, you don't strike me as the sort to hand everything over without a fight. Now, here's what I propose. You and one of my men go up to your bedroom and together the two of you take another look through your knick-knacks. I dare say there's a few bangles or a watch that may have slipped your mind. Better still if you remember some bank notes.'

'I must protest! I cannot allow your, your' – wretches springs to her tongue but she resists it – 'your men to traipse through my bedroom. It's private!'

'My men need arms and ammunition. Your privacy ranks a poor second behind that.'

'But there's a truce in place,' says Cameron.

'Ah, that's only all palaver. A breathing space 'til the war's back on. Now, Miss Somerville, off you toddle and see what you can lay your hands on for us. Or else.' He thuds his Mauser butt end against the palm of his hand, with a meaningful jerk of the head at Loulou, cowering on Philomena's lap.

Cameron takes a step towards the captain and two rifles swing towards him in unison. 'This is naked force. You have no authority or right to do this.'

'We learned it from the English. People like you need to decide where your loyalties lie. Either give your allegiance to the Irish Republic. Or clear out.'

'Great Britain will soon bring you to heel,' says Cameron.

'We're not fucken dogs!'

Edith can see the captain's grip on his temper beginning to fray. A vein has pushed up through his forehead. All of his anger appears to be centred on that pulsing stripe. His eyes belong to a man for whom killing has become commonplace. She takes a step towards the IRA leader. 'My brother meant no offence.'

The captain says nothing. Neither does Cameron.

'Did you, Cameron?'

His face reddens.

'Did you?' She pins him with a look.

Cameron exhales noisily. 'I spoke ... out of turn.'

The captain passes a hand over his eyes. Pauses. Speaks. 'The English won't have things their own way here anymore. The people are ready to see this fight through.' He nods at the man who kicked Dooley. 'Go with her.'

Edith's blood slows in her veins. Anyone but him. She looks at the captain and sees there is no use appealing to him. Very well. She lays Dooley on the floor, uncoils the scarf she wound round her neck when she rose from bed a lifetime ago, and rests his head on it. She can't bear to think of his dear little face pressed to the ground.

As before, she carries the hall lamp, her skin crawling at the knowledge of who is a few paces behind her. He whistles a tune as they walk, but stops to study a collection of fox's masks mounted on the wall, near the staircase.

'Caught in mid-flight, you might say,' says the whistler.

She doesn't answer. He makes a gesture to move her on, and all at once she sees him as a man with experience of herding cattle. To the slaughterhouse, probably. On the staircase, her leg drags as she mounts. She grits her teeth and listens for the chiming of a clock, hoping to gauge the time, but the muteness of the house engulfs them. On the upper landing, under a window looking over the rooftops of rooms added on to Drishane, in afterthought, he removes his cap and scratches his scalp. Edith sees his hair is dark and untidy, like a windblown hedge.

'Your fucken brother'd want to watch his manners round the captain. It's all the same to us if we roast your aul' barn of a house.' He jams his cap back on his head and makes a fist of his hand. 'Whoosh!' The hand opens, fingers splayed, mimicking an explosion. 'It's some sight.'

She points to the grenade, dangling from his belt. 'Do you know the damage that thing could do?'

'It won't do a thing unless I pull the pin.'

'You might end up doing yourself an injury in the process.

'I know what I'm about. Pull, count to three, throw it to Jaysus and hit the ground with your head covered.'

Silenced, she walks ahead to her bedroom door, where she balks. She won't have this Dooley-murdering devil tramping around in the space where she sleeps. 'Wait here. I'll never be able to find what I want with you breathing down my neck.' She thrusts the lamp into his hand.

To her surprise, he remains on the saddle board. Quickly, she retrieves her best evening pumps from a shelf in the wardrobe. Inside one of the shoes, mummified in tissue paper, her mother's ruby engagement ring nestles.

'Show me what you have there.'

'It's a ring.'

'Let me see.'

'Are you an expert on stones?'

He takes two steps into the room, his boots causing the floorboards to creak. She unpeels the paper and holds the ring aloft by its gold band. Inside the lamplight's loop, the ruby glows with the assurance of a genuine stone.

'Grand.'

'Shall we go?' she asks.

'Hold your horses.' His eyes patrol her dressing table. 'We'll have them an' all.' A forefinger points towards an enamelled hairbrush and hand-mirror set, a sixteenth birthday gift from her parents.

She grits her teeth. 'Be my guest. Allow me.' She squeezes past him, carrying them. She must get this beast out of her bedroom.

He hesitates, nothing else catches his eye and he follows her.

'I'll take them.'

She scrapes her fingers through the brush to rake out any hairs lodged there. They can have her brush but not them. She hands over the matched pair and he jams them into a pocket. All at once, slyly exultant, she realizes he missed the comb that completes the set. It's out of its usual place, left on her bedside table. Small victories are as sweet as large.

He whistles the same tune, walking back to the kitchen, its notes grating in her eardrums. By the time they are back, her hip is aching and one of her legs is dragging.

'With my compliments,' she tells the captain, handing over the ring.

'That's more like it. The Republic thanks you, Miss Somerville.'

She notices the whistler hasn't produced the hairbrush and mirror. Could he be holding them back for a sweetheart? He meets her eye, an evil look on his face. She turns back to the captain.

'Can you leave us in peace now, please?'

'We'll need a horse.'

She thanks her lucky stars Mike Hurley found temporary homes for the young hunters. 'We've nothing but old work horses left. They pull the plough. Not much use to you.'

'There's one that looked fresh enough.'

'That's Tara, highly strung. She'll throw any rider. I'm the only one who can manage her.'

'The gentry aren't the only ones who can manage a horse.'

'I'm not suggesting that. But believe me, horse sense is a misnomer in her case. She's skittish. If you have to take a horse, make it Samson. He's well on in years but strong – he used to be a hunter. You'll get some benefit out of him. He's a horse that could leap a house.'

'Very well, Samson it is. We have your men in the stable – they can point him out.'

'The Hurleys – are they really all right?' checks Edith.

'Right as rain. I told you before. Now, ladies, Colonel, I wish you good night. *To sleep, perchance to dream.* Let's gather up, lads.'

'Will we take this yoke with us?' Cameron's old shotgun is waved in the air.

'Ah, firepower. We haven't found much in that department, have we? Colonel, do you swear on your honour as an officer and a gentleman' – his mouth twists, amused by a private joke – 'there are no other guns in the house?'

'None. I handed them over at the barracks in Skibbereen.'

'Make him go on his knees and swear it,' urges the whistler.

'Shame on you,' protests Philomena.

'Can't I tell a lie as well on my feet as on my knees?' says Cameron.

'No need for anyone to get down on their knees,' says the captain. 'Do you swear there are no other guns, Colonel Somerville?'

'I do.'

'Very well, I'll take your word for it. Now, do you have a sheet of paper and a pen?'

'There are writing materials in my study.'

'Mrs O'Shea, surely you have something for shopping lists and the like,' says Edith. Goodness knows what else they'll lift if they go tramping through the house again.

'In the drawer on the side of the table,' says Mrs O'Shea.

The captain pulls out a scrap of paper and pencil, writes on it rapidly, folds the sheet and hands it to Cameron. 'For you, Colonel.'

'What is it?'

'A list of the items we've requisitioned.'

'I don't understand.'

'The Irish Republic will refund you as soon as it has control of our tax revenues. We're not thieves, you know.'

Cameron catches Edith's eye. Neither of them speaks.

'Everybody stay put for the next hour,' continues the captain. 'Someone will be watching the house. If any man or woman tries to leave before time's up, we'll be back another night. And you won't escape so lightly next time.' He bends at the waist in a mocking bow. 'And so *slán agus beannacht* one and all. No need to wish me luck. I have the devil's own.' Hand shoulder high, he signals to the men. 'Time we were away, boys.' They swing around him in a semi-circle.

With the clarity of a flash of light in a darkened room, Edith hears Martin speaking to her. *Remind them about the death coach.* 'Keep an eye out for the *coiste bodhar*,' she says.

Two of the men bless themselves, another babbles what sounds like an invocation.

Even the captain has some of the swagger knocked out of him. 'W-what's that you said?'

'The *coiste bodhar*, the death coach. It rattles along our roads most nights. Headless horses in the harness and a coachman with his head under his arm. They say no one who sees it lives out the week.'

A moan escapes from the Kerry boy in Aylmer's boots. The wind whips a branch and taps it against the window. Everyone jumps.

The captain pulls himself together. '*Piseogs*. Now remember, ladies, Colonel, you're being watched. Let's go, boys.'

The back door opens, and one by one they flit out into the murk.

seven

The four people in the kitchen strain their ears for sounds from outside. A horse's neigh. A man's voice soothing it – not Mike Hurley's. The crunch of footsteps. The clatter of hooves. Silence.

It is broken by Loulou, who scrabbles over to Dooley and begins to sniff him. An exploratory lick of his mouth. Another sniffing session, this time circling the body. Circumnavigation complete, she sits back on her haunches and begins to yowl.

'Bloody well shut up!' cries Cameron.

'Go easy on her, Cam,' says Edith. *She's only doing what I'd like to.*

Mrs O'Shea takes her rosary beads out of a pocket and runs them through her fingers, lips moving.

'How about a nice cup of tea?' There's a tremor in Philomena's voice.

'Good idea,' says Cameron.

'Right so.' Philomena braces her arms on the sides of the chair and tries to stand, but her legs give way and she sinks back into the chair with an 'ooph'.

Mrs O'Shea drops the beads into her lap and reaches across the space separating her from Philomena. The two hold hands. 'There, there, *a stór,*' says Mrs O'Shea. Philomena breathes in, squeezes the cook's hand, and stands up.

'I'll help you with the tea, Philomena.'

'No, you stay where you are and rest yourself, Mrs O. My legs are younger than yours. We've all had a shock. A nice sugary cup is just what the doctor ordered.'

Edith wishes she could hold hands with them, too. But it would never do in front of her brother. She considers taking his hand in hers but knows he'd resent the staff seeing it. 'Can I have a look at that piece of paper they gave you?'

He glances over it, before handing it to her. 'Intolerable conceit of the man. Self-styled captain, too, I shouldn't wonder.' Cameron's foot lashes out, connecting with a table leg.

Edith reads the list, laid out in copperplate script despite the time pressure the IRA leader was under.

> Item 1: one horse plus assorted saddles & bridles
> Item 2: one ruby ring
> Item 3: pair of silver candlesticks
> Item 4: one canteen of cutlery
> Item 5: silver egg cups (7)
> Item 6: assorted earrings, bracelets & ladys watch
> Item 7: one chicken cooked & various foodstuffs
> Requisitioned from Summervilles of Drishane House in name of the Irish Republic by Captain C.P., Cork Division, 19 October 1921

Well. That captain has panache, if nothing else. Edith keeps the thought to herself. Cameron would take it amiss.

Loulou whimpers, and Edith bends over her. 'Loulou looks overheated. Maybe she's thirsty.'

'Shall I fetch you a bowl, miss?'

'No, Philomena, you keep going with the tea.'

Edith tries to persuade Loulou to drink, but she refuses to lap. She dips the corner of her nightdress in the water and squeezes a few drops onto her lolling tongue. Next, she turns her attention to Dooley. 'Would you bring me his blanket, Cameron? It's at the end of my bed. We can't leave the poor boy lying here in his own blood.' Her voice catches, she swallows and clears her throat. 'I'll wrap him up in it. He loves that blanket.'

'First things first, Edith. We need to let our friends know about a gang of armed men roaming the countryside. They could go anywhere next. To the Castle. To Glen Barrahane. Anywhere. No one's safe.'

'First things first means taking care of Dooley,' snaps Edith.

Mrs O'Shea heaves herself out of her chair. 'There's a towel in the drawer here, Miss Edith. It'll cover the poor wee mite for now. You shouldn't kneel there like that with him, you'll stiffen up.'

Together, they lay Dooley on the towel and loosely cover him with it.

'Miss Edith, let me clean you up.' Philomena has a damp cloth in her hand. She strokes it across her mistress's face, wiping away the blood.

'I suppose I should tell the police,' says Cameron. 'Except they'll do nothing. They're afraid to leave their barracks without a battalion of soldiers at their backs.' He cracks his knuckles methodically. First the left hand, then the right.

Edith has a flashback to their mother scolding him about the knuckles habit. She thought he had outgrown it. 'Does anyone have the time? We're supposed to stay put for an hour.'

Cameron consults his fob watch. 'Just after three. Would either of you like to go back to bed? Mrs O'Shea? Philomena?'

'I couldn't sleep a wink!' says Mrs O'Shea. 'These are desperate times, so they are. From day to day, you'd never know when trouble might come knocking on your door.'

Philomena is mumbling over the tea preparations. 'One spoon each and one for the pot,' again and again, like a charm. She's crunching over shards of china broken by the IRA captain, but no one thinks to sweep them up.

'I wouldn't have put it past those scoundrels to torch the house,' says Cameron. 'My heart was in my mouth when you gave that ruffian a box of matches, Peg.'

'I didn't have much choice.'

The whistler comes to mind – that upwards swoosh sketched with his hand. He was only too keen to reduce Drishane to rubble. What was it she heard about windows? Automatically, her eyes turn to the shuttered kitchen window. A blast of wind rattles its panes. That's it. They smash the ground-floor windows of a house to create an updraught for the flames. The Vane-Brownes told her about it. They lost their home that way – hundreds of years of history up in smoke.

As soon as she heard how Easterfield was scorched to a crisp ('Not half a dozen stones left standing,' said Timmy the Post), she had Mike harness Tara to the dogcart and drove to Baltimore to see how she could help. Some portraits, war medals and various items of furniture were salvaged. But the centuries-old manor house lay in ruins, still smouldering fifteen hours later. The family lingered there, poking among the rubble, although neighbours begged them to leave.

The butler – a gloomy man who told Edith, 'Soon you'll be the only gentry left, ma'am' – led her towards her old mixed-doubles tennis partner, Bertie Vane-Browne. Bertie began talking ninety to the dozen about his doorknobs. They were crafted from eighteenth-century silver fob watches, an idiosyncrasy admired by guests, and their loss troubled him. 'Queen Victoria coveted them,' he said.

She tried to comfort him, but he was fixated on the handles.

'Irreplaceable. Those people don't know what they've done. One day, they'll regret it.'

'At least no one's been hurt,' said Edith.

After all, landlords were being shot. The Vane-Brownes were tremendous fun, horsey to their fingertips, but she'd always heard their tenants had no great fondness for them. They were another of the old county families bailing out.

'Stay, rebuild – there'll be compensation money,' she urged Bertie. But he said Angela's nerves had collapsed. His wife wanted nothing further to do with Ireland.

Edith darts a look at Philomena and Mrs O'Shea. For all their words of loyalty to the Somervilles, would they care if Drishane was destroyed? They'd miss the employment but would they be bothered about the house? Edith enjoys crashing out the opening chords of *All Things Bright and Beautiful* when she plays the organ at Sunday service in St Barrahane's, beside the Castle. But sometimes she is uneasy about its assumptions that everyone is comfortable with the status quo.

The rich man in his castle / the poor man at his gate / God made them high and lowly / And ordered their estate.

Automatically, she accepts the cup and saucer, comforted by Philomena's work-roughened skin as she guides Edith's hand to take it. Philomena's hands are as capable as her brain.

'Drink that, now, let you, Miss Edith.'

Edith does as she's told. The tea is strong and sweet, and its energy-giving properties course through her.

'I believe I'll have mine in my study, Philomena,' says Cameron. 'Bring it through for me, would you? I'll go ahead and see if I can riddle up the fire.'

Edith is taken aback. How can Cam contemplate going off to be alone at a time like this? They need to stick together. Has he ever taken tea with Philomena and Mrs O'Shea? She can't recall an occasion. From time to time, she sits in the kitchen at their invitation, enjoying the companionship and local gossip. Storing away some of their colourful phrases for future use. But her brother has lived most of his life away from Drishane, in army quarters. Probably, he hasn't spent real time with the servants since boyhood.

Edith claps a hand to her forehead. 'The Hurleys! They've been tied up in the stables all this time! We need to see to them.'

'Bit of a risk going out just yet,' says Cameron. 'They said someone was watching the house. Intolerable to be given orders by one's social inferiors, but the world's gone mad.'

'We've got to help the Hurleys!' She sets aside her tea. 'They'll want hot drinks and a chance to get warm, Philomena. They'll be chilled to the bone.'

'I'll fetch some blankets. Heat them up on the clothes horse in front of the stove,' says Mrs O'Shea.

'Do.' Edith opens a drawer in the kitchen table and removes a carving knife. 'I'm not leaving Mike tied up for one minute longer, Cameron.'

She steps out into the yard. The night is as black as a bog hole, the moon all but invisible behind a cloud bank, but she'd know her way round the stable yard blindfolded. Sniffing the air, she is surprised to realize it must have rained while they were being held. The ground underfoot is damp, and she can smell fresh horse droppings – poor old Samson. Their sacrificial goat.

Purposeful as a cat, she moves across the yard. The bittersweet perfume of laurel is unloosed into the night air. The leaves are poisonous. She'd like to force-feed them to the whistler. Tara recognizes Edith's footfall and whickers to her. Edith considers calling words of reassurance – but on second thoughts, it wouldn't do to alert a watcher.

The lonely bray of an ass travels across the fields. Tara neighs again. Mike mustn't be able to speak or he'd call out to Tara. Some of those Irish words he uses on her. The moon pops out from behind its cloud cover, as suddenly as a pea from its pod. It is like the surface of a drum, full and round and waiting for something.

Footsteps tread behind. She turns, heartbeat pelting.

'I'm coming with you.'

It's Cameron. Grateful, she nods.

The stables smell of horse sweat, the warm breath of animals and leather harness. None of the lanterns are lit. Cameron produces a torch.

'Mike?' Edith calls.

Tara stamps and clatters her hooves against the side of her stall.

'I'll see to you in a minute, milady. Mike?'

'Hurley?' says Cameron.

Muffled sounds.

'They're in the tack room,' says Cameron.

Tara snorts.

'Just a minute, girl. I'll get back to you as soon as I can,' says Edith.

Edith follows her brother into a wood-panelled room where riding equipment is stored. The torch beam shows Mike Hurley propped against one wall, his nephew Ned against the other. Both are wearing gags and are bound hand and foot, tied to wall-mounted metal rings.

'Mike, Ned, are you hurt?' asks Edith.

Mike shakes his head.

'Give me your knife, Edith,' says Cameron. 'Here, take the torch and hold it steady.' He tears off the gag and begins hacking though Mike's ropes.

'They took Samson,' croaks Mike.

Cameron moves on to Ned Hurley and begins to release him.

'I know,' says Edith. 'Poor old trooper. How are you? Did they hurt you?'

Mike stands up, rope puddling at his ankles, holding onto the wall for support. 'Not me. But Ned took a belt to the side of his head. Is your ear still ringing, Ned?'

A wince and a nod.

'You're bleeding, Ned,' says Edith. 'I can see it along your ear. Come into the kitchen. We can take a proper look at it there.'

'They outwitted us,' says Mike. 'Captured Ned down by the gates and used him to trick me into going to them.'

'I was their bait to trap Uncle Mike.' Ned chafes at the flesh on his wrists. 'One of them gave me a thump with some kind of bludgeon. Even so, I wouldn't call to him like they wanted me to. But there was one lad with a hand grenade. Said he'd pull the pin and ram it down my throat. Meant it, an' all. You could tell. So then I did it. I shouted out. "Mike, Uncle Mike, come here, I want you!" And they got their hands on the both of us.' He shudders.

'You did the right thing,' says Edith. 'Come into the house, the pair of you look frozen. Ned, we'll get that wound of yours patched up tonight. But I'm calling the doctor in the morning. You can't take any chances with head injuries.'

Uncle and nephew reel towards the door.

'What did you make of their leader, Hurley?' asks Cameron.

'That lad in charge has them well in hand, Colonel. When he says jump, they hop to it.'

'Could you identify him to the authorities? Or any of the gang?'

A sense of unease vibrates from the Hurleys.

Edith intervenes. 'Let them be for now, Cameron. You go ahead with the men. I want to check Tara over.'

'You and your horses.'

'Horse. There's only one left now.'

'Damn thieves. Don't hang around, old girl. It's not safe out here.'

'It's not safe in the house either, is it? Anyhow, Tara's had a fright and I'm going to sort her out.'

'Have it your own way.'

Edith enters Tara's stall and speaks softly to her, the horse's nostrils ruffling at her.

'Poor girl, you're missing Samson. Did you wonder what those strange men were doing?'

Tara tosses her head and blows through her nose, a harrumphing sound.

'I bet you'd have thrown them if they tried to mount you. You'd show them.' Edith tangles her fingers in the young mare's mane, chilled skin warmed by Tara's body heat. 'All's well,' she says.

Except it isn't.

———

Back in the house, Philomena and Mrs O'Shea are tending to the Hurleys' needs while Cameron stands about brooding. He signals to Edith to step into the passageway.

'Just a minute, Cam. Jeremiah in the gatehouse. Has anyone thought about him? What if he's tied up, too?'

'They didn't come in by the road,' says Ned. 'I'd have spied them if they had. They came across the fields into Drishane. From up somewhere by the O'Driscoll castle, I'd say. A couple of them crept down towards the gates when I was watching the road, ambushed me that way.'

'They could have been camping out by the O'Driscoll ruins,' says Cameron.

'Even so, we should look in on Jeremiah,' insists Edith. 'He could be bound and gagged, for all we know.'

'I'll find out.' Cameron gives Edith a significant look. 'When I'm back, there's something you need to see.' He lifts the torch and sets off in the direction of the avenue.

There's too much to do to waste time puzzling over what he could possibly mean. She trains a lamp on Ned Hurley's cuts, cleaned by Philomena. They look nasty. One of them is still oozing. She fetches her medical kit from the bathroom to dab on some antiseptic, and afterwards ties a bandage around his head. When that's done, she goes to the little Dooley-shaped mound in a corner of the kitchen and kneels beside it, pulling off the towel used to cover him. He is stiffening already. But he's still Dooley, her devoted companion. Bed will be empty tonight without him. She strokes the leaf-shaped patch above his eye.

The back door opens and Cameron stamps in. 'Old Jeremiah heard nothing. Or so he says. I had the devil of a job rousing him.'

'Sleeps as sound as a pound, does Jeremiah,' Mrs O'Shea puts in. 'Sure the house could tumble about his ears and he'd never stir.'

'Damned peculiar at a time like this,' says Cameron. 'Edith, a word with you, please. Bring a lamp.'

She follows him out to the passageway, past the glory hole, as far as the boot cupboard.

'This is what I was trying to tell you earlier,' he says. 'I checked my study. They searched it, judging by the state of the place, but nothing seems to be taken. Surprisingly, I have to say.'

'Good.'

'But they left something behind.' He stoops and lifts something from the ground. 'Look what I found.' Dangling by the laces from Cameron's hand are the IRA man's discarded brown boots. 'One of those thugs must have helped himself – the cupboard door was lying open. Nincompoop left his own behind. But it's a stroke of luck, don't you see? They can be used against him. *Prima facie* evidence, those lawyer chappies call it. There's a bootmaker's name on the inside.' He pulls aside the tongue to reveal the inner back. *Made by J.J. Carroll of Listowel*. 'He'll know who ordered them. We can trace these back to a member of that cut-throat crew we had the privilege of hosting tonight, and he'll lead us to the others. That ringleader chappie's the one we need to get our hands on. Cut off the head of the snake and the body collapses.'

Edith realizes her good turn is about to send trouble to the door of that boy's family. But she can't tell her brother. 'Cam, we escaped lightly tonight. The house is still standing. They seemed happy enough with what they took. What if they hear about us co-operating with the authorities and pay a return visit? To punish us? Or warn others off?'

'I don't know, Peg. Those blighters could go after the Coghills, the Chavasses, the Bushes – any of us. Would you really care to have that on your conscience?'

'There's no protection to be had from the military or police. We have to help ourselves.'

'I devoted my life to the army. I can call in favours.'

A bank of weariness descends on Edith. 'It's been a long night. Let's discuss it in the morning. We should all think about trying to snatch a few hours' sleep. I expect the Hurleys want to go home to their own beds. But I wonder if we shouldn't keep Ned here overnight, on account of that head injury.'

'That's another thing. The Hurleys. They recognized some of the blighters, I'm convinced of it. But they're insisting they knew none of them.'

'Can you blame them?'

'They owe us their loyalty. We've given their family employment for generations.'

All things considered, their first duty is to their own skins, thinks Edith. But she understands that Cameron feels unmanned by the raid. She pats him on the arm. 'You've done really well, Chimp. No one could have handled things any better. Now, bed for me as soon as I talk to Ned Hurley. We can discuss this again in the morning. *Sufficient unto the day is the evil thereof.*'

———

Next morning, in that dream state between waking and full consciousness, Edith feels something warm and damp on her cheeks. 'Dooley,' she mumbles. He's licking her face to tell her it's time to get up. Abruptly, she remembers he's dead. She sits up, fingers to her face. Her cheeks are wet with tears. Desolation washes over her. Dooley's loss grieves her more than her mother's ruby ring, or Samson's seizure, fond though she was of the game old hunter. She swings her legs out of bed. If she lies on, she'll yield to a weeping fit.

Before breakfast, Cameron digs a grave under an ancient oak tree, majestic in its branchiness, where Dooley liked to scrabble and sniff. Edith waits while her brother shovels, the little fox terrier's body held tight to her chest. He is wrapped in an embroidered shawl she bought in Rome a couple of years earlier, on a trip with Ethel Smyth. She can't part with his blanket, because it retains his smell, but she won't allow him to go into the earth uncovered. When the hole is dug, she finds she can't bring herself to lay him in the pit. Cameron has to take the bundle from her, and Edith looks away as earth is spaded over her Dooley. She gazes at the tree, distancing herself from the mechanics of what's happening. Hardly any leaves left. But he'll have the greenest of canopies next spring.

'There now, nice and deep. And you can visit him here whenever you like, Peg.' Cameron is panting from the exertion.

Incapable of speech, she manages a nod.

'Let's have some breakfast now, old girl.'

Edith doesn't move. She wants to be left on her own with Dooley. Just for a few minutes.

'We must keep our strength up, Peg. You can't survive on cups of tea.'

Appeal brims from her eyes.

'Have it your own way. Come in when you're ready.'

Alone with Dooley, she allows her mind to drift. Such a feisty puppy – fearless from the start. Hated being separated from her. When she went out in the dogcart, he'd scamper alongside, doing his stubby-legged best to keep up until she relented and lifted him in. He was meant to sleep at her feet, above the covers, but there were times she woke to find that damp wee nose a few inches from hers on their shared pillow.

'Martin, will you take care of him on the other side?' she whispers, and a rustle of branches overhead gives the response she needs.

Moving with care, as though in danger of fragmenting, Edith returns to the house. Soon, she is seated opposite Cameron in the morning room, all the familiar trappings about them. Edith looks at her blue duck's egg. The idea of food is repellent but she can't buckle now. She decapitates her boiled egg and dips a spoon in it.

Cameron is fussing with Loulou, who's clingy this morning and begging to be allowed onto his knee. 'Just this once, Lou,' he cautions, and feeds her some buttered toast. The Pomeranian licks his fingers with her disproportionately long tongue, lapping up buttery residue.

'About the boots,' he says over Loulou's head.

'Yes?'

'I've decided to hold on to them. Possible evidence when things are more settled. But for now, I think we should keep our heads down. Not draw attention to ourselves. It's galling to let them off, Peg. But needs must. They'll get their just desserts in the end.'

'Whatever you say, Chimp. I'll be advised by you.'

He touches the knot on his tie, his expression suspicious, but decides to take her at face value.

Edith manages a wan smile at her impeccably turned-out brother. After a lifetime in the army, he always looks spotless. She always looks dishevelled. Except perhaps in her riding habit at the start of a hunt. She smooths down the wings of hair on either side of her face. Last night, she tossed and turned in bed, tearing the top sheet – one of Mama's French linen ones, which she always saved for favoured visitors. How she'd have scolded Edith.

'Nevertheless, Peg, I'll pay calls to some of the neighbouring families and alert them.'

'Good idea. Tara could use a jog out. It'll help to settle her after last night. More tea?'

'Thank you. By the way, I thought you told me our ancestors had thrown a spirit cordon around Drishane and we'd come to no harm? Where were they when we needed them?'

Edith has been gnawing over the same conundrum. 'I heard Martin's voice telling me not to antagonize the men. It was good advice.'

'We could have used something more practical by way of assistance. How did those louts even gain access to the land if our ancestors had the place barricaded?'

'I don't know. I'll ask Martin.'

He glooms over his teacup. 'If you ask me, the locals are up to their necks in rebellion. They're as nice as pie to our faces but they aren't loyal. To us or the Crown.'

'I don't know how loyal the Crown is to us, Cam. The Government has mishandled the situation dreadfully. They persist in treating the Irish as naughty schoolchildren, and make no allowances for the sense of rage that's been building over the past thirty years. A bit more common sense all round would go a long way.'

'You always stand up for the Irish, Edith.'

Why not? I'm Irish, after all. So are you.'

'Not that sort of Irish. And another thing. I'm not happy about Jeremiah in the gatehouse. For all we know, he could be in on what happened last night. I find it damned peculiar, him sleeping through everything. Not sure I believe him. I think we should dispense with his services. Let him find a new billet.'

'He's lived there since Grandpapa's day. Raised a family of six in that little house. Stayed on as a widower after Delia died. You can't turf him out.'

'Oh, can't I? I'm Master of Drishane. I can do whatever I bally well like. Let one of his daughters down in the village take him in. Or his sons. That's a decent-sized farmhouse two of them have on the road to Skib, however they got their hands on it.'

'You know very well they made money in America. Cameron, you're being unreasonable. You don't know Jeremiah had anything to do with last night.'

'I know he was asleep on the job.'

'He's not a night watchman, he's a gardener.'

'It's highly suspicious, him sleeping the whole way through the raid. He must have heard something. Seen lights.'

'The gatehouse is at the bottom of the avenue. You can't see the house through the trees.'

'I don't care. He'll have to go.

'Cameron, stop it. Just stop it. Jeremiah O'Mahony has worked in our gardens for half a century. Our grandfather trusted him. Our father trusted him. If you throw him out, I'll put him up in one of my houses in the village. Rent-free.'

His cheeks flame. 'It's outrageous that armed men should be free to trespass on my land, and walk into my property, bold as brass. As if they owned the place. The world's gone mad.' Cameron pushes back his chair and stands up. 'My land and my property,' he repeats. 'And no one cares. There's no one to complain to.'

'I care.'

'I mean no one in authority. Once, I could have whistled up a police inspector to deal with this. I've a good mind to take this further. I could go into Skib and see the commanding officer of the Sherwoods. I served with his brother.'

'Please don't cause a fuss. It'll only make things worse. The Government has abandoned us. We have to use our own wits to get through this.'

'A lorryload of soldiers driving up and down the road between here and Skib would soon put the frighteners on those scoundrels. No, that wouldn't work, the roads are in pieces. But they could ship them in over water.'

Edith grips the table edge. 'Don't even think about it, Cam. For pity's sake. Imagine if they turned the Black and Tans loose on Castletownshend. The villagers would never forgive you. Our name would be mud forever. The Tans have terrorized the people in other parts of the county – ask the Hurleys, ask Philomena and Mrs O'Shea, if you don't believe me. The truth is, the Government has washed its hands of Ireland. While the war was on, it let the Tans and Auxiliaries behave any way they liked. They've been reined in now because of the truce. But if it falls apart, all hell will break loose.'

Cameron occupies himself with Loulou for a minute or two. 'I just want peace and quiet, Peg. All those years overseas, I kept thinking about Drishane. It was meant to be my haven. But I don't feel the same about it anymore.'

'Because of the IRA raid?'

'Damned rebels. Strutting about. Making threats.'

He wanted to sell Drishane before the flying squad paid them a visit, but Edith doesn't point this out. Her brother needs reassurance. 'I know how you feel, dear. But Drishane will survive – I feel it in my marrow. We just have to lie low. Cam, you'll leave Jeremiah alone, won't you? Let him stay in the gatehouse?'

'Suppose so.'

———

'Take it easy today, Peg. See you at dinner.'

Edith and Cameron, the latter dressed for a journey, are standing on the front steps. He sees Mike Hurley lead Tara and the trap around the side of the house and raises his voice. 'How's that nephew of yours this morning, Hurley?'

'Not too bad, Colonel. It takes more than a dunch on the noggin to floor a Hurley.'

'That's the spirit.' He walks across the gravel and slips something into Hurley's hand. 'For the young fellow's trouble,' he says quietly.

Hurley touches his cap to Cameron.

Edith observes the exchange with approval. Correct behaviour never fails to please her.

The trap bowls away in a whirl of small stones.

'Just a minute, Mike.' She joins him. 'Are you really all right?'

'Not a bother, Miss Edith.'

'Do you think they'll be back? Our night visitors?'

'I can't say. All I can tell you is the Somerville name means something in these parts. The people wouldn't take kindly to outsiders doing you down.'

'Outsiders? Were they all strangers?'

A look, quick, before his eyes turn away. 'Mostly, Miss Edith. The fella they left outside to keep watch over us was from somewhere not a million miles from here.'

'I see. Does my brother know?'

'Not unless you have it in your head to go telling him.'

The wind is chilly, pinching colour into her nose and chin. Edith hugs herself. Lately, she's been feeling the cold. She bends down to pick up a leaf that's the precise shade of the patch on Dooley's face. Dogs – they burrow through your defences and plant themselves in your heart. After they're gone, a piece of your heart is lost with them. Her eyes mist over.

'Miss Edith? Are you intending for to tell the colonel?'

She pushes the leaf into her pocket. She's planning to do a portrait of Dooley from memory and it will be a useful colour prompt. 'I shouldn't think so. Least said, soonest mended.' She hesitates, wondering how to phrase her question.

If the Somervilles are to survive in Castletownshend, it must be with local support. One of her ancestors saved two local men who were Fenians. That hasn't been forgotten. All of them, Somervilles and villagers alike, weathered the Famine and the Land War. But since that Easter 1916 business in Dublin, certainties have eroded and grievances reignited. Something powerful is swimming to the surface. Over the summer, a scarecrow of a travelling man stopped her near the boathouse and said he wanted to buy back his ancestral lands from them, if you don't mind. As though the Somervilles were squatting on something that belonged to others.

Edith is hybrid and can live with her hybridity. But can the Irish, who are bound to take over one of these days, live with it too? No point in asking Mike. He might give her the answer he thinks she wants to hear.

'All the same, Miss Edith, good job we got those young horses away. In the nick of time, it was.' A slow grin stretches Mike's face.

It's catching. She smiles back. 'Every cloud has a silver lining.'

'We pulled one over on the Sinn Féin boyos, so we did.'

'They'd have loved to get their hands on my hunters. Where are they, by the by?'

'Over by Leap direction. Your sovereigns will see them through the winter.' He tips the brim of his cap to her and walks away in the direction of the greenhouses.

Despite everything, she's less melancholy as she strolls towards the lawns overlooking the bay, Drishane at her back. In the 1700s the house was designed to face towards the quays where Tom the Merchant could watch his ships load and unload the goods by which he made his fortune. His heirs, who regarded trade as ungentlemanly, were unable to change Drishane's aspect. Instead, one of them re-routed the driveway towards a different door. Edith thinks of it as a metaphor. Same house, new doorway – things went on as before. Hopefully, things will continue to do that under a new regime.

She watches the progress of a sailboat steering for Castlehaven Bay. It's tacking sideways against the contrary wind. Shading her eyes, she tries to detect which of the local fishermen it belongs to. All at once, she becomes aware she's not alone. For one heart-stopping moment, she thinks the Sinn Féiners are back. Edith lays her hand against her sternum and counts to three before turning her head.

'Hello, Flurry. Where have you been hiding yourself?'

He's watching the boat, too, and doesn't look at her. But he salutes her with a tip of his hat. 'Here and there.'

'We'd a bit of a night of it last night. An IRA captain and his men paid us a visit.'

'Hunters by the sound of them.'

'Boys, Flurry. Younger than you. And decades younger than me.' She sighs. 'We were expecting a call sooner or later. But the nervous strain of waiting grinds one's nerves to powder. I can't help wondering how long the staff will put up with it.'

'Until they can't is my guess.'

'One of them, a chap with his teeth hanging out to dry over his lower lip, had a grenade dangling from his belt. He murdered Dooley. Kicked him to death as easy as he'd squash a fly. Are you listening, Flurry?'

From his pocket, he produces a crushed packet of Woodbines, shakes out a cigarette and lights it by striking a match on the sole of his boot. The whiff of sulphur blows across to her. 'Hunting's what I'm thinking about. Are there many foxes in the woods this season?'

'Oh, Flurry, no one has time to think about foxes or hunting.'

His voice radiates reproach. 'What else is there to think about but horses, dogs and foxes?'

'Keeping Drishane intact for the next generation. Passing it on in good shape.'

Flurry takes a draw, cheeks hollowing, and she smells tobacco smoke. She's always liked it in the open air.

'You mightn't be too keen on handing it over when the time comes. My grandmama has a tight grip on Aussolas. She's always promising to leave it to me in her will. But as sure as eggs is eggs, she'll outlive me. Out of pure spite.'

'Flurry, what should we do? About the raiders, I mean?'

Moody, he studies the glowing tip of his cigarette. 'If there's trouble in store, I'd get your brother away from here. He who fights and runs away lives to fight another day.'

'They can think again if they think they're going to get rid of us!'

'The people won't bother you, Edith. But I can't say as much for your brother.'

eight

'Cam, we need to talk.'

'Mmm.' Cameron is sucking peppermints, lost in Bach's *Italian Concerto* on the gramophone, his foot beating out the notes. Towards the end of his career, he was commander at Kneller Hall in Twickenham, the British army's school for bandsmen. It was his favourite posting.

Edith knows it was an act of kindness to invite her into his sitting room to listen to the concerto with him, but under present circumstances the music is lost on her. She tries again. 'The thing is, Chimp, it's not safe here for you.'

'Wretched troublemakers. I'd like to horsewhip the lot of them!'

'I'm worried about you. You're Master of Drishane. That makes you a kidnap target.'

His eyes snap open. 'They wouldn't dare!'

'You're forgetting about the heir to the Powys estate. He was held for nine days until a ransom was paid.'

He harrumphs and she presses home her advantage. 'Look, Chimp, the winds of change are blowing. Old loyalties can't be relied on. Besides, it's men from outside doing these things. The Somerville name means nothing to them.'

He broods. Crunches his peppermint. Settles the pleat in a trouser leg. By and by, he says, 'Doesn't seem right that our place here should be questioned. It's our native soil, too.'

A spark flies out from the log on the fire, bright as a miniature comet: glory followed by extinction. Edith shivers. 'Of course we belong here. But discretion is the better part of valour.'

'I'd go away if you came with me, Peg.'

'But the house. Somebody has to hold the fort.'

'It wouldn't feel right leaving you here on your own.'

'Nobody would trouble themselves about an old woman like me. Besides, I'd have Philomena and Mrs O'Shea. Mike Hurley's here every day, and Jeremiah O'Mahony's always tinkering about in the garden. I wouldn't be alone.'

'Why don't we shut up shop and leave Philomena as caretaker?'

Edith wants to say that Drishane is more than her home – that her sense of self is tethered to the house. And Martin's presence is powerful here. But she needs to advance a more practical argument to Cameron. 'I'd be afraid of the place going up in flames with none of the family here.'

'Animals. Burning two-hundred-year-old houses. No rhyme or reason to their destruction.'

'The Tans have been torching houses, too.'

'Cabins and shacks. Hardly in the same league.'

'You make us a target by being here, Cam. You know you do.' She waits. He can be as obstinate as a rock if pushed. But she knows he wants to go away.

The music comes to a halt, and he stands up to lift the needle from the disc. 'By the by, I met a Yank in the West Cork today, when I stopped in for a bite to eat. He's a reporter for some New York newspaper or other. I forget which. You want to see what this chap was driving. A ripping roadster made by the H.C.S. Motor Car Company of Indiana. Had it shipped over. Bit showy, to tell you the truth. Couldn't be any more yellow if it was a bowl of custard.'

Edith remembers a man and his chauffeur in Skibbereen, fretting about missing a train. There can't be two such motor cars in West Cork. How odd he's still here. 'You'd think, if it was news he was after, he'd be in Dublin or London.'

'Fellow was proud as Punch of his motor. "I know folks stare but to blazes with them," he said. What do you say we take a leaf out of his book, Peg? Let everyone go to blazes? You and me, we could take a place together in London.'

'Cam, I love London for a visit. But I couldn't live there. I'd turn into one of those lumpen women, from overeating and want of exercise. But you'd enjoy it, I know you would. You could go to concert halls. Stay at your club. Catch up with the family – the boys spend their leave there. I suppose Hugh and Jack think of it as home now.' She frowns, wishing this scattering hadn't happened. 'When everything's settled in Ireland, you can come back.'

'Settled? The Irish question? Fat chance.'

'The politicians are making a hash of things but sooner or later they'll see the light. As sure as springtime, there'll be an end to these distur-bances. But for now, you go and I'll stay. Yes?'

'Let me sleep on it.'

—

'Cameron, can you come and look at something with me please?'

'What's wrong, Edith? You look as if you've seen a ghost.'

'Can you come here? Now?'

Cameron leaves the breakfast table and follows her to the front door, lying ajar. He stands out on the step and gazes down the avenue. 'Well? What is it?'

'Look behind you, Cam. On the door.'

Pinned to the wood is a note. Cameron tears it down with an oath.

'Horrible, isn't it?' says Edith. 'Lucky I spotted it before any of the staff. I was outside picking ferns.'

Flushed crimson, he reads the note aloud.

CROMWELLS SPAWN
YOUR BEING WATCHED YOU LEECHES
YOUR DAYS ARE NUMBERED
YOUR SITTING DUCKS KEEP LOOKING OVER YOUR
SHOULDERS
SIGNED THE PEOPLES DEFENDERS

'Infernal cheek,' says Cameron. 'We were never Cromwellians.'

'Of course not. Though we did marry in ...'

'I see this putrid piece of coercion is anonymous. People's defenders, indeed! Probably some errand boy with no seat in his trousers.'

'You're attracting this, Cam, dear.'

'It's not addressed to anyone.'

'Honestly, Chimp, you're a target. A colonel. A landowner. A gentleman.'

'It would be shabby to bolt. Besides, I refuse to be intimidated.' He crumples the dog-earned sheet and throws it on the ground.

Edith picks it up, and they walk back together to the breakfast room. On the way, she smooths out the page and flicks a glance at the pencilled message. She used one of her graphite pencils. Less chance of the lettering becoming illegible if it rained overnight.

Cameron sits down in his place, expression testy, but Edith goes straight to the fireplace.

'Don't destroy it, Peg, we might need to show it to someone.'

'There's no one *to* show it to. It's vile, let's just get rid of it.' Quickly, she throws the note into the flames.

———

Edith and Cameron say their farewells in the outer hall, Cam holding Loulou, who knows something is afoot because of all the luggage. She licks his face and keeps her dark eyes on him.

'My little, little, Lou-lou-lou,' he says. 'Daddy will miss you. He'll think of you every minute of the day. But he'll bring you back some yummy Swiss chocolate from the Alps.'

A jaunt to Switzerland is news to Edith. 'I thought you were going to London, Cam?'

'Yes, all booked. Rendezvous with the clan, and so forth. But I might go further afield. I've been feeling cooped up.'

Where on earth is he getting the money? Edith bites back criticism. The main thing is he'll be safe.

'Begging your pardon,' says Philomena. 'I just wanted to wish the master a safe journey.'

'Thank you, Philomena.'

'Mrs O'Shea will be up directly. She has a cherry cake baked fresh this morning to put in your picnic basket. You won't go hungry, Colonel, even if the restaurant cars are shut.'

'Everything has gone to hell in a handcart, Philomena. You'll look after Miss Edith, won't you?'

'You can count on me, Colonel. I don't see how you'll get across the water at all tonight, mind you. There's not enough wind today to snuff out a candle.'

'The boats are steam-driven now, Philomena,' says Edith. 'I think perhaps you should go and see what's keeping Mrs O'Shea. The colonel needs to be on the road.'

Just then, Mrs O'Shea huffs up from the kitchen with a basket. 'Colonel, I've a feast in here for you, so I have. There's a couple of chicken legs, ham sandwiches, and I know you're fond of . . .'

'You're an angel, Mrs O'Shea,' Edith interrupts the litany. 'Take that out to Mike, would you, Philomena? Now, Cameron, you really must leave. Miss one connection and they're all at sixes and sevens.'

From a pocket in her vast apron, Mrs O'Shea produces a parcel tied with string. 'Could I trouble you to post this in England for me, Colonel? It's for me brother Francie and his family in Liverpool. A barmbrack made the way our mother always baked them, God rest that hardwork-ing saint of a woman. Francie does be lonesome for the taste of her food. And here's some money for stamps. I hope it'll be enough.'

One-handed, still clasping Loulou, Cameron accepts the package but refuses the coins. 'No need for that, Mrs O'Shea. Stamps won't be a problem.'

Edith ushers him outside, the cook's effusions trailing after them.

'You mustn't worry about a thing, Chimp. I'll keep everything ship-shape here for you.'

'I know you will, Peg. Wish I didn't have to leave Loulou behind. Poor girl is sure to get the mopes. But London's no place for her. Someone would tread on you, wouldn't they? My teeny-tiny baby girl.'

'I'll see to it she has plenty of exercise.'

'And her coat needs brushing every day.'

'All right.'

'Talk to her – she gets lonely.'

'I will.'

'When you're out walking, watch out for large birds. Remember the time that owl tried to fly off with her? Thought she was prey.'

Edith holds out her arms. 'I'll take her now. Off you go, dear, you haven't a minute to lose. You know how messy the roads can be.'

Cameron deposits a kiss on Loulou's nose, hands her over and climbs into the trap.

Loulou wriggles in Edith's arms, trying to chase after him, but is held tight. 'Behave, young lady. I'm going to train you. Your master was too soft with you.'

Hurley cries out 'hup' to Tara and the wheels start rolling. Mrs O'Shea and Philomena wave from the steps.

Edith walks alongside for a few steps. 'Tell the boys their sons really need to spend more time in Ireland.'

'Can't think why they'd want to.'

'How are they meant to take care of Drishane if they don't learn to love it?'

The trap picks up speed. He raises his arm in farewell.

Her brother had a spring in his step. He's sorrier to leave this toy dog than Drishane. Edith knows love of place is seeded in childhood. But it can be learned, too. None of the coming generation grew up in the house, the way she and Hildegarde and their five brothers did. When things quieten down, she'll write to Aylmer and Boyle's sons and invite them to stay. One of them will be Cameron's heir.

Edith expects to feel lonely after Cameron's departure, but the house folds itself around her, as comforting as a patchwork quilt. She plunders the treasure chest of Irish R.M. stories to borrow a line here, a scene there, for her play. It will all culminate in a wedding, of course. 'Journeys end in lovers meeting/Every wise man's son doth know.' Aloud, she quotes Feste, the *Twelfth Night* jester. But a plot that's all romance and no Flurrying would never do. Fortunately, that reprobate Slipper, the boozy, unscrupulous hunt servant, keeps muscling in, and it amuses her to allow him to steal Flurry's thunder now and again. He'll be a crowd-pleaser. A succession of productive writing days follows, and she is conscious of Martin's spirit guiding her pen. Not since the earliest days of their literary career has she experienced such a sense of a mission. No wonder tremendous progress is being made.

Writing those stories with Martin was a joyful time, especially the first collection. That was back in the heel-end of the last century. Martin was pain-free then and, although they had family responsibilities, their shoulders could manage the load. Youth helped. Often, they were doubled over with laughter during the plotting, conscious that Major Yeates's wife Philippa was ten times cleverer than he, and as for Flurry Knox, he was so sharp he'd cut himself to ribbons one day.

She has no need to consult their manuscripts to choose the stories she's using to clothe her play. They remain just-landed fresh in her mind. She does, however, trawl her notebooks, scanning for useful phrases to weave through. Opening those marbled covers never fails to comfort her. It's satisfying to retrieve a sentence written some two decades earlier as an act of faith in the future. That future turned out to be rather more tentative than she imagined. Yet she must make the best of it. Whatever deserts her, courage can never be allowed to fail. A first draft will be completed shortly.

Shortly before bedtime, Edith has an automatic writing session with Martin — it's part of her routine, and tends not to produce anything sensational. Tonight is no exception. After some platitudes, along with reassurances that Dooley is happy in heaven, she sets aside pencil and paper, drinks some warm milk and retires upstairs. She undresses and rubs a skimpy amount of cold cream on her face, eking it out because replacements from the Army and Navy Stores in London can't be relied on. This is the time of day she misses Dooley most. When she knelt on the bedside rug to say her prayers, he'd crouch alongside, paws over his eyes. It's too chilly in the room for lengthy devotions. A rapid *pater noster* and a few invocations, and she slips between the covers, toeing for the hot water bottle. The paraffin oil lamp sighs when she extinguishes it. Edith exhales in sympathy, sinking into the feather mattress moulded to her body shape after decades of faithful service.

—

One day, when a full moon is due, Edith decides to bring her sketching materials to the castle after dinner. It's currently empty, but her cousins, the Townshends, won't object to her setting up easel and sketchpad there. She plans to work up some pastels of the castle exterior. The *Flurry's Wedding* plot calls for a moonlit scene at Aussolas, old Mrs Knox's home, and she's longing to try her hand at the stage scenery. She instructs Philomena to prepare her coffee in a thermos flask after dinner.

Dismay registers on Philomena's face, as round and plain – and yet as comforting – as an everyday dinner plate. 'Do you really think you should go out on your own after dark, Miss Edith? What if you run into those boyos again, knocking about?'

'I'll bring Loulou. If there's anyone lurking, she'll bark to warn me.'

'True for you. No better one. Except. What good's hearing them and you on your lonesome? At least ask old Jeremiah to go the length with you.'

'It's a long time since I've needed a chaperone, Philomena. Look, if I hear anything suspicious, I'll shelter in the Castle. I know how to get inside, no matter how securely it's locked and barred. One of the benefits of a misspent childhood.'

'I don't like it, Miss Edith. I don't like it at all. If you have to go, let it be early, before the night draws in.'

'I want to see the castle by moonlight. I—'

A clatter of hooves stops her, drawing both women to the window.

'Glory be to God!' cries Philomena.

'It's Samson!' says Edith. Riderless, reins trailing, the horse is gallop-ing up the drive.

Edith dashes outside, followed by Philomena. By the time she catches up with him, Samson is in the stable yard, drinking from the water trough. His flanks are heaving and coated in dust. He's thinner, and a quick scan of his legs shows some cuts in need of urgent attention, with a shoe missing from the right foreleg.

'Find Mike,' says Edith.

'He must have escaped from the pups that robbed him,' marvels Philomena.

'Run like the wind. He'll be in Cross Street, at his own place. Tell him I want him.'

Tara whinnies, recognizing Samson, but he's too exhausted to neigh back at her.

Edith pats him. 'Aren't you the champion, finding your way home from goodness knows where. There, boy, there now. You're safe and sound.' When Samson has finished drinking, Edith leads him to a bale of fresh hay inside the stable block. She notices sores on his mouth where the bit was sawed at – an inexperienced rider must have been trying to control him. A savage hope flares that Samson threw the scoundrel head-long into a manure pile.

———

Edith and Mike Hurley work in tandem to doctor Samson. Deferring to his expertise, she takes her instructions from him – Mike Hurley is half horse himself. While he bathes the horse's swollen legs in saltwater, and binds them with bandages, she mixes a solution to apply to Samson's chafed areas.

Mike is incandescent at Samson's condition. 'Poor beast was ridden hard and no care taken of him. He'd drop down dead inside a month with this treatment, Miss Edith. No wonder they have to keep stealing horses.'

'Anyone who abuses a dumb animal should be shot.'

'I dare say them fellas will stop a bullet sooner or later.'

Methodical, he checks the leg bandages are tight enough before turning his attention to grooming. Selecting a curry comb, he uses it in circular movements, its short metal teeth dislodging caked-on mud and other detritus. The horse is accustomed to his handling and stands patiently, despite occasional tremors rippling his shrunken frame. Edith tackles his tail and mane, trying to stay out of Mike's way.

Mike shakes out the curry comb, tutting at the dirt that's dislodged. 'Hand me the brush next to you, please, Miss Edith. Not that one, it's for later. I need the hardest one first.' Using short strokes, front to back in the direction of the horse's hair growth, he sweeps stiff bristles over Samson. 'I wouldn't be surprised if them IRA heroes weren't headed back our way. Stands to reason they'd come after Samson. Makes them look foolish, losing him.'

'I thought the same. That IRA captain may be a fanatic but he's nobody's fool.' What if he sends the whistler? Edith quakes at the idea of meeting him again. Fear must be mastered, she tells herself. But that swoosh with his hand, miming a house being set alight, haunts her.

'I'll sit up tonight in the stables, Miss Edith.'

'After what happened last time?'

'Somebody has to see about the horses.'

'I don't know if that's wise.' She hesitates. 'Would some of our tenants keep watch with you?'

'You know they won't, miss. That's asking them to take sides. I could try our Ned again. His mother won't like it, but Samson won't survive if they take him again.'

Edith falls silent. Presently, she asks, 'Is he able for it? After the blow to his head?'

'He's a Hurley – what's bred in the dog comes out in the pup. We'll stick together this time. It was a mistake to separate.'

'I wish—' Edith is too overwhelmed to continue. She watches Mike's sure hands continue their progress over the horse's hide. 'No, I can't allow it. Try Jeremiah. He'll be company for you, if nothing else.'

nine

Dinner is consumed in jig time, since there is no one to talk to and breeding prevents Edith from propping a book against the salt cellar. Standards can't be permitted to slip. During her meal, she decides that communication by automatic writing with Martin is insufficient at this crisis point. While useful, undoubtedly, it has limitations. Could she hold a seance? Imagine if she managed a materialization! Edith has never been able to effect one. Perhaps, she reflects, a seance is overly ambitious without a medium. On second thoughts, she'll try the Ouija board.

No time like the present. Edith rings the bell for Philomena to clear the table. A knock on the door, and Philomena plods into the dining room, still in the process of unrolling her sleeves. She is inclined to linger and chat, with Cameron's absence narrowing the gap between family and servants. Philomena's strong arms lift and stack. She could follow a plough with those shoulders and arms, thinks Edith.

'Mrs O'Shea and me thought you might like to join us in the kitchen this evening, Miss Edith. It must be desperate lonesome up here for you, with the master away.'

'How kind. Do please send my thanks to Mrs O'Shea. But I have plans for tonight. Another night, I'd love to take you up on that.'

'We have a two-week-old copy of the *Skibbereen Eagle*. I'm reading it out to her. The eyes aren't able for the small print, dear love her.'

'Perhaps tomorrow, Philomena.'

'I hear one of the doctor's boys has taken a shine to Timmy the Post's daughter. Cornelius, it is, the one that's training to be a teacher. He's like hounds after a fox – oh very determined to have her. But his family is against the match. She has no dowry.'

Normally, Edith's ears would prick at such a titbit, noting down its details for future use in a story. But tonight her mind is on Martin and she hears the words without any sense of their meaning. Only when Mike Hurley's name is mentioned does Philomena snag her attention.

'I thought I'd bring him out some sandwiches before I turn in. He says he's sleeping in the stable loft tonight to keep an eye on Samson. You'd be rightly shanghaied, Miss Edith, if the IRA came back for Samson and took Tara, too, out of spite. I heard they drove off a couple or three bullocks on a farmer out Drimoleague way after he wouldn't give them the time of day, let alone a contribution.'

'Mike and Jeremiah will keep a sharp eye out.'

'But there's only Mike. Jeremiah took a turn, lost his footing, and Mike sent him home.'

Concern pinches Edith. A great deal is being asked of Mike Hurley. 'How unfortunate. I'll go out and speak to Mike before I lock up. Could you check on Jeremiah? See if he needs some beef tea, or a hand getting to bed?'

'Very good, ma'am dear. I'm relieved you're not going off drawing pictures, down at the castle tonight.'

'I had second thoughts after Samson galloped up. But I've important work to do here in any case.'

Edith goes upstairs to fetch the Ouija board and other props. On her return, Philomena is still tidying the dining room, and when she sees what Edith is carrying, she sets down the willow-patterned tray and folds her arms.

'Miss Edith, I've served you for thirty years, and I've earned the right to speak me mind. All this divil stuff you're at. It's a sin, so it is. Father Lambe would go pure mad if he thought me and Mrs O'Shea were staying in a house where the mistress calls up ghosts.'

'Miss Martin isn't a ghost, Philomena.'

'What is she, then, and her dead and buried this past six years?'

'She's a caring, loyal, loving ...' Edith is lost for words.

'Ghost!'

'Presence. She's a presence. And there is nothing diabolical about it.'

'Me and Mrs O'Shea, we don't like it. It's not right, Miss Edith. Bothering the dead the way you do. Let them that's gone stay gone.'

'Really, Philomena, I've indulged you quite enough. I won't be told what I can and can't do by a member of my staff.'

'We'll give notice, so we will.'

Edith is alarmed. 'Come, come, you're overreacting. Why don't you make yourself a nice pot of tea and—'

'We'll pack our bags. Or Father Lambe will want to know the reason why.' Philomena blots her eyes with her apron hem. 'You're dabbling with dangerous things, miss. You might maybe be putting your immortal soul in danger.'

'That will be all, Philomena. We'll talk about this when you're less overwrought.'

'I know you're the mistress but ...' Sniff. 'Me and Mrs O'Shea ...' Sniff.

'Off you go, Philomena.'

Truculent and tearful, Philomena trudges out. Edith knows she'll have to pacify her, but not when she's emotional.

Now, to the job at hand. Spiritualists always burn incense to enhance the atmosphere, in her experience. As a stand-in for incense, she has decided to sacrifice a muslin bag of dried rosemary from her wardrobe. It will burn slowly. The smell of smoke is meant to alert those who have passed over. So Jem Barlow claims. Apparently, anything but sage is useful – sage drives away spirits, for some odd reason.

She dims the lamps and sprinkles the rosemary into an ashtray, where it smoulders slowly. A sneeze from under the sideboard, and she realizes Loulou has crept into the room. 'Not a peep out of you, milady.' She bribes her with a cube from the forgotten sugar bowl.

Edith removes the board from its box. It's a black-painted rectangle with gold markings. 'Yes' is stencilled on one side under a sun symbol, and 'No' on the other beneath a moon symbol. The letters of the alphabet are ranged in a double semi-circle, while the numbers zero to nine are lined up along the bottom.

Loulou scoots over, springing for her lap, and Edith settles her there, stroking the bridge of the Pomeranian's nose. Then, emptying her mind of everything except Martin's face, she places one finger lightly on the planchette, the pointer which slides around the board. She uses her left hand, leaving her right hand free for writing. In a clockwise fashion, she moves the planchette from Yes to No and across the letters, followed by the numbers, doing this for some minutes. When the time feels right, she speaks.

'Are you here, Martin? If you are, spell out words to me, dearest.'

Nothing happens. She continues manipulating the pointer. Sudden as a squirt of perfume, a memory swims through her: Martin smuggling Edith's dog through French customs, concealed in one of her enormous leg-of-mutton sleeves. A bubble of laughter bursts from Edith. Martin always looked as if butter wouldn't melt in her mouth. But there was nothing she wouldn't do if the humour took her.

The board vibrates. Has she arrived?

'Martin? Can you—'

The door crashes open. A man enters, toting a rifle.

'Beggin' your pardon, Miss Somerville. I'm to fetch you down to the kitchen.'

It's the voice she recognizes first. His skin isn't blackened this time, showing a face as sleek as apple jelly. But she knows him. It's the young Kerry fellow who raided Drishane.

From the safety of Edith's lap, Loulou sets up a rumpus.

'Hush, Loulou. Stop that racket. Good evening, young man. How are the boots holding up?'

His face splits into a grin. 'Fit me like a glove.'

'I'm glad to hear it.' She looks at the firearm – at least he has the courtesy not to aim it at her. 'How many are with you this time?'

'Just me and Patr— … I can't say his name.'

'The brute who kicked my dog to death?'

'No, ma'am.'

'Thank goodness. Couldn't bear to see him again.'

'He doesn't have much feeling for people, let alone God's dumb creatures. He's as wild as a March hare.'

'Why are you back? We've nothing left to give.'

'The horse. We saw him in the stable just now. He's some animal to find his way here from Fermoy. It must be seventy-five miles, if it's a step.'

'Poor creature is half-dead, whatever you've been doing to him.'

'Tell you the truth, we've had to put two at a time on his back.'

'You'll kill him, you know. Horses need to rest if they're worked. They're not machines.'

A shrug. 'Captain's orders is to bring e'ther him or another beast. There's a fit-looking mare in the stable. Maybe she'd be a better bet.'

'I hope you haven't tied up Mike Hurley again.'

'The aul' fella? Below in the kitchen with the women.'

'Did you hurt him?'

'No need. He came quiet. Where's your brother, the colonel?'

'England. Didn't the others tell you?'

A nod.

'You're checking our story, aren't you?'

A half-grin breaks through his darkened face. 'What's that you have, ma'am? Is it some kind of board game? Like snakes and ladders?' Advancing, he tracks mud into the Turkey carpet. Loulou launches into another round of yelping.

She covers the Ouija board with its lid. 'Not quite. Mind your manners, Lou – pipe down. You seem like a nice young man. It's a shame to see you embark on a career as a horse thief.'

'I'm a soldier of the Irish Republic.'

'And a horse thief besides.'

'Captain's orders.' Sullen now, his gaze sweeps the room, absorbing its grandeur.

What if he decides to do some looting? They still have possessions to lose. To distract him, Edith says, 'Is this really the life you'd wish for yourself? It must be hard on you – on all of you. Haring about the country, sleeping in ditches, hunting and being hunted.'

'It's for Ireland.'

'Your mother must be worried sick.'

'I wish I could send her a letter. Mam made sure all of us could read and write. Said we'd need some bit of lettering so as to write letters home from America, or wherever we wound up. She thought we'd have to go away to make a life for ourselves, d'you see.'

'Was there a school near you?'

'A good twenty miles away. 'Twas Mam taught me my letters. She cut a willow rod, poked one end in the embers to blacken it, and used it to write on the outhouse wall. A was for where the roof beams joined, B was the priest's spectacles, C was the moon. D a bow and arrow – that's me, so it is.'

'What was E?'

'E was a gate.' Unconscious of having given away a clue about his identity, he adds, 'Mam always wanted us to better ourselves.'

'You're going the wrong way about it.'

He gestures with his rifle. 'That's enough aul' blather. Let's go.'

Edith pushes back her chair and stands, holding tight to Loulou. *Remember always use your wits and strike a bargain where you can.* That's what Martin told her in automatic writing. She takes a guess. 'D for Daniel, is it?'

'My friend'll be pure mad if we keep him waiting. Come on, now.'

'Or could it be D for Denis?'

His eyes pop, giving her the answer.

'Denis. Well, well.'

'The captain'll be pure mad at me over this.'

'It can be our secret. So, Denis, your name's not the only thing I know about you. I know you're about to send a storm of trouble raining down on the heads of your family. When you swapped boots here, you left your old pair behind. Colonel Somerville found them. They can be used to trace you – the boot maker's name is marked on them. J.J. Carroll of Listowel.'

He wilts. 'Where are the boots? Give them here.'

'They're somewhere safe. Elsewhere.'

A moan escapes from the boy. 'I don't believe you. I want them back.'

'You said they belonged to your father. Well, your father can expect a visit from the Black and Tans.'

'Please, no, ma'am, you mustn't. It'd kill me mother and father stone dead. Sure, they've had the house burned over their heads already by the Tans. A neighbour's given them an aul' bit of a cattle byre to tide them over. But if that's raided maybe nobody'll take them in. Please don't do this, your honour-ma'am.'

'I have a proposition to make you, Denis.'

'Don't keep using me name.'

She walks around the table and stands beside him, looking into his face. Reading his uncertainty. 'I might – *might* – be able to dissuade Colonel Somerville from handing your boots over to the military commander in your area. But you'll have to do something in return for me.'

'Tell me.'

'Leave our horses alone.'

'Both of them? I can't do that. Captain says …'

'Tell him they weren't here.'

'But what'll I say to the other lad? Sure we saw the two of them in their stalls. And how are we to get back to the lads with no horse to carry us?'

'How did you come here?'

'Managed to hitch a lift in a wagon most of the way. The people is good to us.'

'I have an idea about transport. An alternative to a mount. Something that will make your captain think well of you. He'll be impressed by your initiative.'

'What is it?'

'We'll talk in the kitchen. I'll tell you at the same time as the other fellow.'

'I want me boots. No boots, no deal. I know you have them.'

Edith has seen where Cameron stored them: in a battered old seaman's chest in his study. 'I might be able to get them for you.' In a twist of the knife, she repeats the bootmaker's name. 'J.J. Carroll of Listowel.'

She can smell his fear, although he's trying to mask it with bravado.

'What's to stop your brother landing me mam and dad in trouble? Soon as I leave here, the bootmaker's name could be in the hands of the Tans.'

'Look, if my brother wanted to get you in trouble, he'd have done it by now, wouldn't he? We're not totally unsympathetic to your cause. Play fair by me with our horses and I'll play fair by you.'

'Are you … on our side, ma'am?'

'I'll tell you whose side I'm on. Your mother's. She didn't go to the trouble of teaching you how to write letters to her, only to receive one telling her you've been hanged or shot.'

———

In the kitchen, an unexpected sight meets their eyes. A man cradling a rifle is slumped at the deal table, sound asleep. Philomena, Mrs O'Shea and Mike Hurley are transfixed by him. At Edith's arrival, Hurley puts his finger to his lips, pantomiming silence.

She is mystified why they haven't overpowered him, until she realizes the intruder's forefinger is resting on the trigger. One false move will deal out injury or death. Yet how peaceful he looks.

Quick as thought, Denis sets down his old boots, hooks his rifle over his shoulder and approaches the table. Inch by inch, his hand advances on the metal. Inch by inch, he slides it out from under the sleeper. The trigger is gone from the other man's fingertip but the butt remains under his hand.

'W-What?' The IRA volunteer jolts awake, one hand clamped on his weapon and the other on Denis's wrist. 'Feck are you at?'

'Easy now,' says Denis.

'I said, what the feck are you doing with me rifle?'

'You were asleep. I was afraid of an accident.'

The sleeper's eyes dart around the company. 'Move back. Get over there where I can see ye.'

'We need to buck up,' says Denis. 'We've spent long enough here.'

'Right, so. You,' he waves the rifle at Hurley, 'saddle the horse. And we'll take a spare saddle with us and some extra tackle.'

'Not so fast,' says Denis. 'The animal's half-dead. We wouldn't get the length of Skibbereen on him.'

'So we'll take both. Ride one, lead the other.'

'I've a better idea,' suggests Edith. 'There's a motor car you can use. It's in the West Cork Hotel. Belongs to an American staying there. Why don't you borrow it in the name of the Irish Republic? Your captain would be terribly impressed if you drove up in it.'

Denis directs a look of admiration at her.

'Sure we wouldn't have a notion how to drive one of them yokes,' says the other.

'The owner has a chauffeur. Perhaps he could be encouraged to go part of the way with you, until you get the hang of things. He'd be cover for you if you run into any patrols. Who'd suspect a fancy chauffeur?'

'Just picture the captain's face!' says Denis.

'The West Cork, you say? And he's there tonight?' The sleeper considers it.

Edith crosses her fingers. 'Yes, both he and the motor car.'

Denis leans into the other volunteer and whispers to him. Their conversation is rapid. All Edith can hear is, 'How do we get to the hotel?' from the sleeper.

'Mike could give you a lift in our trap,' she says. 'But I'd want your word of honour that both Mike and Tara are allowed home to us. He drops you on the outskirts of Skibbereen. Then he turns back.'

'No bother,' says Denis.

'Is that a promise?' asks Edith.

'What's to stop him going to the peelers?' objects the sleeper.

'I've never given evidence to the police in my life and I'm not about to start,' says Mike.

'Besides, you know where we live. Your captain wouldn't take it lying down,' says Edith.

The sleeper reflects. 'That'll do.'

'I'll have me boots now, ma'am,' says Denis.

She collects them for him.

He puts them under his arm, and makes for the door. 'Come on, Hurley, let's get the trap on the road. Good night to you, Miss Somerville, and you, ladies.'

Edith catches Mike's eye. 'You be very careful, Mike. Please. No heroics.'

ten

Edith watches the spill of rain turn holes in the avenue into pools of water. Through the downpour, a hunched shape emerges. It is the postman on his bicycle. She hasn't seen Timmy the Post in weeks. Head bent over handlebars, he steers around the side of the house towards the kitchen door. She checks the time and decides to give him twenty minutes to dry off and have a hot drink. But impatience sends her to the kitchen sooner. From the passageway, she hears his voice sharing the latest news.

'The postman beyond in Schull was savaged by a wild dog on his rounds. Some of them beasts would ate you alive and go back for the toenails.'

She clears her throat, to alert them to her arrival, and sweeps in. 'You're welcome to Drishane, Timmy. I hope there's good news in your letters.'

Mug in one hand and rasher sandwich in the other, he springs to his feet. 'Miss Somerville, I'm sorry to be sitting in your kitchen in me bare feet, but the socks and boots are drowned-wet, so they are. Philomena here insisted on drying them by the range.'

'Quite right, too. And it's not my kitchen, it's Mrs O'Shea's.'

Mrs O'Shea, preparing a meat pie at the far end of the table, looks up. 'Timmy O'Driscoll's thinner than a farthing. He needs building up.'

'Indeed he does. Unlike that cat of yours eating our butter.'

A tabby cat, tail as fluffy as a winter muff, is perched on a side table applying her tongue methodically to the butter dish.

Edith claps her hands to startle the cat. 'She should be kept in the barn. And the butter dish should have a lid on it.'

Philomena, who is separating a jumble of fish knives from fruit knives, takes a run at him with a sweeping brush. 'Go on out o' that, ya dirty brute!' The cat jumps down and shelters behind the dresser.

'Really, Mrs O'Shea, I can't think why you permit this. We'll all be poisoned.'

'Ah now, Miss Edith, I just fetched the butter out of the pantry this minute to make Timmy his sandwich. And you know, Tiger is a good mouser. She earns her keep.'

'Sure the kitchen and pantry would be overrun without her dropping in now and again to put manners on the mice,' Philomena chimes in.

'But who'll put manners on her? Look, she's still here, biding her time. The minute my back is turned she'll be at the butter again.'

Philomena opens the back door and calls to the cat, which streaks past her and out through the rain. Mrs O'Shea pounds her displeasure on the pastry beneath her rolling pin.

Edith turns back to the postman. 'I'm glad to see Mrs O'Shea has given you something to eat, Timmy.'

'Fed and watered like a prince, I am. Faith, you're always very dacent to me here.'

'It's the least we can.'

'No truer word. We must be good to each other. When St Patrick met Fionn McCool, he asked was God good to the Irish in pagan times. And Fionn said sure there was no need because were all good to each other.'

Mrs O'Shea and Philomena bless themselves.

'Did you have much trouble getting through to us, Timmy?'

''Asier to swim to America than cycle these parts. But I do me poor best. There's some post from England for you, ma'am. Never fear, I kept it all dry in me pouch.' Toes splayed, he pads across to his leather satchel, dripping over a three-week copy of *Skibbereen Eagle*.

'Thank you, Timmy. And how are things in Skib?'

'You wouldn't believe the goings-on there, ma'am. 'Deed and troth you wouldn't. Sure, wasn't the Yankee gentleman's motor car, a great brute of a machine that's his pride and joy, pinched by the Shinners four nights back.'

A furtive shaft of joy glows in Edith.

'They borrowed his driver, as well,' says Timmy. 'Didn't harm him, mind you, and he got the motor car back last night. But it took a pounding. Dunched, scratched and whatnot. He's in a powerful rage. Talking about taking it up with Mick Collins hisself. Says he wants the men responsible handed in to the authorities.'

'That seems a little ambitious.'

'Collins might soft-soap him. He might even throw him a few pounds towards repairs. But as for turning in his own men? That'll happen when yesterday comes again.'

Edith wonders if she ought to make amends to the American – invite him to lunch or something. Without admitting her own role in his misfortune, of course. 'I should think Mr Collins has bigger fish to fry. But theft of one's property is irksome. Still, all's well that ends well.'

'I'd be banjaxed without me bicycle, on loan from His Majesty King George. The American gentleman, Mr Grun by name, is a journalist. He's over here reporting on the goings-on. So Mick Collins might be a shade more sympathetic to him than to you or me, ma'am.'

'In that case, I expect his motor car is insured and the bill for repairs won't come out of his pocket.' Relieved, Edith downgrades lunch to a calling card left at his hotel as a courtesy, perhaps with an invitation to afternoon tea if he should find himself in the locale.

Meditative, Timmy sucks his teeth. 'There's some say he's been spying for the British. Sure what else would he be doing so long in a place the size of Skibbereen?'

'God bless us and save us! A spy is it?' Mrs O'Shea drops a piece of diced meat on the floor and the cat materializes to pounce on it. The cook flips a cloth half-heartedly at her. 'No, Tiger.'

'How did that creature get back in?' demands Edith.

'Through the pantry window,' says Philomena. 'I left it open. That's a day fit for neither man nor beast.'

Edith gives up and returns to Timmy. 'The American's taking an enormous risk, surely? He's hardly inconspicuous. And the flying columns are particularly active in West Cork. I know there's a truce, but still. You'd hardly know the difference pre- or post-ceasefire here.'

'Hidden in plain sight, that's what he is, ma'am.'

Edith decides she has wronged the motor car owner quite enough without indulging in speculation about his activities. 'I'll attend to my letters now, Timmy. There may be one that needs a quick response – I could deal with it while you're still here, if you wouldn't mind taking it with you to the post office. Whatever you do, don't leave until I come back to you. Oh, and make sure your stockings and boots are dry before you put them on. Wet stockings next to your skin do untold damage.'

'Occupational hazard in my line of work, Miss Somerville, but thank-ee kindly.'

Edith retreats to a chair in the inner hall with her letters. One of them is from her friend Ethel Smyth, announcing her inability to sell the hunters but readiness to pay a visit to Drishane. Would the following week be convenient? She names a day and the arrival time of her train. Edith reflects. She can use the visit as a deadline to force the pace on her play. Ethel Smyth is a disruptive house guest, all-pervasive, like a Castletownshend sea mist – the prospect of her arrival will act as the impetus she needs to finish *Flurry's Wedding*. And perhaps she can circumvent postal disruptions by sending it back to England with her.

She scratches out a hasty note to Ethel telling her she'll send Mike in the dogcart to meet her off the Cork train at Skibbereen station, along with a warning that the unsettled state of the country means little by way of tennis or croquet parties in the neighbouring houses. *We're living as quietly as mice inside a skirting board, trying to avoid the notice of the resident cat*, she writes. Pleased with her analogy, inspired by the rapacious Tiger, she seals the envelope and goes back to the kitchen.

Passing a window, she notices Jeremiah sheltering under the oak where Dooley is buried, puffing on his pipe. Odd, that business where he couldn't or wouldn't sit up in the stables with Mike. The day after Mike delivered the IRA men to Skibbereen, she asked him if there was more to Jeremiah's inability than met the eye.

'He's just old, miss, and has no one to see about him. His daughters call in, but it's not the same.'

That's the trouble with the times they're living in, thinks Edith. You start doubting everyone.

While she's watching, Jeremiah takes something from his wheelbarrow and places the object under the tree, propped against the trunk. Then he lifts the barrow handles and pushes away with it through the mizzle. Edith waits until he's out of sight before throwing on a raincoat and darting out.

Why, it's a white stone, almost an oval, the size of her face. At one end of the stone there's an indentation, so that it resembles a lopsided heart. Some time ago, unable to find anything that satisfied her, she asked Jeremiah to keep an eye out for an appropriate marker for Dooley's grave. He's done her proud.

———

Edith completes *Flurry's Wedding* on the day Ethel Smyth arrives, radiating vitality. Exuberant in a tricorn hat, which lends her a buccaneering air, she brings the smack of the wider world.

'Boney, dear, you're laden down with packages like a Christmas tree. I see you've brought champagne. You clever puss, how did you guess I had something to celebrate?' Boney is her personal nickname for Ethel, because she reminds her of Napoleon Bonaparte, on red alert to conquer the world.

'Intuition,' booms Boney. 'Besides, catching up with friends is always cause for celebration.'

'And so say all of us. Let me show you to your room. Then we can have tea.'

Boney slips an arm round Edith's waist as they walk through the outer hall towards the inner one, leading to the main staircase. She's demonstrative, overwhelmingly so, in Edith's opinion, but perhaps it's understandable after a year apart.

'And how is every inch of you, Edith Somerville?'

'As old as Methuselah and stupid in the head from doing nothing but work. Apart from that, all the better for seeing you.' From habit, Edith pauses at the foot of the staircase, readying herself for the climb.

'We'll have to liven things up a bit round here. All work and no play.' Boney pinches her cheek.

Edith winces. She only attended school for one term – she had to live with a chaperone – but her friend's behaviour is reminiscent of the schoolgirl crushes she recalls from those Dublin days at Alexandra College. 'I hope you won't find it too dull, Boney. There are no race meetings or shooting parties – no jollity at all, apart from social calls, and maybe a few rubbers of bridge.' She begins to mount the stairs, forcing Boney's arm to slip from her waist.

'I'm here to see you, not half the county, dear heart.'

'The thing is, Boney, we're sitting on the lid of a seething pot.'

'I was born in the year of the Indian Mutiny. Nothing fazes me.'

By now, they are on the first floor corridor, where a hissing sound punctuates their conversation.

'What's that?' asks Boney.

'The bathroom pipes. I'm afraid we're having problems. Cold water's all they can manage now – the system simply won't heat.'

'Plumbing is one of the myriad mysteries of this old house. You need a nice, modern place like mine. All the conveniences.'

'Primary among them, a golf course outside your gate. Personally, I like a house that has ghosts flitting through its rooms.' Drishane is peopled by ghosts. Edith knows her own is among them – the ghost of her girlhood. 'Here we are, Boney. This is your room.'

'So far from you? I hoped we'd be next door to one another. Couldn't you billet me in the room where Martin slept when she lived here? We could swap secrets in the night.'

Edith's had the same room since childhood, a large, dim space in a wing convenient for the stables. It's far enough from the other bedrooms to give her privacy and that's the way she likes it – especially when there are guests. 'Martin's room is no longer in use, I'm afraid. But she's delighted by your visit and says to give you her best regards.'

———

Before dinner, they meet in the drawing room, made cosy by flames crackling and leaping in the grate, under an elaborately carved black oak mantelpiece. Edith has changed into a velvet dress for dinner, while Ethel Smyth's sturdy body is resplendent in sequins – lavish for a quiet dinner *à deux* but then she does nothing by halves. Loulou is curled up on the hearth rug, bubbling with snores. Edith feels a twinge at the thought of how Dooley and Loulou used to lie there, bodies overlapping. Once, she'd have replaced him with another fox-terrier puppy, but she's tired of investing her affections in dogs which reach maturity and die long before she's ready to part with them.

At Boney's insistence, the sherry decanter is discarded and the bottle of champagne opened. Crackling with authority, like an officer inspecting troops on the parade ground, she swarms about the room. Words machine-gun from her. She is full of her latest composition, a ballet called *Fête Galante*, and revisions she's made to her opera, *The Boatswain's Mate*. Then there is the woeful performance of another of her works in Hull, where the conductor was such an incompetent blockhead that she left her seat, marched to the podium and snatched the baton from his hands.

'And what of your Irish R.M. play?'

'I finished it today.'

Ethel Smyth's guileless child's smile beams upon Edith. 'Marvellous! It'll run to packed houses in the West End. You'll be lionized! When can I read it?'

'I'll read some aloud to you after dinner if you like.'

'Do it now.'

'You're more impatient than the wind, Boney. There isn't time before dinner.'

Boney refills their champagne flutes and joins Edith on the sofa.

'To company.' Edith clinks the rim of her glass against her guest's.

'To the most agreeable company in the world.'

'Steady on, Boney.' Edith takes a sip. 'I say, do you really think *Flurry's Wedding* will go down well in London? I change my mind from one day to the next.'

'Certainly, it will. Humour is your forte, my dear Edith, and we all need to have our ribs tickled. Especially when times are troublesome. You must come and stay with me in Hook Heath, and we'll attend your opening night together. It'll be a triumph. Your play will be on everyone's lips. I'll organize supper afterwards at The Ritz.'

They relapse into companionable silence, Edith spellbound by the flames in the grate while Boney watches her, and absentmindedly drinks from both glasses.

'I can never decide if your eyes are grey or green, Edith dearest.'

'That's because they're grey-green.'

'Like the sea around here. Was your hair very dark as a girl?'

Self-conscious, Edith pats her pinned-up grey hair. 'I suppose it was dark brown. Martin was fair, with hare's eyes. Terribly short-sighted, though. She was known to shake hands with the butler at social gatherings.' Boney hoots with laughter. 'She was delicate-looking, not rugged like me,' adds Edith.

'I expect she was most awfully clever. But you aren't rugged. You're magnificent.'

'I'm like the Wreck of the Hesperus, you silly thing.'

'I bet you couldn't keep your hair up when you went out riding. I expect you flew over every impossible ditch and somehow kept your seat, but your hairpins went flying. I can just see that mass of dark locks tumbling round your shoulders. And you, laughing and pink-cheeked, too caught up in the thrill of the chase to stop. Absolutely superb – you don't know how to be anything else. A goddess in human form!'

Edith stares. Clears her throat. The fire crackles. A bong sounds.

Edith is on her feet in an instant. 'There's the dinner gong.' Loulou stirs and stretches. 'Yes, you greedy guts, nothing wrong with your hearing. We have some lovely brown trout for you, Boney. Mrs O'Shea cooked it in almonds, just the way you like it.'

En route to the dining room, Edith wonders if she can rustle up another house guest to dilute Ethel Smyth's Ethelness. She's always been exuberant, but it's getting out of hand. A week of her is going to prove trying.

Just inside the dining-room door hangs a set of still lifes, all dead creatures: oils of pheasants, lobsters and so on. Ethel Smyth pauses to study them.

'None of these had a happy end. Not yours, Edith. I can tell. Your use of colour has more brio. We must organize another exhibition for you.'

'Sargent always ripped up a drawing and started over if he didn't like it and I'm exactly the same. It's the first impression that matters. Paint quickly to keep it fresh. Never tinker. That's my motto. Why don't you take this place?'

In a clean, white cap with a pleated frill, hands folded in front of her, Philomena waits by the soup tureen. Edith is proud of her for making an effort. If it wasn't for the hanks of hair escaping from under the cap, Philomena would be as well turned out as any English servant.

'Good evening, Philomena,' says Boney. 'How have you been?'

'The Lord look down on me in pity this day. Me legs are at me since breakfast. Now, Mrs O'Shea has made you a nice creamy parsnip broth, Miss Smyth, on account of you complimenting her on it the last time you were here.' She begins serving.

'*Doctor* Smyth,' Edith corrects her, before Boney complains. 'And I believe I ordered chicken soup, Philomena.'

'Dr Smyth, to be sure,' says Philomena. 'I do be forgetting. Mrs O'Shea was run off her feet today and hadn't the time to kill and pluck a hen. I was busy myself, supervising that Treacy girl. If you didn't stand over her, she'd be away like a wild goose, galloping the country.'

'Thank you, that will be all for now, Philomena. You might see to the drawing-room fire before bringing in the next course – we'll go back in after we dine.'

Philomena sniffs and leaves the room.

'Unfortunately, we can't get coal from Wales any more, Boney. We have to rely on wood or turf.'

Boney scatters crumbs in a dismissive gesture with the hand holding a bread roll. 'I don't know how you manage in this disaster of a country.'

'We grind along as best we can. Besides, I prefer the smell of wood in a fireplace.'

'What's that?'

'I said there's something about the smell of burning wood.' Was Boney more deaf than the last time they met? Edith finds herself obliged to repeat things.

'Coal is more efficient,' insists Boney.

'My dear, Ireland has other attractions besides efficiency. How is your soup?'

'Delicious. You know, there's something I've noticed about you.'

'Go on.'

'You let the servants ride over you.'

'Excuse me?'

'You do. It's being going on forever, so you don't even notice.'

'Mrs O'Shea has a fondness for the hen I ordered her to kill. That's why we aren't having chicken soup. It's a pet of hers, you might say.'

'Which proves my point.'

'Your point being?'

'They lie. They can't help it, and you go along with it.'

'It isn't lying exactly.'

'What else would you call it?'

'It's how it is here. That's all.'

'Lying.'

'Embroidery.'

'Lying.

'They never give the same excuse twice. I enjoy their inventiveness.'

'You know what the matter with you is?'

'I've a feeling you're about to tell me.'

'You've a blind spot about the Irish.'

'Why wouldn't I? I'm Irish.'

'There's no doubting that.'

'Now you be careful before you say another word.'

'I always speak the truth.'

'Well, here's a truth for you. Wasn't your grandfather Smyth Irish?'

'I don't deny it. Permanently pickled and couldn't stop talking. What else would he be but one of your lot?'

'Really, Boney, must you give voice to every thought that crosses your mind? Mama taught us that good manners are an essential shell. Didn't yours teach you the same?'

'Mama was too busy finding fault with everything I did. Papa dined out as often as possible.' Ethel Smyth butters another bread roll. 'She was awfully good at petit point, though.'

A withering mama softens Edith, who had her own experience in that department. 'I was never any use at sewing. Hated being cooped up indoors.'

'Your hands are too large. Beautiful and large, I should say. It's what allows you to handle horses. Mama was a sprite. If she attempted to lift a footstool, Papa would rush to do it for her. Mama had all sorts of rules about dress and behaviour. Clothes being matched to eyes indoors, and hair outdoors. Stockings coordinated with shoes, and so on.'

After Philomena has served the main course, Ethel Smyth says, 'Dear heart, I want you to stay with me after Christmas.'

'I don't think I can, Boney. I need to be here to hold the place together. Empty houses are an invitation.'

'But you must come. Some important news is going to be revealed on New Year's Eve and I'd like you there to share it. I expect my friends will organize a dinner to mark the occasion.'

'What news?'

'I'm honour-bound to keep it secret—'

'Well then of course you mustn't—'

'—But it will be gazetted on the 31st of December. It really is most awfully thrilling. Quite an honour. In fact, a victory! Not just for me but womanhood. Can't you guess from the date?'

'I'm afraid not. I was never any good at guessing games.'

Boney's blue eyes are bulbous in their sockets. 'I know you won't breathe a word to a soul. I'm to be cited in the King's New Year's Honours List. Dame Commander of the Order of the British Empire. I'm the first female composer to receive a damehood!'

'What wonderful news! Dame Ethel Smyth no less!' Edith goes to her friend, pressing her pink-and-white cheek against the other's ruddy skin. 'I couldn't be happier for you.'

'It's in recognition of my genius as a composer. Long overdue, if I say so myself.'

'Ethel the Great. Step aside, Alexander.'

Boney's hand reaches for Edith's, braiding fingers with her. 'And I didn't have the benefit of Aristotle as my tutor, like Alexander. All I had was prejudiced male reviewers complaining my work was either too womanly or not womanly enough.'

'You've shown them all, Dame Ethel, as I shall have to remember to call you. You've hurdled every obstacle.' Edith manages to untangle her hand and returns to her seat.

'I must speak to Henry Wood about including more of my work in his promenade concerts. In fact, he should dedicate an entire programme to me. My *Mass in D* is long overdue a revival. The Hosanna always brings down the house – the trumpet solo is a triumph. And the Gloria utterly splendid.'

Edith casts her mind back to the *Mass* performance she attended. Her impression was of the Almighty being commanded rather than implored to show mercy. It was positively Wagnerian. But after all, Boney is a female version, teeming with *Sturm und Drang*.

'And to think there was a time when I couldn't cadge an invitation to a Buckingham Palace garden party. Will you come to Hook Heath, Edith, and be with me when the announcement is made?'

'I couldn't possibly, dearest. Too short notice, I'm afraid.'

'But I insist on having you with me. It won't taste as sweet without you by my side.'

'I'm thrilled for you, truly I am, but I simply can't.'

Boney wags a forefinger. 'I won't take no for an answer.'

'You must, I'm afraid.'

'I give you fair warning. I shall lay siege to you.'

'Later in January is possible. Perhaps coinciding with the investiture? You'll need the support of a friend then, too.'

Boney taps a forefinger against her lips. 'You have a point.'

She begins talking about dates, while Edith drifts among her own thoughts. How nice if she was made a dame. But Irish people aren't exactly popular in England currently. She might have risen higher if she had based herself in London, embedding herself in its literary circles, but Castletownshend is her centre of gravity. She is jolted back to attention by Boney reaching across the table to tap her on the wrist.

'See, here, Edith, you're turning into a hermit crab. You can't take root in Drishane – we should plan another excursion abroad.'

'I like my routine. I'm a countrywoman at heart.'

'I need to be in the thick of things. I crave variety. It's stimulating.'

'Trips are stimulating, naturally, but the truth is I can't afford one right now.'

'Even with all your irons in the fire? Art, literature, journalism, farming, horse-coping? Am I leaving something out, you talented creature?'

'We can't sell our farm produce, and our horses are stolen from under our noses. Any money I make from *Flurry's Wedding* will have to go on fixing the roof – although the roofer says he'd have more luck plugging a bog pool. You're lucky it hasn't rained today or you'd hear an orchestra of drips.'

Boney jumps up and conducts an imaginary orchestra.

'But I'll visit you in Hook Heath as soon as possible,' continues Edith. 'I do have some business in London, as it happens. I really should speak to Mr Pinker in person about placing *Flurry's Wedding*.'

'He's lacking in theatrical contacts. You mustn't throw away your opus on that jumped-up little money-grubber.'

'Sometimes, I wonder if Martin and I would have written any of our Irish R.M. books without his nagging.'

'Mr Pinker has had his pound of flesh— '

'Ten per cent, dear.'

'Daylight robbery! For work that sells itself! Under no circumstances must you entrust *Flurry's Wedding* to this bloodsucking little tick of a man.'

Secretly, Edith resents that commission. Mr Pinker oughtn't to keep deducting his penny-pinching percentage year after year. She knows it's in his contract. But really, it's ungentlemanly to continue chipping away at her earnings simply because he struck a number of bargains for her with publishers years ago, deals she was perfectly capable of negotiating herself – she's always been able to paddle her own canoe in business. Boney's full-frontal attack delights her.

But she says, 'That's a little harsh on Mr Pinker, Boney. We've had a business relationship for decades. His judgment has proven sound on many occasions. I admit, he's losing his touch and those sons aren't in his league, but cutting him out would be a wrench. We've hunted together. He's bought horses from me.'

'I expect he took up riding especially to wheedle into your good books. Bear in mind this is business, not friendship, with Mr Pinker. You mustn't confuse the two. The literary firm of Somerville and Ross has been profitable for him – the R.M. series alone must have been a money spinner.'

'I suppose. Frankly, I may have to consider severing ties. I can't really afford his commission any longer.'

'Well then, why pay it, Edith?'

'And he could certainly use a little ginger. I wonder if he's quite well? Perhaps I should try and place the play by other means. I'll give it some thought. But wait until you've heard me read from it after coffee. You might think it's absolute tosh and twaddle.'

'I shan't, you darling simpleton. I shall think it utterly brilliant, like everything you write.'

eleven

Ethel Smyth is gazing, rapt, at Edith's face while she reads from the play. She is free to look with intensity because Edith, who has a talent for accent, is engrossed in acting out each character's role. They have reached the point where Flurry is about to abscond with Sally, aided and abetted by his accomplice Slipper. Sally's mama Lady Knox is horrified, but Flurry's grandmother Mrs Knox is delighted – anything that puts Lady Knox's nose out of joint wins her approval.

'Slipper yells to Yeates, "Twas yerself called for 'Haste to the Weddin'', long life to ye!" Old Mrs Knox hurries down steps and has an old shoe and rice. Lady Knox dashes back round house. They meet! Curtain. End of scene three.'

Ethel Smyth slaps her knees. 'What a card that Slipper is! I say, is he drawn from life?'

'He's a combination of people I knew from the hunt.'

'Marvellous!'

'Tell me honestly, Boney, is the play any good?'

'It's a tonic for the spirits. It'll raise the roof.'

'Really?'

'Really – you have turned the place into Stratford-on-Drishane! The only thing missing is music. I could write you some jaunty Irish airs to accompany it.' She beats time against a cushion. 'I can see the framework in my head – the outline of the statues against the sky, so to speak.'

'Please don't trouble yourself. Opera is opera and theatre is theatre and never the twain, et cetera. Apart from Messrs Gilbert and Sullivan, of course.' Edith slides the cushion away from Boney before her fist bursts the stitching.

'But it will perk up the play enormously. Music improves everything.'

'You're too kind. But I'm not convinced the play needs perking up. Music won't be of any benefit to it.'

'Nonsense! Music should be mandatory with all stage performances. It's essential. We can't have too much of it!'

'There can be too much of a good thing, you know, Boney.'

'I disagree. Truly, I'm going to insist on writing the musical score for your play.' Boney's arms flail in time to a beat only she can hear. 'You can supply the libretto. It'll be a team effort!'

Ice penetrates Edith's voice. 'My team efforts are with Martin Ross.'

Even Boney realizes she has transgressed. She searches for an olive branch. 'Have another choccy.' She passes over another of her gifts, a box of Charbonnel et Walker chocolates.

'Really, I couldn't.'

'Just one more. To show no hard feelings.'

Edith selects a rose cream and nibbles at it. 'We must put them away after this.'

Boney pops an entire truffle into her mouth. 'Why? I see no reason not to indulge ourselves once in a while, my little Quakeress. Now, we need to put our heads together and work out how to make *Flurry's Wedding* the smash of the season. I shall have to tackle some big cheese personally on your behalf. You're far too modest to do it yourself.'

Edith realizes her play stands a better chance if Boney champions it. Exuberant she may be, but her heart's in the right place. 'That's terribly kind of you. I do appreciate how you put yourself out for me, dear.'

'We're two sides of the same medal, Edith. I understand you. Better than that family of yours, which takes you for granted. None of them appreciates you for the meteor-like talent you are.'

Edith finds she needs to prop up her head with a hand. It's only Boney's first night and already she's bowling her over. No one is averse to a little flattery but Boney over-eggs everything. 'What's happening in London? Is there much interest in what's going on in Ireland?'

Boney's fingers hover over a violet cream. 'There was quite the hoo-ha when I was passing through yesterday, on my way to catch the boat train. Your chaps were in 10 Downing Street.'

The chocolate is seized and bitten in half.

'Was anything agreed?'

'Didn't hear.'

'Oh dear Lord, I hope there's an end in sight. They've been wrangling over terms since October. What's your sense of the public mood?'

Cheek bulging, Ethel Smyth considers. 'People are war-weary. Keen to have our boys home. But taking up arms against the throne was wrong and those rebels of yours shouldn't be let off with a treaty. Personally, I'd have that delegation sent over by your de Valera person horsewhipped and thrown into the Tower.'

'Hurling Ireland straight back into war. I'm very glad it's Mr Lloyd George who's at the helm and not you, Boney.'

'If I were Prime Minister I should insist on you moving into Number Ten with me.' Boney captures Edith's hand and strokes it.

Edith springs to her feet. 'Time to turn in.' She snaps her fingers at Loulou, dozing by the fire. Instantly, the dog is at her ankles. She holds out her arms and Loulou bounces into them. 'Will you ring for Philomena when you're ready to go up? She'll bank down the fire and so forth. Good night, my dear. See you in the morning. Do feel free to lie on after your journey.'

———

Boney's visit proves to be enjoyable, despite her attempts to persuade Edith to commit to things she has no intention of doing – such as trekking in Turkey's Black Sea Mountains with her next year.

'Everyone will be doing it soon,' says Boney. 'If we go now, we'll be ahead of them.'

'My father always said, "Wherever the world is headed, let you head the other way,"' parries Edith.

Boney also tries to turn the croquet lawn into a miniature golf course so she can teach Edith how to play, and harries Edith to do her portrait – Edith refuses, for no reason that she can easily justify to herself.

'But Sargent sketched me. I don't know why you say it's impossible.'

'It just is, Boney. Don't go on about it, dear. Why not play me something rousing on the piano?'

Boney launches herself at the instrument. A great tangle of notes floods out, a passage from her *Mass in D* – the kind of music Lord Kitchener would have composed if he'd been that way inclined, it occurs to Edith. Unexpectedly, Boney breaks off and buries her face in her hands.

Alarmed, Edith hurries to her side. 'My dear, whatever's the matter?'

'My ear's at me. Booming and singing away. I'm dreading what it means. What if I go deaf, Edith? It runs in the family. How will I be able to compose music?'

'Well, Beethoven,' Edith begins, but stops short at the expression on Boney's face. A compound of frustration and terror. She tries again. 'Have you been to an ear specialist?'

'Not in a while.'

'Promise me you'll make an appointment with one as soon as you're back home.'

———

'I say, Edith, who's that skulking in the flowerbeds?'

Can she see Flurry Knox? Disgruntled at the idea, Edith joins Boney at the window. A young woman is banging a saucepan lid with a wooden spoon.

'That's Nora Treacy from the village. She's helping with the pre-Christmas cleaning.'

'Why is she making that racket?'

'There's a black hen that's an escape artist. It's the one we were supposed to eat on your first night – Mrs O'Shea was too busy to wring her neck.'

'Too disobedient to wring her neck, you mean.'

'I dare say she was right. Black Bess lays the most enormous eggs. You had one of hers for breakfast – didn't you notice the double yolk?'

'I could hardly sit up straight, let alone pay attention to my poached egg. I was exhausted from being woken at dawn by a fearful racket from your rooster.'

'That's Roddy. He believes in rousing the household punctually, whether we like it or not.'

Another crash is delivered to the saucepan lid, along with a roared 'chuckee chuckee chuckee'.

'Really, Edith, you're too slack. She should be in the kitchen or scullery. Not loitering in flower beds. Look at her. She's wandering off now to gossip with your gardener.'

'He's something to her. A grand-uncle, I think. The Treacys and the O'Mahonys are definitely related.'

'This entire country of yours is undisciplined. I meant to tell you about one of the porters at Skibbereen railway station, the day I arrived. Fellow who stank of onions. Asked me where I was destined and when I said Drishane, he told me you were the civilest aul' heifer that ever drew breath. Then he spotted your man, and would have spent half the day chin-wagging with him if I hadn't instructed Hurley to get a move on and take us home.'

'I hope you were polite to Mike, Boney. I rely on him.'

'His boots were filthy. General Smyth would have made mincemeat of him.'

'Mike's not in the army, and neither is he under your father's command. Do, please, try not to antagonize the staff, dear. For my sake. Now, how about a walk in the castle grounds? I'd suggest a picnic, but the weather has a bad habit of going into floods of tears at the mere mention of the word. We used up all our sunshine for the month yesterday. I know, let's call in with my friend, Miss Barlow on the way, invite her to dinner. She lives on Main Street.'

'The medium?'

'Yes, she's back from Belfast. Ever such a gifted sensitive.'

'Anything to Jane Barlow, the writer?'

'A cousin. Martin was frightfully impressed when she discovered it. Literary connections always swayed her in someone's favour.'

'Do you mean Martin knew her when she was alive? Or is this impressed from beyond the grave?'

'Yes, she knew her. I thought we might arrange a seance after dinner, if Miss Barlow is willing. I think you'd find it interesting. You see, a barrier cuts us off from those we love in that undiscovered country on the other side. Miss Barlow's powers help to dismantle the obstructions.'

'I'd rather not.'

'Sorry?'

'I'd rather not have anything to do with that, that – business – if you don't mind, Edith.'

'I didn't realize you felt that way.'

'Well, now you know.'

—

Towards the end of the week, they hire bicycles in Skibbereen and pedal – slowly – out to Lough Hyne, about three miles from the town. It's Ireland's only saltwater lake and a place of enchantment, in Edith's view. Boney pronounces herself enraptured as they perch on a low wall, admiring the view. Clouds coast overhead and the wind gains in momentum. Edith licks a finger pad before presenting it to the air.

'Good, it'll be at our backs on the return leg to Skib. I haven't been on a bicycle in ever such a long time. Didn't think I still had it in me. Used to do it years ago with Martin. It was quite the craze at one time.'

'One year, I galloped everywhere at breakneck speed on a tandem,' says Boney. 'Not just me on board, of course. With a dear friend. A very dear friend. She was … rather special.'

Edith isn't listening. 'Years ago, when Noah was a boy, I won a poster competition to sketch a bicycle and rider in twenty lines or less. The cash prize was handy.'

'What did you spend it on?'

'Can't remember. Art materials, I expect. I thought I was going to be the next Renoir. You know how girls are, building castles in the air.'

'You still do.'

'Sorry?'

'Build castles in the air.'

'About what?'

'Your life in Ireland. You're mouldering here, Edith.'

Edith pretends not to hear her. 'I must have a word with the rector about the list of hymns for St Barrahane's on Sunday. I'm supposed to play "At Thy Feet, O Christ, We Lay" on the organ. But I can never keep a straight face with that one. It inevitably suggests hens to me.'

'I see what you're doing. Changing the subject. You could have a wonderful life with me in England if only you'd take a leap of faith.'

Edith scrabbles her fingers along the top of the drystone wall. They close over a loose pebble. She tosses it in her hand. 'Can you skim stones, Boney? I'm a champion skimmer. Come on, I challenge you to a contest.' Edith walks to the water's edge.

Boney scowls. 'I've a better idea.' She flings her hat on the ground and pulls off her coat. 'Last one in's a rotten egg.'

'You're not serious!'

'Try me.'

'But we haven't brought our bathing costumes.'

'Tosh! Who needs 'em?'

Unbuttoning rapidly, Boney stands stark naked in front of Edith. She catches a glimpse of pendulous breasts with brown nipples like saucers, and a riot of curly grey hair between her legs. With a whoop, bottom cheeks wobbling, Boney makes a run for the water's edge and splashes in, causing a commotion among the waterfowl.

'Whee! Hurry up, Edith!'

'Boney, get out at once! Someone will see you!'

'Let them! I don't care! Come and join me, Edith!'

'You'll catch your death! It must be Baltic in there!'

'It's exhilarating! I love it!' Boney turns on her back and splatters a backstroke.

What an exhibitionist, thinks Edith. But part of her admires Boney's devil-may-care verve.

———

Strolling along a back road parallel with the coast, Edith throws a tennis ball for Loulou. It carries further than she intended, and the dog gives chase into a scrubby field. Under Edith's arm is a piece of driftwood. Now that Boney is packing to leave, she'll have some time to herself again. The driftwood's mangled shape appeals to Edith, and she intends to paint it while it dries out. Afterwards she'll feed it to the fire.

Her back is hunched against a searching east wind, which somehow manages to sneak under her scarf and down the back of her neck. Edith considers the naked landscape: trees pared to the bone, mountains scowling under a raincloud. Desolate though it is, there are compensations. Just ahead, a robin bobs along the ditch, hopping on springs, and she stands to watch. He jerks his head, pulls a worm from the earth and swallows it down. Intent, she misses Tiger's approach along a branch. But the tabby's leap, as fluid as running water, catches her eye. In one bound, the robin is pinioned beneath paw and tooth.

'Shoo!' Edith claps her hands.

But the bird is captured. Still with an inch of worm wriggling from its beak, the robin is stolen away.

'That's nature,' says Flurry. 'Red in tooth and claw. Kitty took that wall with ease. Time was when you could tumble over any wall like a cat yourself.'

'You have a habit of creeping up on me, Flurry Knox.'

He shrugs. 'You look as if you have the weight of the world on your shoulders. What's on your mind, Edith?'

She leans the driftwood against the wall. 'My play needs a little push to get it out into the world. Any fool can write one, but it takes genius to have it staged.'

Flurry tips his bowler rakishly low on his forehead. 'Hasn't your pal offered to help? The one who tosses life like a pancake?'

'True, and she has contacts in the theatrical world. But Boney is a bull in a china shop.'

'Who else do you know in that line of business? Now's no time to be shy.'

'Cousin Lottie's husband is a playwright. But he's puckish. You'd never know how he'd take being asked for a favour.'

'Nothing ventured, nothing gained.'

'He's quite the socialist and fiercely clever. I doubt if my play would be his cup of tea. I don't think he'd have much patience with horsey matters.'

'You're not Old Moore, Edith. You can't predict how he'll react.'

'True. I could ask Lottie to have a word with him. If he likes the play, he might recommend it to a producer. I'm going to send the manuscript back to London with Boney. At least it can't get lost in the postal service. Things are still haywire here.'

'Is he a success, this playwright husband of your cousin's?"

'Enormously. The problem is that once Boney sees the Shaw name on the envelope, she'll gallop down to Ayot St Lawrence to meet him.'

Flurry takes off his bowler, removes a fly for a fishing rod inside it, and replaces the hat. 'Sure, what harm?'

'It's a bit risky, unleashing Boney on them. She has an unfortunate habit of making enemies.'

'I wouldn't like to get on the wrong side of her. She has a face that could stop a runaway horse in its tracks.'

'None of your sauce, you scamp. Perhaps it will be all right. Mr Shaw is quite the eccentric. He may choose to find her diverting.'

'Why not speak to Lady Gregory? She was always hounding you and Martin to write for the Abbey.'

'Certainly not. Augusta means well. But Yeats is boiling over with conceit.'

'He reads detective novels,' says Flurry. 'Can't be entirely bad. But this Shaw fellow might be a better bet.'

The sound of mooing makes her look down the road. A man in a white flannel coat and slouchy hat with its hatband missing is driving half a dozen cows towards them, swishing an ash plant against their hindquarters. His face is as furrowed as a ploughed field. When he draws level, he touches the brim of his floppy hat. 'Afternoon, Miss Somerville.'

'Good afternoon, Thady. The rain held off.'

'That it did, your honour-ma'am.'

After he has passed, she turns back to Flurry. But he has gone, too. Edith opens her mouth to call him, tasting the salty wind on her tongue. On second thoughts, Flurry Knox is not the class of man to appear when summoned. Wings beat overhead – birds flying inland. The threatened storm must be approaching.

She picks up the driftwood. 'Loulou! Where are you Lou? High time we went home. We've a visitor to give a send-off to.'

—

Boney wheels and strides, firing directions at Mike Hurley while he loads her luggage into the dogcart for the homeward journey to England. She's a woman born to wear a uniform, like her father and grandfather before her. But Edith decides Mike needs to be rescued from her attentions.

'You won't forget to write to my cousin, Mrs Shaw, asking if you can call with my play? Rather than just arrive? I've written to her about you. I expect she'll invite you to tea. Promise me you won't simply turn up. They entertain quite a lot and it mightn't be convenient.'

'I shall be humming with work. But I'll take a run down before New Year's Eve. Otherwise it'll be impossible because of all the brouhaha over my news.'

Philomena dashes out with provisions for the journey.

Boney slips two bank notes into Philomena's hand. 'One for you and one for the cook,' she says, in a whisper that's audible a field away.

'Thank you, ma'am.' Philomena bobs a creaky curtsey.

Edith observes the manoeuvre with pleasure. Whatever her faults, Boney is no skinflint.

Boney catches her eye and makes an impulsive movement towards Edith. 'The time has simply careered by, my treasure. I don't believe I'm ready to leave you quite yet.'

Edith steps back smartly, withdrawing up the steps – her body reacting ahead of her mind. Horrified, she grasps that Boney meant to try and hug her in front of the staff. 'Have you packed those eggs from the Home Farm carefully? I'd hate them to be scrambled en route.'

'Yes, yes, they're well padded. I say, Edith, you will visit soon, won't you?'

'Of course. I'll write and let you know my plans.' She must manoeuvre Boney into the dogcart before she finds herself wrestled into an embrace. Departures have a bad habit of heightening Boney's emotions. 'That trunk looks a little insecure, let me check on it for you.' She slips past and pretends to busy herself with testing some straps. 'Mike, would you help Dr Smyth up, please? We don't want her missing her train.'

'To be sure I will, Miss Somerville. Are you ready, Dr Smyth?'

Boney casts a yearning look at Edith, who pretends to be absorbed by checking the fastenings on her luggage. She sighs, ignores Mike Hurley's outstretched hand, and pulls herself on board. *If it were done when 'tis done, then 'twere well it were done quickly*. That applies to most things in life but particularly to catching trains.'

Edith deems it safe to offer a handshake now. 'Don't forget the ear doctor.'

'I won't.'

'Good. By the way, the sooner Mr Shaw reads my play, Boney, the sooner I shall be over.'

Her departing guest presents Edith with a radiant smile. 'I'll write to your cousin on the train. You're destined to realize, my dearest of Ediths, that I'm indispensable to you.'

———

The postal service appears to be working again, and letters are making their way through. The one from Charlotte Shaw, née Payne-Townshend, is everything Edith hoped it would be. She has brought it with her from the morning room into her studio, to re-read for a third time.

I found 'Flurry's Wedding' vastly entertaining, Edith. It brought to mind so many scenes of Rosscarbery and our girlhood, when you and I would spend the entire day on horseback. Ah, the sweet carelessness of youth. Or as the Bard reminds us,

> Youth is hot and bold,
> Age is weak and cold
> Youth is wild, and Age is tame.

I have passed on your charming play to GBS to read. He's busy with his own play about Saint Joan but promises to read it soon.

We saw your friend Dr Smyth's name in the Gazette announcement — Dame Ethel Smyth as she is now. GBS thinks honours are ridiculous affectations but I must confess to being pleased for her. She bounced in on us saying call me Smyth to rhyme with lithe. A most vivacious person. Not quite sane, according to GBS, but he insists sanity is overrated.

Edith folds up the letter and returns it to its envelope lined with pale-grey tissue paper. Nineteen twenty-two is off to a promising start, and the year is still only eight days old. Her eye lands on Loulou, snoozing on the back of her chair, a high-wire act that's bound to result in an accident, but she looks too comfortable to displace. Edith reaches for her pencils and rapidly outlines Loulou's shape.

As she works, she begins to ponder the possibilities that lurk behind that description of Edith as vivacious in Lottie's letter. Did the new dame commandeer their piano and begin playing her suffrage anthem, 'The March of the Women', whether they wanted to hear it or not? Did she rehearse her grievances against the Synge family for refusing to sell her the rights to *Riders to the Sea* for an operatic adaptation? Did she stray into politics and tell them this new Anglo-Irish Treaty was a shameful and cowardly surrender to the gun?

Edith's speculations are interrupted by the thrum of a motor car. Loulou wakens, ears pricking. She wobbles perilously, manages a leap to the floor just in time and begins to dance around, barking. The motor car sputters to a halt at the front of the house, which means Edith can't see who it is from her studio. Keeping an ear cocked, she continues sketching, until Philomena pops her head in to say an American journalist has called. Edith puts aside her pencils. Loulou's legs aren't quite right, but if it'll do it'll do.

'He sent in this, Miss Edith.'

A card on a salver reads:

Theodore H. Grun
Europe correspondent
The New York Times
All the news that's fit to print

'Is there a fire lit in the library? Then show him in there, Philomena. And bring us tea as soon as you can. Tell Mr Grun I'll be with him presently.'

Edith hustles out of her painting smock, washes her hands and tidies her hair. She sails into the library, where she finds Theodore H. Grun flicking through some back issues of *Punch*.

'Miss Somerville, ma'am, I took you at your word about dropping in. Decided to swing by and pay my respects.'

'I've been hoping to meet you, Mr Grun. Now, I've ordered tea. Does that suit you, or would you prefer coffee?'

'Tea's just dandy. A mighty fine place you got here, ma'am.' He flashes startling teeth, luminously white, as if each separate tooth has a built-in electric light. 'Great art and antiques you got.'

'Thank you. Just some family knick-knacks. Where are you from, may I ask?'

'Albany, New York. Gee, I wish my family had knick-knacks in this league. Saw a real old sword hanging up in the hall when I came through. Looked like it would fetch a pretty sum. What d'ya think it's worth?'

Edith frowns. 'My grandfather's regimental sword. We wouldn't dream of selling it.'

'Could guarantee to get you a good price if you change your mind.'

'That's most unlikely.'

'Shifted some stuff for a family by the name of Vaughan in a big ole heap over near Killarney. Lot of buyers for this sort of thing, back home in my neck of the woods.'

She stirs her tea. Allows a pause to develop. 'How long have you been in Ireland, Mr Grun?'

'Middle of August. Guess I didn't think I'd be here this long – figured I'd be moving along after a month or so. But the long and the short of it is these are interesting times here. I see your Irish parliament has okayed the Anglo-Irish Treaty. Though no guarantee the losing side will respect the decision.'

'I hadn't heard about Dáil Éireann approving the Treaty. How close was the vote?'

'Happened yesterday. Sixty-four for, fifty-seven against.'

'Oh dear. I wish it were more conclusive.'

'Dominion status for Ireland isn't a bad result, ma'am. Canada, New Zealand and Australia are able to live with it.'

'It's a vote for peace, that's worth remembering.' The wind loosens soot inside the chimney breast and it patters on the flames. She shivers. 'Someone just walked over my grave.'

'Ma'am?'

'Figure of speech. I wonder if Mr de Valera will stay on as president of the Dáil? He said he'd vote against the Treaty. This result undermines his authority.'

'The Treaty will go before the people to vote on, I hear. That'll be the decider.'

The door opens, Philomena appears with a tea tray, and Mr Grun attempts to take it from her.

She holds on tight, flustered by his gallantry. 'I'm grand, thank you, I can manage.'

'Don't seem right, an itty-bitty thing like you and a great, big tray-load like that.'

Philomena squeals. 'The blarney out of him! Did you hear, Miss Edith? Mind he doesn't try and butter you up.'

Grun winks at Edith.

'I'll be on my guard, Philomena,' says Edith.

Edith waits for Philomena to arrange the tea table and leave before resuming the conversation. 'How does America feel about what's happening in Ireland?'

'America doesn't like to see Ireland bullied by Great Britain. Folks think the Irish have been real plucky.' He accepts a cup and saucer, and chooses one of Mrs O'Shea's shortcake biscuits.

'I was sorry to hear you had your motor car purloined some time ago.'

'I was pretty darn sorry myself, ma'am. Lucky to get it back, I guess.'

'Owning a motor car must be a dreadful responsibility. Do you hunt? I have some magnificent animals I'd be willing to part with. A noble beast, the horse. Reliable.'

'I'm a fan of the combustible engine, ma'am. Shape of the future.'

'If you say so. Where do you intend travelling next for your newspaper, Mr Grun?'

'Oh, I'm not going anywheres just yet. This tussle isn't over by a long shot. De Valera's lining up on one side and Collins on the other. The foot soldiers are split, too. Things are about to get real personal.'

'That's what I'm afraid of.'

'Can you see this Treaty being accepted by everyone who fought, ma'am?'

She thinks of the captain and the whistler. 'No. Some want a republic, do or die.'

'Right. The North is opting out, whatever they decide. Partition.'

Partition. Edith hasn't heard the term before in relation to Ireland. It sounds ominous. She holds the plate of biscuits in his direction. 'Will you try another, Mr Grun?'

'Sure. Great cookies.'

'May I ask, why aren't you in Dublin? Can there really be enough to interest you in West Cork?'

'I come and go. Been to Dublin plenty. Belfast, too. But Skibbereen's as good a base as any.'

'Really?'

'Say, how does your set feel about Irish independence? Are you a union-ist or a separatist? Will you pack up and go once Great Britain pulls out?'

'Certainly not. This is our home. Anyhow, we don't know that Great Britain will leave.'

'Oh, I think it's inevitable. A matter of when, not if. Now, don't take this personally, ma'am. But wouldn't it make more sense for you to bail out? Some might think your family's exploited the Irish for centuries. Payback time's just around the corner.'

'My family has *not* exploited the Irish.'

'No? You're taking a heckuva chance others see things the same way.' Those disconcertingly white teeth make another full-frontal appearance. 'Strikes me you're between the devil and the deep blue sea, if you'll pardon me for saying it. Not Irish enough in Ireland, not Britisher enough in England. But they gotta take you. Whereas you might find you're not wanted here.'

Edith looks at her cup and saucer. If she squeezes the handle any tighter, the fragile object might smash. 'Is that your impression, Mr Grun? Have you heard something to that effect?'

'I hear all sorts, ma'am. How d'ya feel about de Valera? Is he the man to steer the country? Or would you prefer to see Collins run the show, once the dust settles?'

'The dust hasn't settled yet.'

'Heard some people in these parts call de Valera the Dago.'

She pretends not to hear.

'Say, here's a thought. Would you accept a cash offer to go? I know a couple of individuals with deep pockets. Happy to take an old pile like this off your hands for the right price. Confidentially, I've been instructed to sound out some owners, act as go-beween, if you catch my drift. What d'ya say? Get out while the going is good.'

'Are you a journalist or a property speculator, Mr Grun? Or, indeed, something else entirely?'

'Me? I'm all sorts of things, ma'am. A man of many parts. But sure, I'm a reporter, too. Plenty happening here to share with our readers. Real interested in Irish affairs, the *New York Times*' readers.'

'Well, here's something you can share with your readers. Or with whoever it is that's pulling your strings. Edith Somerville is going nowhere. The Somervilles are staying put.'

—

Edith watches the yellow motor car drive away. But it stops on the avenue, where the chauffeur sticks out his head and beckons to Jeremiah. The gardener doesn't budge. While the motor car idles, Grun steps out. He seems to be engaging Jeremiah in conversation. After a minute or two, the trowel is thrown down with a dismissive twist of the hand, and Jeremiah clomps away in the opposite direction. It looks to Edith as if he walked off while the American journalist was still talking to him.

twelve

Tingling from the January cold, leaning heavily on her walking stick, Edith tramps uphill, passing houses with modest facades that open directly onto Castletownshend's main street, and veering left past the landmark twin sycamores which straddle the perpendicular road, splitting it down the middle. Loulou falls behind to nose around the tree roots. Edith is on her way home from the skimmers' beach. In one of her pockets nestles a piece of cobalt-blue sea glass – she can never resist a random find on her walks. Edith waves at two farmers she recognizes on the footpath opposite, on their way into Willy Casey's pub for a bottle of stout. By Tally Ho – another empty house in the village, this one belonging to the Somervilles, but they can't find tenants for it – she pauses to catch her breath. Two figures emerge from the Drishane gateway and walk towards her. As they approach, she sees they are wearing sailor uniforms. They must be from Hugh's destroyer in Castlehaven Bay.

'Afternoon, ma'am,' they chorus.

'Did you have an errand in Drishane? I'm Miss Somerville.'

They whip their cigarettes behind their backs. 'We was just delivering some post we was carrying for you,' says one.

'Thank you, I'm most grateful. I hope the cook gave you a pot of tea.'

'We was offered it, ma'am. Had to say no. More errands to do.'

'Is there any news?' she asks, more in hope than expectation.

They exchange glances, before shaking their heads.

None they're willing to share, then. 'Give my regards to your captain,' she says.

They touch their caps in salute.

Edith looks round for Loulou. 'Look lively, Lou!'

The little dog takes her nose out of a drain and scampers to join Edith, who stomps up the avenue. She trills her fingers at old Jeremiah, busy with the hydrangea bushes. He waves the clippers at her. In her parents' day, there was a crew of gardeners keeping the place up to scratch. They'd spin in their graves to think only one old man was left. She wonders what Grun was saying to Jeremiah the other day. Philomena told her Grun's chauffeur asked a lot of questions while they gave him tea in the kitchen.

Coat and Wellingtons are abandoned in the outer hall. In the inner hall, Edith sees two envelopes propped on the mahogany stand. Both have a London postmark, and she notices that one is from Mr Pinker. It feels as if it contains something – hopefully the cheque for royalties she's been expecting. But the second letter intrigues her with its tiny, exceptionally neat handwriting. The name and address on the flap reveal the sender to be none other than George Bernard Shaw. Excitement fizzes through her veins.

'He must have read the play,' she tells Loulou.

Edith slides both letters into a cardigan pocket, and sticks her head through the doorway to the kitchen to ask for tea and scones in the inner hall.

'And Philomena, take Loulou and give her a scrub, she's more mud than dog.'

Back in the hall, she riddles the fire to encourage a blaze, adds some pine cones from a basket by the side of the fireplace and settles herself in an armchair. Pine scent drifts through the air. She toes off her shoes and stretches out her stockinged feet to the flames. The envelopes crackle and she retrieves them from her pocket, fingers stroking paper. Pinker's first. She slides a finger under the flap and prises it open. Yes, it's a welcome cheque, along with a courteous note. Whatever old Pinker's faults, he always passes on payments promptly. Now to Shaw's. Good news lies inside, she feels it in her bones. Will she wait for tea or gobble up the contents at once?

'What do you think, Martin? Shaw as a delayed pleasure? Or instant gratification?'

'Discipline leads to greater rewards,' says Martin's voice in her head. 'But self-indulgence is necessary from time to time.'

'Then self-indulgence it shall be.'

Shaw's letter is dated 20 January 1922. Her eyes speed-read its message.

> *Laugh at dirt, worthlessness, dishonesty and mischief ... You write like a lady in the worse sense of the word ... Never seems to occur to you that poor people are human being ... Stick to your pen and let the stage alone.*

Shaw loathes *Flurry's Wedding*! He's telling her it's hopeless and to give up playwriting.

The rattle of the tea trolley announces Philomena. She bustles about, lighting oil lamps and making the room cosy.

'You'll ruin your eyes, Miss Edith, trying to read without the light on. I'll draw the curtains. It's hardly day before it's night, this weather.'

A slumped Edith gazes into the fire. Her silence alerts Philomena.

'I hope there wasn't bad news in one of your letters, Miss Edith?'

Edith straightens her back. 'Not especially. Thank you, that will be all, Philomena.'

Alone again, she pours a cup of tea, adds a splash of milk and reads the letter carefully. It's about as damning as it can possibly be. There isn't a ray of light anywhere. Shaw knows exactly what he's saying, judging by his final line.

> *Forgive me if you can.*

Months of toil wasted. No fat fee to keep Drishane afloat. Better too much of a lady than not enough of a gentleman. She pities Lottie, married to such a person. If she can't write, how is it that Somerville and Ross's books were read by royalty, no less? Queen Victoria and King Edward VII were always delighted to receive copies as gifts.

But that was when Martin was alive.

She examines the letter's contents for a third time.

As far as it has any thread at all it deals with the marriage of Flurry and Sally. That is to say, it proposes to entertain the spectators with the marriage of a decent young lady to a blackguardly horse thief, dirty and disorderly when not dressed up for some special occasion, unable to learn an honest living, and in no way distinguishable in culture, in morals, in interests, or in decency of language from the poorer rascals whom he orders about by virtue of the social position which he disgraces ...

Poor Flurry, denounced as a horse thief by an underbred fortune-hunter who got his clutches into Cousin Lottie's trust fund.

Later, stung though she is, Edith decides Shaw gave his honest opinion – one professional to another. She'll write at once, explaining the play was meant to be humorous and not one of his social satires, thank him for his kindness in reading her work and trouble him no further.

Then what?

Edith butters a scone, adds a dab of Mrs O'Shea's blackberry jam and finds she's no longer hungry. She pushes aside her plate. Martin's advice is needed – she'll arrange a seance with Jem Barlow. The last time they did it, a materialization was almost achieved.

———

Despite the short notice, Miss J.E.M. Barlow, known as Jem, consents to a seance that evening. Edith has been saving some early blooming African violets, grown in one of the glasshouses. She snips them now, arranging them in a cut-glass bowl in the library. They'll wilt before morning but their sacrifice is necessary. Violets will help to lubricate the channel of communication because of their association with Violet Martin.

Edith taps her lower lip. Objects associated with the person on the other side of the great divide are useful. A brainwave sends her to her studio, known as the purlieu in her mother's time, where she riffles through a storm of papers until she tracks down the original manuscript for *An Irish Cousin*. It was their first book together, that shilling shocker whose success changed their lives. The manuscript, handwritten in dark-blue ink, is a fair copy executed by Edith because Martin's script was evil (to quote Nannie Martin, her mamma), but here and there an amendment has been scribbled by Martin. The pages are yellowing, their edges foxed, and a doubled length of green tape holds the stack together. A faint scent of violets drifts from them.

'Darling old thing.' Edith strokes the manuscript.

In solitary splendour beneath portraits of her ancestors, she eats a light meal of scrambled eggs on toast, intending to offer Miss Barlow supper after her exertions. A seance takes its toll on the medium. Philomena's disapproval was visible in every line of her body when she served the eggs, but Edith refused to discuss it with her.

'By all means take it up with Father Lambe, but you can't be allowed to dictate to me, Philomena. Now, please see to it that the library fire is lit and everything left ready, as per my instructions.'

She's waiting in the library when Philomena shows Miss Barlow into the room with a moody crash of the door, not troubling to knock or introduce her.

Edith ignores Philomena's display of temper. 'Punctual as ever, my dear Miss Barlow. I do appreciate your surrendering your evening to me at such short notice.'

She shakes hands with a ladylike person in a feathered hat and silver fox-fur stole, somewhat younger than Edith. They are similar in height and frame, but when Jem Barlow fixes the pale-blue light of her eyes on someone, she seems capable of seeing right through to their spinal cord.

'All that's surrendered is a rubber of bridge, Miss Somerville. And I always lose. You've saved me half a crown, at least.'

'In that case, may we get started, Miss Barlow? I thought it might be a good idea if we turned out the lamps and used candles. I have some here.'

'Excellent idea. More atmospheric.'

'Out you go, Loulou.' Edith turns the door knob and points.

Loulou stands her ground, tongue hanging out. She is stared down, knows it and shuffles to the door.

Miss Barlow scans the room, sits at a small table in an alcove and removes her hat and gloves. Edith takes the seat opposite. The manuscript lies between them. Edith counts back. It's almost forty years since she and Martin worked on that novel together, back when the earth was flat.

'Our dear departed will stretch out their hands to us if at all possible, Miss Somerville. To see them, we must look with our inner eye.' The medium reaches out and takes a firm hold of Edith's hands. Next, she lowers her eyelids and breathes rhythmically, face tranquil.

She could be cogitating on the next day's menu to be agreed with her cook, thinks Edith. Instead, she is a daring explorer in that mysterious country where Martin now lives.

Edith tries to look with her inner eye, but is distracted by the heat from Jem Barlow's hands. She waits, aware of complementary sounds in the room, which grow louder as the seconds tick by on the mantelpiece clock. Miss Barlow's even breaths, the fire crackling, a beam shifting in the ceiling. Outside the window, a bird gives a drowsy series of chirps.

All of a sudden, the grip on her hands tightens. 'Are you there, Miss Martin? Are you able to make contact? One who loves you on the earthward side of the veil is anxious to speak with you.' Her eyes spring open. They are glassy, the pupils reduced to pinpricks. 'Miss Martin? Can you make your way to us? Please try. We're waiting for you, Miss Martin. Waiting and hoping.' She lowers her voice. 'Call her by name, Miss Somerville.'

'Martin!' cries Edith. 'I need you. Do try to come to us, my dear. It would mean so much to see you.'

Still holding Edith's hands, Miss Barlow inhales abruptly. 'She is here! I sense it!'

Edith feels some shift in the atmosphere.

'She is with us! A materialization!' exclaims Miss Barlow.

Edith's heart skips a beat. The flickering candlelight causes the shadows in the room to bend and waver. Perhaps she does feel some tremor, like the vibrations left after a hand has drifted across harp strings.

Is it her imagination or is there a stronger scent of violets?

Miss Barlow cocks her head. 'You'd recommend it?' She is all attention. 'Naturally we'll be advised by you. Yes, I'll tell the sitter. Miss Somerville, my spirit guide, Melville, says you may pose questions through him and he will convey your requests to Miss Martin. She can show herself to us but may not speak directly. I fear the obstacles are too great for her to communicate with her own voice tonight. But she is near. Very near.'

Edith's eyes circumnavigate the room, but detect nothing. Yet how to explain that prickle on the back of her neck? Her gaze latches onto an armchair beside the window where Martin used to curl up and read. Perhaps the air is thickening there. Has it shaped into a woman's contours?

'Miss Somerville, do you have a question you wish to put to Miss Martin?'

Edith's blood drums in her ears. Her throat is parched. She swallows. 'Martin, what should I do about our play? I've had a setback. Should I abandon it – or persist?'

'She is communicating her answer now through Melville,' intones Miss Barlow. 'She says go to London, use your contacts there. You're too remote from the centre of things here.'

'So the play will be staged? It will be a success?'

Miss Barlow listens intently to Melville, nodding and pursing her lips. Edith's eyes remain fixed on the armchair where that dense shadow has appeared. Is it Martin? Along Edith's spine, the skin feels stretched too taut.

'You must believe in yourself,' says Miss Barlow. 'Your new work will stir interest and comment. Believe in yourself.'

'I'm riddled by doubt,' says Edith.

The medium's shoulders hunch in concentration. She squeezes Edith's hands. 'Miss Martin says people become like horses refusing a jump. Uncertainty is their enemy, not inability. You must not surrender to uncertainty. You have achieved great things in life, and are destined for further triumphs.'

Edith becomes conscious of a friendly presence. It's as if an invisible hand is resting lightly on the small of her back, in a gesture of encouragement. A patch of warmth heats her skin there. 'Dare I believe, dearest Martin?'

'You must. What is there but belief to sustain us?'

Other messages follow, inconsequential but heartening. Their gist is that she is to seek the help of well-wishers with influence. In answer to a question from Edith, Martin says she has never wanted to be back in her body again.

'I feel no sense of separation,' she says.

'Oh, Martin, I confess that sometimes I do!'

Jem Barlow heaves out a lengthy sigh, and lays Edith's hands on the table. She opens her eyes, blinks twice, stretches her back. Her pupils are normal. The trance has passed. 'How did it go, Miss Somerville?'

'Very well, thank you. We communicated beautifully.'

'There was a materialization?'

'Perhaps. I ... I'm not certain.'

'But the psychic energy crackles still! Can't you sense it?'

'I may have seen something ...'

'My dear, there's been an indisputable force in this room tonight. There can be no doubt of a breakthrough. I confess, I feel positively drained – always a sure sign.'

'Allow me to offer you some refreshments, Miss Barlow.' Edith rings the bell for Philomena. 'Will you take some sherry while supper is fetched?'

Miss Barlow consents to a glass. Edith pours some dry sherry into two Waterford crystal glasses, and while the medium drinks hers Edith quizzes her on the dream state she entered.

'I have no recollection of details. It's a kind of semi-sleeping condition, yet I feel more illuminated by knowledge than in my waking state. That said, the part I play is passive. I know my role is simply to listen and convey messages from those who have gone before us to another plane.'

'Passive, but essential,' protests Edith.

'I do what I can, Miss Somerville.'

'It gives me such comfort. I miss her dreadfully.'

Miss Barlow clasps her hands together, a topaz ring winking in the candlelight. 'My dear Miss Somerville, you should never doubt Miss Martin's friendship. It remains as true as ever. I feel her affection for you in this room. It is flame-bright.'

'Do you suppose you could materialize her again? I – I think I could make out her form. But it was really only a dim outline.'

'No wonder it was dim. Her energy has to travel here from such a long distance.'

'If I could only see her face again.'

'Believe, Miss Somerville. Believe and it will happen.'

'I do. Oh, indeed I do.'

But she can't help feeling a little deflated. Her dearest Martin. So close and yet so far. There but not there. Her words but not her voice. Her shadow but not her face. Within touching distance – but she couldn't touch her.

—

The letter from Charlotte Shaw is dated the night of the seance. Edith refuses to regard it as a coincidence. She reads it over breakfast.

My dear Edith,

A thousand apologies on behalf of my insensitive husband. I hadn't an inkling GBS was going to send you such a letter. He told me only that he'd read your play and was intending to give you some advice. Naturally I presumed he meant constructive advice. But alarm bells rang when your own impeccably courteous letter arrived, thanking him for his candour, and I asked to see his rough copy of what he'd written. I was aghast! This is not a concert review for one of those London rags you used to scribble for, I told him. This is one of my Castletownshend cousins. You've dined at Drishane!

He concedes that he may have been a little hasty in his 'abandon hope all ye who enter here' analysis. There is much wit and joie de vivre *in 'Flurry's Wedding' and I feel certain that it can be salvaged, with a little judicious pruning and re-ordering. GBS agrees with me. Won't you come and stay with us for a few days, Edith, and the two of you can discuss how to make progress with your play? He can be tactless and somewhat flippant, but he does understand the theatre world and undoubtedly you would benefit from his expertise. The stage is a different storytelling milieu and some guidance might not go amiss.*

Do say you'll come to Ayot St Lawrence. It's just a country cottage, really, and we don't go about much when we're here. The seclusion is agreeable compared with London's hurly-burly and GBS finds it conducive to work. Come for my sake if not his. I am in agony with neuralgia at the moment and your visit would be a welcome distraction. Besides which, a visitor from Ireland is the next best thing to being there. With things so unsettled these past few years, I haven't been able to visit as I'd like to do, although we have high hopes the Treaty will hold, and men of good sense on both sides will see this thing through. Wire us your plans. I have your play put by safely. Strike while the iron is hot!

Fondest love,

Lottie

'I'll need a mackintosh, Philomena. It'll be foggy in London. It generally is. Lamps have to be lit all day, sometimes.'

Edith is supervising while Philomena packs her trunk. On her itinerary are a weekend in Ayot St Lawrence, a few days in Ethel Smyth's Hook Heath house and a longer stay with her brother Boyle and his wife Mabel in London. She also intends calling on Mr Pinker, and has written suggesting a meeting on February the fourth. It's time for her to part company with her literary agent. She hopes there isn't a row. But she's determined, like Hamlet, to 'drink hot blood, and do such bitter business as the day would quake to look on'.

'What's London like, Miss Edith?'

'London is like the ocean, Philomena: vast, bottomless and it refuses no one.'

'I'd love to see Big Ben, so I would. Is it true there isn't a corner of London where you can't hear it?'

'Not quite. But its bongs do carry.'

A sudden swirl of dust near the door makes Philomena cross herself.

'Why did you do that, Philomena?'

'That dust's a sign. One of the good folk is on the move. You will come back, won't you, Miss Edith? I'd hate to think of the Somervilles up-and-leaving Castletownshend altogether, the way some of the gentry does be packin' up and goin' to the North or England.'

'You can bank on me coming back. There'll be Somervilles in CT as long as there's a CT. Tell you what, I'll send you a postcard of Big Ben.'

A loud sniff. 'God is good and so are you, Miss Edith. I'll stick it in my scrapbook. Best send Mrs O'Shea one, as well, if it's not too much trouble. She'd take it amiss to be overlooked.'

'We couldn't have that. Now, don't pack my walking shoes because I'll need them for the crossing. I may have to leave my cabin and go on deck if the sea is choppy. The air's like wrapping yourself in a damp sheet. But needs must. Less chance of queasiness outdoors.'

'Will I pack your black hat with pheasant feathers in the hatband? You'd never know when you might have a funeral to go to, and you with so many family and friends over there.'

'I wish my family were all here in Ireland, Philomena. But my brothers had to make their way in the world. Yes, pack the hat.'

'They'll find their way home, please God.'

Edith thinks about her tribe of brothers: Cameron, Aylmer, Boyle, Jack and baby Hugh, born when she was fifteen. All of them joined either the army or navy and travelled the world. How many will find their way back to Castletownshend? Boyle, for sure, at least. He loves this cranny of Ireland.

'Miss Edith? Will you be needin' your painting things?'

Philomena's voice yanks her back to Drishane.

'Just a sketchpad and some pencils but I'll take care of them myself.' As she leaves the room, she touches Philomena's work-roughened hand.

Philomena stops folding and smoothing clothes.

'Am I doing the right thing, leaving Drishane? You haven't heard anything that worries you in the village, Philomena?'

'Nobody will lay a finger on this place while I have breath in me body, Miss Edith. We'll keep everything as safe as if it was in God's own pocket.'

———

There are no foot-warmers on the Dublin-bound train and the cushions feel crusty. An inexplicable halt on the line occurs in the middle of nowhere – Edith guesses Kildare from the flat landscape. For a time, she watches a small boy starfish his hand against the window, making mooing noises at cattle in the fields. 'Moo-cow, Mama, moo-cow,' he tells his mother, until she puts aside her magazine and moos along with him.

At the waiting room in Amiens Street, where Edith is passing time until she can board the Kingstown train to connect with the ship, the air is blue with tobacco smoke. Why does the fire in every station waiting room smoke, but not burn, she thinks fretfully. She leaves her bags with the young mother, whose son is now sleeping on her lap, and steps outside onto the street. The smell of unwashed human bodies attacks her nostrils. It's the same in Cork city, of course, but she objects more to the odour in Dublin. Perhaps, as a Cork woman, she's inclined to make allowances.

She looks in the direction of the Liffey. Beyond it, across the rooftops, lies St Stephen's Green. Once, she'd have broken her journey with a stay there, in her aunt Louisa Greene's house. Aunt Louisa is gone now, too. Another name crossed out in her address book. A man with a sandwich board roped to him shuffles past, advertising *Little Red Riding Hood* at the Gate Theatre. A woman stops a constable, in the distinctive, steel-spiked helmets of the Dublin Metropolitan Police, and asks for directions to Jammett's. Someone is going to dine well on French cuisine, thinks Edith, as the constable points the way to Nassau Street. Barefoot newsboys with marzipan-coloured skin scurry about, shouting the headlines. 'Latest Treaty news! Dev snubbed! Overseas Irishmen support the deal!'

Edith fumbles out a coin to buy one. Before she can reach a newsboy, she is intercepted.

'A penny for the babby. She needs milk.' A woman with a child wrapped inside her shawl holds out an upturned hand.

Edith considers her. It's a Madonna-like tableau, one to which she has always been susceptible – in art and in life. The woman is tidy, with a knob of hair on top of her head, but scrawny, as though she hasn't seen a solid meal in months. She can well believe such a woman isn't able to produce enough milk for her child. She gives her the shilling she's holding, and adds another shilling to it.

'May your soul fly straight to heaven, ma'am.'

Edith buys a copy of *The Irish Times*. 'Last Days of Robert's Sale' is trumpeted across the front, but she flicks past lists of hemstitched tray cloths and embroidered duchess sets at knockdown prices to arrive at the news section inside.

At the Irish Race Conference, Mr de Valera and his friends have been disillusioned completely about the attitude of overseas Irishmen towards the Treaty. The wild idea of asking the Conference to declare against the peace settlement is not likely to be pressed now, because some of the most influential Irishmen throughout the world are in favour of it.

So, support is growing for the Anglo-Irish Treaty. Perhaps 1922 will bring stability to Ireland. Relief flows like running water through her. She pleats the newspaper, folding inwards its dateline of Friday, January 27, and returns to the waiting room.

———

The mail boat rumbles to the sound of its engines starting up. Edith leaves her cabin to go up on deck, passing a small boy at play with a peashooter. He ignores his mother's urging to wave goodbye to Papa. Edith finds little boys more interesting than girls, whom she tends to ignore. But there are other sights to watch here, and she leans on the railings, inhaling the smells of sea salt and rot. The quay is thronged with people waving hands, handkerchiefs, hats and newspapers at friends. Their shrieks are good-humoured but indecipherable. Further along on the skyline she sees cranes, and other vessels at anchor. It's an invigorating scene, an antidote to her weariness after a day dealing with talkative porters and uncongenial waiting rooms.

A flock of seagulls perches on the railings just along from her, the birds' insouciance making her smile. They hitch a ride until the Hill of Howth recedes to the west, its lighthouse piercing the twilight. Smoke billows from the funnels, a foam wake churns behind. Now the seagulls rise into the air with a few lazy flaps, but instead of turning back to shore they follow the ship, letting rip with their screams.

The city lights begin to recede, the evening draws in. Edith considers going below for dinner but lingers still, enjoying the sensation of being on the move again after so long at Drishane. Men with cigars pace the deck. She takes a turn, getting her sea legs. Out of the corner of her eye, she notices one of the stewards watching her. His demeanour has an intensity which puzzles her. When he sees her spot him, he backs away, into a passageway. Just as she is about to challenge him, the boat sways and turns, and a cloud of steam is blown directly into her face. The toxic combination of machinery oil and cooking smells sends a rush of queasiness racing through her. It feels as if her stomach is being driven through her back. She staggers downstairs to her cabin. The vessel pitches and rolls all night long and she skips dinner, spending the crossing in bed with her head beneath her arm.

'Like a sick hen hiding under its wing,' says a voice suspiciously like Flurry's.

But when she lifts her head the cabin is empty.

thirteen

Charlotte Shaw stands in the doorway of her Ayot St Lawrence home, arms open to embrace her cousin. 'My dear, it's wonderful to see your rosy cheeks again. How was the journey? Was it too, too dreadful?'

'Not for a travel-hardened old warhorse like me, Lottie. Besides, I broke it by staying at Boyle and Mabel's place in London last night.'

'Come inside, you dear thing. You must go upstairs and freshen up. Then I want to hear all about home. Every little detail.'

'You won't like what I have to say.'

'Won't I?'

'I'm afraid not. Ireland's changed.'

Charlotte frowns and is about to speak, but Fred Day, the chauffeur, approaches with the luggage. 'Day, leave Miss Somerville's bags in the hall, please. Mrs Higgs will take care of them.'

Edith is ushered into a modern, red-bricked villa, a rectory before the Shaws took possession. It feels distinctly suburban and unlovely to her. She is shown upstairs to her bedroom, where she removes her hat and coat, and pats her hair into shape. En route to the drawing room, she passes a room with its door open, and catches sight of cameras, type-writers, an ancient exercise bicycle and a Bechstein piano. The house is a jumble of paraphernalia.

Charlotte has tea waiting, and she accepts a cup gladly. Knowing her cousin, it will be made from some superior blend – her cousin has always been fond of creature comforts. Edith takes in her surroundings. This room, too, is jammed with furniture and bric-a-brac. What a magpie Lottie has turned out to be. Despite the clutter, it's an oasis of ease and warmth, cushions and footstools positioned at strategic angles and the air perfumed by hyacinths in bowls. Books, books and more books are piled, stacked and shelved everywhere the eye falls, along with maga-zines, pamphlets and train timetables.

'Is George away from home?' Anxiety underpins Edith's question.

'No, he's in his writing hut in the garden. The GBS routine is sacro-sanct. But he'll take a break for a cup of chocolate at four-thirty and you can catch up then.'

Edith sets down her cup and saucer and picks her way to the window. Snowdrops flock in beds beneath the lintel, lawns lie beyond them, while at the bottom of the sloping garden a belt of conifers stands sentinel.

'What a charming situation, Lottie.'

'Hertfordshire doesn't hold a candle to West Cork, but it's nice enough, in its way.'

'The garden looks delightful.'

'Our fruit trees give GBS no end of delight. He risks life and limb on wobbly ladders, picking apples and pears to squirrel away. We have a pigeon cote and beehives, too.'

'I always thought you were a city person. After you inherited Derry you never actually lived in the house.'

'Its upkeep costs too much. Those old houses suck your blood and grind your bones.'

'Not if you love them, Lottie.'

Charlotte flushes at Edith's reproof. 'I love Derry. But it makes sense to rent it out. My life is no longer in Ireland.' She strikes a deliber-ately jolly tone. 'You should see GBS and me helping Mr Higgs with the garden – sawing logs, digging, planting, whatever needs doing.'

'Really? Both of you?'

'Of course. *Et in Arcadia ego*. We love the quiet noises of the countryside.'

Edith tries and fails to imagine the man she thinks of as the Genius – not entirely admiringly – chopping wood or weeding a gravel path. She hopes Lottie handles the axe because her husband is too clumsy to be allowed near a blade.

Charlotte lifts a framed photo of two girls on horseback off the mantelpiece. 'Look at us, Edith. We never knew what freedom we had.'

'Was that taken in Derry?'

'Yes, long before I changed my name to Shaw. You thought nothing of riding the twelve miles to Rosscarbery, to spend all day roaming with me. How light-hearted we were.'

'Those were the days.'

'You always suited a riding habit.'

The Payne-Townshends had lashings of loot compared with the Somervilles – Uncle Horace made a packet on the London Stock Exchange. That girl on horseback beside Edith was known as the heiress of County Cork. Lottie and her sister Sissy had the pick of husbands, thanks to their £4000 a year apiece. She notices, not entirely kindly, that her cousin has piled on weight since their girlhood – she doesn't so much sit down as subside into a chair, clotted cream draperies fluttering.

'How are all your doglings, Edith?'

Now isn't the time to tell Lottie about Dooley. 'Inconsolable at being left behind.'

Staccato footsteps announce the arrival of George Bernard Shaw. He has a salty beard, hair that clumps at his jacket collar and a shirt cuff undone.

'Darling, it's only three-thirty!' says Charlotte.

'A wise man knows when to obey rules and when to ignore them. I left Saint Joan to her own devices and came up to say hello to Edith.'

He jerks forward to shake her hand, putting Edith in mind of a grasshopper. From behind his back, with a magician's flourish, he produces a russet apple, bows and presents it. 'For the lady convinced Castletownshend is the apple of some god or other's eye.'

Edith is beguiled, while Charlotte looks indulgent.

'Now, Edith, tell me at once, how's this Treaty going down in Ireland?' asks Shaw.

'There's a sense of bewilderment and unreality in the country.'

'But will Ireland accept it?'

'Not if Mr de Valera can help it. He sets my teeth on edge.'

'Darling,' Charlotte intervenes. 'Don't start a cross-examination the moment you lay eyes on Edith. She hasn't even finished her tea yet.'

'I don't mind, Lottie,' says Edith. 'I hope it's accepted, George. But you never can tell. The people say one thing and think another. The old certainties are gone.'

'And good riddance to them,' says Shaw. 'How are things on the ground?'

While Charlotte rings for his chocolate, Edith updates Shaw, who fidgets with a Staffordshire figure of Shakespeare and listens intently to her litany of landlords shot, houses burned and old county families bailing out.

'Is Derry at risk?' askes Charlotte.

Edith pulls a face. 'Ancient scores are being settled. Murdering our houses is one way of doing it. Why should any of us hope for our own to be saved? Yet we do.'

'Perhaps it's not always murder. Maybe some of the houses are committing suicide,' suggests Shaw.

Edith and Charlotte stare at him.

He gives a twitch. 'The houses have been complicit in the subjugation of the people. They symbolize division.'

They continue to gape.

'Are the people united about self-rule?' asks Shaw.

Edith pulls herself together. 'They are united by suffering. Ireland's been in a state of unrest and ferment for so long now.'

'I really can't imagine how self-rule would work,' says Charlotte. 'The Irish are too excitable, and under the thumb of their priests. The Catholic farming class all wanted to send a son into the priesthood – that's their idea of achieving respectability.'

'Many of our neighbours have given up and left,' says Edith. 'If the Sinn Féiners take over, there's a good chance they'll do like the communists in Russia and seize everything. May as well sell up and take what we can get now, they say.'

'Neighbours?' Shaw has a glint in his eye. 'Do you mean the villagers?'

'Well, no. People like …' she hesitates. Takes a deep breath. Says it. 'People like us, I mean. The upper classes.'

'I was a clerk in Ireland,' says Shaw. 'I don't count as *us*.'

'Your people were the right sort,' says Edith.

'You mean opportunists?'

Charlotte begins to pat the twist of hair on the back of her head. Edith imagines she must be resigned to her husband's behaviour.

'You mustn't use terms like upper and lower classes,' continues Shaw. 'Besides, you're not the sacred ascendancy any longer. You're the descendancy, incarcerated within your demesne walls. You know that, don't you?'

'Would you prefer the clean and dirty classes?' says Edith.

'Ah, now we reach the nub of it,' says Shaw.

'Water costs nothing.'

'Heating it does. And washing is an effort. You don't launder your own clothes, Edith, you might be less particular if you did. Working people are bone-weary at the end of the day. You must have faith in your community – throw in your lot with your people. And I don't mean the gentry. Your class are pterodactyls and have outlived your age.'

'Whatever I may be, I shall be digging in, not clearing out. The violence has to end sooner or later.'

Charlotte chips in. 'How on earth do you cope?'

'Good manners and a sense of breeding – we try to do what our ancestors would expect. A sense of duty, I suppose you'd call it.'

'I believe the violence isn't all one way,' says Shaw. 'The Black and Tans have done dreadful things, by all accounts.'

Edith sighs. 'There's a wildness in the Tans. If they don't start bad, they soon turn that way. It's been a trial of strength between the military authorities and the IRA.'

'But the Government condones what's been done in Ireland,' says Shaw. 'With one side of its mouth, it insisted there were no reprisals. And with the other, it said what an effective deterrent they were.

Anyhow, killing and terrorizing can't be justified on the basis of "keeping the peace".'

Edith nods. He's put his finger on the crux of the problem.

'English people don't know what's happening in their names,' says Charlotte.

'The people are frightened of everyone with a gun, Lottie. Whichever side they're on,' says Edith.

'Fighting solves nothing,' says Shaw. 'Pacifism is the only solution. If you don't know that, you know nothing about history.'

'You may say I know nothing of history, but if I haven't read it I've lived it – and I can assure you it is very unpleasant,' says Edith.

'Will the IRA foot soldiers fight on? Regardless of what the politicians cook up between them?' asks Shaw.

'If they think the Treaty is unfair, yes. They've paid a high price already. Surrender is unthinkable. The Roman Catholic priest in Castletownshend claims St Columcille prophesized the day would come when men would become scarce and not one would be left to saddle a horse or drive a plough. That day could be closer than we think.'

This silences her hosts. Charlotte brushes cake crumbs from her lap into her hand. 'We can talk again at dinner. Now, why don't I leave you two writers alone to discuss literary matters?' She fires a meaningful look in her husband's direction.

As soon as they are alone, they settle down to discussing her play, which he tells her has too much padding.

'A play must be nimble, not bulky, Edith. That's something you ink-slingers in the novel-writing game need to learn. And another thing. A play that's heavy on Flurrying and light on reality will never do.'

She supposes he has a point. What a strange creature he is, though.

He produces her manuscript and takes her through it page by page, showing where cuts can be made. They spend more than two hours combing the work. His advice is constructive. She's unsure how much of it she'll actually follow – he wants an enormous amount of material cropped, and really can't abide Flurry, who is the play's focal point – but it's useful to hear him talk character and staging.

'Is Flurry your male alter ego?' Shaw asks at one point. 'You are inordinately forgiving of him.'

Edith is flummoxed.

'And another thing,' he goes on. 'I don't know why you're setting the play in the 1890s. Place it in the present day. More relevance that way.'

Absolutely not, she thinks. Besides, that's rich coming from a playwright working on Joan of Arc, who lived in the fifteenth century.

—

Edith changes for dinner, wishing there had been time for a rest beforehand – but when Shaw was willing to work with her, she didn't like to lose the opportunity. Back downstairs, Shaw is exactly as she left him, except he's reading the *Economic Journal*. He sets it aside at once and stands up. Why, he's still wearing his tweed jacket and knickerbockers. In small matters and in large, he does not behave *comme il faut*.

'You know what you remind me of, George? My youth.'

'How so?'

'Enthusiasms came more easily.'

'As we grow older, we mustn't forget our youth. It's a lighthouse showing us the way we once wanted to go. I've been thinking about your play. Tell me, is this a first effort for the stage?'

'I've written for amateur productions. Fundraisers and so forth.'

'Let me guess. Did they have elves in them?'

'One did. *A Fairy Extravaganza: In Three Acts, by Two Flappers* – it raised money for prisoners of war and the hunt's fowl fund.'

'I see. It's not the best apprenticeship for a career in the West End.'

Charlotte appears, dressed for dinner, and scolds her husband for not offering their guest a drink.

'He should be a monk, Edith. No meat, no alcohol, no tobacco. Pour us both a glass of sherry, darling.'

Shaw might as well be a Presbyterian minister, thinks Edith.

'You don't mind a vegetarian dinner, Edith? We never serve meat. But Mrs Higgs is a marvel with her root vegetable casseroles.'

As suddenly as a pea shooting from its pod, Shaw vanishes from the room. Over his shoulder, he calls, 'I forgot to check the scales.'

'Piano scales?' asks Edith.

'Weighing. He likes to check his weight several times a day.'

'But there isn't a pick on him.'

'Exactly. And he wants it to stay that way.'

Edith studies her cousin. Charlotte has an untouched look, like a new candle. She wonders at the compromises which must happen daily to make a success of this unconventional marriage.

Shaw catapults back in. 'Still eleven stone on the nose.'

'Marvellous,' says Charlotte. 'I wish I had your willpower.'

'Have you two been gossiping about Ireland's fuchsia-tasselled hedgerows and featherbed boglands while I've been away?'

'Of course, darling. And sharing our thrice-told tales of being the belles of West Carbery. Shall we go through?'

Shaw offers both of them his arm, jeopardizing a Sèvres shepherdess on a side table.

'About your play, Edith,' says Shaw. 'Once you've knocked it into shape, why not send it to Yeats and Lady Gregory? For the Abbey?'

'Mr Yeats and Augusta have an obsession with the ancient heroic ways. I don't want to be part of that fakery.'

A smile breaks free of his beard. It's answer enough for Edith.

In the dining room, the table is laid with a spotless damask cloth and well-polished silver and crystal. A Victorian epergne crammed with out-of-season fruits squats in the centre. The meal is entirely without taste – parsnips, potatoes and onions stewed into a gloop. Peasant food. Wholesome, of course, Edith concedes that. At least the wine is excellent, although Shaw sticks to barley water, which he tells her is made to his specification by Mrs Higgs.

'It's too bad there are only three of us, not enough for a rubber of bridge after dinner,' says Charlotte. 'I should have invited some people over.'

Edith is glad she didn't. This is a working weekend.

Dessert is strawberries in syrup, bottled by the couple the previous summer, as Lottie tediously describes. Whenever she tells a story, Edith's mind invariably wanders. Fortunately, Shaw cuts in and quizzes Edith on spiritualism.

'It helps me to navigate my life.'

'Sounds like tomfoolery. And worse. The vulnerable and recently bereaved are exploited.'

'I'm not the exploitable type.'

'I'd like to try automatic writing,' says Charlotte.

'A parlour game for the susceptible,' says Shaw.

It occurs to Edith that he's amusing himself with her, as a cat toys with a mouse. Two can play at that game. She pivots to her cousin. 'We can try some automatic writing after dinner if you like, Lottie. Would you care to join us, George?'

'Certainly not. It's the unconscious mind at work. And of my own unconscious, I am – naturally – unconscious. That's the way I prefer it.'

'Do you really speak to the dead, Edith?' asks Charlotte.

'The so-called dead. Of course I do.'

'The messages are part of a repressed personality,' says Shaw.

'Then perhaps useful for self-discovery, darling?'

'If you were drunk would you say it was the real you emerging? How can a trance be any more true? It's self-delusion. Utter poppycock.'

'Darling, you're being dreadfully cranky.'

'Having now reached the age of Methuselah, I'm entitled to be cranky.'

Edith happens to know she is six months younger than Shaw.

'But I am a mere man, what do I know of any afterlife?' he continues. 'I shall turn in and read over some notes on Joan of Arc's trial. Good night, ladies. Don't let me stop you playing with ghosts. Though on your own heads be it.'

fourteen

Shaw's departure sucks all the energy from the room. Edith and Charlotte have a stab at automatic writing but make no progress. Privately, Edith thinks Shaw has put his evil eye on it. If he'd wanted to commune with the spirit world, they'd have been table-tapping into the wee small hours. 'Sometimes it just doesn't work,' Edith tells her disappointed cousin. They decide on an early night.

The next morning, Edith reworks her play, and over lunch picks Shaw's brains for theatrical contacts. He tells her on no account should the play be submitted before it's ready. Redrafting, followed by further redrafting, is essential.

'Take me, Edith. I've been thinking and reading about Joan of Arc since her canonization the year before last. I hope I'll be able to translate my French peasant girl to the stage, but there are no guarantees. The Maid continues to resists me. Better no play than a shoddy one. Remember that.'

'The hotter the work the sooner the finish,' says Edith. 'Or so our housemaid Philomena insists.'

'Once, the English might have liked that little gem,' says Shaw. 'Not now. We're in their black books.'

'But Flurry is loved. Isn't he, Lottie?'

'Of course he is, Edith. But GBS does have a point,' says Charlotte.

Shaw fixes his eyes on Edith, who has a sense of being under a microscope.

'*Was* loved,' he says. 'But times change. Keep up or be left behind. With theatre, the subject must have relevance, and I don't see how Flurry Knox fits that requirement.'

'You're working on a play about Joan of Arc. How is she relevant?'

'The Maid is the queerest of fish. We've all been quite wrong about her, myself included. I once thought her a half-witted genius, like Admiral Nelson, but now I realize she was gifted with exceptional sanity. She may have been a Roman Catholic. But if you ask me she was the first Protestant martyr.'

'I don't see how Protestant martyrs are relevant,' Edith persists.

'When the world is upside down, as it is now, martyrs appear sane. And people believe they can help us,' says Shaw.

'Really?'

'If they make us think, and question things, yes. But your Flurry isn't capable of making anybody think. He's a wastrel.'

'My Flurry has a good heart.'

'Your Flurry is heartless, Edith. But worse than that, he's something absolutely unforgivable for any character on the stage. Flurry Knox is simply not believable.'

———

In the afternoon, they climb into what Shaw calls his 'Henry' – although it's not a Ford but an AC coupé, he tells Edith. Shaw is in the driver's seat, his chauffeur beside him, with Edith and Charlotte in the back. Shaw pings on some goggles.

'How do I look, ladies?'

'A veritable Beau Brummell,' says Edith.

He chortles, and lets out the clutch abruptly, causing the motor car to judder.

Edith winces.

'What is it?' asks Charlotte, from under her fashionably squashy hat.

'Nothing,' says Edith.

'Perhaps you're cold. Here, share my rug.' Charlotte tucks her in, and Edith is obliged to suffer the fussing and patting.

The motor car continues to shake.

'Day, I think some nuts on the wheels need tightening,' says Shaw. 'Something feels not quite right here.' His foot is pressed on the accelerator, roaring the engine.

'You need to let off the brake, sir.'

'Excellent suggestion.'

Shaw releases the brake and the motor car kangaroos along the driveway.

Edith can't hide her grimace.

'Are you in pain, Edith?' asks Charlotte.

'A bit of arthritis. In the hip and leg, from riding side-saddle since I was four. All pleasures must be paid for sooner or later.'

'Poor thing. Have a *marron glacé*.' Charlotte produces a box of sweets and unties the ribbon. As soon as Edith has helped herself, Charlotte leans forward to Shaw. '*Marron glacé*, darling? I can stretch around and pop one in your mouth.'

'Not now, beloved. I'm concentrating.'

'Easy on the accelerator,' says Day. 'You need to take the gate slow, sir.'

Shaw's speed doesn't alter. He shoots through the gate, scraping against one of the posts, and bursts onto the laneway.

'We're doing twenty miles an hour now,' Shaw calls over his shoulder. 'Look at the speedometer!'

'Both hands on the wheel please, sir,' says Day.

'Marvellous, darling. But don't go any faster, will you?' cries Charlotte.

Edith peers out at barns and farm gates flashing past. Two ramblers with haversacks tramp across a path between fields.

'I'm always terrified he'll take a spill,' confides Charlotte. 'He's such a daredevil. But at least a motor car can't topple onto you, unlike a motorcycle. He has one of those, too. GBS is obsessed with modern gadgets. He makes me feel like Rip Van Winkle's mother.'

By now they are in the village, passing timber-frame houses. Shaw sounds his horn and waves at everyone they encounter. Some wave back or call out greetings swallowed up by the thunder of the engine. The majority scuttle away, dragging their children and pets with them. Edith spies a general provisions shop, some scattered houses the colour of fondant creams, a couple of church spires and a sprawling, half-timbered inn called the Brocket Arms.

'The inn was a stopping-off point for pilgrims on their way to St Albans Abbey,' says Charlotte. 'It's said to be haunted by a monk who hanged himself there. Or was he murdered?'

They're through the village now. Edith tents her forehead with one hand, trying to take another look at the Brocket Arms, fast disappearing into the distance.

Charlotte leans forward and taps Shaw on the shoulder. 'Darling, did the monk commit suicide or was he done away with?'

'What's that?' Shaw turns his head. Day grabs the wheel.

'Never mind, we can talk about it later,' shouts Charlotte. She addresses Edith. 'There's not much to Ayot St Lawrence. GBS says the last thing of note to happen here was the Norman invasion. But we like it. We've put down roots.'

They continue for five miles along narrow country lanes, as far as the small town of Harpenden, where they park and stretch their legs with a riverside walk. Edith notices how orderly everything is: English towns are so spick and span. She watches a family of swans on the water, only half-listening while Shaw and Charlotte debate whether or not to take tea. He says it supports local business, while she has reservations about the cleanliness of the teashop he's recommending. Shaw gives way and they return to where motor car and chauffeur are waiting, Day sitting on the running board. At their approach, he pinches off the tip of his cigarette and puts the remainder in his pocket.

'I'm glad to see he's not smoking in the motor car,' says Charlotte.

'Fred Day knows better. I've explained about your weak chest,' says Shaw.

'Why don't you let him drive us home, darling?'

'My dear, I've been deprived of Mrs Percy's Battenberg cake, you surely wouldn't deprive me of the joys of driving, too?' With Day holding the door open, he hands his wife into the backseat.

Day goes around the side of the vehicle to open the other door for Edith.

'Darling,' whispers Charlotte, 'it's silly to keep a dog and bark yourself. You'll do Day out of a job. Let him drive.'

Shaw refuses to lower his voice. 'There's no danger of that. Day can do all sorts of things I can't, like fiddle with leads and things under the bonnet. No, I believe I'll drive back. I find it relaxing.' He produces his goggles and snaps them over his face.

The drive home is uneventful, until Shaw insists on showing Edith how he can reverse into the driveway.

'Shall I hop out and guide you, sir?' offers Day.

'Not necessary,' says Shaw.

'Why not let him give you directions, darling?' cries Charlotte. 'The light's beginning to fade.'

'Oh, very well,' says Shaw.

Both Day and Charlotte vacate the motor car, followed by Edith, who only realizes she ought to when Charlotte pops her eyes at her.

Shaw screeches through the gears searching for reverse.

'Easy, sir. Don't forget the clutch. This way, sir. Left. No, left!' calls Day.

Despite Day's best efforts, his employer flies back and demolishes a flowerbed.

Everyone is somewhat shaken, apart from Shaw, who hobbles as he walks back indoors.

'Darling, have you hurt your leg?' asks Charlotte.

'Yes. And the worst of it is, it's my favourite leg.'

Over dinner, Shaw talks about his admiration for the Soviets.

Edith weighs in. 'If you lived in Russia you'd be muzzled like a dog or put up against a wall and shot. Unlike the authorities here, they don't allow you to be critical of the state,' she says.

'You like to see yourself as advanced and freethinking but you don't have an idea in your head that your grandmamma didn't have,' says Shaw.

He's nettled. Edith twists Martin's Claddagh over her knuckle, before pushing it back down onto the finger, taking Shaw's criticism as a triumph – it's not easy to score a point off him.

Charlotte intervenes. 'Edith, what was that you were saying in the motor car about your literary agent?'

'You see how my wife saves me from myself?' says Shaw.

'You know him, darling,' Charlotte tells her husband. 'Mr Pinker. He represented you in the past.'

''Course I know him,' says Shaw. 'Gets his hands on most of us, sooner or later. Persuasive chap.'

'He takes ten per cent I can ill afford,' says Edith.

'He knows what sells. And I dare say he could pinkerize your play for you, if you gave him a free hand.'

'I think that would be most unwise.'

'Pinker knows his business. If I were you, I'd follow his advice.'

Edith shakes her head. 'My friend Dr Smyth – Dame Ethel Smyth, I should say – believes I ought to part company with him.'

'Ah yes,' says Shaw. 'The stage front woman with the demented hat. A person of forceful opinions. Shared at least a dozen with me in the space of half an hour. Expresses herself well. But she's a composer. What does she know about literary agents?'

Edith hesitates. He has a point. But the sight of Shaw stroking his goatee beard, mischief blistering from every feature, stiffens her back-bone. 'I'm inclined to take her advice. I have an appointment with Mr Pinker on Tuesday in London.'

'Pinker may dig in his heels and refuse to let you go,' warns Shaw.

'Oh, I do hope not. It would be an unfortunate end to things. We've worked together since the 1890s, when all's said and done. But I'm not getting any younger and running Drishane isn't getting any cheaper.'

'Presumably you're under contract to the agency?' says Shaw.

'Well yes, but *Flurry's Wedding* is new work, because it's for the theatre.'

'He might argue, with some justification, that it's adapted from existing work. So you may find you're still under contract.'

This isn't what Edith wants to hear. 'Mr Pinker has dropped hints about retiring and passing on the business to one of his wastrel sons. I don't see why I should be handed over. I'm not a parcel.'

'Again, it depends on your contract,' says Shaw.

A clock chimes. He bolts off to weigh himself.

During his absence, Charlotte confides, 'She has a flop on you, you know.'

'Who?'

'Ethel Smyth.'

'We're friends,' says Edith. 'Just good friends.'

'A huge flop. Plain as the nose on your face. Why would you take advice from someone with a flop on you?'

From outside comes the hiss of sudden rain. Edith avoids answering by talking about the weather.

After she turns in for the night, she finds herself unable to sleep. The dawn chorus is limbering up before she nods off.

———

On the morning of her departure, Shaw pays her the compliment of inviting her to see his writing hut in a leafy nook at the bottom of the garden. It's a revolving cabin built on a turntable, an innovation he is ridiculously proud of.

'I just set my shoulder to the side and give it a push every now and again, and around we spin. We follow the sun, my hut and me. It reduces the need for artificial lighting, and keeps the place warm. Sunshine helps us to stay hale, hearty and happy. What you see before you, Edith, is a simple but effective health measure.' He points to the shed's furniture: a wicker chair, table with flap and narrow bed. 'In case I need to take a catnap.'

'So this is where those successful plays are dreamed into being,' says Edith.

'Some are more successful than others. Everyone has their disap-pointments.' He hesitates. 'I know I've picked your play to pieces from start to finish. I hope it hasn't been hurtful.'

'I'm not easily hurt and I make it a policy never to bear grudges.'

'I have an urge to improve people. Charlotte says I should have been a missionary.'

'Perhaps if you weren't an artist you'd have been a reformer. Is there anything you miss about Ireland, George?'

'I miss everything about it. But I can't live there. I'm amazed you stick the place.'

'It's home.'

fifteen

Stations flit past on the Piccadilly line of the London Underground. Edith reads the stops, each one bringing her closer to the moment when she must pin her courage to the sticking-place. Mr Pinker suggested taking her to lunch but she declined, although it would be easier to deliver the *coup de grace* in a public place. After more than twenty-five years of doing business together, she must give him the opportunity to say his piece without the worry of waiters overhearing. The escalator at Covent Garden raises her towards street level, past advertisements for Mecca cigarettes, pocket-sized moustache combs and ready-to-wear frocks apparently suitable for all occasions, according to Debenham & Peabody. Clustered outside the Underground entrance are flower-sellers. Normally she would linger over their cheerful parade, but she bypasses them, steering towards Trafalgar Square. The National Portrait Gallery is an old friend on the right, while St Paul's dome rises ahead, effortless as birdsong.

She pushes on for the Strand along pavements fretful with people, trying to ignore the throbbing in her leg, and arrives at Arundel Street.

A flight of granite steps leads up to number nine, Talbot House. The swinging doors rotate, and a slight woman in a neat-fitting jacket and skirt emerges. She has a face that would fit into a teacup. For a heart-beat, Edith imagines it's Martin. Every time they entered this building together, they pinched one another because they were successful authors. But when they draw level, she sees the woman is decades younger, and her eyes are not as fine as Martin's.

In a marble hall, Edith is faced with the option of lift or staircase. Her leg makes the decision for her. 'Third floor,' she tells the lift operator, and exits onto a corridor where typewriters clatter from behind closed doors. This building is an ants' nest of industry. She reaches an opaque door.

James Brand Pinker
Literary and Dramatic Agent

Since when was he a dramatic agent?

Two women are working inside, one at her typewriter and the other attempting to put some order on a leaning tower of manuscripts. 'Ulysses' and 'James Joyce' are printed on the top manuscript. Boney sent her an extract the previous year, published in some magazine or other. For Edith, it read as if scratched out by a semi-literate working man. She saw, she sipped, she shuddered. 'Tasteless, puzzling and anar-chic. "Ulysses" deserves to sink without a trace,' was her verdict. Boney, on the other hand, lauded Joyce as a genius and window-breaker. 'He lets in the fresh air,' she told Edith.

Both secretaries have cropped hair and trailing strings of pearls. They address her respectfully as Miss Somerville, recognizing her before Edith introduces herself, which is gratifying. The older of the two invites her to take a seat while she alerts Mr Pinker to her arrival. He's on a transatlantic call, but she's certain he'll be with her as soon as possible. A blue-and-white tea service sits on a lacquered side table, and the second secretary offers her refreshment, which she declines. Edith does, however, consent to flick through a magazine.

Pinker emerges from his office, slight, bespectacled and clean-shaven, and bows over her hand. Amid the bustle of welcomes, he ushers her

into his office and settles her into a Chippendale chair beneath an electric chandelier lit up already on this wintry day. As ever, she is struck
by the gentleman's club atmosphere of his office. Pinker is dapper in a
mustard-and-pink polka-dotted bow tie (only a caddish or underbred
person would wear such a creation, thinks Edith). He sits opposite her
rather than return to his carved-oak desk, reminisces about West Cork
and extends courtesies from Mrs Pinker. Edith notices his face is flushed
and his voice, always somewhat hoarse, is wheezing.

'As you know, I've written a play, Mr Pinker.'

'Naturally I'll do what I can for you, Miss Somerville. Do you have
it with you?'

'I'm afraid not. You see, I'd like to try placing it myself.'

His smile doesn't falter. 'Is that wise? My job is to spare you creative
people the trouble of haggling and bargaining. Leave you free to direct
your genius to your craft.'

'We can't always afford the luxury of being employers, Mr Pinker.'

'What price peace of mind?'

'I must put my cards on the table. I'm not ungrateful for your efforts
on our behalf – quite the reverse. But the fact is, my income from writing
is declining.'

'Tastes change, alas.'

'I simply can't afford your commission. I have expenses to meet.'

'We can talk about money another time, Miss Somerville. Why don't
I read your play first? Is it ready for submission?'

'I certainly hope so. I've worked most awfully hard on it.'

'Excellent. Well then, the best thing is for me to take a look at it and
see what we can do. The theatrical realm is unpredictable. So many proj-
ects come to nothing there. They begin with high hopes, but the march
of events intervene.'

'I'm optimistic about my play's prospects, Mr Pinker.'

'As am I, Miss Somerville. As am I. But the theatre world is a jungle.
I wouldn't like to think of you venturing into it without a guide.'

'I'm not aware you have any experience of the theatre, Mr Pinker.
Your forte is placing novels and short stories.'

'On the contrary, dear lady. One of my authors, Arnold Bennett, has adapted the script for the biggest box-office smash in London currently. *The Beggar's Opera*. It's been running since 1920 and still no sign of the public losing interest.'

Pinker's voice has always been whispery, but now it seems to be emanating from deep in his throat. Is he unwell? He seems most unlike himself. Fidgety and on edge.

He continues, 'Nigel Playfair – he's the manager of the Lyric – has struck gold. Naturally I dealt with Mr Playfair on Mr Bennett's behalf. I could have a word with Mr Playfair about your play. Arrange a luncheon for the three of us. All managers like to be courted a little. But first, I should cast an eye over the play.'

Edith vacillates. Pinker has always been adept at spotting opportunities. But if she shows her play to him, it commits her to a business arrangement.

Pinker watches her carefully. 'Have you met Mr Bennett? An energetic man. Almost as industrious as yourself. He reposes a great deal of confidence in me.'

'We've nodded at one another.'

'I choose my authors with care. I hope I've never disappointed their confidence in me.'

Edith wishes he wouldn't witter on about Arnold Bennett – probably, she thinks sourly, he's made a mint from him.

All of a sudden, Pinker's face turns ruddy and he fingers his collar. 'Stuffy in here. Need some …' He stands up and wrenches open the window. Traffic sounds float in – horns, wheels, horse hooves. Pinker leans forward and inhales the grubby air. When he resumes his seat, perspiration beads his hairline and he blots it with a handkerchief. 'Now, where were we, Miss Somerville? Your play. Is it a musical?'

'No, it's a play.'

'Musicals are enormously popular with the public. You mustn't think they're lowbrow. *The Beggar's Opera* is a case in point. Mr Bennett says it's a forgotten masterpiece.'

'I must try for tickets.'

'Mrs Pinker and I went to the opening night. Most amusing.'

'Is that the one about a pirate?'

'No, a highwayman, Macheath, in a scarlet coat and long, curling wig. Mrs Pinker was very taken by him. The Lyric is an intimate little venue, of course, but I believe it's full ...' He blinks hard, twice. 'Full most nights.'

'Doesn't sound particularly amusing.'

'Ah, but it is. What did you say your play was about?'

'Flurry Knox steals a horse from his grandmother. Major Yeates is embroiled by accident.'

He scrubs at the back of his neck with his handkerchief. 'Readers are fond of that scallywag of yours. But I should warn you. These past years have left us a little out of sorts with our friends in Ireland.'

'Ireland is my inspiration. I draw my best material from there.'

'I suppose as long as it has plenty of intrigue, we can drum up inter- est. The West End enjoys action and adventure.'

She notices his handkerchief is sodden. He must be perspiring heavily. 'I'm afraid, Mr Pinker, I'm not here about placing *Flurry's Wedding*, but to explain I can't afford to retain your services.'

'A wedding – now that might fly.' His speech speeds into a staccato burst. 'Plenty of spectacle in it? Matched pair of white horses, plumes on their heads, leading the wedding carriage, and so forth?'

'There *is* a horse but I presumed it would be a mechanical animal. I say, Mr Pinker, are you quite well? You look a little warm.'

'It does feel close. With your permission.' He unbuttons his waist-coat jacket. 'You see, audiences must have spectacle. They've become accustomed to real swans swimming about on stage, monkeys dressed up as pages and whatnot. Mrs Pinker and I saw some ... some cowboys. From the American, ah, West. Spin ... spinning ropes.'

'I don't believe I'd care for specialty acts. That's not the audience I'm writing for.'

'Excuse me. Water.' He stands, misses his footing, catches at the chair back.

Edith is by his side in an instant. 'Mr Pinker, do sit down. Let me help you to some.' She guides him to his chair, before pouring a glass of water from a jug on his desk.

He slumps in his seat, the heel of his hand pressed against his sternum. His face reminds Edith of a broken doll. But he rouses himself to take the brackish London water from her, finds an enamelled pill box in his waistcoat pocket and taps out two white discs.

'Shall I call one of your assistants, Mr Pinker?'

He shakes his head. 'Thank you, no … tell you the truth … little under par.'

'You do look careworn.'

He finishes the water and recovers somewhat. 'Mrs Pinker says I, ah, I fatigue myself. On my authors' behalf.' He mops at his face and neck again. 'But my interest goes beyond the financial. I care about my authors, Miss Somerville. I want your talents fully recognized.'

Edith can't decide if he's intentionally trying to make her feel guilty. Deliberate or not, it's working. 'Couldn't you manage a holiday? The winter can be tedious.'

'Not at the moment. I'm obliged to travel to New York to handle a business matter. Frankly …' His eyes dart around the room. He lifts a magazine from a side table and fans himself. 'Yes, truth be told, I'm dreading the journey. But I can't postpone it. Time and tide wait for no man.'

'Shouldn't you ask your doctor's advice before undertaking such a long voyage?'

'Doctor advises against it. But, as you know, my son Eric is running our American office, and the silly boy has got himself into a spot of bother. Needs his dad to untangle things.'

'I hope it's nothing serious, Mr Pinker.'

He hauls himself to his feet, knocking over the glass, which shivers into fragments. She bends to lift some of the largest splinters.

'I beg you not to, Miss Somerville. Miss Baker will take care of it.' Skin clammy, he shakes her by the hand. His smile is as cheerful as a corpse's. 'Send over your Flurry Knox play and we'll put our heads together and see what we can do with it.'

'I don't think—'

He cuts her off. 'Been wonderful to catch up with you, Miss Somerville. Meeting you brings back Miss Martin to me. Such a loss to literature.'

'It's a poor thing to outlive one's friends. Don't see me out, Mr Pinker, I can find my own way.'

———

Outside on the Strand, Edith pauses by a bus stop to adjust her hat pin. A figure loitering there catches her eye. Hasn't she seen that face before? It reminds her of the road sweeper outside Boyle and Mabel's house this morning. He bends down to tie a shoelace, and she forgets about him, tasting instead her vexation at not accomplishing her mission. Mr Pinker simply wouldn't listen. There's no help for it, she must dispense with his services in writing. Perhaps she should hold off until she has a definite offer from a theatre. Walking past the Savoy, she purges her guilt by remembering his admission about his son. That clueless young man has been up to something shady, if she's not mistaken. He has educated his boys to be gentlemen but blood will out. Mr Pinker's father was an East End barrow boy.

———

Edith consults with Boney, who saw *The Beggar's Opera* a year ago and pronounced it a rattling good evening. She doesn't need Pinker to act as go-between, she decides, and composes a letter to Nigel Playfair, manager–director at the Lyric. The missive emphasizes her connection with Shaw. 'You're laying it on thick,' hisses her conscience. 'Contacts must be harvested,' whispers another voice. Martin's?

Dear Mr Playfair,

Forgive this direct approach from one who has admired your work for years. My close friend and relative Mr George Bernard Shaw recommends that I offer you first refusal on my new play. He says it's ideal for the Lyric. Might I hand over 'Flurry's Wedding' to you personally? I'll be attending 'The Beggar's Opera' on Thursday night and it would be a convenience to do it then. Yours will be the first eyes, apart from

Mr Shaw's, to read my play, which is inspired by the Irish R.M. stories I wrote with Martin Ross.

I'm very much looking forward to seeing your revival — I hear it's the toast of London. It has been remiss of me not to attend a performance sooner but I am only an Irish country mouse. However, as soon as I knew I had business in the city I made haste to purchase tickets.

Yours sincerely,

Edith Oenone Somerville

The following day he writes back, inviting her to have a glass of wine with him half an hour before curtain-up.

———

Nigel Playfair looks like a cross between a bishop and a butler, although one with bulky objects jammed into his dinner-jacket pockets. Apart from a blazing fire behind a dented metal guard, a threadbare Turkey carpet is the only concession to comfort in his office. He is genteel and deferential, pouring her a glass of decent Burgundy and conversing in a voice capable of wooing the world. She remembers he was a successful actor before becoming a manager, and still accepts character roles.

'Your Irish R.M. stories are classics, Miss Somerville. My nephew told me they were sent out to our boys in the trenches and helped to pass some difficult times.'

'Did he come home?'

'Left a hand behind at Ypres — but the rest of him came back. The Great War took many men. Sad days. It's our duty to distract the public from those unhappy memories. I look forward to reading your play. Is it your first?'

She removes the manuscript from her leather satchel and sets it on the low table beside them. 'Not entirely. I have adapted work in Ireland for the stage.'

'The Abbey?'

'No, for local productions in County Cork. Charity fundraisers. Humble little affairs, but popular. This is my first professional play.'

A flicker of doubt glances off his horn-rimmed spectacles. 'We're looking for something with bite to take the place of our ballad-opera when it runs its course. Something for my artistic team to sprinkle their fairy dust over. I don't mind so much about the critics — *The Beggar's Opera* had cool notices in its early days. No play is critic-proof, of course. But I had faith in it. And I was justified.'

'My play is *pour rire*. People need license to laugh.'

'Indeed. Well, I'll read it as soon as I possibly can.' He lifts it, juggling his hand as though weighing the manuscript. 'Feels a little thick.'

'I cut it down considerably, with Mr Shaw's assistance. Naturally, I'd be happy to effect more cuts, as necessary.'

His jowly face clears. 'Mr Shaw — keeper of the public conscience. Still, if Mr Shaw had a hand in this, it will be a treat to read.' Hastily, he tacks on, 'And, of course, the same applies to anything from the pen of your good self.' The first curtain bell rings and he stands. 'Duty calls, dear lady. You have tickets for tonight's performance?'

'In the stalls. I'm accompanied by the wife of my brother, Admiral Somerville. She's waiting for me in the foyer.'

'Permit me to swap your tickets for my personal box. You'll be more comfortable.'

'Too kind, thank you.'

By now, Playfair has his fob watch in his hand, checking the time. He guides her to the corridor outside his office, beckons to a junior stage manager and instructs him to take good care of Miss Somerville and her guest. Another staff member approaches Playfair and complains about some missing props.

Quickly, Edith asks, 'When might I hope to hear back from you, Mr Playfair?'

'I could promise you the sun, moon and gingerbread, Miss Somerville. But whether I could deliver them is another matter. The best I can say is that I'll read it at my earliest opportunity.'

———

Edith and Mabel Somerville are transported. Light massed into a single beam is trained on the dashing Macheath's face. He is pleading with Lucy Lockit, the turnkey's daughter, a young woman whose virtue he stole before abandoning her and their unborn baby. The highwayman needs her help to escape from Newgate Gaol or he'll dance at the end of a noose. Edith has to acknowledge that, visually, the show is daring and innovative, while the fusion of song, dance and drama is a crowd-pleaser. She has never seen anything to compare with the pared-back simplicity used to recreate Georgian London in all its glamour and squalor – there are scarcely any scene changes.

When the final curtain falls, Edith and her sister-in-law wait for the crowd to thin out before leaving the box. Engrossed in possible stage sets for *Flurry's Wedding*, she lends only half an ear to Mabel's prattle about the daisy-fresh appeal of Polly Peachum's pink-and-green gown. On the street, she recalls her leather satchel left under the seat and hurries back into the almost-empty theatre. She finds it where she left it, in Nigel Playfair's box.

'Wouldn't do to lose that.'

Edith whips around. It's Flurry Knox, lounging in the doorway.

'It's empty. Mr Playfair has my play on his desk.'

'Don't you mean *my* play? Whose name is on it?'

'You're the inspiration, you silly boy, but you're not the author. What are you doing, frivolling around London?'

'Taking a look at the place. So this is the theatre where you're planning to make a fortune from me. It's on the small side.'

'If it's a hit, we can transfer to a bigger theatre.'

'If you were going to start small and build, you could have begun in Dublin.'

'Don't be ridiculous, Flurry. Success in Dublin doesn't count. It's London that matters.'

sixteen

While she's waiting for news from Nigel Playfair, Edith takes a run down to Surrey to spend a night at Ethel Smyth's house. It's only half an hour from Waterloo Station, but when she steps out at Woking it feels like an entirely different corner of England. Through a swirl of steam on the railway platform, Boney's face emerges.

'All hail the dame!' Edith performs a mock curtsey.

'I've ordered new calling cards. I'm furious they haven't arrived yet. Come on, I have a hansom waiting outside for us.' She links arms with Edith and stumps her towards a bay horse with protruding ribs. 'It's not everyone I'd cut short rehearsals for. I'm conducting the Woking Choral Society Choir. We have a performance in two weeks, and they aren't ready yet. Not by a long chalk. The only thing they've learned properly is my *Hey Nonny No*. Hardly surprising when it's head and shoulders above everything else in the programme.' She addresses herself to a burly cabbie, pudding rolls at the back of his neck. 'We're ready to go now. Hook Heath. No luggage. I hope you did as I told you and gave that horse a drink of water.'

'He's better fed and watered than me, missis. Can you hop up under your own steam or do you need a hand?'

'We can manage.' Boney rolls her eyes at Edith.

They heave themselves into the cab and Boney raps on the roof with her knuckles.

'Walk on,' calls the cabbie.

'There was no need to meet me,' says Edith. 'I could have found my own way to the house.'

'Of course, you could. But I didn't want to miss a minute of your visit. What news of *Flurry's Wedding?*'

'It's with Nigel Playfair of the Lyric.'

'He'll snap it up if he's any sense.'

'I shouldn't count my chickens before they're hatched. But he was most encouraging.'

'He knows what's what. I'm glad you sacked little Pinker and took charge yourself. A writer of your stature needs no agent. Your name is your entrée.'

Edith is ashamed to admit she hasn't exactly parted company with her agent – although neither did she send her play to his office. 'He was about to go to New York when I saw him. Some difficulty or other involving his son.'

'A Pinker pup!' Boney screeches.

Edith winces. She sounds like a Skibbereen apple woman. Then she remembers Ethel Smyth cutting short rehearsals to collect her. 'In fact, there are two Pinker pups.'

'Hah! Have they inherited his wee, upturned nose and shiny button eyes?'

For some reason, the image sets them off squawking, and Boney becomes so helpless with laughter that she has to rest her head on Edith's shoulder.

'We're like bacon and eggs, the way we fit together, Edith!'

They pass Woking Golf Club and arrive at her house. Boney pays off the cabbie and together they push past gorse bushes to reach the front gate. Coign is a rambling, mock-Tudor cottage. A bench rests beneath the drawing-room window, for visitors to miss none of Ethel Smyth's virtuoso assaults on the piano when they take the air. Climbing rose bushes are trained along the walls. To the casual eye, the house has stood there for centuries. But Edith is aware that an American patron of the arts, Mary Dodge, gave Boney the money to buy a plot and build on it ten or twelve years ago. She chose the location for its convenience to the golf club.

The interior walls are white and rough cast, while none of the furniture cost more than a pound or two. Even so, Edith is surprised anew by how comfortable the set-up is. The housekeeper, a Sphinx with straw-coloured hair, as economical with words as Ethel Smyth is effusive, appears in the hall when she hears Ethel's key in the lock and waits silently.

'Breaded veal cutlets for lunch,' announces Boney. 'When will they be ready, Sadie?'

'At one, mum.'

'Excellent. Time for a pre-prandial first.' She leads Edith into the sitting room, where she tries to persuade her to take a glass of sambuca.

'It's a digestif, Ethel!' protests Edith. 'I'll have to go for a siesta if I start drinking liqueurs at this time of day.'

'Ah, what's time? I ordered it from the wine merchant in memory of our trip to Sicily.'

'A mouse trotted across my pillow in Taormina.'

'You turned it over and went right back to sleep. Nothing fazes you, divine creature. Now, how about a small glass?'

Edith is obliged to acquiesce, although she doesn't finish it.

Lunch is devoted to Ethel Smyth's account of her investiture at Buckingham Palace, including what the King said to her and, more importantly, she said to the King. Beside her place setting rests a shoebox containing congratulatory telegrams, which she insists on reading aloud one by one.

As soon as decency permits, Edith makes a suggestion. 'How about stretching our legs?' The outdoors dilutes Boney's turbulent presence. 'I haven't had a proper walk in days.'

They stroll along the perimeter of the golf course, Edith keeping an eye out for flying balls, her hostess in full flow about the club's attractions.

'Golf is the most stupendous exercise,' says Boney. 'It's exhilarating.' She rolls the r sumptuously. 'You should try it.'

Edith's mouth turns down.

Boney holds up her hands in surrender. 'It's not for everyone, I accept.'

It's a relief to Edith to be led into the clubhouse. Inside, Boney orders a pot of tea and plate of biscuits, 'fancy ones, not plain', but almost immediately a member engages her in conversation about caddies. Left to her own devices, Edith flicks through some newspapers on the table next to them.

In the *Daily Mail*, a headline on page five catches her eye.

Literary Agent's Death

The esteemed literary agent Mr James Brand Pinker has died of influenza in New York leaving a widow and two sons. Among the authors he represented were Henry James, Joseph Conrad, Arnold Bennett, John Galsworthy and Compton Mackenzie.

She tries to catch Boney's eye, but her friend is holding court. 'Never lost a golf ball ... utter carelessness ... insist on my caddy hunting for it.'

Edith returns to the newspaper and reads through half a column about the unexpected nature of Pinker's death and how doctors were unable to save him. The report continues:

Mr Pinker was a shrewd judge of what the public enjoyed reading. He could spot a bestseller quickly. From modest beginnings in East London, he became a clerk and later a newspaper journalist before setting up his agency in 1896. He spent the past quarter of a century in the service of some seventy-five authors, including stars in the literary firmament.

No mention of Somerville and Ross. Edith feels aggrieved.

He always made a special point of helping young authors in the early stages of their career, when they most needed the aid of an adviser with a thorough knowledge of the literary world and publishing trade. His sons Eric and Ralph Pinker will continue the family business in London and New York.

Edith sets down the newspaper. Now she won't be obliged to have a confrontation with Pinker. Her relief is followed by a prickle of shame. She must write to Mrs Pinker. Perhaps a floral wreath, too. Does she have their home address? Her forehead puckers. The Pinkers leased a country house in Reigate. What's it called? Bury's Court, she's almost certain of it. She'll send flowers there. Martin stayed a night or two with them once, it must be a decade ago. Tasteless furnishings, she reported back. But opulent. 'He certainly feathered his nest,' according to Martin. Pinker married money.

A crash of chair legs as Boney sits beside her. 'Is anything the matter, Edith?'

She points to the headline.

'By George, what a stroke of luck! It means he can't interfere with your Playfair contract. The timing is perfect!'

That expression of Edith's inner thoughts shames her. 'In fairness, Boney, he negotiated some excellent deals in his day for us.'

'His deal-making days are behind him now.'

—

The next afternoon, Boney travels to London with Edith. She'll stay at her usual quarters, a hotel in Lincoln's Inn. Meanwhile, Edith is return-ing to Boyle and Mabel's place in Chelsea.

During the train journey, Boney slaps the palms of her hands against her knees. 'I say, let's you and me go to Hammersmith and see Playfair. Insist he make an immediate decision about your play.'

'Stand down your war chariot, Boney. He's hasn't had it a week. Anyhow, it would be impolite not to make an appointment first.'

'You and your good manners. I'd turn up on his doorstep and brook no refusal. Very well, how about this? What do you say to lunch at Simpson's tomorrow? My treat. We haven't celebrated my dameship properly.'

'Tomorrow I need to spend the day at the British Museum Library. I'm researching a newspaper article.'

'The day after, then.'

'I can't. Mabel has invited some friends to tea. I'm to give them a reading from *Flurry's Wedding*. I need an hour to practise.'

'Oh, may I come to tea? I love hearing you read.'

'It's not my place to invite you. I'm a guest there, singing for her supper. I thought you had appointments?'

Boney's answer is shouted down by a whistle blast as the hurrying train enters the tunnel leading into Waterloo Station.

'What did you say?'

'I'm supposed to be at rehearsals for *The Boatswain's Mate* in three-quarters of an hour. I shall have to shake a leg. Get there *tout de suite*, as they say in gay Paree.'

'Gay Paree feels a universe away. Do you know, I think that's where I was happiest in life.'

'Because you were devoting yourself to art?'

'Yes, at the Délécleuse and Colarossi studios. My drawing was a little weak, but my teachers were encouraging about my use of colour.'

Wheels and brakes screeching, the train draws to a halt. Someone yanks open a window and a puff of acrid smell gusts in. Edith looks out at grey-tinted London and hankers after a field of daffodils.

'We should go to Paris,' says Boney. 'Why not? As soon as Playfair pays you something we'll take off on a jaunt. You're a real workhorse – you need a break.'

'This is a break.'

'Nonsense, it's all family duty and business. I mean a break away from it all. I'll go with you. What larks we'll have! Oh, my dear, your knot has worked its way loose. Allow me.' She leans forward and adjusts Edith's tie. 'There now, I've given you a lovers' knot. That'll hold 'til the end of time.'

Edith slides to one side, levers herself to her feet and checks the seat for lost belongings. She lurches out to the train corridor, Boney in her slipstream burbling about picnics in the Bois de Boulogne.

I am *not* going to Paris and that's that, Edith tells herself. Boney no sooner thinks of something than she does it – she has obligations to no one but herself. Unlike Edith.

A ticket collector takes her return stub. Behind her, Boney causes a hold-up by forgetting where she put hers.

Edith glances over her shoulder. 'Inside your hat.'

'*She opens her mouth with wisdom and the teaching of kindness is on her tongue.* On our next trip, Edith, you can take charge of the tickets. Parisians are less patient than Londoners.'

Edith forges ahead towards the Underground station. Saying nothing is the path of least resistance. Boney chomps through opposition like a weevil through biscuits.

———

Mabel Somerville has made a home in Netherton Grove and any member of the clan is always welcome, even when Boyle is away with his ship, as he is currently. It's not the most fashionable end of Chelsea — too close to St George's Union Infirmary, and distinctly un-grove-like — but Edith is glad of a berth in their three-storied terraced house.

A large, thick envelope is waiting for Edith. She doesn't wait to unbutton her coat before opening it. Inside, a letter from Nigel Playfair rejects her play and returns it to her.

> *Quite unsuitable for the stage* ...
> *Far too many scenes* ...
> *Impossible to put on.*

The ripple of piano scales drifts downstairs. She lifts her head from the letter. Mabel must be in the middle of her daily practice. Edith's play has been turned down, yet life continues as normal for others. All at once, her insides feel emptied out. She sits on a hall chair, the manuscript thudding to the floor. But the letter is still gripped in her hand. She risks another look.

> *Old-fashioned* ...
> *Muddled message* ...
> *Unconditional refusal.*

Should she have implanted more of Shaw's suggestions? Is it possible all her efforts with *Flurry's Wedding* are a misfire?

Almost at once, she overrules the thought. The play simply wasn't what the Lyric wanted – she'll offer it to another producer. Boney will suggest a home.

Mabel Somerville appears on the landing. 'I thought I heard the doorbell. Welcome back, Edith. How was your trip to Woking?'

She puts the letter behind her back. 'Enjoyable, thank you, Mab.'

'My friends are terribly excited about your reading tomorrow.' Edith's heart sinks. It will be an ordeal to read from a play that's just been turned down – what was that odious word? – unconditionally. 'You are still willing, dear? The invitations have gone out.'

'Of course, Mab. You know me, any excuse to show off. By the way, would you mind if I invited Dame Ethel Smyth? She happens to be in town this week and expressed an interest.'

'Your composer friend? Certainly. Perhaps she'd play one of her compositions for us.'

'The difficulty, Mab, would be stopping her.'

———

The rooms are small in Boyle and Mabel's house – space was sacrificed for a suitable address and handsome frontage. To accommodate guests, a set of glass doors between dining and drawing rooms is opened. Edith perches on her sister-in-law's piano seat and faces her audience of a dozen. She has butterflies in her stomach and a frog in her throat. While Mabel says a few words of introduction, she drinks half a glass of water. But as soon as she starts reading, her nerves vanish.

The guests avoid rattling their teacups and laugh on cue – especially when the script calls for a brogue. Is it possible they're enjoying it? Her delivery gains in confidence.

Ethel Smyth sits not more than six inches away from Edith, eyes fastened on her. Afterwards, she rumbles about how the play is a *tour de force* because Miss Somerville strains words through a trellis of loveliness.

Her increasing deafness forces people to shout back at her that yes, it's a masterpiece. Edith cringes. After all, her magnum opus has been refused.

But at least the audience asks for an encore – and with enough persistence to make the request appear genuine. During the applause, Edith notices Mabel's pretty face is rosy with relief. She knows her sister-in-law finds it daunting to entertain in London, having grown up in Sydney. But her Waltzing Matilda cake, topped with pineapple slices and pecan nuts, is a triumph.

After the guests have departed, and Mabel is directing her servants to rearrange the furniture, Boney whispers to Edith about the two of them taking some air.

'It's dark out, Boney.'

'There are streetlights. You aren't in the middle of West Cork now.'

'Mind the paintwork!' cries Mabel.

'Look, I can't hear myself think with your sister-on-law fussing over her furniture. She should use a spirit level and be done with it if she cares so much about straight lines. Do come out. I've hardly seen you. Everyone wanted to monopolize the great playwright.'

'Let's sit in the morning room,' says Edith. 'It'll be quiet in there. As a matter of fact, I want to show you something.'

'Rather,' says Boney.

Edith raises her voice. 'You don't mind, do you Mab, if Dame Ethel and I have a little chat in the morning room?'

'Go right ahead.'

When they are seated in the small, bay-windowed room overlooking the street, she produces the damning letter. The paper feels forlorn between her fingertips, as if knows its contents are unwelcome. She watches Boney read it.

'How beastly, Edith! I shall boycott his theatre.'

'He takes rather a dim view of *Flurry's Wedding*.'

'Pearls before swine.'

'I thought casting might be the issue – suitable Flurrys can't be found under every gooseberry bush. But I never dreamed the work itself would be rejected.'

'He's talking nonsense. You are Edith Somerville! You have magic in your fingertips!'

'But Mr Playfair isn't even willing to give me a short run. I could have undertaken rewrites, I could have, I don't know, done whatever was ...' Edith's voice trails off.

'Don't be downhearted, dearest. He's not the only impresario in London.'

'Can you recommend one?'

'Of course. Your play will have its day in the sun. But first, you must stand up for yourself. March straight over to the Lyric, tell Playfalse he's an imbecile and plant a tomahawk in his skull!'

'What good would that do, Boney? Other than relieve my feelings? I'm not really in a position to stick in the spurs here. I don't have the power.'

'Never underestimate relieving your feelings.'

'Maybe he has a point ...'

Boney is on her feet and stamping from one end of the room to the other. 'Here's what we'll do. You and I will call on Mr Playfair and ask him to indicate the scenes which he regards as' – she consults the letter – '"self-indulgent", "unfunny" and "laboured".' A little humiliating, I admit. But his feedback will help you to reshape the material and find it a more deserving home. He's a boor, but he knows his onions.'

Edith sifts her options. Boney has a knack for quarrelling with people. Equally, she gets things done. But it's mortifying to ask for help from someone who has just rejected her play in the bluntest terms.

'I say, Edith, how about changing the setting? Make your characters Cossacks instead of Irish. You lot really are out of favour in Britain. That might be why he's turned you down.'

'I know nothing about Russia, Boney.'

'Haven't you read their novelists? Pushkin, Dostoevsky, Tolstoy?'

'Afraid not.'

'Their playwrights? How about Chekhov?'

Edith shakes her head.

'Really, Edith, you ought to be more systematic about your reading. It can't all be Shakespeare and the English classics. The Russians are exhilarating. There's a Russian saying, "The Cossack will starve but his horse will have eaten its fill." See? Just like your precious Irish. Converting your play would be no trouble.'

Edith is transfixed by an image of Flurry in a fur hat, racing across the steppes. It's tempting. But no, she couldn't manage it. 'I'll have you know this is an Irish play, not a Russian one, Boney. But some feedback from Mr Playfair would be useful. Maybe I should go and see him. I'll think about it.'

'I'll meet you at Hammersmith tube station tomorrow evening at six. Fricassee Playfair as an hors d'oeuvre, and we can dine together afterwards.'

'I said I'll think about it, Boney. Don't rush me.'

Boney looks off to the side. Uncharacteristically tentative, she says, 'Do just bear something in mind about Stage Land, Edith. It's a hair-trigger business. No one can ever predict whether the public will take to a play. If I were you, I'd start work on another novel. You know what you're doing there.'

'You mean give up on *Flurry's Wedding*?'

'Good heavens, no. I mean don't put all your eggs in one basket. Get going on another novel while this theatre business rumbles away in the background.'

———

That night, Edith consults with Martin.

youwill set the westend alight

She studies the automatic writing, wondering why she doesn't find it reassuring.

seventeen

Edith stutters about London, licking her wounds and reflecting on whether or not to beard Nigel Playfair in his den. She feels ghosted — insubstantial, humiliated and out of step with this world which once appreciated her talents. When she looks around, she sees faces where the features are blurred. But perhaps she is the one being rubbed out?

Yet London is beguiling in the particular way it knows how to be. Sometimes, she avails of its pleasures by catching a red double-decker omnibus drawn by three horses — her leg won't allow her to climb to the top, unfortunately — at other times, she walks the thronged streets. A visit to Hatchard's at 187 Piccadilly allows her to check its stocks of her books. She finds her latest title, plus all three of the Irish R.M. collections, but considers their placing could be more prominent. Furtively, she rearranges the shelf display.

Outside on the street again, she makes an effort to conjure up Flurry. Inside her head, she says: 'The setting: Piccadilly Circus. Flurry Knox strolls into view wearing evening clothes. He stops by the statue of Eros to light a cigarette.' But he refuses to be invoked.

Thanks to her network of relatives and literary contacts, she is invited to a merry-go-round of social events. A distant cousin on her mother's side summons her to luncheon in an unattractive house close to Hyde Park Corner, whose interior has an extravagance of plush which injures her eye everywhere it lands. Her hostess is resplendent in a burnt sienna frock with a sheen as if raindrops were captured in the cloth. Edith is relieved she took Mabel's advice and wore her most boastful hat.

'My dear, may I ask, is your *chapeau* from Paris?'

'Skibbereen,' says Edith.

Her hostess recovers herself and points to a man with a weathered face and lavish moustache, glumly inspecting some cloisonné eggs. Although he's not wearing uniform, he radiates a pukka, military-type aura.

'Field Marshal Sir Henry Wilson, dear. Chief of the Imperial General Staff during the war,' she hisses in Edith's ear. 'He's just been elected Member of Parliament for North Down – somewhere in the north of Ireland, apparently. Resigned from the army especially to stand. I'll introduce you.'

Edith shakes hands with a tall man, a year or two younger than her, with the face of a hanging judge. He has a brisk manner and old scarring above his left eye. They have never met, but she expects they know people in common. Cameron told her Wilson was one of the people pushing hard in 1918 for conscription to be extended to Ireland, but Lloyd George knew it wouldn't fly.

When they are seated for luncheon, she finds herself beside the field marshal. A conscious look passes between her and their hostess on the opposite side of the table. Edith is being given a place of honour. In return, she's to keep the great man amused.

Over pea and mint soup laced with an excess of salt, Edith makes conversation. 'I believe you grew up in Ireland, field marshal?'

'Just outside Edgeworthstown. The Currygrane estate.'

'The dear friend of an ancestor of mine lived in Longford, too. Maria Edgeworth. Perhaps you're familiar with her work?'

'More of a Kipling man. *We know, when all is said, / We perish if we yield.*'

'Yielding can take strength. Sometimes, it's the right thing to do.'

'Nonsense! Can't think of a single instance.'

'I can.'

'Well, naturally. You're one of the fair sex. You're predisposed to yield.'

'Am I really? Anyhow, I believe Britain ought to grant Ireland dominion status.'

'That would be a mistake.'

'Because it looks like weakness?'

'Because surrendering to those renegades in Ireland would have a deplorable impact on Palestine, India and Egypt. There are larger issues at stake, Miss Somerville. Irish self-government doesn't suit the strategic unity of the empire.'

A die-hard. Edith sets down her soup spoon and prepares to do battle. 'How is there to be a peace settlement if concessions aren't made?'

The arrival of beef wellington interrupts their conversation, and Edith makes small talk with her neighbour on the other side. Conscious of eye signals from her hostess, she returns to Wilson, determined to avoid politics.

'Do you hunt, field marshal?'

'When I can.'

'I have a couple of topping young hunters for sale. One of them could jump St Paul's Cathedral. You might know someone in the market for a mount?'

'Afraid not.' He drains his glass of claret and nods at the footman to replenish it. 'I suppose you're an admirer of Collins.'

'I haven't met him.'

'Second-rate chap. All he's good for is spreading atrocity propaganda. Every law of civilized warfare's been ignored by that rabble he runs. Better men did their duty in Flanders, up to their eyes in muck and blood. Better men are buried there.'

'And some of them were Irish.'

He spears a piece of meat. 'Ulster did her duty during the war. We stand by Ulster now. Anything less would be a betrayal. That's why we've partitioned Ireland. Ulster Unionists won't live under a Roman Catholic government and I, for one, don't blame them.'

'But you aren't standing by Ulster, field marshal. I understand this new Northern Ireland territory consists of six counties, not nine. Donegal, Cavan and Monaghan are to be included in the southern state.'

A gridwork of broken veins on his cheeks pops up. Loudly, he says, 'Better for two-thirds of passengers to save themselves than for everyone to drown.' The eruption of passion simultaneously repels and intrigues Edith.

Their hostess leans across the table, around a dramatic silver centre-piece composed of two swans with their wings outstretched for flight. 'Miss Somerville has written some topping novels, field marshal.'

Wilson clears his throat. 'Yes. Splendid.'

'Do you read novels, field marshal?'

'Not much. Lady Wilson' – he nods down the table – 'is susceptible to them.'

Edith casts round. 'Are you a playgoer?'

'Now and again. You?'

'When I have the opportunity.'

'And have you managed to see anything during your current stay in London?'

'Indeed, I made a point of it. I had a most enjoyable evening at *The Beggar's Opera* at the Lyric Hammersmith.'

Unexpectedly, his tone of perpetual exasperation softens. 'Lady Wilson and I saw that production. It's a little off the beaten track but we're enormously taken by the show. Hoping to go again, as a matter of fact. Tickets are in short supply. But I've left my name at the box office for cancellations.'

'What draws you back to it, field marshal?'

'Lady Wilson is musical. She rates the songs.'

'Miss Somerville is on close terms with Dame Ethel Smyth,' says their hostess.

'Ah, the composeress,' says Wilson. 'Lady Wilson was favourably impressed by one of her operas. Ships in it. Didn't make it along, myself.'

'*The Wreckers*. And what do you like about *Beggar*?' asks Edith.

'Seeing that degenerate Macheath get his comeuppance.' The field marshal's fingers seek out his moustache. 'Although I must say, the young

lady playing Polly Peachum is most awfully talented. It's well worth a
return trip for her alone.'

—

'Mr Playfair, how do you do?'

Nigel Playfair looks as surprised as if Edith has just fallen from the
sky at his feet. Armed with the knowledge of his arrival time, which he
told her was a golden rule on performance days, she has been waiting by
the stage door in advance of the matinée.

'Miss Somerville, to what do I owe the pleasure?'

'Might I tell you my business inside, Mr Playfair? It's a little chilly
out here.'

Courtesy wars with prudence on his face.

She hunches her shoulders in a shiver. 'I'm hoping for a few words
of advice. Nothing more.'

'Of course, forgive me. Do come in.'

He settles her into a chair in his office – even more shabby by daylight
– but offers no refreshments. She understands this meeting will be brief
and takes out her copy of the script, along with a notebook and pencil.

'I hoped you might do me the courtesy of showing me where you
felt my script could be trimmed. It's an imposition, I know, but I'd be
terribly grateful.'

'Miss Somerville, with the greatest respect, I simply don't have
the time to go through your work line by line. You said you wanted my
advice – here it is. Abandon playwriting and return to novels and short
stories, where you excel.'

Abandon playwriting? She feels winded, as if thrown from a horse.
'I've no doubt.' She clears her throat and starts again. 'I've no doubt
Flurry's Wedding could use some spit and polish. But you'd … consign it
… to the scrapheap?'

'Madam, let me be clear. You've taken bread and turned it into stones.
I wish I had happier news. As regards playwriting – many are called but
few are chosen. You have other gifts. Concentrate on them.'

'Is it because my play is set in the 1890s? I could advance it a few decades, set it just before the war, perhaps.'

'It's not the period, it's the material. You've seen what Bennett did with an old John Gay play – he fashioned new clothes for it. Bennett's a novelist like you, but he took a vicious political satire, out of copyright, and transformed it. He didn't just salvage it. He unpicked it, reimagined it and revolutionized it.'

'But surely that's what I've done. Taken my own material and re-worked it.'

Playfair stands. 'I'm afraid you haven't. Your characters are drawn with a blunt pencil. Your plotting is unintentionally farcical. And you have written so many scenes, it would require a platoon of stagehands to change them. In short, your play is beyond redemption. And now, Miss Somerville, if you'll excuse me, a great many matters are pressing on my attention.'

He opens the door and walks into the corridor. She has no choice but to jam the script back in her bag and follow him.

'You, there!' Playfair clicks his fingers. "Fellow with the paintbrush.'

A stagehand in overalls is touching up a piece of scenery. He looks over his shoulder. Then, still holding his paintbrush and pot, he walks off in the opposite direction.

Playfair calls again. 'I say, are you deaf? Come back and escort this lady out, please.'

The stagehand sets his brush on the paint-pot lid, pulls the peak of his cap over his forehead and moves towards them.

From a distance, his face is fuzzy. But prickles on Edith's skin identify him. Her heartbeat lurches and judders, before resuming at a staccato skip. Aghast, she looks to Playfair for help, but he is in the process of bowing, retreating and closing the door.

She's alone with the whistler.

The stagehand keeps his eyes on the floor. 'This way.'

She doesn't budge.

His tongue darts across his lips, moistening them. 'This way, lady.'

She remains pinned to the spot.

'Want to get me the sack? Guv'nor says show you out.'

The accent is pitch-perfect Cockney, but she isn't fooled. Those eyes like rain-drenched pebbles – she'd know them anywhere.

'*He'd kill a fella and ate him after.*'

This is the beast who kicked Dooley to death. The adrenaline of fear mixed with outrage gives back her voice. 'Why should I care if they sack you?'

He stretches out a meaty hand and pushes her in the small of her back. 'Time you was going.'

Like it or not, she is propelled along by the force of his hand. 'Robbed many horses lately?'

'Dunno what you mean.'

'I don't believe you.'

'You're mixing me up wiv someone else.'

'I never forget a face. We met in Ireland last year.'

'Never been in Ireland.'

'Liar!'

'Served nearly four years in the Norfolks. 'Onourably discharged after the war ended. Robbing 'orses ain't in my line.'

By the stage door, Edith manages to shake free. She purses her lips and whistles a few bars of the tune she heard from him in Drishane.

Oh Danny boy, the pipes, the pipes are calling
From glen to glen and down the mountainside

His eyes slit. He pushes one fist into the other. 'We can do this naice or we can do it nasty. Now, if I was you, I'd run along 'ome and put your feet up. While you still can.'

'Scoundrel!' she cries.

He catches her by the shoulders and gives a shake that sets her teeth rattling. 'There's more where that come from.' Abruptly, he lets her loose and lumbers away.

Outside, Edith is obliged to lean for support against the brick wall of the laneway, smearing dirt onto her coat. Her vision blurs – the buildings in front of her appear to be wobbling. She shuts her eyes and fights to regain control.

What should she do? She could go back inside and tell Nigel Playfair he has an IRA man on his payroll. She could alert Scotland Yard. Or the Home Office. Or the Prime Minister. But what if the whistler tracks her down and pays her back for interfering? Or takes it out on some other member of the Somerville family?

Holding the wall for support, she inches out to the street and flags down a hansom cab. Expense be hanged, she doesn't feel able for the Underground.

—

'I expect those Republicans of yours are intending to blow us all to kingdom come,' says Boney. 'I bet they have barrels of dynamite hidden in the theatre. Your chaps are notorious for dynamiting.'

'That was the Fenians,' says Edith. 'And it was decades ago.' Her gaze wanders across the stucco ceiling of the Lyons Tea House where they are meeting. 'I can't puzzle out why the whistler is working in a theatre.'

'It's cover for him to spy and plot without drawing attention to himself. Stage Land is a free and easy world. People come and go all the time. On no account must you go back to the Lyric, Edith – he might do something desperate.'

'I wasn't intending to.' Apart from anything else, Nigel Playfair has shown her the door.

'Promise me, dearest. I know how plucky you are. But I'm older and wiser than you. I couldn't bear it if anything happened.'

'I promise, Boney. Although you know perfectly well you're only ten days older. It doesn't really count.'

'I wonder if he followed you over here for some reason?'

'Highly unlikely. He looked as shocked to see me as I was to see him.' Edith shifts position on her decidedly hard chair. 'Is there a target near the Lyric, do you suppose? Someplace Irish separatists might want to attack?'

A barge hoots, passing under Blackfriars Bridge, which is within sight of the white-and-gold teahouse frontage.

'That's it – the river,' cries Boney. 'The Lyric is close to the Thames. It's elementary, my dear Watson!'

'Why does that matter?'

'It's a highway. Your rebels could reach all sorts of destinations by river.' Her blue eyes bulge from their sockets. 'The Houses of Parliament are by the Thames. I bet they're planning to do a Guy Fawkes!'

'Steady on, we don't have any proof.'

'Proof be hanged. I have a gut instinct about this. What does yours tell you?'

That the whistler is a bad lot – he'd stop at nothing. 'Perhaps we should go to the police.'

'Delay could be fatal. We'd never forgive ourselves.'

'You're right. Where's the nearest police station? Is there one around the corner on Fleet Street? Or up towards St Paul's?'

'There's a station at Charing Cross. Let's go at once.' Boney signals for the bill.

'You're coming with me?'

'Naturally, you darling dimwit. We're two horses harnessed to the one chariot.'

'What a ripper you are.'

Boney rushes her out to the street, where a gust of wind from the river causes Edith to clamp a hand onto her hat. As she does, a loose folio marked with newsprint flies past. Looking behind, she notices a man in a brown derby hat struggling with his newspaper.

———

As soon as he sets down his pen, Edith realizes the desk sergeant is a doubting Thomas. He shifts from one foot to the other, boots creaking. Probably, his bunions are acting up. Policemen always have bunions, in her experience.

'So, let's get this straight. You believe there's an Irish rebel working in the Lyric Theatre who intends to blow up Parliament. Is that correct?' he asks.

'Yes.' Bullish, Boney answers for them.

'And you base this prediction on a hunch, madam? Is that it? Or a premonition?'

'On the fact he's a known IRA member. He's part of a nest of cut-throats who trespassed at the home of Miss Somerville, where they robbed her of horses and other valuables. Look here, my good man, you're not treating this with the seriousness it deserves. Fetch us your superior officer.'

'I'm afraid you have to deal with me, madam. The duty inspector is otherwise detained.'

She slaps her calling card onto the incident book. 'Send in this to him. *Dame* Ethel Smyth. I'm sure he'll squeeze us in. We can wait, if necessary.'

Mentally, Edith groans. Ethel Smyth is going all Ethel on her. Two heads aren't better than one when one of those heads is Boney's.

The sergeant sets his elbows on the desk and leans across it, his metal uniform buttons tapping against wood. 'Madam, the inspector has no time to squeeze anything in. We have a murder case on our hands. A young woman has been found strangled in her bedroom in Farringdon.' He turns his attention to Edith. 'Now, what was that about trespassers in your home, Miss, um, Somerstown. Whereabouts in London was that?'

She reads his name badge. Holohan. Why, he's one of theirs. Although his accent is Kent, if she's not mistaken. 'Not London, sergeant. I live in County Cork, in southern Ireland. We were raided several times by Irish Republicans.'

'Did they threaten an explosion at any stage of your acquaintance with them, madam?'

'She doesn't have an acquaintance with them.' Ethel Smyth gives the sergeant a look that could slice and dice onions. 'They're not neighbours, or people she knows from church. These men broke into her home and tied up her and her brother, Colonel Somerville. It's a miracle they escaped with their lives.'

'Did you report the break-in, madam?' the policeman asks Edith.

'Naturally,' says Edith. 'But it won't make much difference. Sergeant, I'm sure you have members of the public landing in on you with all sorts of stories about crimes. Some of them utterly implausible.'

'It has been known, madam.'

A snatch of drunken song bursts from one of the holding cells. Something about a sailor's life on the ocean wide.

'Pipe down, Taffy,' calls a police constable.

A door is rattled. 'We was promised tea an hour ago,' shouts another voice.

'You'll get it when I'm good and ready,' says the constable.

The sergeant raises his voice. 'Bring them in a cuppa, Acheson. It'll calm things down. I can't hear myself think here. Now madam, where were we?'

Edith holds his gaze. 'Believe me, I am not given to imaginings. I have learned to trust my intuition. But why should you, sergeant? Doubt me, by all means. That's common sense on your part. Nevertheless, it's highly suspicious that a chap from one of Michael Collins's flying columns is hanging around London, pretending to be someone he's not. The evidence I'm laying before you is circumstantial, nothing more. But I would be failing in my civic duty if I did not report it.'

He opens the incident book and lifts his pen again. 'Working as a stagehand in the Lyric, you say?'

'Just so.' Ethel Smyth jumps in. 'You should haul him in for questioning.'

'We need to have reasonable grounds, madam.'

'You have. He's an Irish rebel. Miss Somerville's just told you.'

'England's had a dose of Ireland to last us for years. But we can't go hauling in every Mick and Paddy knocking about London. The holding cells would be chock-a-block. Now, could you give me a description of the man, Miss Summers? And do you know what name he's going by?'

'Edith, why not draw him? Miss Somerville is frightfully good at portraits, Sergeant.'

'Words would be preferable, madam. When you're ready.'

Quickly, Edith provides him with height, build and colouring. 'You have my name and London address. I'll be here for several more weeks.' She turns to Boney. 'I think we've occupied enough of Sergeant Holohan's time. Good day.'

Edith leaves, and Boney has no choice but to follow her out into Charing Cross Road.

'That fellow was borderline insolent,' grumbles Boney.

'He's the first line of defence, that's all. It's a responsible job.'

'He had all the authority of an amateur organ-grinder. Did your governesses teach you nothing except the multiplication table, Edith? You need to lay down the law with these people. We really should have refused to leave until we saw an inspector.'

Boney is always so emphatic. Edith thinks longingly of an afternoon nap. 'I don't blame him for being dubious. The story does sound a bit far-fetched in the cold light of day. I think I'll run along home now, dear. You were very kind to come to the police station with me.'

'You know there's nothing I wouldn't do for you, Edith.'

'What a passion you have for slaying dragons.'

Despite her best efforts, Edith limps as she makes her way towards the Underground station. She half-turns, intending to wave at Boney, and glimpses a man in a brown derby hat disappearing into a tobacconist's shop.

'Rest up, my treasure,' trumpets Boney.

———

The following day, riffling through the late edition of the *Evening Standard*, Edith is transfixed by a headline on page four.

Police Raid On London Theatre

STAFF were shocked today at a London theatre when members of the Metropolitan Police raided the premises with an arrest warrant for a scene shifter lately arrived from Ireland.

The drama unfolded at the Lyric Theatre in Hammersmith, home to the successful and long-running musical The Beggar's Opera. The man did not turn up for work today and police believe he was tipped off in advance and absconded.

Police conducted a search of his lodgings but it yielded no trace of the fugitive. It seems likely the Irishman fled overnight. Neighbours reported sounds shortly before dawn indicating the wanted man making his escape.

An upstairs back window was found lying open by his landlady, Mrs Thelma Barnstable, who is assisting police with their inquiries. A subversive Irish publication was found under the mattress.

'The man was ever so polite and helpful,' said promising young actress Miss Rosina Bridewell, who has a small but key role in the popular show. 'He sounded as English as roast beef. I'm amazed to hear he's an Irish rebel. I'd never have put him down as one.'

Scotland Yard is asking the public for information on John Green, described as just short of six feet tall and well-built with brown hair and a full moustache. He may also use the name Sean Crowley.

'I was right,' says Edith. 'Just wait 'til Boney hears.'

eighteen

The mistscape stifles everything. Murky and yellow, the fog rolls along, deadening sound, obscuring shapes, pinching extremities. Edith shivers as she gropes her way down Netherton Grove. Her sister-in-law warned her against leaving the house. But Mabel was a 'laugh in the morning, cry by nightfall' sort of person, always predicting the worst possible outcome. As soon as she advised Edith to cancel her appointment with Mr Herbert Tring from the Society of Authors, Edith was determined to get to Westminster and keep it. An omnibus from the Fulham Road, only a few minutes away by foot, would carry her almost to the society's front door.

No sooner has she descended the front steps and walked a few paces than she realizes her error. What looked like a few foggy feelers a little earlier in the day is now a fog in full bloom. It never fails to surprise Edith how quickly it develops in London. She is enveloped in great, smelly buffetings. Within a few paces, she feels damp to the skin. She ties her scarf across her nose and mouth, but the strip of material offers inadequate protection – soon, her eyes are stinging, her throat is raw.

The fog slows her progress to a snail's pace. At least the streetlights have been lit early. She knows she has to turn right somewhere near here, but street signs are impossible to read and distance can't be gauged. And does she really want to risk crossing the street? What if she steps straight into the path of an omnibus?

If there was a policeman about, she could ask him to help her across, but it's as if London has been depopulated overnight. The occasional clop of horse hooves and sputter of a motor engine tell her she isn't by herself – vehicles are passing – but almost no one else is on the streets. Her heart jumps when a woman holding a lantern looms out of the fog bank and almost collides with her.

'I say, could you—' begins Edith, but the woman vanishes as quickly as she materialized. She's alone again. If only she'd sent Doris, the parlour maid, to the post office on Tothill Street. A telegram to Mr Tring would have taken care of the meeting. Crablike, she edges along, holding onto the sides of buildings and railings. Her foot kicks against something that makes a clatter. It sounds like an empty bottle. She tries to feel for it with her sole, in case it trips her up, but the object has bowled away. The fog gives her the impression she's been walking in circles. Perhaps she should go into a shop and check her directions. She passes a bakery, but it's bolted and shuttered. A few doors along is a public house, which appears to be open judging by the glow from its windows and fanlight above the door. She can hear the rise and fall of voices inside. No, she won't go into a pub. There's bound to be some other establishment open.

All at once, the metal beneath her fingers turns to air. She pauses, nervous of taking a misstep and stumbling. Swiping through the advancing clouds with her walking stick, she peers ahead, disorientated. It occurs to her that the safest course would be to do a volte-face. An I-told-you-so from Mabel is preferable to a broken leg.

From behind, a disembodied hand cups her elbow. She smothers a cry.

A muffled voice speaks. 'If you'll allow me, Miss Somerville. I'll see you safely to where you're going.'

'Who's that?'

'A friend from home, ma'am.'

'I know that voice.'

'Do you?'

She turns to face the figure emerging from the haze. 'Is that you, Denis? Denis from back home?'

'None other, Miss Somerville.'

A scarf covers the lower half of his face. Peering, she recognizes a pair of blinking green eyes. 'Could you help a lady in distress, Denis?' Fog enters her windpipe and her breath becomes laboured. 'I had an appointment. But I've changed my mind.'

'At your service, ma'am.'

'I'd be most glad ... of your arm ... to take me home. It's only a few minutes away.'

'I've a friend with a motor car near here, he'll give you a lift to wherever you want to go.' He pulls his scarf away from his mouth, cups his hands around it and cries, 'Helloooo!' He waits, eyes watering. Repeats the call. 'Helloooo!' Covers his mouth again with his scarf. 'He's not far off but you can't see further than your hand here. I'd go looking for him but then I mightn't find you again.'

'You're very sweet to take this trouble on my account.' She sneezes, finds her handkerchief by touch in her bag and blows her nose. 'But really, my brother's house is quite close. It's just back up this street.'

'Let's give it a minute. My friend is nearby. I thought the sea mists at home were bad but I've never known the like of these fogs.'

'No comparison.'

'You'd wonder how people manage at all.'

'In Castletownshend, the people say if you go astray in the mist' – she hacks out a cough – 'you'll find your way home by turning your jacket and hat inside out.'

'Whisht, now, ma'am. Don't try to talk. The fog's getting at your chest.'

She knows he's talking sense. But something about the isolation caused by the weather conditions forces her to speak. 'A *piseog*, I dare say. But I'd almost try it today.'

She can tell he isn't listening.

'Let me chance going to look for him, Miss Somerville. He can't be far – I'd stake my mother's life on it. You stay put now.'

'Don't leave me!' She clamps her hands on his lapels.

Gently, he shakes himself loose. 'I'll be back before you know it. I'll count my paces. That way I can count my way back to you. One, two …' He plunges away, swallowed up in the swirl.

The rhythm of his footsteps echoes back at her. Listening intently, Edith hears a faint 'Helloooo.' She grips the railings, straining to hear it again. Other sounds seep through the fog. The despondent blast of a foghorn, the howl of a dog. Perhaps it's lost, like her. Alone amid these poisonous vapours, Edith's doubts spiral. It would be easy for someone to prey on her – snatch her bag or knock her over. Denis told her to wait but he's a country boy, she begins to doubt his ability to plot a course through a fog-laden city.

'What should I do, Martin?' she asks. Her voice sounds timid. It shames her. She can't turn into a faint-hearted old lady. Edith Somerville must fend for herself.

If she stays in a straight line and retraces her steps, she must reach home. Clamping her hand on the railings, she begins to work her way backwards, stamping as she goes to stop her feet from turning numb. But she must have taken a wrong turn because the glimmer of the Underground sign tells her she's at Fulham Broadway station.

Any port in a storm. Pursued by tendrils of tobacco-yellow fog, Edith manages to gain the station. There's a bench near the ticket office. She sinks onto it to catch her breath. A burst of coughing overtakes her, and she pulls down her scarf, takes some deep breaths, and massages her throat with gloved fingers. Some lozenges in her bag might help. She retrieves the packet and sucks on a sweet.

Pages rustling inside the ticket office indicate an employee with nothing but the newspaper to occupy him. By the ticket barrier, she sees another uniformed functionary in an attitude of resentful inactivity. The station is deserted otherwise.

'I say,' she calls out to the ticket collector. 'Excuse me, are the trains running? I need a westbound one.'

'They are, mum, but there ain't a westbound train due to pass through here for another forty-five minutes. Fog's playing havoc with the timetable.'

'You didn't wait!' Panting, Denis bursts into the station, boots thudding across the tiles.

'I thought you weren't coming back. Why, you look terrified!'

'You gave me a fright. I thought something must have happened to you. Come on, now, Miss Somerville. I managed to scare up my pal. He's outside the station.'

'I'm not sure about a motor car, Denis. You hear such dreadful stories about collisions in the fog.'

His voice turns wheedling. 'He's a careful driver, my friend. You'll be in safe hands. Door- to-door service.'

His tone is oddly insistent. 'Have a cough drop while I catch my breath,' she suggests.

'No.' He goes to the exit, waves at someone, hurries back to her. 'Won't you come with me, Miss Somerville? I can't leave you here like this. It wouldn't be right.'

Edith studies him. He's over-excited, quivering like a dog on the scent of a fox. The paralysis which overcame her in the fog has worn off. Now that she's warmed up in the station, she is starting to wonder about the coincidence. First the whistler, then Denis. Two members of the same West Cork flying column here in London. What are the odds? 'Quite a fluke meeting you, Denis. How on earth did you fetch up in London?'

'I had to … I wanted … I needed a change, ma'am.'

'I'm glad you took my advice and got away from those disreputable friends of yours.'

He doesn't respond. She notices that he's still wearing his scarf over the lower part of his face, masking his identity. Her suspicions multiply.

'How *did* you happen to run across me today?'

'Luck, ma'am.'

Larded with anxiety, she continues to watch him. It doesn't take a detective to see he's ill at ease. All at once, her thoughts untangle. She's convinced he loitered outside the house and followed her. He must be mixed up in the same business with the theatre as the whistler. Edith realizes she has to shake off Denis. She's in a public place, there are members of staff nearby – he can't kidnap her in plain sight. But the minute she climbs into a motor car with him she's in his power.

She forces a smile to her lips. 'What a prize fool I was to leave the house today. Now then, I don't believe I'll take you up on your kind offer. I'll just rest here a while and wait for the fog to lift. Goodbye, Denis.'

He bends down and puts his mouth close to her ear. 'It's not goodbye yet. I've a friend who's keen for a word with you.'

'Is he in the same line of business as yourself?'

'He is. I'm under orders to bring you to him.'

Her eyes flicker to the ticket collector.

'I'm thinking you'd be as well coming quietly. Your brother's wife, the Australian woman. At home alone, isn't she? She'd make a useful hostage.'

'She's not alone. Your information is incorrect.'

Something about their interaction alerts the ticket collector, who stares openly at them. Just then a flock of passengers, tired of waiting for trains, disgorges from the escalator and he is forced to attend to his job.

Denis keeps his voice low. 'Don't tell lies, Miss Somerville. You can't count on the servants. They wouldn't lift a finger to help her.'

Edith recognizes the truth in his words. Mabel's staff aren't fond of her.

'Do as you're told and nobody gets hurt,' he says. 'You'll get home safely, I promise you.'

Her face is immobile but her eyes blaze. 'Your promises are worthless.'

'Look, we've wasted enough time. The man I'm bringing you to meet isn't the patient sort.'

Edith's eyes roam the station in search of someone she can appeal to for help. But there is no discreet way to do it. And if Mabel falls into this gang's hands, she'll wither away. Her nerves would never recover.

'Let's go,' says Denis.

Just then, the man in the ticket booth pulls down his hatch and appears through the office door. Slowly, Edith stands up. The ticket seller pays no attention to them as he locks the door and joins the ticket collector for a chat. But Edith changes course and hobbles across to them, waving her walking stick.

'I say, excuse me. Would one of you gentlemen kindly oblige a lady?'

'What are you at, you aul' bitch!' mutters Denis.

'I need someone to call me a policeman.'

'No need, it's taken care of,' cries Denis.

'Could you help me, please? I'd be most awfully grateful,' says Edith.

'No problem, mum,' says the ticket collector. 'Glad to take a look. Though I wouldn't bank on any being out and about in this pea-souper. Somefing the matter?'

Denis joins them, so close Edith smells the fresh sweat from his armpits. 'Bit of a mix-up here. I have a motor car waiting for us.'

'I don't want to go with him.'

'Are you bothering this lady, Paddy?' The ticket collector moves between them.

'I'm not, indeed I'm not.' Denis widens his arms, conciliatory. 'We know each other from home. I have a car outside for the lady. She's worried about a friend called Mabel. Jumpy sort, the kind that'd leap right out of her skin if you said boo to her.'

'No,' says Edith. 'Leave her alone.'

'Mabel goes to a bridge club every Wednesday afternoon, doesn't she? Coleridge Gardens.'

They know Mabel's name and her movements. She's outfoxed and knows it.

'Lady?' The ticket collector turns to Edith.

'I – I. Sorry. Thank you. I'll take him up on that offer of a lift, after all. I shouldn't have troubled you.'

Denis tries to catch hold of her arm. Straight-backed, she bats him away and stalks to the exit. Outside, patches of London street are popping up and vanishing, as foggy coils shift about, revealing snapshots before blotting them out again. A motorized hackney chugs by the kerb, its window shades pulled down. Edith thinks of the *coiste bodhar*, the death coach.

Denis hustles her into the vehicle and fists the back of the driver's seat. A jolt, and they begin moving.

'You took your bleedin' time,' says the driver. He's wearing a brown derby on the back of his head.

'I did the best I could,' says Denis.

'I did the best I could,' mimics the voice in a falsetto.

A Liverpool accent, Edith notices. Its nasal inflection is distinctive. She makes out the back of his neck, two hairy hands on the wheel and one hairy ear.

Denis pushes back his cap and wipes his sleeve across his forehead. He burrows into the corner behind the driver, draws his feet to his chest and curls into a hedgehog.

He's still wearing Aylmer's boots. They've changed for the worse in his care – unblacked and unacquainted with a boot tree. Big Ben chimes the hour, causing him to uncoil momentarily, lift one of the blinds and look out. They must be somewhere near Westminster. He frowns, tugs away his scarf at last, and settles down to gnaw at bitten fingernails.

She reviews her dwindling options and considers it politic to be pleasant to her kidnapper. 'You're a long way from home, Denis.'

A grunt. He's been practising at the whistler school of charm.

'How do you like London?'

He shrugs. 'I'm not here to see the sights.'

'Why are you here?'

'To pull the lion's tail.'

'Ah, Denis, this won't end well for you. You should go on back to Ireland while you can.'

Denis rubs the heel of each hand into his eyes. When he drops them, the whites are veined and reddened. He looks utterly exhausted.

Edith says 'I remember how difficult I found it to sleep at night, the first time I visited. We're spoiled for silence in Ireland.'

Now his eyes twitch towards her. 'The noise does never be stopping here. Night and day, there's no difference betwixt them. And the people everywhere! More people than I thought the world could hold, all bunched up together. Roaring like a pack of heifers. Your head'd be melted by this place.'

Edith leans forward. 'Denis, I don't know what you're up to and I don't want to know. It's none of my business. Can't we leave it at that? Let me out. I'll forget I ever saw you and you can forget you ever saw me.'

'No. I've to deliver you to somebody.'

'Who?'

'That's for me to know and you to guess.'

'I was never any good at riddles.'

He shrugs.

'So, you didn't cut loose from those friends of yours, after all. All your talking in Castletownshend was only that. Talk.' She leans her forehead against the window shade, not caring that it's soiled and smelly. 'It's not too late, Denis. Let me go. You're better than them.'

He broods, until all at once he flares up. 'Shut your face! You wrecked months of work. You were seen at the police station. You're an informer, that's what you are. Lowest of the low.'

nineteen

The hackney slows, the driver says something about gates.

'Stay here.' Denis jumps out.

Edith tries to see where they are but all she catches is a patch of wire fencing. They could be anywhere. Now she feels the vehicle roll forward, taking its time. Voices. Male. Barking instructions. The motor halts, its engine is cut off. Cautiously, Edith lifts a corner of the blind. They seem to be inside a building.

Denis wrenches Edith's door. 'Out you get.'

She tries to stand but her bones have stiffened, and her ankles give way – she topples forward. Denis hops onto the running board and catches her. His hands are moist on her body. She wishes she could shove him away, the thankless reptile, but can't manage without his help. Her body creaks as she descends.

'My bag,' she says. 'It's still in the motor car.'

'It's grand there. Nobody'll touch it,' says Denis.

'Thieving's not in our line,' says the driver.

The space feels cavernous. Two strangers holding tilly lamps are standing beside Denis. A dense, yeasty odour fills her nostrils. Packing cases line the walls and she realizes she's inside a warehouse.

HUNTLEY & PALMERS
READING & LONDON

is printed in red and blue ink on the outside of the boxes. 'Sweet Kinds' is stamped on some, 'Unsweetened Kinds' on others.

She shifts her attention back to the men beside Denis. They are dressed like dockers but somehow don't strike her as labourers. For starters, they aren't muscled. Men who earn their daily bread by hard labour have a physical presence, which these two lack. Besides, when one of them walks behind the motor car to close the warehouse door, she sees he has a pronounced limp – his knee doesn't bend. She looks at the shape beneath his trouser leg. Perhaps it's an artificial limb.

'Is he in the back?' Denis asks.

'In the office. Been askin' after her for the best part of an hour.' A Cockney accent. But that long chin is Irish. He hands his lamp to Denis.

Denis catches at Edith's arm to hustle her along. Feeling her unwillingness, he says quietly, 'We'd best not keep him waiting.'

She allows herself to be led through the warehouse. This person waiting for her must have heard their arrival but he's sitting tight. It's a way of emphasizing his authority – Cameron told her they were taught that in officer school.

Her body is leaden but her mind races. Denis called her an informer. Informers are murdered. Is she a lamb to the slaughter? Imagine never seeing Drishane again. She'd be reunited with Martin, of course. But her skidding heartbeat tells her she's not yet ready to die.

Perhaps they only want to warn her off. There's no need to drag her to a biscuit warehouse to kill her. Denis could have done it in the fog – left her in a crumpled heap in a doorway and no one the wiser for hours. By now they have reached the back corner, where temporary walls and a door create a room. It's lying ajar.

Denis knocks. 'She's here now, Camel. I have her with me.'

'Send her in.' A Scottish voice. Educated. 'Then shut the door and clear the fuck off.'

By the lamp's flare, Denis's moss-green eyes are troubled. Beside his mouth, a tic has shoved up through the skin. She realizes he's frightened. Her heartbeat trips.

The room is windowless, the lighting shadowy. Its occupant is in profile. He sits side-on at a desk, legs outstretched, a cigar smouldering between his fingers. A handsome man in his late twenties, clean-shaven, with slicked-back hair as black as a sweep's face. He's like one of those actors from American cinema she saw in a magazine in Pinker's office. Valentine? Valentino? On the desk are an ashtray, a mug and a novelty Huntley & Palmers tin shaped like a milkmaid. Across the top of the biscuit tin lies a foot-long knife in a sheath. Edith's eyes glide over it, refusing to look directly at the object. He must have placed it there deliberately.

The occupant of the office does not acknowledge her presence. He turns the tip of his cigar towards him to examine the burning ash, and takes another draw. A blue spiral of smoke drifts towards her, pricking her throat. The silence stretches. Her right leg throbs. Her glance darts about for a chair but there is nowhere else to sit. She thinks with longing of her walking stick. Even something to lean on would ease the misery. She must have left it in the hackney or maybe the Underground station. Can't be helped. Edith shifts her weight onto the left leg and plaits her fingers together, keeping him in her line of vision without staring.

At last he moves, knocking some ash from his cigar onto the ashtray. Still without looking at her, he speaks. 'You've been sticking that over-bred nose of yours into places it doesn't belong.'

He waits. As does she.

'Going to the peelers.' He sighs, twitches a trouser leg, brushes off a fleck of ash. 'That wasn't nice.' A rummage in the desk drawer produces a pencil and box of matches. 'You're a risk.'

His voice is chiselled, thinks Edith. No mercy in it.

He tosses aside the pencil, strikes a match and watches its flame. 'And in my line of business, we eliminate risks.' A puff of air and the flame is extinguished.

Edith understands he's trying to menace her. She must exert will-power and block him. But her body refuses to be schooled by her mind. Dread shivers through her. In an effort to keep it dammed inside, she wraps her arms about herself. Her mouth dries out. She licks her lips.

He turns his head a little and reads the worm of her fear. The longer he observes her, the more insubstantial Edith begins to feel. Even if she speaks now, no one will hear her. If Denis or any of the others came in, they might step right through her. If she tries to open the door, her hand won't be able to grasp the knob. Her sense of humiliation intensifies. This is what he wants, she tells herself. Don't surrender to him. She pits her willpower against his.

I am Edith Somerville of Drishane House, Castletownshend. I will not be bullied.

'Have you ever ...' he halts, reflects, picks up the thread again. 'Eaten potatoes boiled in seawater?'

Could she have misheard him? Inconsequentially, her mind fastens on that Scottish accent. The Somervilles have Scottish blood.

'Have you?' he repeats.

She clears her throat. 'No, I don't believe I have.'

'No taste to match it. Lends a certain *je ne sais quoi* to the dish.' He ruminates, toying with the matchbox. 'Maybe you don't bother with potatoes? See it as peasant food?'

'I eat potatoes.'

'Grown on your own land?'

'Where possible.'

'Been in your family long, the land?'

'Since the seventeen-hundreds.'

'Sir Walter Raleigh brought the potato over from Virginia. Quite the adventurer. Came to a sticky end, mind you. Lost his head on the block. Didn't he have an estate in Ireland? Somewhere near Youghal, I believe.'

'If you say so.'

'Yes, quite an unpleasant end. *A fronte praecipitium a tergo lupi.*'[1]

---

1 A precipice in front, wolves behind.

Show-off. Edith doesn't know what it means. But she knows he's trying to browbeat her with this talk of execution. Somehow, she injects a sliver of ice into her voice. 'Really, Mr Whoever-you-are, I'm dog-tired. I've been dragged here against my will. Perhaps you'd kindly tell me what you require from me and allow me to be on my way.'

He turns his head fully. Edith sees him face-on for the first time and forgets herself. She gapes. The left side of his face is a reddened mass of scar tissue. The lash-less eyelid is closed. The ear is a stump. The mouth is twisted downwards.

A flick of the eyebrow on the unspoiled side of his face. To blazes with you and your shock, it says.

'Oh, I don't know if we can allow that. The truth is, we're disappointed in you, Edith. Going to the peelers like that. Unwise. Most unwise.' He shakes his head. 'A sensible person would have chosen not to notice.'

She bites down hard on her lip. Perhaps it was ill-advised. In fact, standing here, terror drumming at her temples, she has to agree it was extremely reckless.

'We understand you met Wilson,' he continues.

'The field marshal?'

'None other. Sir Highly Decorated himself.'

Her antennae quiver. These people have Sir Henry Wilson in their sights. 'Yes, we met.'

'What did you talk about?'

She's afraid of saying anything that might put him in jeopardy. 'Nothing memorable.'

'Nothing? Come now, Edith, you can do better than that. I have it on the best authority the pair of you were deep in conversation.'

The servants, she thinks. She pinches the bridge of her nose, concentrating. 'People we knew in common. The weather, I suppose. Kipling came up.'

'Ireland?'

'Yes, in passing.'

'Flog the savages, and so on and so forth?' She nods. 'Anything else?'

'Not that I recall.'

'Did he mention any plans while he's in London?'

She remembers him saying their names were left at the Lyric in case of cancellations. The Lyric. Where the whistler was working. Her heartbeat is a gigantic metronome. 'Not to me.'

'Any travel plans? Belfast, maybe?'

'No, nothing. We just talked about … gardening.'

A finger against the crimped wreckage of his mouth, he weighs her answer.

Pinpricks of perspiration break out and Edith is desperate to leave. The longer he detains her, the more she fears she'll say anything to get away.

Hesitant, she risks a question of her own. 'Is that all … are you finished with me?'

'Finished? That's a good question. Are we finished with you?' That single eye glares at her, every drop of his rage and misery visible in it.

Edith's courage falters, folds and deserts her. He's ready to rain down fire and brimstone on her head and there's nothing she can do to stop him. 'Please. I just … want to … go home.'

He stubs out his cigar. 'We don't care tuppence for what you want. It's less than nothing to us.' Purposeful, he pushes against his chair so that it clatters to the ground and reaches for the knife, which he pulls from its holder. When he begins to walk towards her, she sees his left hand is twisted into a claw.

This is the end, she thinks. Her heartbeat accelerates even as time slows down. She listens for some comfort from Martin – *I'm waiting for you, dear Edith, we'll spend eternity together* – but hears nothing. Apart from the rush of her own blood, this scarred stranger's voice is the only sound in her ears.

'Your wishes don't weigh one feather with us,' he hisses.

The odours of tobacco and coffee are rank on his breath. Involuntarily, she shrinks back, stumbles and bangs the back of her head against the door. She leans against it, tremors coursing through her body. The knife is aimed at her throat. Her heart lurches. She can't take her eyes off the blade. Pointed. Sharp. Close. Closer. Her scalp lifts away from her skull. Death is concrete a presence – a third person in this room.

His voice is pitched barely above a whisper. That web of skin with its puckered mouth is a few inches from her face. A guttering light gleams in his one, beautiful eye. 'You've caused us a great deal of trouble, Edith, and I can't think of a single reason to excuse you.'

The air crackles. The room holds its breath. A spurt of defiance drives Edith to cross her arms and raise them chin high, warding him off. He thrusts aside her arms and strokes the edge of the blade against her cheek before laying it in the hollow at the base of her throat. Inside its cage, her heart skids to a halt. She knows death is brushing up against her.

A tiny flick of the hand and her skin is nicked. A thread of blood dribbles out. Her eyes well with tears.

He smiles. Waits. Studies her.

In no hurry, he withdraws the blade. 'Chin up, only the good die young.' Mouth pursed, he studies the blood on the tip of his knife, leans forward and wipes it on the front of her coat. 'But if I have to speak to you again, I'll make mincemeat of you and enjoy doing it.' His voice slows down, its tone becoming apocryphal. 'I am. An instrument. Of vengeance. If you ever. Go. To the peelers. Again. About anything. Even a runaway dog. I'll track you down. Personally. Whether in Buckingham Palace. Or that fancy Irish house of yours. And slit your throat. From ear to ear. Leaving you. To bleed. To death. And when I've done that. I'll work my way. Through your family. Bairns included. Do we. Understand one another?'

She is incapable of speech.

'I'm waiting. And I'm not a patient man. Do we fucking well understand one another?'

The ghost of a nod.

'Is that a yes?'

'Yes,' she whispers.

'I CAN'T HEAR YOU!'

'Yes.'

'Excellent.' He returns to the desk, sets down the knife, picks up the chair. With his back to her, he says, 'Now, sod off back to Ireland on the next boat. And keep your trap shut.'

She's too petrified to move.

'Fucksake, do I have to do everything myself?' He strides back, sweeps her away from the door, opens it and calls to the men in the warehouse. 'We're done here.'

Denis runs up and hovers in the door jamb.

'Get rid of her.'

Edith hears a humming in her ears.

'Where?' Denis asks.

The buzzing intensifies.

'... Cross.'

He's changed his mind about letting her go. He intends to have her crucified! Edith moans. The room blurs. She staggers. The man with scars catches her by the shoulders.

'Careful there.'

He passes her over to Denis, as casually as a pound of sausages. Tottering, she leans on Denis, who half-carries her into the warehouse.

'Are you going to kill me?' she manages to gasp.

'Saints preserve us, no, Miss Somerville. I'm to see you as far as King's Cross.'

She manages to turn her head and look at him. Is he telling the truth? What if he isn't? She should make a run for it. But she's floppy. He guides her to the motor car and bundles her in. Slumped down, her hammering heartbeat is the only thing in the world she's conscious of – it feels as if that organ might tunnel through her chest.

'There, there, Miss Somerville, we're finished now. Fog's lifting. You'll soon be safe home,' Denis murmurs.

The motor car has started up and Edith's stomach begins to react against its swaying. She groans. The colour drains from her face and the contents of her stomach corkscrew and curdle. The vehicle takes a sharp corner, and the manoeuvre unravels her self-control. She clamps her hand against her mouth, scrabbling for the window catch.

'Jaysus, not in here!' Denis springs to his feet, pulls up the blind and forces open the window.

A slimy mass of semi-digested food erupts into her mouth. Somehow, she manages to push her head through the gap and evacuate down the car's outer flank. After she has finished heaving, she hangs over the side, breathing in the air. Dimly, she becomes conscious of the driver cursing and Denis telling him to mind his own effin' business.

Edith wilts back into her seat. Denis takes her handbag, roots about, and pushes a handkerchief towards her. She holds it to her mouth.

'Shut the bleedin' window,' says the driver. 'What if she spots a copper and lets out a yell?'

Edith forms prayer peaks with her hands, begging Denis to leave it open. The breeze is making her feel less queasy.

'She mightn't be finished throwing up,' says Denis. He whispers to her, 'He's not a bad skin, really. Try and breathe in the air. It'll help.'

By and by, she gasps out, 'Who was that? In the factory?'

'I'm not allowed to say, ma'am.'

'He's insane.'

'Mad as mischief,' Denis allows.

The drive is smoother now. Her stomach begins to settle. 'How on earth did you get mixed up with him?'

'I was sent.'

'They used you to get to me, didn't they? How did they know to use you?'

He wriggles in his seat. 'I might have said we were friends.'

'Friends? Really?'

His eyes slide away to the side.

'Is this how you treat your friends?'

He doesn't answer. Finally, he says, 'Camel is a man wouldn't give this' – he snaps his fingers – 'for either me or you. But he knows what he's about. He'll show the English what's what.'

'He's a killer. I don't know how you can have it on your conscience, getting tangled up with him.'

Something in the clench of his jaw tells her Denis has made his choice. She doesn't know what happened to change his mind – war steals some part of a man's soul, she supposes.

'You look to your conscience and I'll look to my mine,' he says.

All at once, the smell of vomit on her handkerchief revolts her and she hurls the scrap of linen out of the window. 'What happened to his face?'

'He was a pilot. Shot down by his own side – friendly fire, they call it. A miracle he survived. Managed to land his plane but as soon as it touched the ground it went up in flames.'

'Was he in the Royal Air Force?'

'Well, he wasn't fighting for the Germans.' He hesitates. 'Whatever he told you to do, I'd do it, Miss Somerville.'

'You heard him. I'm to go home and speak to nobody.'

His eyes turn as distant as a bird in flight. 'Going home's no hardship. This place is too flat altogether. I grew up in the shadow of a mountain. Spoils you for anywhere else.'

She's only half-listening, thinking back over her encounter with Camel. He ran a risk, letting her go. A man with his scarring is easily identified. It's almost as if he has a death wish. But she certainly doesn't. Edith has no intention of making a return trip to a police station.

Denis is still gabbling about his damned mountain. 'It crouches over the village, guarding us. Never looks the same two days running. I like it best when there's a cloud of mist wrapped round it, blue as Our Lady's gown. Sure, the mountains on the moon is nothing compared to mine.' His voice thickens. 'I hope to God I'll see that mountain again.'

You don't deserve to, you stupid boy, throwing in your lot with killers like Camel. For a moment, she thinks she was unguarded enough to speak her thoughts. She checks Denis's face. No, she can't have said it. Steady there, Edith. You're not out of the woods yet. 'It wasn't very kind of you to take me to him.'

'I know, Miss Somerville. The things I've done. Sometimes, when they come to me, I feel my head will bust open like a rotten cabbage.'

'Has it never occurred to you that you could give them the slip, here in London? It's a big place. Easy to lose yourself in it.'

'I can't. It's hopeless.'

'Nothing is hopeless. When you're as old as me you'll know that, Denis.'

'I can't desert my comrades. This is a fight to the finish. And with men like Camel on our side, we're bound to win.'

'Win what, exactly?'

'Our country's freedom, of course.'

Edith feels blunted, incapable of another word. Men and their causes. If she had the energy, she could tell him he'd be no better off in a republic. That what's happening in Ireland is a playing out of romance versus reality. That the dream of patriotism is being exploited by lies and propaganda. But he wouldn't listen.

The motor car pulls over, its engine running. The driver turns his head. 'This is it.'

'Time to get out, Miss Somerville,' says Denis.

'Where am I?'

'King's Cross station. You'll be able to find your way from here. See? The fog's lifted.' He turns the door handle and helps her to the running board but stays inside. 'Best of luck to you, now.'

'Luck is always temporarily on loan from someone else, you know. Sooner or later it runs out.'

He makes a helpless gesture with his hands. Edith glances back at him. He's shrivelled up inside his skin.

'This is a murdering world, so it is, ma'am. But God save Ireland.'

The driver crunches the gears, and the vehicle pulls away, its door swinging shut.

A chilly twist of night air nicks her hat brim, making it flap. Her skin pimples. There are just a few foggy tatters now. By the light of the moon, profligate in its radiance, Edith can see railway arches. A row of houses with muslin curtains at the windows. A queue of motorized hackney cabs. Unexpectedly, she feels ravenous for a pot of tea and lashings of hot, buttery toast. She waits for a motorcycle to splutter past, leaving an evil cloud in its wake, before crossing the road to the hackneys.

'Netherton Grove, Chelsea,' she tells the cabbie.

Edith's knows she's had a narrow escape. Something precious has been restored to her.

Life.

twenty

'Edith, were you insane going out in the fog?' It's Boney, who has parked herself in Mabel and Boyle's house.

'My dear, thank goodness you're home safe. Dame Ethel and I have been worried sick about you.' Tension is visible in Mabel's pursed-up mouth – partly as a result of Boney's thunderclap presence, Edith guesses.

'I'd sell my soul for a hot bath. Might I have one, do you suppose, Mab?'

'Of course. I'll send Doris up to draw it for you right away. Do sit down, Edith. You look all done in.' She melts away to issue instructions.

'Tell her not to stint on the bath salts. Lavender if you have them. Good for rheumatism,' Boney calls after Mabel. 'I say, you've been sick all over the front of your blouse, Edith.'

'Putrid, isn't it? I took a funny turn. What are you doing here, Boney?'

'I came to invite you to the highlight of the music season. But when I saw how worried Mrs Somerville was, naturally I stayed to support her. I'm directing the overture to my Cornish opera, *The Wreckers*, at the Royal Albert Hall next week. They had an unexpected gap in their programme and asked me to oblige. Queen Mary may attend – I've been in touch with one of her ladies-in-waiting about it. My sister met her at a supper in Lady Shelby's.'

'I'm afraid I won't be here next week. I have to go back to Ireland as soon as possible.'

'Nonsense, you can't possibly leave. I won't hear of it.'

'Boney, I don't have the energy for a row.'

'You're overwrought, Edith. Nobody's rowing.'

'You are.'

'I really do need you at the Albert Hall next week.'

'And I simply can't be there, I'm afraid.'

The door opens and Mabel's head appears through the gap. 'Your bath's ready, Edith. I've left a glass of brandy beside the soap dish. You look like you could use a pick-me-up.'

'You're an angel, Mab.'

'Shall I come up and keep you company while you bathe, Edith?' asks Boney.

Mabel's eyebrows are scandalized.

'Would you mind not, dear?' says Edith. 'I'm too exhausted to concentrate on a word anyone says.'

'Quite right,' says Mabel. 'Edith, don't trouble to come downstairs afterwards. I'll send you up some supper on a tray. You can have it in bed.'

'But I need to talk to you about my overture.'

Edith waggles three fingers in farewell.

'I'll come over in the morning. Directly after breakfast,' Boney tells her back.

———

Later, checking on Edith in bed, Mabel remarks, 'I thought she meant to stay the night, invited or not.'

'Dame Ethel Smyth no sooner thinks of something than she does it.'

'You look worn out, Edith. I wish you'd stayed home today.'

'Me too, Mab. But I was safe as the Bank of England, waiting out the fog with Mr Tring in Tothill Street. He was kindness personified. I think I could sleep now, if you don't mind.' She makes a mental note to send Mr Tring a telegram in the morning. She never turned up for their appointment – although he may have been unable to keep it, too.

'Not at all, my dear,' says Mabel. 'I'll take your tray. Sleep tight.'

Exhausted though she is, Edith finds herself unable to drop off. Camel's face is planted in her mind. That single, awful eye. The way his mouth coiled into a sneer. She clicks on her bedside light, fetches paper and a pencil, and props herself up against pillows. An automatic writing session is bound to help. Habit helps her to enter a state of trancelike stillness. Soon, she is communicating with Martin.

'That swine has me in a bit of a funk,' Edith says.

> nowonder hes a loathsome skunk high ti me you returned to
> drishane

This is exactly what Edith wants to hear, although it feels as if she's being cowardly. 'But what about *Flurry's Wedding*?'

> you can make copies at home and send it to other theatre managers
> one swallow doesnt make a summer nothing canbe read from one
> rejection

'Will I be safe in Ireland? Will that monster come after me?'

> he was born to dangle on the endofaroperoperope
> skippingskippingskipping rope mope soap

And nothing else is forthcoming from Martin that evening.

———

True to her word, Boney is back in Chelsea next morning. To spare Mabel, Edith takes her walking as far as Brompton Cemetery, where there are seats near the main avenue. A morning in bed to recuperate would have been preferable, but Edith has decided to leave London on the Irish mail that evening, and there are errands to run before she goes. The eight forty-five train from Euston connects with the overnight sailing from Holyhead to Dublin. Mabel received her decision without comment, apart from promising some Scotch eggs and ham sandwiches for the six-hour train journey through England and Wales, and volunteering Doris to help pack her trunk. Boney is being less cooperative.

Edith rests on a bench beside a barbered patch of grass, watching a woman in deepest mourning attend to a grave. Boney is too agitated to sit. She rampages around, crushing early primroses underfoot – her feet hitting the ground as decisively as drumsticks against goatskin.

'This may be your last opportunity to see me direct my own work, Edith.'

'There'll be other triumphs I can share.'

'Not like this. I insist, Edith. I absolutely insist on having you in the audience.'

'You won't miss me with Queen Mary there.'

'I'd always miss you, whoever was there. Change your plans. Do, please.'

A shadow touches Edith and she flinches, until she realizes it's only a man walking past to join the mourning woman – her son, perhaps. He takes her arm and they walk along the central avenue towards the chapel.

'Edith?' says Boney. 'You aren't listening.'

'Yes I am. You want me to change my plans. But I can't.'

'You must.'

'The world doesn't revolve around you, Boney.'

Ethel crashes down on the bench beside Edith. 'Don't you understand? I'll never conduct again. This is probably going to be my last time. You see, it's not just one of my ears troubling me now. Both of them are booming and singing.'

'You mean your other ear has started acting up?'

'Not all the time, but often enough. Soon, I'll be as deaf as a post.'

Edith is appalled. Poor Boney. Her refusal to stay must seem heartless. For once, that vivid face beneath its tricorn hat looks vulnerable. She touches her friend's arm. 'I'm so sorry, dearest.'

'That's why next week is madly important. I'm going to storm the gates of heaven with my music. If it's to be my last performance, by jingo it will be my finest. If I have to bow out, it'll be with a bang and not a whimper.'

'Good for you. I'm proud of you, you splendid thing.'

In a small voice, Boney says, 'Except I'm not splendid. I couldn't admit this to anyone else. But I'm frightened.' She lays her head on Edith's lap. 'I'm staring defeat in the eye. But I won't go down without a fight.'

Edith pats her back. 'You'll be magnificent.'

'I am, usually. But these stupid ears are liable to let me down. With no warning. I could be standing in front of the orchestra, baton in hand, royalty in the box behind me – and bong! Deafer than deaf. Dearest, life has never seemed blacker. I'm feeling utterly desperate. I can't bear to lose you, too.'

Edith is in a quandary. Is there any way to explain why she has to leave London? Not without revealing she was abducted – and Boney will react to the news by trooping straight off to Scotland Yard, with or without her. Her conscience pricks about the field marshal. But he'll be fine, surely. He must have protection. A phalanx of it. When she went to the police about the whistler, she ended up kidnapped. There's no telling what might happen to her if she goes to the authorities about Camel. Sir Henry Wilson will be fine.

Boney lifts her face from Edith's knee, eyes moist. 'Say you'll stay with me, Edith. Help me to face whatever lies ahead. You're so stout-hearted, you'll infect me with your pluck.'

'Oh Boney, if only you knew how spineless I am.'

'Well then, move into Coign with me, why don't you – there's plenty of room for two – and we can be spineless together.'

Edith recoils, but tries to hide it. She eases Boney's head off her lap. 'Oh look, your hat's crooked. Let me fix it. I wish I could stay for your overture. Believe me, I do. But it can't be helped.'

'You force me to tell you about the surprise I was planning for you.'

'Surprise?'

'I mean to dedicate the concert to you. I was going to announce it from the stage.'

'Oh, Boney.'

'Now will you stay?'

'I can't. I simply have to go back home to Ireland.'

'Why now?'

'I have my reasons.'

'Give me one good reason. Just one. I'll shut up if you do.'

'I've spent long enough away from Drishane. My duty is there.'

'Drishane is your brother's show. Why should you have the trouble of it?'

Because he doesn't know how to run it. Because it feels as if she's the only Somerville interested in saving the house for the next generation. Because apathy will root out the family more thoroughly than the IRA, if they're not careful. 'Do we have to go through all this again?'

Boney's mood pops as abruptly as a soap bubble. She springs to her feet and begins prowling about again. 'You're living in a fool's paradise. Don't you know the wonderful life you could have if you shrugged off Drishane, and your family, and Ireland? I thought we meant something to one another.'

'Of course, we do. But don't you understand? Drishane, and my family, and Ireland are mostly what make life wonderful for me. It wouldn't be the same without them.'

'Ireland? Wonderful? With murder gangs roaming the countryside?'

'Drishane is a safe place.'

'If it's safe, how come your unspeakable countrymen order you about at gunpoint? How were they able to stroll in and steal your horses and jewellery?'

'That was last year. Old grievances are settled now. There's a treaty. Listen, Boney, I really must get going. I've ever such a lot to do if I'm to catch the boat train. I want to go to Fortnum's for Bath Olivers and madeleines, I need to order flowers for Mabel and I saw a tortoiseshell moustache comb in Regent Street that's perfect for Cameron. Plus I have to send a telegram to Drishane.'

'You treat your family as if they're semi-divine. Spend your money on yourself, why don't you?'

'On what? I need nothing.'

'We could travel.' Boney halts in front of Edith and stands there, rocking on her heels. 'If you won't come and live with me in Coign, at least let's take a trip, dearest. Remember what fun we had in Sicily? We could go to Egypt and see the pyramids together. You've never travelled by dromedary, have you? There's nothing to match it. Please, Edith, say you'll come away with me. Somewhere far, far away. Just the two of us.'

Boney is keyed up, unpredictable. Her urgency unnerves Edith. 'I couldn't possibly.'

'You've changed. You've forgotten what it's like to be spontaneous.'

'Don't be ridiculous!'

'What's the last spontaneous thing you did? See? You can't remember. You think of yourself as an artist, but you're a Victorian maiden-miss — conventional to your fingertips. It's not experience you lack, it's emotion.'

'And you have too much. You're emotionally extravagant.'

'I'm offering you a lifeline, if only you knew it.'

'You're hectoring me.'

'I've never hectored anyone in my life.'

'You're the high priestess of hectoring!'

'Is it any wonder, when you try to leave me in the cloakroom for months on end, like a forgotten umbrella? I deserve more. I demand more!'

Edith measures out her words. 'Stop it, Boney. Just stop it. I'm sorry about your ears, honestly, I am. But I see rocks ahead for us if you insist on pursuing this ridiculous line. You always want more than I can give you.'

'I'm greedy for life. I make no apologies for it.'

Edith sighs. She offers an olive branch. 'Why not spend Easter in Castletownshend? You can criticize my organ-playing in St Barrahane's. It'll be warm enough for boating, and we can walk together in the blue-bell woods. The bluebells won't mend your ears, but they'll raise your spirits, I promise. Say you'll come and stay in Drishane.'

'Draft-ridden, ramshackle barn! I'd rather die in a ditch!'

'In that case, I shan't ever invite you again.'

'Oh, don't sulk. You know I don't mean it.'

'Why say it?'

'Because you keep on retreating into your Irish world where I can't follow you.'

'I've just asked you to stay.'

'You know precisely what I mean. You're unavailable to me there, somehow, surrounded by your Irish mists and bogs. I know Castletownshend is Shangri-La to you, but I've had enough of the place. I want to be with you – but elsewhere. With no distractions. How about New Zealand? What an odyssey that would be! I've always had a hankering to go. You haven't really travelled until you've been on another continent. Won't you consider it? For my sake?'

'No, Boney, and you must stop pushing me. It's tiresome. I haven't the money for such a trip. And before you offer, I don't want to borrow it from you. My mind is made up. I spoke to Martin last night and she agrees it's time I went home.'

Boney says nothing.

Edith rises, gathering her umbrella and bag.

A dam burst explodes in her path.

'Your automatic writing is muddle-headed tosh! You use it to suit yourself!'

'You don't have a psychic bone in your body. How would you know?'

'I know codology when I see it. Martin's dead, Edith, dead and gone. But I'm here. Living and breathing. And loving. You can have *me* if you want me.'

Shocked to the core, Edith chooses to disregard the second part of what she's just heard. 'Martin is as real to me now as she ever was. Death changes nothing.'

'She's a figment of your imagination. That automatic writing comes from your consciousness, not hers.'

Edith covers her ears. 'Enough! I won't listen to another word!'

Boney tugs away her hands. 'I'll make you hear this if it's the last thing I do. No wonder you can't write for the stage – every ounce of your imaginative power is bound up in the spirit world. An artist must mean what they're doing. But you're too busy pretending.'

'Goodbye, Boney. I'm off to Fortnum & Mason's now. I shan't have time to see you before I leave. Good luck at the Albert Hall.'

'You don't know what to do with my love, Edith Somerville. That's your misfortune. And one day you'll regret it.'

twenty-one

Ireland's morning skies are brooding, like a forehead wrinkled in thought. Edith disembarks in the prosperous port town of Kingstown, just outside Dublin, and transfers by train to the city's Westland Row railway station. Under its glass dome, a troop train is preparing to depart. So the newspapers are right – the regiments are being called back to England. The men are boisterous, and she listens to their banter while a porter collects her luggage.

'I'll miss the black stuff,' shouts one.

'Won't miss the Micks,' yells another.

'Apart from the girls, Nigel,' cries a third. 'Bet you've left a little Nigel or two behind.'

The porter trundles up from the platform with her bags and crooks his eyebrows in their direction. 'Can you imagine the havoc those boyos would have wreaked, day after tomorrow, if they had the chance?'

'Why the day after tomorrow?'

'St Patrick's Day, ma'am. Soldiers always drink the pubs dry then.'

Mid-March already. 'I suppose the natives give them a run for their money.'

'Not them boys. The Lancashires. They'd drink the eye out of a cat.'

Edith doubles his tip in honour of that dash of local colour, but not before instructing him to wheel her luggage down the ramp to the street and hire a hackney cab for her.

It carries her along Dublin's noisy, smelly quays to Kingsbridge station, from where she travels on a series of stop-start trains towards Cork. None of them with a restaurant car. Good job she saved some of Mabel's provisions. The landscape unspools through the centre of Ireland, magic-lantern fashion – from the flat plains of Kildare to the lush meadows of Tipperary. She sees churches with weathervanes, a bridge across a river, a round tower. What a pre-Industrial Revolution world this is, compared with London's chimney stacks. The further south-west she advances, the less substantial England becomes in her mind. The engine's rhythmic drone lulls her into a state of quiet joy – she knows it's no Eden, yet the landscape fills her with a sense of the divine.

Sometimes, the tracks run so close to the road that she catches glimpses of people going about their daily business. Motor cars are less commonplace here. She spots a messenger boy fiddling with his bicycle wheel, perhaps patching the tyre, and notices a farmer's cart stop to give a lift to some children on the roadside. Sheep and cattle freckle the hill-sides. A brindled greyhound lopes alongside the train for a few minutes, before dropping back.

At Limerick Junction, where the train crawls into the station, people emerge from their whitewashed cottages to watch its arrival. They are picturesque, with their thatches and half-doors, often with a horseshoe nailed on for luck. Low hedges have clothes draped over for drying. When the train whistles, the occupants of the cottages wave, as if greeting old friends. Edith has visited enough of those cabins to imagine what lies inside: a smoke-blackened kitchen with low *súgan* chairs and stools, a wooden settle which doubles as a bed, a spinning wheel in the corner, a kettle hanging from a metal crane over the glowing turf. She's eaten their bread baked in a pot under woody ash, which lends it a distinctive flavour, and drunk their sweet, stewed tea, sometimes with a splash of *poitín* in it. The crathur, they call it. They have holy pictures on their walls – tasteless art, she thinks of it – and prints of Robert Emmet and Daniel O'Connell, or maybe Lord Edward Fitzgerald. She supposes de Valera and Collins will be added to the repertoire, in time.

'Change here for Limerick or Waterford,' carols the train guard.

She beckons to him. 'I have bags in the luggage car that need to be transferred onto the Skibbereen train in Cork city. Somerville, three pieces.'

'No bother, ma'am.'

'You won't forget? You look young to be a train guard.'

'Me, is it? Sure, I'm as old as a pot of last week's tea.'

Whooping with most unladylike laughter, she slips him a coin.

The train idles as passengers disembark and embark. Two men in homespun tweed pass along the corridor, engrossed in conversation.

'Act for ourselves ... give the people a chance ... an end to inherited privilege,' she overhears.

All this talk of Ireland's independence makes her impatient. What difference will a change of regime make to the people? Their cottages will still be overcrowded, their children will still emigrate. It's just how it is in Ireland. The train shrills its departure. Wheels grind and screech. Automatically, Edith waves at the country people raising their hands shoulder high, faces wreathed in smiles. She used to believe that if they didn't own much, yet they never seemed to want much. Were they deceiving her – or was she deceiving herself?

She considers this world through the train window – there is a sense of fixed places within it. Just as the patchwork fields are fixed into place by the stone walls separating them. But she knows that unchanging quality is no longer the case. Three years of war in Ireland have shaken something loose. *Come what may, we'll always have Drishane and its lands, or at least most of them.* But is that another of her fictions? Her thoughts, chug-chugging to the engine's beat, make her uneasy. She fidgets at the cuff of her new, grey suede gloves.

The train's approach to Cork city distracts her. Here, single cottages give way to a straggle of terraces and then to tall houses and warehouses, placed so tightly they catch one another at the heels. Amid clanging doors, puffs of steam and bellowing porters, she steps onto the platform at

Glanmire Road railway station. As if on a signal, a small, white missile anoints the back of her right glove. She looks up. Pigeons are fluttering about the station roof's metal fretwork. That dropping is meant to be a sign of luck. It means she's been singled out. Dashed inconvenient, though.

She hurries into the public convenience to dab at it, before crossing over to another platform. There, she joins a smaller train waiting to carry passengers to Bandon, Clonakilty and Skibbereen. On board, passengers mill about, blocking the aisles and carriages, arranging themselves and their belongings – mostly secured with leather belts and lengths of string – to their satisfaction. The train releases a series of authoritative blasts. Metal heaves out a groan, the engine jolts and they are shunted forward to the accompaniment of slamming doors. Advertising hoardings for health tonics, ladies' fashions and a music hall production swim past. As they exit the station, the door to her second-class carriage opens. A figure in clerical black enters, nods at his fellow travellers and takes a seat next to Edith. He removes a book and spectacles from his bag, and places it in the overhead luggage rack. From habit, she looks at his reading matter, expecting it to be his breviary. It's *Whitaker's Almanack* – the only book Flurry Knox reads.

Edith wonders what Flurry will make of her failure to place *Flurry's Wedding*. She half-expects to see him reading the yearbook over the priest's shoulder – he's addicted to its information about postage rates, cab fares, government salaries, the opening hours of the British Museum, Easter, Passover and Ramadan dates, and miscellaneous anniversaries including the death date of Napoleon III. She met the emperor's descendants in Sicily with Boney. A refined little bandbox duke, with a sister in pearls the size of hen's eggs. Poor Boney, she's her own worst enemy. Things will never be the same between them.

'Excuse me, Father. I've been away for a while. Are we out of the woods yet, do you suppose? Is the country settled? It's just that I saw a regiment evacuating from Dublin.'

'Not yet,' he says. 'But please God we're getting there. The generals are pulling out their men very slowly, to be on the safe side – still plenty of boots on the ground in Dublin, Cork and the Curragh.'

'The barbed wire has come down in Dublin.'

'Do you say so? That's a good start.'

'It would be lovely if the peace held. The country people have suffered dreadfully.'

'Indeed and they have. Mankind has an extraordinary capacity for war. But peace always breaks through, regular as the tides.'

She returns to the passing scenery, wilder now, the fields irregular and separated by gorse bushes, the horizon a purple blur. The sea isn't far away. If she rolled down the window she could inhale its saltiness, but soot smuts from the engine are liable to blow in. The glass is grimed with it. How clear the terrain is beyond this train. Some of that clarity seeps into her thoughts. London wasn't real life – this is reality. Ireland is where she belongs. And nothing will dislodge her.

———

Mike Hurley meets her at Skibbereen station, Tara in the trap. He tips his hat – 'Miss Edith. Your telegram arrived this morning. You've been missed' – before collecting her luggage from the porter.

Tara neighs, pawing the ground with front hooves until attention is paid to her. While Mike fastens Edith's bags into place with rope, the mare nudges her palm for sugar, and Edith conjures up a lump saved from her cup of tea at Kingsbridge. A donkey and cart clops up, the driver's feet dangling either side of its tail, his wife sitting on a sack behind and facing in the opposite direction. Daylight is nearly leeched from the sky, but Edith recognizes Barney and Lil Egan, who farm a few acres near the famine graveyard. They had a son who ran the holding with them, but he was executed in Cork jail a year ago. She wonders how they manage on their own. The younger boy was said to be willing to come home from Boston, but his father wouldn't have it – said he couldn't risk losing a second son.

'Grand, soft evening, Barney, Lil,' Hurley calls out.

'Miss Somerville, Mike. The rain's held off, thank God,' answers Egan.

'Good evening, Barney. Good evening, Mrs Egan. I trust you're keeping well?' says Edith.

Egan mutters a few words, but his wife neither looks at Edith nor speaks – it's said not a word has passed her lips since her son was hanged.

Edith and Hurley watch them recede into the distance.

Hurley sighs. 'A hard fate.' He laces his hands, palms outward, to give Edith a footrest.

She clambers aboard and sits side-on to him in the back of the trap, drawing comfort from his stable-yard smell. She's content for him to take the reins. He's a natural-born horseman.

Beyond the town, a dash of light rain tickles her face, but the shower is over almost before it began. They jingle along, her eyes rested by the raindrops glinting on the foliage, caught in the arc of their passing lights.

'How are things in Drishane, Mike?'

'No complaints.'

'And in the village? Are they for Dev or Collins?'

'The Treaty doesn't please all. And them that's not pleased is a contrary bunch. Father Lambe reads them the riot act in his sermons.'

'How do the people take it?'

'There's some mutter "Up the rebels!" but not so loud he can hear them. Father Lambe runs a tight ship.'

'I had a letter from the colonel in Switzerland. He's planning to come home soon.'

'Hmm.'

'Don't you think he's been gone long enough?'

'No harm for him to sit it out a wheen longer. 'Til he sees what way the wind blows.'

'It doesn't sound as if Michael Collins is in charge of his own men.'

'There's anti-Treaty boyos the length and breadth of the country not too fond of him. Particularly here, in his home county of Cork. They're calling him a sell-out. Trouble's coming, Miss Edith. Things'll be a sight worse before they're better.'

Edith's mind sheers away from images she prefers not to dwell on.

'How's your comrade? The one that's powerful fond of music?' asks Hurley. 'Sorry to see you go, I dare say.'

Comrade? That's the best description she's heard yet of her relationship with Boney. 'I suppose she was sorry. But she's a busy person. Plenty to occupy her. I meant to say, I found a buyer for Pilot and Trumpeter in England. Friends of the George Bernard Shaws. Didn't get what I'd hoped for them, but beggars can't be choosers. I'll be asking you to travel over to Oxford with the horses, as soon as we can pin down the arrangements. They're still with your friend in Leap, I take it?'

'Still there, Miss Edith.'

Tara pricks her ears, rounding the bend towards Castletownshend. Without waiting for Mike to direct her with a click of his tongue, the mare veers to the right, carrying them through granite gateposts and along a shady, tree-lined avenue.

In the minute or so it takes them pass along the driveway, Edith resolves to write a letter to Boney before bedtime. She rehearses it in her mind:

You must make arrangements to see that Viennese ear specialist you mentioned. He may have a cure. I'd like to go with you if you're willing to have company. I should be able to get away again after Easter. Meanwhile, you mustn't play golf or tennis in the rain. And thank you, dear, for putting up with my vagaries. I cannot change friends as readily as my gown – and so you remain stuck with me, if you'll have me, as a comrade.

They swing right again, towards the front door, which lies ajar despite the night air, lamps lit in welcome either side of it. Loulou bolts out, yapping up a storm. Poor Dooley, there'll never be another like him. He was always first to greet her. Still, this salutation from Loulou is gratifying. Mike Hurley jumps off and extends a hand, and she is forced to admit she needs his help to guide her down from the trap. The Irish Sea crossing has multiplied her aches and pains. She has some mustard plasters in her overnight bag. By and by, she'll put hot poultices on her back and neck.

Loulou darts about like a fish, tail quivering, before making a flying leap and landing in Edith's arms. Lavish with saliva, she licks Edith's entire face including both ears, displacing her hat. This excess of affection charms Edith into forgetting her stiff joints.

'What a little kangaroo you are. Clearly, absence makes the heart grow fonder.'

For a few moments, she stands and looks at the house. In an unpredictable world it remains unchanged. Drishane restores her to herself. A half-remembered Bible quote drifts through her mind. Something about the peace which passeth all understanding.

On a whim, she goes around the house to the kitchen window and looks in. Philomena is in her favourite armchair, smoothing buttermilk over her eczema, while Mrs O'Shea is kneading dough at the table. Tiger is poised on the tabletop, vigilant for whatever can be hijacked. The cat's ears prick up and she turns her poisonous, pond-green eyes on Edith. Edith gazes her fill. How satisfying it is to reach journey's end.

She raps on the window and Philomena and Mrs O'Shea's faces light up. But Tiger's triangular face registers alarm and she flits away.

Edith and Philomena meet in the outer hallway, each hurrying towards the other.

'You're as welcome as the flowers in May, Miss Edith!'

'Each time I make it over and back to London, it feels as if I've accomplished something as difficult as Hannibal crossing the Alps. Any chance of a pot of tea?'

'Of course, Miss Edith. You'll have it in jig time. Sure, the kettle's always boiling. We've supper ready for you, whenever you've a mind to take it. How was London town?'

'Oh, I lolloped about enjoying myself. But after a while, you realize there's no place like home.'

'No truer word. Where would you like your tea?'

'With you and Mrs O'Shea, of course. In the kitchen. I'll just wash my hands first. I'm dusty from travelling.'

'Mrs O'Shea has one of her cherry cakes baked fresh for you.'

Philomena trots ahead, taking a passing swat at a dusty rubber plant with the hem of her apron. It occurs to Edith that Philomena knows Drishane in intimate ways she can never match. At floor level from scrubbing, at cupboard level from tidying and itemizing contents, at ceiling level from balancing on a ladder attacking spiderwebs. Philomena is familiar with its plates and glasses, its knives and napkin rings. She beats its rugs and airs its curtains, polishes its windows and sweeps its passageways. It may have been commissioned by Edith's forebear Tom the Merchant, it may be her family history embedded in the brickwork. But it's still habitable because of Philomena Minihane, and other Philomenas before her.

Each to their own, thinks Edith, and nuzzles Loulou before setting her on the floor. 'You're heavier than when I went away, Lou. Someone's been feeding you treats.'

'Sure how could a body refuse that crathur a morsel of sweet cake?' says Mrs O'Shea, puffing up from the kitchen to join them. She has gained an extra ruffle of skin under her chin in Edith's absence. 'Welcome home, Miss Edith. You were missed. Now, as soon as you take the weight off your feet, I've a message for you from my sister who's cook to the Salters. They've a new litter of fox terriers, born to a sister of Dooley's. The pick of the litter is yours for the asking.'

Edith unpins her hat. 'I couldn't possibly.'

'Yerrah, time's a great healer, Miss Edith.'

twenty-two

Frisky as a lamb, Edith jump-steps across a brook frothing like wedding lace over pebbles. Even her damp shoes and the twinge in her leg as she lands don't cause her regret. Sometimes in life, a leap must be taken. It's summertime. A sun-gilt morning in late June. Just ahead is Pinker, her new fox terrier pup, who yipped as she splashed through the water and doubled back to repeat the manoeuvre. Edith tried to entice out Loulou for some exercise, too, but she point-blank refused to leave Mrs O'Shea's kitchen.

The day has been set aside for sketching. In a satchel, strapped across her front, are a collapsible easel and painting materials. Grass swishes against her legs, seagulls whirr overhead and the sea breeze is at her back. The climb is steep going – once she raced up these Carbery hills on horseback, following the hounds – but she won't indulge in nostalgia for what has been. Besides, she has a flask of coffee and sandwiches packed to revive her when she reaches the top.

She picnics on springy ground clotted with clover and buttercups, bees bumbling among them. Somewhere nearby a thrush chants its matins. Pinker curls into her lap, paws on Edith's breastbone, and begs prettily for scraps. On an impulse, she unpins her tam-o'-shanter to feel the sun on her scalp, and the woollen hat is snatched up as a plaything.

'Drop it, Pinker. Drop it. Do as you're told. Let go.'

She wipes it off with a handful of heather. The puppy is learning. It'll take time.

Edith leans back on an elbow and shades her eyes to take in the view. That line where sky meets sea never fails to enchant her. The land makes jagged forays into the sea, and corners of it have broken off and floated out to form islands or crops of semi-submerged rocks. Foam-coated waves hint at the restless motion of the pilgrim ocean. Fishing boats with white sails bob along near Reen Pier. Her painter's eye notices how light searches out water and bounces off its surface. In the distance, if she squints, she can distinguish the ruins of the O'Driscoll castle, clan chieftains here before the potato came to Ireland. St Barrahane's is easier to pick out, where Martin lies in the churchyard. One day, she'll be buried beside her. But not any time soon.

There is no longer a destroyer in Castlehaven Bay. The British evacuation from Ireland is almost complete now, and Michael Collins is chairman – such a funny title, she thinks – of the new Irish Free State. Not a republic, after all, but a dominion with a role for the King, and a hived-off slice at the top called Northern Ireland. The longed-for peace has splintered into civil war, bitterest of all conflicts. Brother versus brother, friends versus friend, Free Stater versus Republican. A point of no return has been passed.

Cameron is home again, meticulously following political events – as closely as Edith watches him, in case he sells any more of Drishane's lands. Her brother is a Collins man, he tells her, and predicts he'll have crushed all resistance before the summer is over. And then what? Her spirits are wearied by the lot of them. Yet war seems distant on this hilltop. Life is what she feels in this place. Perhaps even eternity.

Near a windblown tree, Edith sets up her easel. She pins paper to it, unfolds her sketching stool and sets to work. Even in summertime, a palette of mossy colours is needed to capture the scene. Pinker romps around, chasing imaginary enemies, her doggy burbling folding into the peaceful background noise. But when she begins scuffling at the trunk of the tree, it interferes with Edith's concentration, and she puts aside her work to investigate. Pinker has unearthed some bones belonging to a small animal. She pours water over them and admires their bleached purity. A fox may have feasted on a rabbit on this hilltop. She's not the first picnicker. Pinker is reluctant to yield her find but is bought off with a triangle of chicken sandwich. The bones belong in Edith's picture.

This is one of those days when she wishes she'd devoted more of her life to art than literature. It was Martin who pressed them to become writers. Left to her own devices, she'd have been an artist, instead of juggling both. Edith knows art is the finest part of her.

That's enough preparatory business with pencils. Pig-hair brush in hand, she begins to paint with watercolours. While one corner of her mind concentrates on transferring what she observes to paper, another considers an idea for a new novel that's nibbling at her. It's a decaying Big House story; perhaps that's why she felt compelled to include the bones. Long ago, she and Martin discussed the outline. It concerns a minor dynasty in Ireland, which rises and rules and riots before crashing in ruins — yet clinging by its fingernails to the ancestral home. An ambitious project — is she capable of tackling it? Even with Martin's help?

Hours pass during which Pinker explores the hillside, vomits up some earthworms and takes a nap, Edith working steadily all the while. Finally, she stops and examines her sketch. It seems to her she's caught something of the essence of the landscape — mountains, sea and sky funnelled onto the page. Despite the sunshine, her scene is melancholy, an effect caused by the arrangement of the shadows. Or it could be because of those tiny, picked-clean bones. 'If it'll do, it'll do,' she says, and packs up her equipment. Time for home. She intended staying out for longer — Cameron had business in Skibbereen and planned to lunch at the West Cork Hotel — but her limbs have stiffened. Her sixty-fourth birthday crept up on her in May. Boney sent a card with a saucy message.

She whistles for Pinker, who abandons her games and dances around Edith's ankles, before scooting ahead. Going downhill is as challenging as the uphill trek with this lame leg of hers. Still, she'll be able to work those sketches into a decent landscape. On the flat, she realizes she's lost Pinker again. Standing still to catch her breath, she finds herself holding it. A russet fox with a black mask is a few feet away. A dog fox in the whole of his health, with a fine brush. He appears through a gap in the hedge, sniffs the air, and listens, ears cocked. Catching her scent, he turns his yellow eyes on Edith and holds her gaze momentarily, before sliding away. It's almost as if he dissolves into thin air. If she can hold his image in her mind, she'll paint him.

Pinker rushes up, twitching with excitement, and noses the ground where the fox stood. 'Too late,' she says. 'Anyhow you're not big enough to take on a fox. Give it time.'

She continues homewards, listening to a chorus of country sounds – clucking, mooing, honking, bleating. Hens are perched on half-doors, hopeful of food. A flock of geese commandeer the road, and she waits in a ditch until they've passed, holding Pinker, who's inclined to give chase. A barefoot goose girl, skirt kilted at her knees, calls out a greeting. One of the Treacy girls, by the look of her. Nora Treacy has gone to Chicago. Would her sister be able to help with the cleaning at Drishane? She must mention it to Philomena.

Back at Drishane, a motorcycle with sidecar is parked outside the front door. Mike Hurley emerges from around the side of the house.

'Visitors, Miss Edith. A couple of lads from that new Civic Guard.'

Edith turns waxen. 'Is it about Colonel Somerville?'

'Didn't say what it was about.'

She presses her hands together, readying herself. 'Take Pinker with you, would you Mike? I don't want her biting strangers' ankles. That's how we lost Dooley.'

Waiting in the inner hall, leaning against a desk where her grandfather once sat to accept his tenants' rents or their excuses, two men in dark-blue uniforms and peaked caps are waiting. The Civic Guard, a police force set up to replace the recently disbanded Royal Irish Constabulary, hasn't bedded down yet. Tensions keep flaring between its members – some of whom are ex-IRA, while others belonged to the RIC. Cameron claims the IRA men enlisted for the sole purpose of destabilizing it.

Edith enters, composed of sharp edges, determined to deal with them quickly. The warning from that Camel creature isn't easily set aside. The men straighten at her approach.

'Miss Somerville?' The burlier of the two addresses her.

'I am she.'

'My name is Sergeant Maguire and this is Guard Tomelty. We'd like a word with you please.'

An Ulsterman – Monaghan, maybe. Once, she'd have known the local policemen. There are strangers everywhere now. She notices neither man appears to be armed. Of course, the Civic Guard was established deliberately on that basis. If she must have strange men in uniform about the place, it's a relief they aren't pointing weapons at her.

'How can I help you, sergeant?'

'It's about these.' He jerks his head at the constable.

The younger man has what appears to be an old pillowcase wedged under his arm. He loosens the drawstring and pulls out a pair of riding boots. Shyly, he holds them out, like a salesman inviting her to admire his stock.

Edith strokes the leather, apple-skin smooth beneath her fingertips. She knows whose they are. Still in want of a lick of polish, too.

'I see you recognize them,' says Sergeant Maguire.

'I believe so. They look like my brother's. Aylmer Somerville.'

'Show the lady.'

Guard Tomelty rolls down the top of one of the boots.

Aylmer Somerville
Drishane House
Castletownshend

Her synapses begin clicking through the permutations of what this means. Denis must have been caught. Odd that she should care, but she does. It was only a matter of time before his gallop was halted. Maybe it's better for him to go to jail for a while, out of harm's way. 'What happened to the man who was wearing them, sergeant?'

'Hit by an omnibus.'

'Is he … did he … is he in hospital?'

'In the ground is where he is. Dead and buried.'

'Dead?'

'As a doornail.'

The sergeant's outline appears to waver and recede. She blinks hard, several times, clearing her vision.

'That's right, ma'am. Killed on the spot. In the middle of an act of stupidity. I suppose he'd call it patriotism.' He shakes his head.

'I don't understand.'

'He was running away. Being chased by a crowd. In London, it was. The police there contacted us for help identifying him. On account of them boots he was wearing.'

'The boots. Yes, I see. They were stolen during a raid here last October. Another brother, Colonel Somerville, Master of Drishane, reported it.'

'Write that down, Tomelty. Aye, I've read the report. There's no mention of any boots stolen. A horse, some jewellery and silver, is all.'

'I suppose Colonel Somerville didn't think it worth mentioning. The boots aren't of much value. But one of the intruders helped himself to them. The colonel can corroborate what I say, and two members of the household were also present. Our cook and housemaid. They're here at the moment if you need to speak to them, but I'm afraid my brother is attending to business in Skibbereen.'

'Guard Tomelty will need to take statements from whoever was on the premises during the raid.'

'Of course. Do you mean now?'

'No time like the present.'

'If you'd care to follow me, guard.'

'You can't be there when he interviews them, Miss Somerville,' warns the sergeant.

'Naturally not.'

Edith leads the young civic guard to the kitchen, where Philomena and Mrs O'Shea start talking about making him something to eat to build him up. 'But I don't need building up,' he protests. 'I'm here on official business.' She leaves him alone to fend them off, if he can.

Back in the inner hall, head on one side, Sergeant Maguire is study-ing her grandfather's regimental sword mounted on the wall.

'That'd do right damage, if it was kep' sharp.'

When Edith was a small girl, Grandpapa told her he sliced off noses and ears with it. She used to think he was teasing, but in later life won-dered if there might be some truth in it. 'It's ornamental, Sergeant Maguire. I expect it saw action in its day. But that was a long time ago. In the middle of the last century, in India.'

'Relatives of mine served in India. Now, about the boots. A decent, sturdy pair, I grant you. But what happened to his own if he swapped them? Did he leave them behind? Would you happen to have them?'

She can see the boots in her mind's eye. Brown, ankle high, *Made by J.J. Carroll of Listowel* on the inner back. 'I'm afraid he took them with him.'

'I dare say they were a battered aul' pair, in flitters.'

'No, they were new, but too tight. His father's boots.' She feels a catch in her chest at the thought of the news making its way to that family in Listowel. A family where the father gave his son the boots off his feet before the boy left home. 'May I ask the name of the man cap-tured wearing Aylmer's?'

'An *amadán*. That's who he was. Don't know that I ought to go handing out his name yet. He was a young fellow from Ireland, got mixed up in a bad business.'

'What kind of bad business?' She hopes he'll tell her Camel has been put behind bars.

'Did you hear about what happened to Field Marshal Wilson, across the water?'

Edith stiffens. She had a sleepless night after reading about his death in the newspaper, convinced Camel must have been tangled up in it. If she'd gone to the police, the field marshal might be alive. On the other hand, she would have turned herself and her family into targets. It's a circle she's unable to square. She made a decision knowing someone might suffer by it. *But what choice did I have?*

She brings her hands together, knuckles showing through the skin. 'I read about Sir Henry in the newspaper. Dreadfully sad. I hope he didn't suffer. I hate to think his wife saw it happen – it said in the paper she did. But perhaps that's one of their exaggerations?'

'Hard to miss gunfire on your own doorstep. He was shot right outside his house. Eaton Place. He'd just stepped out of a hackney cab. Coming home from unveiling a war memorial in Liverpool Street station. Three men were waiting for him. Irregulars. One of them was wearing these boots.'

Edith's throat tightens. She swallows past the constriction. 'I'm sorry, did I hear you correctly? Are you saying the man wearing these boots killed Field Marshal Wilson?'

'Not sure who pulled the trigger, but he was part of it. They fired on Wilson, left him bleeding to death and made a run for it. Some members of the public chased after them. One of the gang panicked and dashed out in front of a motorized omnibus. Driver couldn't stop. It rolled right over him.'

He's still talking but Edith doesn't take in what he's saying. Her mind is clutching at alternatives. Perhaps it wasn't Denis wearing the boots – he could have lost them, with that vagabond lifestyle of his. Or it might be a case of mistaken identity. What if he lent the boots to the whistler, or one of the others? There's a stabbing pain in her palm. She glances down and realizes she is digging her nails into it. But if it's really Denis who died, then he was part of an IRA gang that assassinated the field marshal. It sounds like the sort of affair he'd be involved in. After all, he lured her to that bloodthirsty pilot with the ravaged face. Who'd have slashed her from ear to ear, if the humour took him.

'I'd take it as a favour—' She halts, regroups and tries again. 'I'd be most awfully grateful if you'd tell me. Confidentially, of course. What's the name of the young man who died?'

'Ach, I suppose it'll all come out in the wash. I dare say the newspapers will print it. Denis Brophy, that's who he was. Nineteen years of age. Came from Listowel in County Kerry. Used an alias, forbye. Dan Keane.'

Denis Brophy. So it was her Denis. She never knew his surname. There's an inevitability to his death. She can't say it's a tragedy, or that she's truly shocked. But she does feel regret clot inside her. Denis took the wrong fork in the road.

'Such a waste.' Edith walks to the nearest window. Pinker is digging up a flowerbed, decimating her mother's dahlias, but she hasn't the energy to rap on the pane. 'And the other men he was with? Do you know anything about them?'

'Caught alive. More's the pity for them, maybes. Young fellows, aged twenty-three or twenty-four. Grew up in England, the pair of them. But, you know yourself, Irish parents.'

She turns back to him and finds a brooding expression on his face. 'What will happen to them?'

'They're in Wandsworth Jail now. There'll be a trial, the law will run its course. Ex-soldiers, they are. Fought in the trenches. One of them lost a leg at Ypres. That's why they didn't get away. He fell, his pal doubled back for him, and they were surrounded. Poor beggars. They weren't the ones pulling the strings. Mark my words, there's others behind this hit.'

So, they'll hang. At least Denis escaped the noose. Edith wonders if they might be the two men with tilly lamps in the warehouse. She realizes she's been holding her breath, and lets it escape. 'Where will it all end?'

Sergeant Maguire clears his throat. 'Maybe that's what them'uns who ordered the killing want. For none of it to end. For the fighting to go on. And on. Why do you think Mick Collins shelled the Four Courts, the week after the field marshal met his maker? Pressure was put on him to sort things out, if you ask me. You do it, Sonny Jim, or we'll do it for you.'

Edith leans her forehead against the windowpane. 'Such a waste. Boys, all of them.'

'Aye, but they caused a mountain of trouble. After the field marshal went west, the English said the Treaty was broken. That's what tumbled us back to war. And war agin our own kind, this time. Mick Collins made a choice to stand over the Treaty. It was either fight the empire again, a long, drawn out handlin', or fight ourselves – and hope for a swift finish.'

'Will it be? A swift finish, I mean?'

'Aye, I dare say. Ireland's had enough of revolution.'

Guard Tomelty returns, notebook in hand. A look snakes between him and his senior officer. The guard nods. Edith's story has been validated.

Sir Henry Wilson didn't approve of the Anglo-Irish Treaty, Edith recalls. A shameful and cowardly surrender to the gun, he called it. 'Is it true the field marshal drew his sabre and ran at them when he saw their weapons?' she asks.

'So the newspapers say. I wasn't there,' says the sergeant.

'Odd, to survive that slaughterhouse of a European war and end up felled on your own doorstep.' Guilt jabs at Edith again. She should have gone to the London police with her suspicions that he was a target. But that Camel creature terrified her. She shudders. 'At least Sir Henry was wearing his uniform. A man like that would hate to die in his nightshirt.'

'Up to his neck in blood, he was,' says the young guard.

'That'll do, Tomelty. Speak no ill of the dead.'

The sergeant's tone of reproof causes a blush, pink-tipped like a daisy, to creep over Guard Tomelty's cheeks.

Suddenly, Edith wants these functionaries of the new Irish state gone from Drishane. Their presence reminds her she ought to have contacted the authorities, scared or not. 'Now that I've solved the mystery for you, sergeant, is there anything else I can help you with?'

The tilt of his chin shows his resentment at being dismissed. 'Not at present. I'll bid you good day.'

Guard Tomelty gathers up the boots and jams them into the pillow-slip. Irrationally, she feels an aversion to the idea of Denis's boots being taken away, and perhaps used as exhibits in a trial. 'Do you need to keep them, sergeant? I should prefer to have them, if that's at all possible.'

'May be required for evidence, Miss Somerville. If not, they'll be returned to you.'

———

Edith and Cameron are sitting on the lawn by a sundial, which claims *I onlie count the sunnie houres*. Pinker dozes on Edith's lap while Cameron updates her on the news from Skibbereen. She only half-listens, distracted by a cloud of bluer-than-blue butterflies rioting among the glossy leaves of magnolia bushes, and the hum of industrious bees settling and rising from one flower to the next.

'Shall we have a game of backgammon after dinner?' suggests Cameron.

'If you like.'

'Here's Philomena now with the drinks.'

Philomena deposits the tray with gin decanter, soda siphon and glasses on a wrought-iron table. 'Faith, but the Lord God himself would look down and pity me this day, Miss Edith.'

'Your eczema?'

'Exactly. The pair of yiz look as broody as hens on a clutch of eggs on them low chairs. Personally, if I sat into one of them there deckchairs I wouldn't be fit to stand up again.' She lowers her voice, although it is still perfectly audible. 'Have you told the master about them boyos calling to the house, asking questions to beat the band?'

'Indeed I have, Philomena. He's sorry to have missed them, aren't you Cameron?'

'I wish I knew what happened to those boots I left in the seaman's chest,' says Cameron. 'They'd have been jolly useful for the investigation.'

'Thank you, Philomena, that will be all,' says Edith. She waits until they are alone. 'But they have the men who shot Sir Henry. They have visual evidence – they don't need circumstantial proof.' She accepts a glass from her brother. Idly, she tries to separate out the swallow's sweet twitter from the wren's piercing note. Over by the rhododendron walk, her peripheral vision catches a figure in jodhpurs, hacking jacket and riding boots. Polished ones, unlike Denis's.

'I seem to have pins and needles in my foot, Chimp. Won't you excuse me? I believe I'll take a constitutional around the garden. Here, take Pinker.' Pinker opens her eyes and licks Edith's hand as she passes the puppy across, then snuggles onto Cameron's knees. 'I walked the legs off her today.'

'Only a matter of time before it's the other way around, Peg.'

'There's life in this old dog yet.'

'Nobody doubts it.'

Flurry Knox is lounging with his back against a horse chestnut tree, one slim, horseman's leg crossed over the other. His bowler hat is resting on his chest and a scent of hair oil rises from him.

Despite having changed for dinner, she lowers herself to the ground and settles beside him on the grass. 'Mr Fox himself.'

'None other.'

'Flurry, do you ever wish time could run backwards?'

'I do not. That's a waste of a wish when there's so much else you could be wishing for.'

'Such as?'

'You tell me. You're not too old to dream up your own wishes, gerrill.'

'*Flurry's Wedding* a West End hit?'

'Ah, what's the West End to us here in Castletownshend? When we have heather to rest on, the thunder of swans' wings in flight to listen to, and the great vault of the sky above us?'

'You've turned lyrical since I saw you last. Anyone would think you'd fallen in love.'

'I have. With a long-backed hunter that's within the black of my thumbnail off sixteen hands. Which reminds me, I can't lie round here gabbing. I need to push off and seal the deal.'

A puff of laughter billows from her.

He scrambles to his feet and, by way of farewell, makes her a mock bow from the waist. 'There's a stench off the past and that's the truth of it. The future's where you want to point your nose, Edith Somerville.'

Author's Note

In 1925, three years after the end of this novel, *The Big House of Inver* was published. It proved to be Edith Somerville's most successful solo novel – although she still insisted on using the dual Somerville-and-Ross signature.

She never did get *Flurry's Wedding* staged, despite revising it repeatedly over a seventeen-year period. But the Somervilles held on to Drishane House, largely thanks to her efforts, and the family continues to live there.

Acknowledgments

Thanks are due to:

Dr Carlo Gébler, Dr Paul Delaney, Dr Philip Coleman and Dr Kevin Power of Trinity College Dublin, who read early drafts and gave endless encouragement, as did my nephew Justin Blanchard.

Trinity's librarians for whom no request was too much trouble. Also Queen's University Belfast for sharing its extensive Somerville and Ross archive; the staff in Special Collections were a joy to deal with, especially Roísín Scullion.

The family of Professor Fitzroy Pyle for awarding me the Fitzroy Pyle Postgraduate Bursary during the course of this work at Trinity's Oscar Wilde Centre, where it formed part of a PhD in literary practice.

The Somerville family of Drishane House, Castletownshend, Co. Cork, for kindly allowing me access to their private family archive, sharing memories and anecdotes, and giving me the freedom to wander around their home and its grounds. In addition, Robert Salter-Townshend for his family stories about Edith. And the people of Castletownshend who always make me so welcome during my frequent visits.

Antony Farrell, The Lilliput Press's publisher, who took to Edith at once. Also to the Lilliput team for their enthusiasm and hard work.

The volunteers at Shaw's Corner, Ayot St Lawrence, with whom I spent some happy hours. Writer Lia Mills and photographer Simon Robinson shared the adventure there – what larks we had!

Writer friends Sarah Webb, Ciara Ferguson and Anne-Marie Casey with whom I discussed the novel during its genesis. Also, Lorraine

Curran, Kathleen Barrington and Imelda Reynolds who were always ready to listen to my Edith-ing. And my neighbour Lise-Ann McLaughlin, who played Sally Knox in *The Irish R.M.* TV series. Such unexpected connections magnify life's joy.